PROOF COPY

The [illegible]y is Not Enough

June O'Sullivan

Poolbeg Press

This book is a work of fiction. References to real people, events, establishments, organisations, or locales are intended only to provide a sense of authenticity, and are used fictitiously. All other characters, and all incidents and dialogue, are drawn from the author's imagination and are not to be construed as real.

PROOF COPY ONLY. NOT FOR RESALE.

Published 2026 by Poolbeg Press Ltd.

123 Grange Hill, Baldoyle, Dublin 13, Ireland

Email: poolbeg@poolbeg.com

A catalogue record for this book is available from the British Library.

ISBN 978-1-78199-559-4

Not final ISBN. For proof copy only.

www.poolbeg.com

PRAISE FOR *THE LIGHTHOUSE KEEPER'S WIFE*

"An evocative and authentic debut." ***Irish independent***

"Tense and Terrifying read. I couldn't put it down." ***Sue Leonard, The Examiner***

"A compelling, albeit heart-rending read from a powerful new voice." ***Sunday Business Post***

"It's well paced ; keeps you turning those pages and is moving in an authentic way." ***Sunday Independent***

"This is a stunning debut." ***Donal Ryan***

"A powerful & evocative debut historical novel world." ***Joseph O'Connor***

"It is a truly beautiful piece of storytelling. I loved this book." ***Fíona Scarlett***

"A very poignant & vivid debut." ***Swirlandthread.com***

"What an amazing read." ***Dundalk FM Radio***

About the author

June O'Sullivan is originally from Limerick but lives on an island in County Kerry with her family. This is her second novel. *The Lighthouse Keeper's Wife* was published in 2025. A graduate of the MA in Creative Writing at the University of Limerick, she also enjoys writing flash fiction and short stories. Her obsession with lighthouses has now been supplemented with an obsession with aviation.

Dedication

To Sophie Catherine Theresa Mary Peirce-Evans
Per Ardua Ad Astra

Footease

Which peace is best, the peace before a storm,
When one must fear the menacing unknown,
Or the peace afterwards, when safe through harm,
Craft into quiet haven is gently blown?

From *East African Nights* (1925), by Sophie Eliott-Lynn

PROLOGUE

Knockaderry, County Limerick, 1897

The only things moving outside the house are the leaves of a shadow-darkened tree. It rustles with a deep intensity, as though aware of its burden, its responsibility to maintain the ebb and flow of life in this dying place. The door to the kitchen is solid wood, set low in a deep frame. When it opens, the bolt on the inside rattles, loose and no man to fix it.

Never mind. There is no need for bolts and locks anymore with nothing left worth stealing. The heavy door opens onto a large kitchen, empty of the servants who should fill it with their toil and their gossip. It is bare, save for a dresser, a table, two chairs and a wrought-iron fireplace in which some wet sticks flicker into occasional, hopeful bursts of light and heat before returning to a smouldering hiss. The fire throws resentful shadows around the room.

The shadows capture a silhouette on the brick wall. A woman, seated on the edge of a wooden chair, pulled up close to the fire, hunched and motionless. A child, barely one year old, on the floor, her back to the wall. In her hand a rag, worried to fraying by her mouth and fingers.

There is another shadow in the room. The thread that binds all this together and if it breaks there will be hell. He is at the elbow-worn table. A stocky man with a dog at his feet who he kicks away, but each time it slinks back again. The man is hunched over too, one hand supporting his head, the other fisting a crystal glass of amber liquid. His power in the room is tangible. He can make the woman by the fire flinch with the smallest movement.

He can make the child disappear with a darkening of his tone. She scuttles now, seeks out a secret place where she can hide until the dark clouds pass over or the storm that bursts from them exhausts itself. She squeezes into the corner beside the wooden dresser. The shelves overhead glitter with broken glass.

It is coming now. The tension echoes off the bare walls of the room. The stringy mongrel feels it too. He rises and slinks away to his corner. Outside the wind in the trees begins a whistling and gusting rhythm.

It begins.

'Why would he not stay?' the man moans, thumping a fist on the table.

There is no answer.

'*Answer me!*' he shouts, dashing his glass at the hearth.

The woman yelps but does not move away from the broken shards. She pulls her shawl tighter about her, a swollen lip quivering. He is on his feet now, unsteady, but quick. He passes by the corner where the child hides. Something is banging upstairs. A window come undone? His voice is low now.

'You know well, of course, don't you, Mrs Peirce?'

She is shaking. This low tone of his voice is worse than the shouting. The shouting she is used to and she knows, like his mongrel, to dart away from it, out of reach. But this low, creeping voice sneaks up out of the darkness until there is no way to escape it.

'You know why the Hannon lad wouldn't stay, don't you? It's because you are a whore! A dirty whore! And a good lad like him doesn't want to be caught in your presence. Isn't that so?'

His face is beside hers now – he is staring at her with naked hatred. She is trying to turn to stone but the fear in her body betrays her and she shakes. His hand is on her shoulder, pressing down hard until she caves from the pressure, whimpering. Then she is thrown to the floor. She screams. And now he is shouting again.

'*I should never have married you! You tricked me, you bitch! Saw me here alone in this big house and you said to yourself "Here's my meal ticket"!*'

She crawls along the flagstones but there is no escape that way. Only a dark corner. And he will find her there.

'You tried your luck with William Power but he knocked you back so you turned your cursed sights on me. Look what you've done to me!' He waves his arms. 'Not a penny to my name. Not a neighbour or friend in the world to look me in the eye. Do you see how low you've brought me? *Do you?*'

He finds her and drags her screaming out of her corner by the hair, strands ripping wetly. She tries to speak. She is on her knees by the hearth.

'I didn't, Jackie. I swear. Please!'

'So I'm a liar?'

She has said the wrong thing. She slumps onto her haunches and lowers her head, ready to receive the blows. And now they come.

A punch to the side of the head lays her out flat. He has a stick now. Or is it the leg of a broken chair? He wallops her with it. Anywhere. Everywhere. She is a crushed bundle. Her eyes are squeezed tight and the pain of each blow ripples through her. She has stopped screaming, is almost silent, just moaning. Her body jerks and contorts.

'*You did. You did!*'

He punctuates each statement with stick on bone.

'You came here and you took everything. You tricked me. You told the guards I bate you. You opened your legs to me and you not even my wife. You told me there was a baby. So I had to marry you. Then you tried to get rid of it. You had my baby, my son. And you let him die! *Why?* You were sent by the Devil. I see him in your eyes. You dirty Devil whore. I'll drive him out of you. Or I'll drive you out. *Get out! Get out!*'

The stick rains down on her now. She is silent. The force of the beating moves her but she doesn't react.

He throws the bloodied stick to the floor and wipes sweat from his forehead.

'Oh, Jesus Christ! Oh, Mother of God! Look what the bitch made me do!'

He falls to his knees beside her, pulls off his coat and wraps her in it.

'You're cold. You cratur, I'll warm you. Come here to me, my Kate.'

He drags her to the chair and hauls her onto his lap. He rubs at her arms, her legs. He kisses her lips. Outside a dog is barking. He gets to his feet and lowers her to the ground. He is barefoot, his feet making bloody prints on the floor. He rubs a hand across his lips, as if wiping away the last trace of her.

'Oh Jesus! I'll swing for this.'

The door bangs open. The loose bolt rattles as he races out into the night. Then there is silence. The child crawls out of her place in the corner and comes to sit beside the bundle of her mother. She creeps under her mother's shawl, snuggles into her back, and sleeps.

Chapter One

Hereford, England, April 1926

The plane rises. I close my eyes and savour the feeling of being up in the air, light and free, every other earthly sound muffled by the roar of the engine. I tilt back as we soar then level out. At fifteen hundred feet, I reach forward and tap Lawson's shoulder. He gives the signal and before I have time to think I step out onto the wing. The air rushes at me and past me and through me. The parachute rig on my back is tugged by the wind and I am reassured by its presence and the tightness of the harness straps around my one-piece trouser costume.

I see the crowd below, specks of people, watching and waiting in the exhibition ground. The April sun glints on field glasses held aloft to better observe my jump. These people are my lifeblood, my bread and butter. Without their interest I could not earn my living in this way and I will not disappoint them. I take a breath and I am about to step off into nothingness when I hear it.

The silence.

In the same moment the plane drops and I am plummeting with it, clinging on to a strut, one foot on the wing, one still on the carriage step of the Avro 504K. The engine has failed. We are hurtling down, down. The wind pummels my face and rips at the parachute pack. My fingers ache with the strain of holding on. If I drop now my parachute won't have time to deploy and I will fall to almost certain death. It is as though the wind is trying to rip the parachute from my back and me from the wing. The ground rushes towards us. I see the roofs and chimneys and treetops as we skim over them. We are coming in hard to land and I see a scattering below us on the ground. It is only once we thump to a stop that I realise where we are. The plane has come to a halt on the goal line and the players, whose football match we just interrupted, stand in silent shock. One man picks up the ball as though to keep it from harm.

Lawson rests his head on the instrument board. I jump down. My legs are shaking.

'What happened?' I ask.

He is out of the plane now, lighting a cigarette with trembling hands.

'Bloody thing just lost power. You OK, Sophie?'

'I'm fine. You do know it was just me who was supposed to come down like that? With my parachute?' I lean over and take the cigarette from between his fingers, take a deep pull and pass it back. 'How long before we can go up again?'

He flicks the cigarette to the ground and stamps it out. 'Are you completely mad? You could have been killed. I didn't even know where you were until we landed.'

'I'm not sure I'd call that a landing,' I say. 'I've seen better. And yes, we go again. That crowd didn't come to watch you clipping the hedges.'

I crouch down and check the plane's underbelly, smoothing my hands along the panels as though soothing a spooked horse. 'There's no damage here.'

The football players crowd around us, peppering us with questions as Lawson peers in at the rotary engine.

'It looks like one of the connecting rods has broken,' he says. 'We won't be going up anywhere. Not until I get that fixed.'

I unbuckle my parachute pack, throw it on the ground, pull down the one-piece costume and step out of it. I leave it puddled where it falls.

This is not good. Today was to be the day I became the first woman in Britain to complete a parachute jump and now it is all ruined. I need to salvage what I can.

'Any of you boys got a car? I need a lift to the exhibition ground.'

'What about me?' Lawson asks.

'I'll see you back there. Oh, and if you wouldn't mind terribly, bring my costume and parachute with you when you're coming.'

I give him one final glance as I hop into a footballer's motorcar. Lawson is scooping up my clothes, shaking his head.

We speed back to the grounds. The spectators are still there and they don't need to know that I feel sick from the fright of that near disaster. They only need to know that I am brave and undaunted.

'What's your favourite stunt?' I ask my new friend.

'The loop the loop.'

'Then I shall do one especially for you,' I tell him as I hop out.

In minutes my Moth is ready for take-off. I do the loop the loop, as promised. I do it many times. And I nosedive and roll and side-slip. I prefer being the pilot, in control of my own craft, not at the mercy of another and their flimsy connecting rods.

The crowd cheers loudly when I come back down. I haven't given them what they came for but I've given them something.

The next day our send-off is more subdued. Word has spread about our near miss. The danger is more apparent now and the spectators know they are complicit. We could have died. Could still. But if the alternative is staying grounded then I'll take my chances. I lean forward and squeeze Lawson's shoulder. He's a good sport to take me up again. I know he'd rather be in the clubhouse attacking his third brandy. We ascend and this time it is even more beautiful. Lawson gives the signal and I climb out. The blue ocean of sky surrounds me so I dive straight out into it before anything can go wrong. I am dropping fast, my heart falling away from me. I pull the cord. My parachute opens immediately and I am jolted from my glorious free-fall. I feel the loss of it but now I am floating, drifting, under a canopy of silk, eighteen feet in diameter. Green stalks of rye wave to me and I wave back. I drop into a freshly ploughed field with a thud. My parachute wafts to earth behind me and I unshackle it.

I can hear the cheers from the spectators. Lawson has landed. As I meet him he swings me into the air. Hands reach out to shake mine and a newspaper man in a neat tweed suit fires questions at me.

'How was it?'

'Absolutely splendid. Although that field could have been a bit softer. The fields here are harder than back home in Ireland.'

They laugh, eating out of the palm of my hand.

'Did it hurt?'

'No more than jumping from a five-foot wall.'

More laughter. Some applause.

'Was it dizzying? Were you very afraid?

'Not one bit. In fact, I enjoyed viewing the scene below me as I came down. I just wish it had lasted a bit longer. It felt like less than a minute.'

'*Sixty-four seconds!*' Someone in the middle of the crowd holds aloft a stopwatch and the newsman scribbles the detail in his notebook.

'Was it thrilling?'

'Somewhat. But that was more to do with the novelty of the thing.'

'You are the first woman in Britain to complete a parachute jump. What will you do next?'

I ponder this for a moment. What will I do next? Suddenly this moment seems less important than whatever comes after.

'I'll just have to find a new thrill.'

I join in the laughter this time as the men hoist me onto their shoulders.

Stag Lane, London, June 1926

'Up a bit. Now that side. Perfect!'

One of the other flying instructors puts the finishing touches to the party decorations in the hangar. The banners flutter in the warm breeze. Tables have been placed around the planes outside in the airfield. They are set with plates of cucumber sandwiches, pound cake, scones and fresh strawberries sweating in the June heat.

'Do give me a hand, Sophie!'

Mary Bailey is struggling towards me, weighed down by bags. There is the unmistakable sound of clinking and I grin.

'Now where might we put these so that they'll stay cold?' Mary grabs a passing pilot. 'Would you be a sweetheart and fill some buckets with the coldest water you can find?'

He grins and nods.

'Champagne?' I ask.

'Of course!' Mary leans in for a kiss. Left cheek, then right. 'So much to celebrate. The first Airwoman's 'At Home'. Genius idea, by the way. We've never had a gathering like this before. Two hundred guests coming to meet the pilots of the fairer sex. But, more importantly, the first woman pilot to secure her commercial 'B' licence. And an Irishwoman at that. One of our own. Bloody well done, you!' She takes my hand, spins me in a twirl then pulls me in again for a tight squeeze before releasing me. 'Hang on. We need to do this right.' She pulls a bottle from the bag and wrestles with the cork. It pops, sighing gently. She raises the bottle in my direction.

'To Britain's first officially recognised female commercial pilot!' She takes a deep swallow from the bottle then passes it to me.

The bubbles tickle my tongue. It is clearly expensive stuff.

'That is simply delicious,' I say. 'And it's very good of you. I don't think anyone was expecting more than tea.'

'Tea is for old ladies.'

'I feel like an old lady some days.'

'Stop that! You're a spring chicken!'

'I'm almost thirty, Mary. Nothing springy about that.'

'And look at what you've done already. You have a world record for the high jump, a world record for the javelin. You've more athletics medals and trophies than anyone else I know – and now this! To be honest, it's mildly irritating. Now stop looking for compliments and enjoy this expensive champagne. Where is the good in me being lumbered with an ancient, wealthy husband if I can't toast my friend's success?'

'I need to get one of those.'

'What?'

'An ancient, wealthy husband. Know any going spare?'

We laugh.

'Trust me. They're not all they're made out to be.' Mary flops into a chair and leans across for the bottle. I sit down beside her. 'Abe Bailey is the main reason I took up flying, you know. Him and the children. I fly to get away from the prams and all that dull drudgery.'

'Starting without me?' John approaches, his brown eyes glittering with good humour.

'Are you an airwoman?' Mary demands. 'I think not. You are a mere airman. Off you go!'

He ignores her and pulls up a seat between us, taking the bottle. He takes a small swig then passes it to me. Our fingers touch, the burn of his flesh contrasts with the smooth chill of the bottle.

'Anyway,' Mary continues, 'we're trying to sort out a problem for Sophie.'

'A problem?' A shadow of concern crosses his features. 'Can I help?'

'I doubt it.' Mary lights a cigarette and blows the smoke towards the roof. 'I don't mean to be hurtful, darling, but I doubt there's a problem on earth that this lady is incapable of solving herself. But,' she sits bolt upright, 'you don't know any wealthy widowers, do you?'

John laughs and shakes his head. 'I'm almost afraid to ask but what do you want one for?'

'Sophie's in search of one. Rich, old, preferably nearly dead. For a husband.'

John stands and walks away. 'I'll go see if I can rustle up some glasses. We may as well pretend to be civilised.'

'And see what's happening with our buckets of cold water!' Mary calls after him.

I love how he strides with purpose no matter where he's going. I hope we haven't upset him with our talk.

'We shouldn't joke really, Mary. It's in poor taste. Anyway, have you forgotten? I already have a husband. Old, yes, but not wealthy, more's the pity.'

'And?'

'And?'

'And what good is he to you, dear? You've thrown away years on him, running off to the jungles of Africa to run his blasted coffee farm and what do you have to show for it all? He's broke, Sophie. From what you tell me he always will be. But look what you've achieved since you moved back to London. You've changed the world.'

I laugh. It's typical of Mary to be so hyperbolic. William isn't a bad man, he's just had bad luck. It's true, though, we are estranged. Maybe a divorce would be for the best, if I could find the time. And the grounds. Desertion? But who has deserted whom?

The hangar starts to fill with new arrivals and I'm glad to pause this conversation for now. I don't want to think about William at a time like this. The laughter and chatter buoy me and I stand to the side for a moment to take it in. I want to store these moments away, like treasure, so that I can take them out and gaze upon them when things get tough.

John, my dear constant companion, comes to stand next to me.

'Good spirits,' he says, nodding at the crowd of women. 'All because of you.'

'I just made some sandwiches.' I shrug.

He bumps me with his shoulder. 'You did much more and you know it. And I know it hasn't been easy, even if that's what you want everyone else to believe.'

He reaches down and grasps my hand, standing close so no one can see. I squeeze his fingers. He has always been there for me.

'Go and enjoy your party,' he says. 'I'll stay here.'

I let go of his hand but he takes it again.

'I'm sorry I'm not rich.' His eyes search my face as if looking for proof that it doesn't matter. But we both know it does. He has given me so much. Those warm eyes, his strong arms, his kind heart, his ability to make me laugh. But I need more.

'I'm sorry I'm not free,' I answer.

I join the crowd. Sir Brancker is arriving, shaking hands.

I climb onto a chair. Everyone turns to see me, all six foot of me, reaching almost to the low ceiling.

'Ladies and gentlemen, but mostly ladies!'

They whoop.

'I wish to thank you from the bottom of my heart for being here. Not just today, but all the days. Today is a celebration of what we have achieved together and a commitment to do even more in the future.'

They cheer and I raise my hands to quieten them.

'I must, however, apologise to Sir Brancker for a slight bending of the Air Ministry's rules. As you all know, only recently have we women been granted the right to get our commercial licenses.' The room fills again with whoops and cheers. 'And, of course, this has prevented us from making money due to the ban on us taking paying passengers. Well, the time has come for me to confess that at times I have been creative, in circumventing this ban. I have taken passengers who didn't pay me a guinea for the flight but who did coincidentally pay me a guinea for a signed photograph of the airplane. I do hope that was alright?'

I stare directly at Sir Brancker, a smile teasing my lips as everyone erupts into laughter. Someone hands me a glass and I raise it.

Sir Brancker raises his in return and christens me 'Lady Hell-Of-A-Din'. It stings, the way he twists my married name, Eliott-Lynn, into a barb about my boisterousness. But, I suppose, I've earned it.

Chapter Two

Hamble, Hampshire, May 1927

I glide my plane to a standstill and pull off my goggles. They have started to frost over and I feel like the cold is in my bones. It's hard to believe it's early summer on the ground. I'm certain I've broken the record. According to my altimeter I topped 15,700 feet. Mary, my enthusiastic passenger, turns around in the front seat and gives me a thumbs-up.

I see a man running towards me now.

He climbs onto the wing, leans into the cockpit to see the instruments on my dashboard and then shouts to the gathered crowd, '*Fifteen thousand, seven hundred and forty-eight!*'.

They erupt into cheers.

Another world record. But I am numb. So what if I climbed a bit higher? Next week someone else might go to fifteen thousand, seven hundred and fifty. Then this won't count for anything.

I know the others will want to celebrate this but it's too small. I need something bigger, bolder. Something no one can touch. Something that will be mine for a long time. But for that I need money.

At lunch I let Mary carry the weight of the conversation. I sip at my gin, trying to work it all out. When John excuses himself to use the bathroom Mary leans in.

'I'm sorry.'

'What did you do?' I drain my glass and gesture for another.

Mary swats my arm. 'I heard about William. I didn't say anything before, I didn't want to bring it up in front of John. I'm so sorry.'

I nod. 'I'm sorry I ever met him. What kind of woman ends up with a dead husband floating down the Thames with a single copper penny in his pocket? And, you know, he always blamed me for being reckless with his money. I know I should feel sad but I don't. I haven't seen him since I left Kenya three years ago.' I blink hard. I am angry. With him, for being so useless, for falling into the Thames, or throwing himself in, or whatever he did. With myself for marrying him. With it all.

'So now you can.'

'Can what?' I ask as John returns.

'Find yourself a nice, rich, old widower!' Mary slaps her thigh.

I feel John looking at me. I know if I turn I will see hurt in his eyes. So I compose my face and give nothing away about how much I love him and how much it really doesn't matter.

'I'd better start looking then,' I say.

The gin has slowed the angry tide of my blood to a sluggish ebb by the time we get to my lodgings. John shakes my hand at the front door. How bizarre. I look down at my hand as though it might contain a secret message.

'Good luck,' he says and turns to walk away.

There is still that long, purposeful stride but his shoulders are reaching towards his ears.

'John? Good luck with what?' I call after him.

'Finding a new husband.'

I run after him and grab hold of his jacket.

'Don't go, please. Let's talk.'

He follows me back to my tiny sitting-room, hovering like someone come to deliver bad news. I sit in the armchair by the cold fireplace and light a cigarette.

'You're angry,' I say. 'I know. But, really, you shouldn't pay any heed to Mary. You know how she is. How she runs away with things.'

'It's just a bit difficult, Sophie. To drown her out. And to continue ignoring the thing that is staring me in the face.'

'You knew I was married.'

'Not at first, in Boscombe.'

'I was living in married quarters, for God's sake!'

'But you never talked about William. You let me believe you could be mine. But that was never the case and I'm a fool for hanging on.'

'I couldn't be yours.'

'Not then. But we could be together now. Properly.'

I quench my cigarette in the ashtray, taking my time to stub it out, avoiding looking at him so he won't see the answer in my eyes. *No. I love you, but no.*

'I should have known!' He thumps his fist on the mantelpiece. 'I was charmed by you, flitting in and out of my life. Tearing across France on your motorcycle, disappearing to Africa for months on end to play coffee farmer, the running, the flying. Why are you so desperate to get away, Sophie? What are you running towards? I thought it was me. But now I know it has nothing to do with me. I would have given you anything. It doesn't matter. You're just going to keep running.'

'*Buy me a plane.*' My words are crystalline.

'*What?*' He turns to look at me.

'Buy me a plane. You said you would give me anything. That's what I want.'

'You know I can't.' His voice wobbles. 'Not now, not yet. But we could work towards that, together.' He comes and kneels beside my chair. 'We could build a life, a marriage.'

'That's no good to me, John.' I run my hand through his thick, dark hair. 'I tried that. I thought marriage would bring me freedom. But it's just a different type of prison. No better than my aunts rotting away in the living mausoleum in County Limerick that my grandfather made for them.'

'You're not your aunts.'

'I know.' I rise and step away from him.

He takes my place in the chair, his head in his hands.

'I never intended to be them. I worked damn hard and made sure I never would be. But I don't have forever. I'm thirty years old. The world is moving so fast. Every success, every record I break vanishes with the morning mist. The faster I make them, the faster someone comes and takes them from me. Someone younger, richer. So, yes, I could live an ordinary life with you, John. But then I wouldn't love you, I'd hate you. I know it's callous but I need someone who will back me, financially, to go after what I want. Love will have to wait.'

He stares at the floor, then stands. 'I understand. And I do wish you luck. And I hope love waits for you, but I can't. I won't be here when you come looking for love again.'

He leaves, pulling the door to a final, quiet, resolute click.

I slump to the floor and sob.

The days go by in a haze of gin and self-pity. I struggle to leave my bed only to find myself back in it mere hours later. My brown curls resemble an abandoned nest and I can't decide if the smell tainting the atmosphere is coming from my body or my bedroom. And I don't care. Eventually Mary runs out of patience. She sweeps into and through my rooms, tidying and nattering, and before I know it I've been bullied into washing and dressing and agreeing to dinner later. I say yes so she will stop bothering me. And she does but leaves behind a parting gift to incite me: today's newspaper. My clever friend knew exactly what she was doing.

The newspaper lies folded on the kitchen table but I can see the picture and under the **Weekly Dispatch** banner I read, '*Lucky Lindbergh's Lone* —'. I can't see the next word but as I unfold the paper I know it has to be '*Flight*'. I stand and read. Charles Lindbergh, at twenty-five years of age, has made the first solo transatlantic flight, leaving New York and crossing the Atlantic to arrive in Paris. His first words on stepping out of the *Spirit of St Louis*: 'Hello, boys, I'm here!' My mind wanders to what my first words might be when I make history. Then I notice his Orteig prize money. My eyes water. Twenty-five thousand pounds. What I could do with money like that! I read through the rest of the article then throw the paper back down on the table. That's old news now. It's made him a rich man, a free man.

I have to get going.

I take a page of writing paper from my bureau and start to jot down names. Men with money, without a wife. Bachelors or widowers. Widowers preferably. There's something amiss if a wealthy, single man can't convince someone to marry him. Or it may be that he doesn't desire it. Either way not much use to me. I draw a line through that column to concentrate on the bereaved. I need to go to the shop for a copy of the *Telegraph* or the *Standard* to browse the obituaries. It is macabre to do such things. Strange. Some might even say mad. I go to the mirror and survey the flushed face staring back at me, the wild hair. Am I mad? Going mad?

I tell Mary I'm going to restrict myself to just three drinks at dinner.

'Oh Sophie, you're not going to turn sensible on me?'

'Small chance of that. But I am planning something and I need to keep my thoughts clear. I can't allow myself to wallow.'

'Still pining after John?'

'Yes.'

'He's definitely gone for good then?'

I nod and take a large mouthful of wine.

'It's a shame,' she says. 'He's a sweetheart but the simple truth is that it doesn't pay to be romantic if you want to get ahead. If I hadn't agreed to marry Abe I might be mouldering away in Monaghan. You read about Lindbergh?'

'Of course I did. How clever of you to ferret me out of my misery like that. You knew it would light a spark in me.'

I'm dying to tell her my ideas but afraid the light of day will cause them to turn to dust and evaporate. At this point they're all just dreams.

'I have some thoughts about attempting a similar challenge. Similar, but different. Something that's all my own. I need to work it out some more. And my spark needs fuel.'

'Fuel?'

I rub my fingers together.

'Ah, funds. How did Lindy do it?'

'Lindy?'

'That's what they're calling him. "Lucky Lindy".'

'I see. He raised funds from businessmen in St Louis.'

'Is that something you could do?'

I roll my eyes and point at myself. 'Can you imagine the sombre moneymen of London backing this horse?'

'Well, if anyone could convince them it would be you.'

'No. It would take too long. I can't afford to wait. I've started a list.'

'A list?'

'Of potential suitors.'

Mary laughs hard, almost choking on her chicken. When she recovers she leans closer. 'I don't suppose you've brought it with you?'

I am a little bashful as I take it from my purse and slide it, still folded, across the table. She opens it, flattens it out on the table, scans it, then refolds and passes it back.

'A solid list. I might be of assistance.'

I wait.

'Come to dinner Saturday with me and Abe. I'll introduce you to someone. He's already a big fan apparently.'

I place my knife and fork down and dab at my lips with the linen napkin. My famous appetite has deserted me.

'I like that name – Lucky Lindy. I need a new name.'

'You have one.'

'Do I?'

'Lady Hell-Of-A-Din. You have to admit it's clever, how it rhymes with Eliott-Lynn.'

'That is not how I wish to be known, thank you. Eliott-Lynn or Hell-Of-A-Din. I like the Lady part though. I think it could suit me very well.'

'Indeed.' Mary smirks.

Dinner at the Baileys' proves to be a resounding bore. What is it about men that they feel compelled to pontificate for hours on the dullest topics? Finance, coal, steel. On and on they go. It is with a great sense of relief that we watch them retire at last to the drawing room to bore each other some more.

Mary signals to her butler for glasses of port. He presents us with two delicate crystal glasses bearing the Bailey monogram and I take a deep sip.

'Well? First impressions?'

'Of what? I'm afraid I was mostly asleep.'

She tuts. 'Sir James, of course. He seemed spellbound when you spoke of your time in Africa practising javelin-throwing with the natives. I'd say he thinks you're a wild thing.'

'I'd say he's right.'

We both laugh.

'Although have you noticed how men love to think they can tame that wildness out of a woman?' I say. 'Let's see how things progress. He must be twice my age.'

Mary raises an eyebrow. 'That and more! When I told Sir James that you were our other guest tonight he lit up like a child on its birthday. He said he's been following your exploits the last few years.'

'Yes. Our paths have crossed. We've often attended the same luncheons and functions.'

'I believe he's keen to get you to himself. A private audience. I think it's worth giving him another shot. Leave it with me, I shall play Cupid.'

Chapter Three

Knightsbridge, London, September 1927

No one can ever say that Mary Bailey isn't true to her word. For here I am, walking in the front door of the Berkeley to dine with Sir James Heath. It has taken longer than expected as he was travelling all summer but I have no doubt that she pounced on him the moment his feet touched English soil again. I'm dressed carefully, nothing too outlandish. I don't want to frighten the old chap.

As I'm led to a private table near the back wall I feel a shift of energy in the room. All the eyes and gossiping tongues of London society susurrate in my wake. It makes me think of the velvety seagrass on the dunes in Ballybunion, my favourite beach in County Kerry. I wish I were there now.

Sir James stands to greet me. 'Mrs Eliott-Lynn. How kind of you to accept my invitation.'

We kiss on the cheek and sit.

I wait until the waiter leaves us.

'Sir James, may I make a request?'

'Certainly.'

'Could you address me as Sophie? When people call me Mrs Eliott-Lynn I am reminded of my late husband.'

'Of course, I am sorry for your loss, such a tragedy.'

'Yes. Unfortunately, life didn't work out for William. He believed the farm in Kenya was his winning ticket but it turns out it's difficult for a man from Liverpool to cultivate coffee on an unknown continent. It ruined him financially. And then malaria finished off his health. That put the final cap on it, I'm afraid.'

The waiter takes our order and returns with our aperitifs. The pause gives me a chance to reflect. Am I letting my mouth run away from me? Making a poor impression? I steady myself with a drink.

'You must think I am cold, Sir James, to speak so critically of my late husband. But we were estranged for a number of years, so when I heard of his passing I was sorry for him but felt no great loss to myself.'

'I understand perfectly, dear girl. I am an old man and I have seen many a chap scarper off to some far-flung godforsaken place, sure of his fortune, only for it to break him. And I know something about doomed, romantic entanglements too. As I'm sure you've heard, if the gossips of London are any good.'

I have heard. Sir James recently disentangled himself via annulment from a brief union with a second wife.

'Now my first wife, Euphemia, I truly did mourn her loss. She was a good woman who gave me two children.'

'Do they live in London?'

'No. Percy, my only son, perished in nineteen fourteen. My daughter, Hylda, spends much of her time at Oxenden Hall, busy with her own children. You're only a few years younger than her, I'd guess.'

'It was a terrible thing to lose your son.'

'It was a terrible war. Did you serve?'

'Yes, I joined the WAAC in nineteen seventeen. I was a student at the time, at the Royal College of Science in Dublin. I knew some fine young men who signed up and I felt I should do my bit too. I was a motorcycle dispatch rider and at times I drove an ambulance. But I believe airplanes will be the big thing if there is ever another war.'

'How brave!' Sir James' faded blue eyes twinkle. 'Did you have brothers who served?'

I take a subtle breath. I am ready for this question. Prepared to lie.

The waiter arrives with our *hors d'oeuvres* and Sir James orders a bottle of Bordeaux.

'No. I am an only child. An orphan, really, you could say. My father died before I was born and childbirth took my mother. My grandfather raised me. And my aunts.'

I smile at the memory of Aunt Cis in the big house in Newcastle West, painting portraits of grandfather's beloved dog Rugs.

Sir James' hand advances across the table and rests on mine a moment. It is dry, an autumn leaf.

'That is a sad story, Sophie.'

He withdraws his hand to saw at his smoked salmon and I resist the urge to wipe my hand on my napkin. He chews. 'But what a success you've made of yourself!' he continues. 'That parachute jump! My God. I said to myself that day, that girl is either the bravest I've seen, or the maddest.'

He laughs and I see pink fibres stuck in his teeth. He must notice because he starts to suck at them. When he is happy with the outcome, he asks, 'So what's next? As an avid fan, can I be privy to your future plans?'

I smile. I need to approach this carefully.

'I won't say too much, Sir James, if you'll forgive me. But did you take note of Charles Lindbergh's flight?'

'Did I? If I'd known about it sooner I'd have made my way to Paris to shake his hand as he stepped off that plane. Marvellous stuff!'

I lower my eyes and look at him from under my lashes. 'I want to do something like that. A real record-breaker that shakes the world.'

His white moustache seems to expand as he smiles. 'I like the sound of that.'

'But,' I sigh, 'I'm afraid I don't have access to the same funds as he had.'

I pause. Have I gone too far? Is it too obvious?

He takes a sip of wine.

'A clever girl like you,' he says. 'I'm sure you'll figure something out.'

'Well, I've had to be pretty resourceful up to now.' I am laughing again. 'I must tell you about the time I landed in a field in Poland because I needed to post a letter. The locals were so mad at me.'

Before I can say more we are interrupted by a red-faced young man.

'I'm sorry to intrude. But I was wondering if I could have your autograph?'

He proffers a cutting from the newspaper. It is a picture of me, taken from a distance, dangling from my descending parachute. I sign it and talk with him for a few moments about that day and he walks away, buoyed up.

When I turn back to Sir James he is looking at me warmly.

'I must say it is quite a thrill dining with a famous aviator.'

'Then we shall have to do it again,' I reply, lowering my voice to a husky intimacy. 'Perhaps Sir James would like this famous aviator to take him for a joyride in her famous plane?'

The wrinkles around his eyes crinkle and deepen as my request draws another smile. 'I'd like that very much.'

I am in the hangar at Stag Lane making my final checks when Sir James arrives.

'You don't have anyone to do that for you?'

I wipe my hands on a rag and laugh. 'Goodness, no. Everyone here does everything for themselves. And, besides, even if there was someone I'd insist on doing it myself.'

'Why is that?'

'A lesson I learned during the war. When we women drivers first got to the base at Abbeville some of the men weren't happy. We were replacing them, you see, which meant they could be sent to the front. They had no problem tampering with our vehicles, loosening the brake cables, putting sand into the fuel tank. You wouldn't believe what they got up to. So I learned early on not to let another person touch mine.' I start to wheel the plane out. 'If something had to be fixed, I worked out how to fix it.'

'I bet you did.'

'I always said, on my head be it and no one else's. The same goes for flying. When I'm the pilot my plane stays up or it comes down on my know-how. If it crashes then it's my fault.'

He looks up sharply at '*crashes*'.

'Of course,' I continue, 'flying is infinitely safer than driving. No other traffic to contend with. Two levers. Even a child could learn.'

'Can I be of assistance?' Sir James offers as I roll the light plane along behind me.

'Absolutely not, you are my guest.'

'Don't you need to change?'

I'm wearing my Sunday best. 'Flying is just like driving a motorcar, Sir James. Nothing at all stopping me from flying about in my fur coat and heels.'

When we reach the airfield I unfold the wings and secure them in place, fully extended.

'We'll have a nice relaxed flight and then, if you like, when we land I'll go back up again and show you some of my tricks.'

'Splendid!'

His shoulders relax. He was probably terrified that I'd attempt to loop the loop with him on board, or strap myself to a parachute and jump out.

Conditions are perfect and I swoop across great expanses of sky until I glide us to a stop and help Sir James to disembark. Then I take off again and paint the sky with loops and turns. Even though I am showing off for him I soon forget that and enjoy my wheeling and twirling, like a little girl with her first pair of skates.

I land and he applauds as I remove my helmet, climb out of the cockpit and take a bow.

'Absolutely marvellous!'

'I'm glad you enjoyed it. Shall we have lunch?'

Over lunch I regale him with stories from my flight around England to survey all landing sites.

'Eighteen hours in the air!' he exclaims. 'Were you not exhausted?'

'Not a bit,' I dismiss it. 'I was so comfortable. I made seventy-nine stops with time for a snack and to refuel. It was a breeze.'

He sits back and looks at me. 'You have done so much. Do you think you'll ever tire of it? Say, "that's enough now"?'

'I don't believe so. Definitely not yet. Not until I realise my big idea. I haven't even discussed it with anyone else. But I feel I can tell you.'

'I am honoured, Sophie.'

I lean towards him and lower my voice. 'I want to attempt a flight in Africa, flying the entire length of it.'

'My word. That is a whole other kettle of fish. Africa is vast, unexplored in parts. Quite frankly dangerous in others.'

I wave my hand. 'I spent time in Kenya and Tanganyika, you know. I just think, if I could do it, it would prove to the whole world that anything is possible. That anything we can achieve here at home can be attempted in Africa. That our civilising efforts there are not in vain. The Empire can do much good and a feat like this would prove what good has already been done, don't you think?'

'I think you could certainly do it.'

'I could. But my plane cannot.'

'You want me to buy you a new plane?'

His tone is serious. Do I detect disappointment? I take a deep breath. I didn't expect him to be so direct.

'No, Sir James. I value our friendship more than that. If you were to help me, in any way, then I would want you to be part of the adventure. As a companion, not a backer. I hope you feel the same. You enjoy my company too?'

'Oh, I do, very much. I'm sorry if I was abrupt. I am often approached by people looking for a handout.'

I place my knife and fork down noisily. 'I have got to where I am under my own steam, Sir James. I am certainly not looking for a handout. I find the suggestion insulting.'

'I didn't mean that. Please, don't take offence. I think you're marvellous. I was talking about other people.'

'These other people. Do they ever offer you anything in return?'

'Usually, once they get what they want they disappear.'

I take his hand. 'I'm not like that. I think you and I could be very good friends.'

'I do like to help good friends.' He squeezes my hand.

'I mean a lasting friendship, lifelong.'

'I may not have much of that left.'

'Nonsense. But, think, what do you want from life now?'

'I like the sound of friendship. Companionship, someone to welcome me home, a bit of fun, someone to take care of me.'

'Someone with nursing skills. Say, a former ambulance driver?' I raise an eyebrow.

We both laugh and I raise my glass to his. 'I think we both know what we want.'

'It seems so,' he says. 'Come and see me in a few days at my place in Wilton Crescent. I'll send a car.'

Sir James's driver opens my door and I step out. The Wilton Crescent townhouses soar skyward and wrap around me. I try not to gawp as I am led to the drawing-room. Grandfather's house in Newcastle West was grand in its setting but a hovel in comparison to this grandeur. Austere men frown at me from portraits cluttering the walls, interrupted by a pleasant lady, in pride of place over the mantle. Lady Euphemia, I presume. I bow my head. Am I disrespecting her memory with my plan to ensnare her husband? Maybe, but if not me then it will be some dull-as-ditchwater society lady. At least I can show Sir James a good time.

Here he comes now, gathering me to him to kiss my cheek.

'How have you been, Sir James?'

'Invigorated. My heart is still beating fast from our exhilarating flight. It's taken years off me.'

He hands me a gin. I sip. Perfect. He seems to have taken notice of how I like it. He sits on the couch beside me and I lean against the cushioned arm so I have a clear view of him.

'I've been thinking also, about your predicament,' he says, 'and I would like to make a proposition.'

I am afraid to blink.

'As you know, I am in the marriage market since I secured the annulment from that wretched woman. And no doubt my name is being added to lists of potential matches by keen mothers all across London society and beyond.'

I feel my cheeks redden. Where did I put my list? I must burn it when I get home.

'But what is a good match? I feel it is a relationship of mutual benefit, not unlike a business partnership, where each half brings some worth. That is what I had with Euphemia and that is what I long for. To be frank, you have something I need and I have something you need. You need my money to pursue your dreams. And I need your vitality, your openness to life, your adventurous spirit. I want to be there with you when you get your world-shaking record-breaker. I want people to say, "That's Lady Heath". I want to be part of that.'

My heart is thumping. Is this what I think it is?

'I also think you have a kind heart. And when you are finished with your adventures, you can turn your energy to taking care of me in my old age. It would be quite nice to have a companion by my side when that time comes. However ...'

He stands and moves away from me. I do not like 'however'.

'I do not mean to offend when I say this but I'm not a fool. I'm a man of considerable means and I must protect my assets, for myself and my successors. To that end, Sophie, I propose we marry and I will settle an annual income on you. Ten thousand pounds and not a penny more. You will live here with me and what you do with that income is your own business. What do you say?'

I am speechless, for once. I don't like feeling that I am being purchased. What's worse is that I'm complicit – this was my idea, until I convinced him it was his. Now it feels cheap. I feel cheap.

I stand. 'Sir James. Can I take some time to consider?'

He deflates. 'I don't see what there is to think about but I suppose so.'

He is used to getting what he wants. But he hasn't got me. Not yet. I need to talk to Mary.

Chapter Four

London, October 1927

'The cheap bastard!'

I nearly spit out my tea.

'Mary. It's hardly cheap. That's a lot of money any way you look at it.'

'No. He's being cheap. Do you have any idea how much he's actually worth? Not as much as my Abe, of course, but he's not short of a few bob. I'll talk to him.'

'I'm not sure. Maybe I should accept. I just didn't like the feeling that I was being bought. William and I fought all the time about money, I had to account for every penny I spent. I can't bear the thought of having a man in control of me like that again.'

'That's why you need to make sure it's enough. More than enough. Then you can do what you like. If he does want you, I'll make damn sure he pays the right price. You sit tight. I'll send word as soon as I have news.'

'Thank you.' I see her to the front door.

'Say, what do you need the money for anyway? What are you brewing?'

I give her a quick squeeze. 'If you pull this off, I'll tell you everything.'

Word comes from Mary. God knows what she said to him but Sir James has agreed to twenty thousand pounds a year. I'm relieved and begin deciding which plane to purchase. But first there's the matter of a wedding.

Christ Church is hastily booked and I phone around. A few friends assemble. Nobody from back home in Limerick or Ballybunion, no school friends from Cork or Belfast, none of my college friends from Dublin, but it's the best we can do at short notice.

Mary is waiting for me outside the church in Mayfair.

'You're wearing black?' she says. 'It's not a funeral, you know.'

'It's my lucky colour,' I tell her. I don't tell her that I feel a sense of mourning that it's not John who is waiting for me inside at the altar. My perfect match in age and everything else.

'Well, it must work because you are very lucky Sir James' daughter hasn't got wind of this. By all accounts she's not at all pleased at the thought of "that dreadfully mannish, Irish flying woman sniffing around her father".'

I tut. 'I'm sure Hylda and I will get on just fine. And with manners like that it sounds as though she'll benefit from having a new stepmother.'

I walk through the doors and stride to the altar. The vicar, Reverend Farran, performs the ceremony with little fanfare. The only words he speaks directly to me outside of the practicalities of the ceremony come when we are signing the register. Sir James describes himself as a widower and me as a widow. I list my father as a gentleman. We are laying our foundation on a bed of lies. I sign my name: *Sophie Catherine Theresa Mary Peirce-Evans*. The vicar comments that it is the longest name he's ever seen.

'And now it is simply Lady Heath,' I say.

We leave in a taxi. At Mary's suggestion we are taking a train to catch the boat to Ireland for our honeymoon. She thought it best if we made ourselves scarce.

'Lady Heath, are you pleased?' Sir James asks.

'Delightfully so.' I can't deny the thrill I feel at hearing my new title. Think of the doors that will open. No more having to kick them down with sheer will. 'We should invite your daughter to dinner on our return. I'm keen to get to know her.'

'It might be best to let Hylda cool off a while. I can't see why she doesn't want her old man to have a bit of fun. And if she's worried about me being taken advantage of, she needn't. As my only living child she is the sole beneficiary of my will.'

I jerk my head up. I stand to inherit nothing?

'Jolly poor timing of me – I am sorry,' Sir James says but he's laughing. 'Yes, my dear. You'll have your income until I die and then it's all hers.' He kisses me hard on the cheek. 'So you'd best take good care of me so that I stick around for a long, long time.'

I manage a smile. No. I'll take good care of me and this opportunity so that I never have to go husband-shopping again.

Dublin, Ireland, October 1927

We live the high life in fine Dublin hotels. I have to bite my tongue and refrain from pointing out the flea-bitten cafés and hangouts of my student days when I studied in the Royal College of Science. Sir James does get a kick out of my wilder side, though, so I treat him to one or two of my safer anecdotes. Like the one about the time I was dared to climb out of a window on the first floor of the college and jumped from sill to sill until I popped back into the laboratory, startling the class there.

He takes me to Barnardo Furriers and spends an outrageous amount of money on a fox-fur coat. I think for a moment about William sending complaining letters to Aunt Cis because I bought a new winter hat. She showed me the letter. He had concluded that my idea of marriage was to extract as much money as possible and have as good a time as possible and speculated that my faults were hereditary and that I should be more pitied than blamed! If extracting money and having a good time was my ambition with William then I failed miserably. I resolve not to think of him anymore, he belongs in the past.

It is this fur coat I'm wearing when we drive down to Aunt Cis's place in Ballybunion and I immediately regret it. The Peirces were never ones for flashy things. The shine of the motorcar and the glint of our gold wedding bands seem vulgar. And they illuminate the shabbiness of Doon Cottage and dear old Cis. I slide the fur coat from my shoulders as soon as we're inside and feel more like myself.

Aunt Cis is her usual charming sweetness, showing Sir James her portraits. She suggests getting out the family album and I baulk. Would she show him the one photograph of my father, wild-eyed, wild-haired, in a fine suit, a caricature of a gentleman? There are no such records of my mother. Her family hadn't the means and my father never thought to capture her image. I whisk Sir James away instead for a walk along the beach.

Cis has invited the usual gang for dinner – the D'Arcy cousins and that cretin, Cunningham. No doubt they're all dying to get a look at my millionaire. Well, let them. I'm more than able for them now, fortified by my wealth.

My D'Arcy cousins greet me warmly. They're happy to see me, dying to hear all about my escapades. I hold forth with my stories of flying and London life. I dodge out of an embrace from Cunningham and make sure when I'm seated that he's out of my line of sight. But that blasted man must make himself seen and heard, foisting his tainted company on every gathering.

'How did you come to meet Sir James?'

It sounds like an innocent question but I know him better. I am cagey and give him nothing.

'We move in many of the same circles.' I peer at him over my wine glass.

'You're being humble.' Sir James reaches for my hand. 'In truth, I was very much a fan of this famous aviatrix. I read so much about her in the papers and I was present at a number of her marvellous events. Our meeting was inevitable.'

I can't keep the grin from my lips. I blame the wine and the joy of Sir James speaking so highly of me. It just might be enough to shut Cunningham up.

'Yes. Inevitable.' I'm on the brink of giggling.

'Miss Peirce,' Sir James says, 'I must commend you.'

Poor Cis startles. 'What for?' She looks in confusion at the dried-out roast chicken she has served us.

'It is my understanding that you were instrumental in the raising of Sophie. Like a mother to her in the wake of the tragic loss of her parents.'

Cis still looks confused. My stomach churns and I grip the stem of my glass. Will Cis think I've told Sir James the truth? Of my housekeeper mother murdered by my lunatic father? Cunningham sniggers and the sound jostles her into a response.

'We're family. We did what must be done, no more.'

I release my grip on the glass. My family's silence on this matter was a source of frustration when I was younger and wanted to know more. Now, it is a relief. She smiles at me and I try to communicate all the love I feel for her. Sir James is right. She did raise me, mother me.

'Nevertheless, I commend you. You did a damn fine job.' He raises a glass in her direction and I could swear she's blushing. 'And if I may, Sophie. I would like to raise my glass in memory of your departed parents. I would very much like to have met them.'

I hear Cunningham muttering 'Lunatic asylum'. Cis shoots him a look. I shouldn't have brought Sir James here. It could ruin everything. He's still talking.

'I would be curious to meet the people who produced such a rare specimen of woman. I have travelled far and wide and have not met another like her. You knew them well, I presume?'

He glances around the table and is met with silence and panicked expressions.

Rosie D'Arcy leaps in, bless her.

'The Peirces were fine people. You'd be hard pressed to meet finer than Sophie's grandfather, Doctor George, that's for sure.'

Sir James smiles. 'It's a pleasure to meet all of you too.'

Cunningham pipes up again. 'We always make it our business to meet Sophie's husbands. I hope you'll have more luck than the first one. Poor man couldn't get her to settle down one bit.'

'I have no desire for her to settle down,' Sir James says. 'I want her to soar.'

I could cry with happiness. I have tolerated the thorn in my side that is Cunningham since I was a young girl. But to see him wilt now under the imperious tone of my husband is glorious.

'What are your plans, Sophie?' Rosie asks.

'I'm planning a trip,' I say, giving little away. 'But I shall need a new plane. For longer distance.'

I look at Sir James.

'Of course,' he says. 'You should get the latest model.'

I smile and wonder when I should tell him that I have already placed an order for the Avro 594 Avian.

'I'm going to walk the beach.' I am already halfway to the door before anyone can react. I see Cis glance towards the mantel clock. It is nearly midnight. But I am too restless to stay. The dining room is full of pipe smoke and small talk and the grating drone of Cunningham's blather.

Sir James takes a final swig from his brandy snifter.

'I will chaperone you, my dear.'

He sways on his feet as he pulls on his jacket. I can't say no, he'll have to come.

I try my best to match his slow pace as we stroll across Nun's Beach but the salty air fills my lungs and I have to move faster or I will explode. I race across the sand, the glow of the moonlight on my face. The breeze is soft and warmer than I expected. I reach the dunes and before my mind can register my decision my hands have begun their work. Within minutes I have stripped to my chemise. I run to the edge of the water and let the freezing Atlantic ripple over my toes. I can feel the spray from the waves. I hear Sir James calling to me as I start to plough my way in and through to the calmer water beyond the breaking waves. I am down and then I am under. A whoosh floods my ears, the chill engulfing me then turning to a spreading heat. How is this possible? Ice turns to fire and instead of being afraid I feel dangerously alive. I know this feeling well. I have it too when I'm in the air, when any rational person would be on edge, thinking of the danger. But I know only peace and calm in the skies.

I kick my legs behind me and carve a path through the swell. I love how my own strength propels me forward. I reach Virgin Rock, known to the locals as Carraig na bhFaoileán – Seagull Rock – and turn to face the shoreline. I can see Sir James, an insignificant speck, standing back from the water's edge, a hand shielding his eyes from the glint of moonlight on the water. I wave to him. Will he wait for me or wander off? It's equal to me either way.

I'm not ready to swim for shore yet. A wild notion takes me. I will swim into the arch in the rock. Silvery light flows through it, beckoning me in. I breaststroke with my arms and kick hard until I'm under the arch. Then I turn to lie on my back and look up at the rock. The moonlight picks out rust and shadowy jagged points. I don't like the sense of my world being capped. I prefer the infinity of the sky. I want to float on my back and watch the stars overhead.

I turn over and start to swim through to the other side. I will exit there, round the rock and make for the shore. But the sea has other ideas. It pushes back against me, making every effort exhausting and pointless. I concede and turn to swim out the way I came in. But the swell thwarts me there too. It tosses me towards the jagged ceiling and throws me against the rock walls. So this is how I will die? Lost at sea. Swimming in the dead of night, in October. When people hear that they will think I killed myself. That's what they said about William. And all before I've really lived. My legs are numb and a cut above my eye stings from the attack of the salt water.

But this is not my element. It cannot have me.

I grasp a rock with my fingertips. Then another, here and there and here, and pull myself along. I take some breaths and dive under, going as deep as I can. I swim underwater, feeling blindly in the pitch dark for anything that might hinder me. I stay under until my lungs burn for air and, as I surface and suck in mouthfuls, I see that I'm almost at the opening of the arch. I'm out of danger and can move through the water more easily now.

Once I am free and in open water again I lie on my back and breathe hard, regaining my strength. It feels less like I fought my way out and more like the sea relinquished me, decided not to have me after all, gave me back to the world.

As I push myself shoreward I promise myself that the sea will never have the chance to claim me again.

Sir James is nowhere to be seen. Shivering, I pull my clothes onto my wet sticky skin. I'm glad he's not here to see me like this, hurt and afraid. I catch up to him on the road on the way back to Cis's cottage.

'*Bloody hell, woman! I'm on my way to raise the alarm!*'

I laugh. 'Raise the alarm? For me? Really, Sir James, you should know better. I am more than capable of getting myself out of trouble.'

He is sour. 'It seems to me that you are more than capable of getting yourself *into* trouble.'

There is no point in arguing when I agree with him. I thread my arm through his, wincing when the material of my dress grates on raw skin at my elbow.

I pour us two generous brandies back at the house. One for his nerves, one to toast my survival.

'Let's leave tomorrow,' I say once the warmth of the brandy has stilled my chattering teeth.

I want to get back to London and make plans. I am impatient now to live.

Chapter Five

Stag Lane, London, November 1927

Mary bursts into the hangar at Stag Lane, disturbing my peace. She trails raindrops from her umbrella as she rushes to hug me.

'Look at you! All cooped up in here. You shouldn't work too hard, you know.'

I have been cooped up and I've been enjoying every moment. After a few weeks of being a social butterfly I crave solitude. And I wasn't really working. Truth be told, I was admiring every inch of my new plane and its exquisite paintwork.

Mary whistles. 'Look at this beauty! I do love the colour.'

'The newspapers said it was "womanish" of me to have it painted.'

'Better than being mannish. Newspaper men are hardly connoisseurs of fashion or flying, my dear. Pay them no heed. I think it's stunning. Why this colour?'

I hold aloft my right hand. On the fourth finger is a plain band with a turquoise stone.

'To match my favourite ring.'

I try to keep my tone neutral. It was a gift from John. Before. A promise of sorts. Unspoken. He told me the turquoise stone came from an ancient temple dedicated to Hathor, the Egyptian goddess of love among other things. I know he only bought it in a flea market but I'm not ready to part with it. Even though the twin finger on my left hand glitters with my new wedding band.

Mary produces a wad of envelopes from inside her coat. 'I hope I managed to keep these dry. I popped around to check on your place while you were gadding about. Fan mail, no doubt. Lots of it. And maybe a poison-pen letter from Hylda.'

I snort. I keep forgetting that Hylda exists and I am much happier to continue doing so. Mary rounds to the front of the plane and hunkers down to admire its underbelly. I rifle through the post. I stop when I recognise the writing. I look at the front. A postcard from Le Havre. So he's gone back to France. I turn it over again.

'*Dearest S, Congratulations. I hope this makes you happy. Love always. J x.*'

'Something from John?'

Mary watches as I struggle to swallow down my tears. She's already read it, I'm sure. I put the bundle down.

'Just congratulations. Kind of him to send a card. So, what do you think?'

'I think you're not over him.'

'I'm not. But I can't wallow in the past. My thoughts have to be on the future and my new baby.'

'*Baby?*' Mary shrieks.

I drape myself across the wing. 'This baby.'

'Oh, thank goodness! I shouldn't like to lose you to motherhood. Tell me, what are you planning? A beauty like this can't be shut away in a hangar. No more than you can.'

'I have no intention of it. Sir James and I are taking the RMS *Saxon* to South Africa. And I'll be taking this along too.'

'On the liner?'

'Yes. Why not? She can be stowed quite easily.'

Mary perches on an upturned box. 'I have missed you. Who else would be daft enough to think of packing a biplane in their holiday luggage? When do you go?'

'Later this month.'

She stands. 'Meet me for dinner tonight? If you're taking off again in a few weeks I want to see plenty of you. And I want to hear all about Ireland and your honeymoon.' She pinches my arm, teasing.

I quail. The details she wants are ones I do not wish to relive.

Then she's gone, admitting a flurry of winter rain in her wake. I pick up the postcard again and sit in her spot reading and rereading his words, trying to answer my questions. Does he mean it when he says he hopes I'm happy? Is he still angry? Does he love me? I kiss the card where he signed his initial. It looks angry. But the 'x' softens it. I slide the turquoise ring off my right hand and onto my left and kiss the stone.

Left After

And there are other lovelier things,
The spring, the hills, the sea.
What matter it if love be gone,
If these be left to me.

From *East African Nights* (1925), by Sophie Eliott-Lynn

Chapter Six

Cape Town, South Africa, December 1927

I stand on the dock and watch strong, dark natives unloading my Avian. I hope they are treating her kindly. Sir James doesn't know but many times during our seventeen-day voyage aboard the RMS *Saxon* I sneaked away to check on her, to make sure the rolling and tossing of our old ship wasn't roughing her up. My shoulders relax now as I see her emerge intact. The men stand to admire her. One of them runs his large hand over her furled wing and it is as though it is my hand. I can feel the cool smoothness of her surface, as he must. My plane is to be brought to the airfield and reassembled by George Henderson, an old friend from Brooklands Flying School, and I am determined to take her out for a ride at the first opportunity.

I turn away reluctantly and make my way to Sir James, who is waiting with our luggage in the motorcar. The driver has kept the engine running. Our evening ahead is a packed schedule of drinks parties, dinner and dancing. I had my fill of that onboard. I long to be elbow-deep in engine oil. But I must fulfil my duty. Sir James expects it of me, his famous young bride who he wishes to parade through South African society like a show pony. I am bored with cocktails, polite talk and formal dinners but Christmas in Cape Town must be tolerated, I suppose, and I will do my best to enjoy it, keep a smile on my face and my husband happy. But then, let no man stand in my way.

The fog of smoke in the heaving ballroom stings my eyes. I make my way outside to the balcony. There are too many people out here too, small groups talking in raised voices even though the thrum of the band is muffled by the closed French doors, and couples tucked away into corners. I shut my eyes and breathe in great lungfuls. It's almost midnight but the air is still heavy with the heat it has shouldered all day. My breaths transport me back to Kenya and for a moment I wish I was there, packed for a hunt, heading into wild bush with my native companions and a fully loaded rifle in my hands. Instead, tonight, I feel like the prey. All evening I've been hunted by the society wives of Cape Town keen for a look at the new Lady Heath. I prefer the amateur aviators wanting to know what flying I plan to do while I'm here. But I'm frustrated by their enquiries and the scratch of my sequinned dress and the echo of the question crashing through my mind. I know what I want to do here but how will I go about it?

I snatch a glass of champagne from a tray held aloft by a passing waiter and swallow its contents in one gulp. The poor man looks appalled. I have besmirched his display.

'Happy New Year,' I tell him. I replace the empty glass and go back inside.

My husband is where I left him, at our table. All the inquisitive wives have been replaced by men. They parry and thrust through a veil of cigar smoke and I listen to catch the thread of the debate.

'It's a dream, my boy. A fine one but I wager it will remain so.'

Sir James is addressing a man I've never seen before. He looks to be closer to my age. Then again everyone seems so much younger compared to Sir James. He is tanned with smooth skin and his brown eyes bring to mind my John. I pause for a moment, side-swiped by the memory. The man stands, his height matches mine, and he gestures for me to take his seat. I do and another champagne flute appears before me. My mouth is dry and I look around for a waiter. I need a gin and tonic to revive me.

'Here now is someone whose opinion will count,' Sir James says. 'May I present my wife, Lady Heath. This is Mr Emil Millin, the motoring editor of the *Rand Daily Mail*. And dreamer of the latest daft notion to arrive in Cape Town.'

The men erupt into laughter and I feel a pitying kinship with Mr Millin. Moreso as I know many of these men only laugh because Sir James does. I scowl at them then turn my attention to Mr Millin who has secured himself a new seat on my left.

'Tell her. Go on.' Sir James gestures with his cigar.

'It wasn't my idea, to be honest. But I'm very glad to be part of it. It could change Africa forever and for the better.'

My stomach clenches. This sounds very like my own plan. Is it about to be snatched away from me?

Mr Millin regards me seriously. 'I believe you are someone who might appreciate the audacity of it.'

His eyes connect with mine, seeking an ally. But I can't take sides. Not yet.

'The dream, the idea, the notion,' I say. 'Good God, will someone enlighten me? What is this grand endeavour?'

Mr Millin opens his mouth to answer but I spot a waiter. I put my hand on his arm to pause him and signal for service. The waiter nods at my request for a large gin. The others at the table place their orders and all the while my hand remains on Millin's arm. I feel the subtle flex of muscle through the sleeve of his dinner jacket and know that he is conscious of my touch. I remove it and turn to him.

'Go on, please.'

He reaches into an inner pocket and pulls out a map of the continent. 'Very simply, the plan, or the grand endeavour as you put it, is to traverse the length of Africa and on to London.'

I hold my breath as he continues.

'By motorcar. A Chrysler 72 Sedan.'

I exhale. 'By car! But there are no roads. Is that possible?'

'We shall find out.'

'Will you go alone?'

'I'll have the assistance of the accomplished racing driver, Gerry Bouwer.'

'And finance?' I'm peppering him with questions, I know, but my mind is racing ahead to my own calculations.

'Sir Abe Bailey. My own paper, the *Rand Daily Mail* and the *Sunday Times* will carry reports of our progress and Mobil will supply us.'

I'm silent, taking it all in. Pieces of the puzzle are starting to fall into place, except one. Abe is financing this? Mary didn't say a word about it.

'Lady Heath wants to do the same thing. But by plane,' Sir James announces from the other side of the table.

His flushed cheeks tell me he's quite drunk. I wish I was close enough to kick him under the table. I narrow my eyes to silence him. He'll ruin everything and I regret ever telling him about my ambition.

'She told me all about it on one of our first dates.'

I take a long sip from my glass. 'Silly Sir James! I was just trying to impress you.' I raise my left hand and wiggle my heavily jewelled wedding finger. 'Did it work?'

The table erupts with laughter.

Before Sir James can respond the waiter is upon us again with a tray of champagne for the New Year's toast. Sir James gestures for me to join him as he makes his way to the dance floor. I stand to follow him then lean down, close to Mr Millin's ear so he can hear me. The band is revving up for a rousing countdown.

'I want to know more. Let's talk again.'

I don't dare to turn back as I walk away but I can feel his eyes on me.

The champagne and gin have me awake early next morning seeking out cool water. Sir James is snoring with the intensity of a bear and our room is stuffy and confining despite it being one of the Mount Nelson's most spacious suites. I need to get out and fill my lungs with fresh air before the later heat steals it away.

I've nearly completed my first brisk lap of the grounds when a pair of shoes, dangling from a bench, stops me. The shoes, and the legs they belong to, lower to the ground and there is the noise of someone groaning into a stretch. I could turn away and go back the way I came but I prefer to exercise in a loop. And I'm curious. Who is this party debris washed ashore on the first dawn of 1928? I pick up my pace again to go by.

'Lady Heath.'

I halt. 'Mr Millin. Are you camping out?'

He pulls on the dinner jacket he wore last night, now creased and worse for wear. As is he.

'I guess so,' he says, laughing. 'My residence seemed too far away last night and this bench looked invitingly comfortable.' He stretches again and stands, looking down on the wooden bench. 'Deceitful thing.' Then he looks at me. 'Are you a night owl or an early bird, Lady Heath?'

'I rarely sleep well after a party. I've had my rest. My mind woke me early with questions and now that I've bumped into you I may find some answers.'

He looks at me quizzically.

'Will you accompany me to breakfast?' I ask.

We fill the time over our food with polite conversation. He asks about my flying exploits. He is well-informed, not surprising for a newspaper man.

'Are you married?' I ask.

'Yes, my wife, Ivy, is at home in Montagu. Our first child is imminent.'

'How lovely.'

'You have no desire for children?'

His question, which sounds more like a conclusion he has reached after some thought, catches me unawares. He's not the first to make the assumption. To presume that my ambition trumps any maternal leanings. The actual truth of the matter remains between me and a dead man who expressed his disappointment with my deficiency in that regard with a pathetic beating. I took it because I felt he needed me to. To make him feel more of a man. But when his last blow landed I swore if he ever laid a finger on me again it would be his last moment on earth. I say none of this to Mr Millin. I have never said it to anyone. I serve him my usual, public answer.

'I have chosen flying, Mr Millin.'

'Does it have to be a choice? Doesn't Lady Bailey have a full brood?'

'Yes. And a full staff. Besides, that is her preference. I believe that running a home is a full-time job. A woman who has to look after a household and a husband and a family should do nothing else if she wants her home to run well. This may surprise you but I think the woman's place is in the home.'

He puts his coffee cup down loudly. I have surprised him. Before he can say anything I deliver my punchline.

'But, failing that, in the aerodrome.'

He laughs heartily and I enjoy the look of him. His eyes crease with small lines and I see in them the handsome older man he will be some day.

'Do all of your profound statements come in rhyme?'

'Not always. Although I did try my hand at poetry in my East African days. I even published them. I find them hard to read now, though. So full of youthful optimism and naiveté.'

'Are you not still an optimist?'

'I'm a pragmatist.'

'Have you shared your view of family life with Lady Bailey?'

'She chooses her path and I choose mine. She enjoys the escape of flying, she told me that herself.'

'Is that why you do it? To escape?'

I'm starting to realise I need to be vigilant around this man. These are the questions of a journalist.

'I like being up there. Above the clouds. Five hundred feet in the air. It's very peaceful. No people to spoil it. It gets so crowded down here, don't you think?'

He smiles. He knows my game. We are like two tigers, circling, warily beginning our courtship.

'Sometimes.'

'And you? Is your plan to drive the length of Africa your escape?' From your pregnant wife, I muse, but do not say.

He shrugs. 'It's an assignment. A job. But I'm excited. We could really change Africa. For the better. Really do something important. Do you know what I mean?'

'I do. A driving route from end to end would open the continent up, certainly. But I think it's impractical. The terrain, the climate, the natives. So much to get in your way.'

'The pragmatist speaks!'

The dishes are cleared and we move to the covered verandah. I light a cigarette and ponder my next move.

'I'm going to share something with you, Mr Millin.'

'Emil. Please. If you're going to confide in me then you must call me Emil.'

'It's not a confidence. Or, maybe it is, something like it. I haven't fully thought this through but I think I'm going to go for it. I want to fly the length of Africa. Cape Town to London. Solo. I think an air route from end to end is much more achievable than a road network. Dick Bentley has just completed a trip from London to Cape Town in a Tiger Moth. I want to prove it can be done starting from the colonies.'

I sit and drag on my cigarette and wait. Will he tell me I'm crazy? Point out all the risks and reasons why I, a woman, shouldn't even consider such a feat.

'What do you need to do that?' he asks.

I grin. A perfect response. 'Not much. I have my plane. I have a route in mind. I need some maps.'

In my mind the planning has started. I'm calculating what supplies I can pack into the Avian, the distances between landing points, the weather, sources of fuel.

'Maybe we could work together,' he says. 'Follow a similar path. Our expedition could serve as a guide for you and you could recce our route ahead.'

'It sounds to me like you've given it some thought already, Emil.'

'It crossed my mind. When I heard that the daring aviator, Lady Heath, had packed an airplane I said to myself, "This lady is not here on honeymoon. Even if her husband thinks so".'

I laugh. Am I so transparent? 'So it's a deal?'

He leans over and offers me his hand. 'I'll have to run it by Gerry and my editor. But you can count me in.'

He sits back in his chair and stares at the clear blue sky doming over us. 'I think I would quite like to look up and see you there.'

Chapter Seven

South Africa, 10th January 1928

I wait to hear from Emil and meanwhile focus on spreading the love of flying. The days and weeks are a joyous whirlwind. South Africans have accepted me as a flying celebrity and are hungry to rub up against that fame, to fly, to be as progressive as their peers throughout the empire. I am more and more enthused about my plan every day that I meet these people. I fly to Port Elizabeth and present the local aero club there with a decent Westland Widgeon and they immediately name it *The Lady Heath*. I give some joyrides and win a race. I'm growing comfortable with the fact that I have enough money for myself so I gift anything I make from joyrides or prize money to the local clubs. How wonderful it would be to leave a legacy of fledgling flyers in my wake!

I'm invited to Port Alfred but fail to find it from the air, hidden under cloud. I feel awful. Apparently they had a welcome ceremony arranged for me there and the local chief was to present me with my own *assegai*, a light spear. I have no idea where I would stow such an item on my Avian.

The other thing I'm leaving in my wake is a disgruntled husband. It might seem deliberate that no sooner do I land in one place than I'm taking off again. But it is not my fault if he can't keep up. I keep him informed of my schedule as best I can but he must understand that flying is dictated not by our whims alone but weather and the condition of the aircraft and many other factors. Tomorrow we are to meet in Durban where he insists we will stay a few days in the Country Club. Grudgingly I will comply even though the thought of standing still sets my teeth on edge. It will allow me an opportunity to outline my plan in detail to him.

We depart for Durban in formation with my Avian leading Major Miller, a pioneer of South African aviation, in his Moth and in the rear a local enthusiast follows in his Widgeon. I savour the peace of the morning sky. It is lit softly by the just-risen sun and it feels as though Mother Nature is displaying her finery just for me, peeling back the shadow of the night and unveiling, in startling clarity, the splendour of the land below me. I guide my plane up and over some mountains then descend again so that I can observe the tiny huts that cling to the slopes, each with its own patch for cultivating crops. Would I be happy there? The simplicity appeals to me. I could rise with the sun and tend to my garden. I toy with the image for a few moments but I know that life is not for me. William and I tried for something similar, on a larger scale, in Kenya and it nearly drove me mad. The slow pace, the repetitive days, the suffocating boredom. As I recall it now I push the stick forward, obeying my natural instinct and accelerating away.

We circle the town of Umtata, but there is no obvious landing spot. On to another smaller town, the surface pock-marked by ant heaps. I smile at the thought of their frenetic industry. That's more my style.

We land and climb down, stretching the two hours of flight time from our limbs. A sign tells me we are in Tsolo and all of its residents now are rushing towards us. I take a breath and ready my smile. Little children of all colours swarm the plane, a few daring to climb into the cockpit as the adults shake our hands.

'I'm Lady Heath,' I tell them, in case the news of our journey hasn't reached them yet.

It appears it has, though, as the crowd makes way for the important men. One, I presume, is the Mayor, a round, sweaty man in a crumpled, cream, linen suit. And the other – a vision – a tall, lithe native, his legs clad in animal hide, chest bare apart from a curtain of coloured beads. His headdress is ornamented with even more strings of blue, white and red beads that sway with every movement. I think of a young bride, letting her hair hang free at night, alone with her husband. I guess that he is the town *sangoma*. It interests me how the modern and primitive co-exist in these colonies where the Mayor and witchdoctor come to greet visitors. There are echoes of Ireland, where pagan beliefs echo beneath the proper religions. Is he here to cast a spell on me? To curse me? To protect the town from my aerial wizardry? I watch bemused and unafraid. However tall he is, so am I, and I am better nourished.

He steps forward and speaks to us in his own language of words and clicks. He stretches out his arms and presents me with a beaded headdress. I bow and accept it. Should I put it on? I look to the white Mayor for rescue.

'As a sign of our esteem, Lady Heath, our *sangoma* offers you this token. The white and blue beads will help you to navigate in the real world and in the spiritual – the red connects you to your ancestors, as we all must be.'

I smile to cover my grimace. Navigation help will always be welcome in a country with few mapped routes but the thought of being connected to my ancestors – well, those I'd rather leave behind.

'Thank you.'

'This headdress is worn by those who make magic,' the Mayor says.

'But I am no magician!'

He gestures to my plane. 'You fly, like a bird. In the eyes of the *sangoma* and all of us that is a great magic.'

I lift the headdress and place it on my head. The swish of the beads is pleasant, like the ripple of a breeze through sea-grass or bamboo. I feel transformed by it. I have a new perspective on my flying and, yes, now I can see that it is wondrous. The crowd cheers and begins to sing and we attempt to move along with their rhythm. When the celebration ends we are quickly brought back down to earth by the news that refuelling here is impossible as supplies must travel over a hundred kilometres by ox-wagon.

We backtrack to Umtata then onwards again to Durban.

Sir James is waiting for me as I land in the airfield opposite the Country Club. I kiss him warmly on the cheek, suddenly filled with gratitude for what he has made possible for me, and what he is about to. I must find the right moment to tell him my plans but first there is a swim to be had, a long soak in the bath and a cool drink on the terrace. My reluctance to break my momentum fades as I give in to the luxuries of the club. I'm aware that my next few weeks will not be so comfortable so I allow myself to indulge.

I arrive to breakfast next morning, well-rested and eager to get on the tennis court. I'm halfway through my omelette and recounting the witchdoctor episode to Sir James when I am interrupted by the waiter.

'A telegram, ma'am.'

I slide it from the silver tray. **Don't worry. You'll be next. E.M.**

E.M. Emil. What does he mean? I don't like when people tell me not to worry. It worries me.

'News?' Sir James asks.

'Of a sort. It's from Mr Millin. We met him at the New Year's Eve party. Remember?'

'Ah yes, the brave fool who wants to drive the length of Africa.'

I smile but his words cut. Is that what people say about me?

'What does he say?' Sir James is eyeballing the telegram.

'I'm not sure. It's somewhat puzzling.' My attention strays to the lobby where several guests are studying the morning papers. I leave the table and approach an older lady.

'May I?'

Before she can answer I snatch the *Rand Daily Mail* from her grasp. There, in the bottom right-hand corner of the front page, is a familiar face. And underneath the caption, "Lady Champion Aviator of the World".

Mary. My friend. My protégée. My student. I taught her everything she knows about flying. All those early mornings at Stag Lane when she crept out of her house to learn in secret. When she told Abe she had earned her 'A' licence, he immediately bought her a plane. My blood fizzes with the unfairness. She has been handed it all and now this. I should be happy for her. I scan the article. '**First woman to receive the honour of being crowned Lady Champion Aviator of the World ... defeated Lady Heath at Birmingham air pageant ... holds height record for light aeroplane ...**' My mouth twists at the memory. Weeks after my own world record Mary outdid me and set her own. She has always been on my heels and now it seems she has passed me out.

My name is mentioned only in reference to that one defeat! And what of my records? My achievements? Nothing. No recognition. No international honour. I am a fool. While I was congratulating myself on having a plane named after me in some backwater town, here she is, Lady Champion Aviator of the World, neck and neck with Lucky Lindy. I want to be proud of her, to celebrate her success and what it means for all of us women aviators but I cannot. Not yet. I must surrender to my more immediate bitterness. I have worked so hard.

Of course, Mary and I are not the same, no matter how much I try to pretend. She emerged, cosseted by the privilege of being a Westenra, raised in Rossmore Castle, and has sailed through life, gliding from her father's wealth to marriage to one of the world's wealthiest men. I clawed my way out of the austere townhouse of a country GP, the daughter of a lowly Catholic housekeeper and a lunatic. My claim on high society is as tenuous as tissue paper. I am doomed to be overlooked and under-appreciated and, truth be told, I think high society would turf me out the door onto the street at the first chance.

I toss the paper onto the woman's lap and storm out. I find a partner, grab a racket and wallop balls at the poor man for over an hour until he pleads injury. I'm bathed in sweat and have managed to calm down a little.

'If you give up flying,' he quips through ragged breaths, 'you could try tennis as your next hobby.'

Hobby! I resist the urge to fling my racket at him.

I return to my bedroom and close the drapes. I lie on the bed and allow my heart rate to slow down and I think. **'You'll be next.'** Emil's words. The next champion. But next is no good. She is the first now and always will be. I must progress my plan. I can be the first at that, at least. I clean myself up and go to find Sir James. I'm a little shamefaced at how I abandoned him at breakfast. As I wander through the corridors of the Country Club I consider my next steps. A telegram to Emil. A telegram to Mary. But first, a conversation.

Sir James is silent and I wonder if he's going to tell me it's a terrible idea. Or that he won't allow it. I am doing it. With or without his blessing. But with his money.

'It could work.'

I smile. 'It will. Once the Chrysler dash sets off I'll accompany them, survey their route, pass messages, generally keep an eye on them, from the air.'

'What do you gain from this alliance?'

A word pops into my head. *Emil*. It surprises me. I haven't thought about it. Not really. But there it is. Of course, I won't say it out loud.

'Publicity,' I say. 'A degree of security.'

'Won't it slow you down? You'll be able to travel much faster than a motorcar in terrain with no roads.'

'I'm not in a hurry.' I see a shadow cross his face and quickly backtrack. I don't want him to think that I'm keen to be away from him for months on end. 'It shouldn't take more than three weeks. But my aim is to get safely to London, not break any speed records along the way. There's much to be gained for the Empire from both these expeditions, don't you think?'

'Abe certainly seems to think so, if he's willing to put his money behind it. But, what of your safety?'

'Mine?' I'm surprised. It's not a concern he's expressed before.

'This is Africa, my dear. Wild animals, swamps, hostile natives, cannibals.'

I raise an eyebrow. He's being melodramatic.

'I'll be up in the air, safe and sound. And the expedition will keep track of my whereabouts.'

'You could crash, run out of fuel.'

'It hasn't happened yet. Probably never will.'

'What about your friend?'

'My friend?'

'Lady Bailey.'

'She seems to be getting on just fine.' Neither of us have mentioned the news of her being awarded the title of Lady Champion Aviator of the World. Maybe he doesn't know or maybe he's sparing my feelings.

'She nearly had her head chopped off.'

I laugh, although I shouldn't. Poor Mary wandered too close to her propeller last year and scalped herself. Her good friend Geoffrey scooped the missing chunk off the ground and some very expensive doctors made the best of reattaching it. Mary, in typical style, turned it into a fashion statement, sporting a different turban every day. Most importantly of all – she kept flying.

'I'll make sure to stand clear of the blades,' I respond drily. Sir James should know I am too accomplished and careful to make such an amateur mistake.

'When do you go?'

'I need to speak to Emil – Mr. Millin,' I correct myself. 'It's down to them really.'

Sir James takes my hand. 'Make sure you come back to me.'

I permit him to hold it a few moments longer but my patience is limited. I am itching to message Emil. And I suppose I should send Mary my congratulations.

Return Jo'burg 28th. When do we depart? Sophie.

Dear Champion Friend. Warmest congratulations. Sophie.

Chapter Eight

Baragwanath, South Africa, 29th January 1928

I await a reply from Emil and grow more irritated by the day. I cannot abide it. I have spent years stalled, awaiting approval, sanction, permission from every organisation and institution that stood in my way. And here I am again. But this time it is preposterous. Why am I waiting on a motoring journalist who works for a newspaper that is organising a motoring expedition? Why am I tying myself to their adventure instead of striking out alone? They will be of some use to me, I'm sure, but as soon as they no longer are or as soon as I'm hindered by them in any way I will part company. Maybe even sooner. Emil must know I'm back from Durban. If I don't hear from him in the next few days then it's off!

My sour humour is not helped by worries about my plane. A leak in the petrol tank and torrential rain have caused some engine damage. I think it has been sorted so I'll try her out today at Baragwanath. They are hosting me for Ladies Day. Perhaps if my engine performs well and I manage to see Emil I will feel more hopeful.

When I arrive at the aerodrome I am swept away by a Mrs Evans and her daughter.

'Lady Heath, what an honour!' The elegantly dressed lady extends a gloved hand. 'We are in an absolute heap, I'm afraid. It's such a joy to have you but the crowds ...' She waves her white glove in the direction of the airfield.

Her daughter, a young girl of about sixteen, takes up her point.

'What Mother is saying, Lady Heath, is that this is the largest crowd we've ever seen in Jo'burg. You've proved quite the draw. Look!'

She leads me to a large window overlooking the runway where thousands of cars are spewing their passengers out. I had no idea my celebrity had risen to this height. What has been happening in my absence? I spot a familiar face in the crowd, notebook in hand, and he must sense it for he turns and seeing me, salutes. I return it, smiling. Is this all his doing? Has Emil been drumming up a frenzy around me and my flying? My hopes for the trip soar again. He does know what he's doing.

Mrs Evans fans her drenched brow with a programme. The sight of officials struggling to control the crowd is clearly bothering her.

I turn to her daughter.

'I'm sorry, I don't believe I got your name.'

'Muriel.'

'Shall we escape the crowds, Muriel? Get some air? It would do your mother good.'

Muriel nods. 'But where?'

I extend my finger and point. *Up*. 'Have you ever been in a plane?

Mrs Evans has forgotten about the crowds by the time I land. Her first joyride has left her still flushed, but now it's from exhilaration. She takes to the makeshift platform to introduce me.

'*And today, ladies and gentlemen, you will be witness to South Africa's first air race!*'

Her exuberant words are lost in the furore of cheers and she whoops with laughter as the crowd surges forward, surrounding the planes.

I step onto the platform and shout over the melée. '*Dear friends, the air race cannot happen if the planes can't fly! You must move back, give us space! And then we will give you a spectacle to remember!*'

Finally, the spectators are herded off the runway and we can manoeuvre our planes into position. There are four of us competing: my friend Lieutenant Bentley, fresh from his flight from London to Cape Town, Lieutenant Bellin, Major Miller and me. I take off last and chuckle as I see Miller has completely missed the belt of trees we have to round. That's him disqualified. I make my turn at a high altitude, swooping upwards on the bend, giving me an extra push for the home straight. I pass Bellin, then Bentley, then the finishing post.

I climb down, waving at the cheering crowd and am hoisted onto waiting shoulders and paraded throne-like back to the platform.

Emil is waiting for me when the formalities and prize-giving are completed.

'Are you enjoying yourself?' he asks.

I laugh. 'It is tremendous fun.'

Today has reminded me what I love most. The thrill of the flight. Never mind the honours and the damaged engine. This is what it's all about.

'Now, where can a winning pilot get a drink?' I ask.

'I'll bring you one. But first you have to do an interview. For my paper. Let's find somewhere a bit quieter.'

His hand is on my elbow, leading me away from the party. I stop walking and turn to face him.

'You want to interview me? Somewhere quiet?' I know this is bold but I keep my tone light. I can feign humour if I've got this wrong.

He takes a small step towards me. Not so much that anyone else would notice but enough that I can read his intent.

'I would like nothing more.' He steps back and takes my elbow again. 'But, unfortunately, I am a mere motoring journalist.'

In a quiet back room an older man in a grey trousers and jacket waits for me, pencil hovering over his lined notebook. His hat sits on the table and he wipes at his brow with a handkerchief. He pockets it now and stands to greet me.

'Lady Heath. Pieter Cranch. Thank you for agreeing to speak to me.'

'I'm not sure I did,' I reply.

His brow creases and he glances at Emil.

I'm being grumpy. I'm too warm, I want a cool drink and I'm irritated at Emil making arrangements without consulting me.

I take a breath. 'But I'm sure we'll have a wonderful chat. Emil, be a darling and bring us two ice-cold drinks. And I hope you don't mind, Mr Cranch, but it is far too hot for jackets.'

I slip my arms from mine and take a seat at the table. He does the same – the armpits of his shirt are soaked through with sweat.

I call after Emil, '*Make them large ones!*' then smile at my interviewer. 'Shall we begin?'

'I won't keep you long, Lady Heath. Your hosts won't be pleased if I do. But your arrival in South Africa has garnered much interest. You are the first woman pilot that South Africa has seen. What do you think of that?'

'Well, I think it's wonderful and I hope I will spark the interest of some young ladies to give flying a try. There's no reason at all why South Africa shouldn't be teeming with women pilots.'

'You think flying is a fitting pursuit for a woman?'

'Of course.'

'A married woman?'

'I don't see how having a ring on your finger might affect one's aviation skills. Major Miller is married, is he not?'

Mr Cranch coughs and shifts about in his seat. I feel a little sorry for him but then he did ask a stupid question. I could tell him what I really feel but I want to keep his readers on side. I soften my shoulders and smile.

'I'm being glib, Mr Cranch, forgive me. Sometimes I find I'm quite giddy after an air race. Let me give you a more considered response.'

Emil sneaks back in and places the drinks before us. Gin and tonic and plenty of ice. I take a big sip. Strong too, just how I like it.

'Mind if I sit in?' Emil says. He seats himself quietly behind us.

Mr Cranch drains half the glass, then glances at his notebook. I twirl an ice cube with my finger then suck the cold liquid from it. He peers at me over his glass, jaw clenched, pencil poised. I can tell he isn't sure if he likes me or not.

'One must choose one's priorities,' I say. 'If you want a thing to be done well you must give it all your energy. Home-running is a full-time job and a woman who has to look after a house, a husband, a family and run a home should do just that and nothing else.'

He's scribbling furiously now but I can see his features have relaxed. He likes what he's hearing.

I continue, 'As I'm sure you're aware I am recently wed to the wonderfully understanding Sir James. He does not need me to run his home. He is quite well-cared for already. And that leaves me free to put all my energies into my career.'

Mr Cranch smiles a little. I have put him at ease. He can print my words without the fear of every South African housewife whipping off her apron and abandoning her brood to take to the skies.

'No children?'

Always this question! Why must he ask a question to which he already knows the answer?

'I wouldn't ever have them in a plane, Mr Cranch. That would be reckless.' I tilt my head down and look at him from under my eyelashes.

He bursts into laughter. 'How true, Lady Heath! Meddlesome little buggers. But how do you keep going? You are rarely in one place for any length of time. Do you ever sleep?'

'Oh, I love my sleep. Eleven or twelve hours is ideal. It's even possible to have a little nap while I'm flying.'

'I don't believe that. You make it sound like a stroll in the park.'

'It's a lot more glamorous than that but no less comfortable.'

'Glamorous? Are you hosting cocktail parties up there?'

'I wish! I'm always ready to attend one when I land. I'm never without my black beaded evening dress, my embroidered shawl and a decent pair of evening shoes for dancing in.'

'What else?'

His pencil flies across the page as he tries to get it all down. This is gold. The party girl in the cockpit. His readers will eat it up, just like he is now.

'Well, a girl has to be practical too, Mr Cranch. I take a black leather coat, my flying helmet, long leather boots. Some clothes that fold easily: a well-tailored coat and skirt, a silk shirt, some silk undergarments.'

I hear a stifled snigger from Emil behind me. Mr Cranch is blushing from his neck to the tips of his ears.

'Oh dear, I've said too much. Please don't print that last part, Mr Cranch!'

'Of course not. Discretion is vital.'

'The part about the silk undergarments, I mean. It's a practicality when flying but it may be improper. If we could just keep that between us two?'

'Yes, of course.'

'Do you have enough?'

My glass is empty, the ice cubes melting to water.

'One final question, if I may. Flying is your passion, it's easy to see. But what do you do for fun?'

'I play tennis and dance. And hunt. I'm a damn fine shot. In my home in London I have a leopard-skin rug and the head of a hartebeest. Both my own kills.'

He puts his pencil down and leans back in his chair to regard me.

'You are quite a woman, Lady Heath.'

I laugh softly. 'You're too kind.' I stand. 'Now, if you feel you have enough I would like to rejoin my hosts. I'd hate for them to think me rude.'

I extend my hand. He rushes to his feet and grasps it.

'Not rude, certainly not. Formidable and, if I may say, charming.'

We shake hands and I leave. I hear Emil exchange some words with him then he is hot on my heels.

I untuck my shirt to allow some air to cool my sticky skin. I need to freshen up before dinner.

Emil catches up and matches my stride.

'You have a new fan there,' he remarks.

I shrug. 'I find that if you get a journalist on your side they write more kindly about you. I have a decent following here now and I want to make sure they stay with me. Do you think it will make the front page?'

'No doubt. But why the act?'

'The act?'

'The way you played up to Cranch back there. All girlish and all that talk about a woman running a home. You said it before but I'm not sure I buy it. It's not who you are.'

I stop and spin on my heel to face him.

'How would you know? You barely know me. Maybe this is me. Maybe I would like to be a homemaker, with my own brood.'

Emil snorts. 'If you wanted that you wouldn't stop until you got it. But you're so daring and able. Why hide it? Why hide your power?'

'It scares people.'

'Not me.'

'Other people. I get called "mannish" much more than "girlish". If I come across as less feminine they see that as a threat. Then they start thinking about their own wives and daughters and what might happen if they decide to follow their passions and suddenly they're afraid. Then they might try to destroy me. So, I give them what they want to hear – evening dresses and so on.'

'You're a suffragette?'

'Of course. I flew over the Equal Rights march in London a few years ago to show my support. But it's another thing I learned in the war. Progress must be gained piece by piece. No matter how much I want to kick against the rails. Piece by piece or you'll startle the horses.'

'That makes sense. Will we sit and have a drink? We have a lot to discuss.'

'I need to change. But, yes, I want to talk about the expedition.'

'I want to talk about the silk undergarments.'

I tut and stride away but I feel a smile threatening to appear.

'One hour – member's lounge,' I say.

I hear 'Yes, ma'am' as I turn the corner.

Chapter Nine

Baragwanath, South Africa, 29th January 1928

The members' lounge is full and noisy, fizzing with the excitement of the day. The airfield has never before welcomed such crowds and I'm happy to notice that there is a distinctly feminine vibration to the chatter. The women here are excited, enthused. I have achieved something.

I turn my attention to Emil. His jacket hangs on the back of his chair and he has rolled up his shirtsleeves. He produces a small pencil from behind his ear and starts to unfold a large map between us. I move our drinks to one side.

He smooths the map with his hands then circles *Cape Town* and *Johannesburg* and continues tracing a route up the continent.

Bulawayo, Victoria Falls, Broken Hill, Abercorn. On and on until *Alexandria*.

'Then we sail to Italy and drive across Europe.' He draws a large, emphatic circle around *London* then looks up. 'What do you think?'

I think it is wonderful and crazy. The map laid out in front of us shows a flat, empty continent. It is a tidy rug of green, traced sparsely with spidery routes that end abruptly at ladybird spots where the towns sit. It is pretty and utterly useless. Nothing to show where the terrain will cripple you or the weather will turn on you, which natives will greet you with sharpened spears or where a swamp waits to swallow you whole. You and your Chrysler Sedan 72.

'I'm thinking,' I reply.

I am thinking of distance and speed and how much fuel I will need and where my landings will be and how long I will stay grounded for at each. And where I can find a better map. Dick Bentley must have something from his flight that I could use. I have more questions than answers but they are for me, not Emil.

'I'll fly ahead and loop back if I see anything of note. We'll have to work out a system of signs, for communication. Something you'll see easily if I fly low.'

'And we'll rendezvous?'

'At times.'

I want to do this alone. I need to do this alone. But I'm tempted by the idea of having company. I'm also wondering if I will have the patience to wait for this expedition. They will slow me down.

'When is the announcement?' I ask.

'Any day now. There's no point waiting.'

'Do you have a date for departure?'

'A few weeks, I imagine. I'm going back to Cape Town tomorrow. I might know more then.'

'You know you're driving into rainy season?'

'Yes. That's a concern. But Gerry said for this expedition to be of any use we have to see the place at its worst and conquer it.'

I lean across and clink my glass against his. 'To conquering!'

He smiles and takes my free hand in his.

'Are we celebrating?'

A crisp voice cuts through our moment. I stand, sloshing wine from my glass and Emil dives to rescue the map.

'Sir James. You remember Emil Millin? He sat with us a while on New Year's Eve.'

'Mr Millin. Of the *Rand Daily Mail*. Indeed, I remember. And I believe you plan to steal my wife.'

Emil reddens. His hand hangs mid-air where he had extended it towards Sir James who is ignoring it. I come to his aid.

'Now, now, Sir James. He only means to borrow me. Or rather my flying skills. And it is going to be of great assistance to me for my own endeavour. I will come back to you and there's a better chance that I will be in one piece thanks to Mr Millin's expedition. We were just discussing the agreed route.'

'Marvellous. I wish you luck then.' Sir James shakes Emil's hand but there is no warmth in his face. He turns to me. 'Do you think I could pin you down for dinner before you take off again?'

'Of course.' I shake Emil's hand formally. 'Send me a telegram, won't you? I'll be ready.'

I slip my hand into the crook of Sir James' arm and accompany him to the waiting motor car. There is a sourness to him.

We return to our hotel in Johannesburg and I spend that evening trying to jolly him into good humour. But I'm tiring of this game. When we go to bed I listen to the sound of his snoring and imagine it is the rumble of my engine taking me to the skies.

The Light Aeroplane Club has agreed to let me spend a few days doing routine work on their Cirrus engines for practice. I need to know how to make repairs myself when the time comes and I'm more familiar with the Viper and Gypsy engines. Now, I can call on friends to help. I won't have that luxury when I'm in the jungle or on the burning sands of Sudan.

Sir James is becoming irritated at my distraction. I'm all the time rushing here and there as soon as I think of something that needs to be done. When I'm with him he has to constantly repeat himself as my mind is elsewhere. Today at tennis he almost beat me and he flung his racket down in disgust. He knew I was barely going through the motions.

It's true. All I can think about is a map. Where can I find a map? All this preparation will have been for nothing if I don't have a reliable way to chart my route. And I can't rely on the motorcar expedition now that I've seen Emil's useless map.

Johannesburg, South Africa, 5th February 1928

I am dining again with Sir James, wilting from the boredom of the same menu and same conversation, when I see someone through the glass dining-room doors. I drop my fork onto my plate with a clatter and bolt out to the lobby.

'Dick!' I grab his arm. 'I need your maps.'

The slight, dark-haired lady on his arm recoils and Dick bursts out laughing.

'Nice to see you too, Sophie. May I introduce my new wife, Mrs Dorys Bentley. Dorys, this is Sophie, now Lady Heath.'

I shake hands with her hurriedly, muddling a hello and congratulations. I know I have completely abandoned my manners and I see a look registering on her face. Ah, I imagine her thinking, that Sophie! Now it makes sense.

'I'm awfully sorry to be so abrupt, Mrs Bentley. You see, I was just this morning thinking about where I might find a map and now Dick walks in.'

I'm not making the situation any better, I know. I take a breath and try to regain control of myself.

'Are you dining?' I say.

'Yes. Or rather we hope so. But we didn't make a reservation. We've been rather distracted.' Dick raises his eyebrows at his new bride who is blushing prettily.

'Why don't you join us?'

Before they have a moment to resist, I summon the maitre'd and a startled Dick and Dorys join a confused Sir James at our now extended table.

'May I introduce my husband, Sir James Heath. Sir James, this is Lieutenant Richard Bentley, a good friend of mine from London and his new wife, Dorys. Dick has just completed a trip from London to Cape Town in a Tiger Moth.'

I widen my eyes at Sir James. I hope he remembers how cross I was on New Year's Eve when he blurted out my plans to a whole table full of guests. I had to explain, in business terms, why my trip needs to remain a closely guarded secret until the last second. I beckon to the waiter to take the Bentleys' order then turn to Dick.

'I want to hear all about your amazing trip.'

I sit on my hands while I listen to Dick recounting his flight from London. Dorys clearly hasn't tired of hearing this story as she hangs on every word. I make mental note of anything that I think may be of use to me.

'Turbulence and heat bumps at low altitude.'

'Follow the railway when you can. Easier to be rescued if needs be.'

'Sandstorm dust will affect visibility.'

'The mosquitoes and leeches can be devilish in monsoon season.'

I am as able a pilot as Dick and, before he finishes an anecdote about stripping his cylinder to find the source of an errant engine noise, I know the gudgeon pin wasn't the cause of it.

We finish our meal and I order champagne to toast the newlyweds.

'Where will you honeymoon?' Sir James asks.

Dick reaches for Dorys's hand, raises it to his lips and kisses it. 'We haven't decided, have we, darling? We have the whole of Africa at our disposal. My Moth will take us anywhere we want to go. This is a sort of honeymoon for you too, isn't it?'

'A sort of honeymoon, yes.' Sir James raises his glass to Dick. 'May you have more success keeping track of your bride. It seems bringing Sophie to such a vast continent may have been an error.'

I shoot him a thunderous look. I'm growing very weary of his complaints.

'Could you spare me your maps, Dick?'

Dick takes a long drink from his champagne flute.

'You seem to really want them, Sophie. Will you tell me why?'

'I can't. Not yet. But, yes, I do really want them.'

'Then I'm sure we can come to an agreement.'

'Name your price.'

Dorys puts her flute down hard on the table, dinging it against her water glass. I know I'm being crass but I know that Dick wants me to buy his maps and I don't have time to feint and parry over it.

'Let's talk tomorrow, Sophie. Will you be here?' He stands and Dorys follows his lead.

'Yes. I will stay in the hotel until I hear from you.'

I stand to shake their hands and catch a sympathetic glance between Dorys and Sir James. I almost laugh. She pities my husband but doesn't understand yet that Dick and I are alike – both driven half-mad by our dreams of the air.

A waiter hovers discreetly until they are gone then steps forward with a silver tray bearing a folded page of Carlton Hotel paper.

'A message for you, Lady Heath.'

I take the note and unfold it.

'We announce tomorrow and leave on the 8th. I hope you're ready. E. M.'

I pass the note to Sir James. The motorcar expedition has been moved up and they leave in two days. I'm glad I didn't dither in my preparations. Sir James purses his lips as he reads then hands the note back to me. I raise my champagne flute but he ignores it so I finish its contents and stand up.

'I'm going to get an early night,' I say. I know I will probably lie awake going over my calculations and my route. But I want to be alone.

Chapter Ten

Johannesburg, South Africa, 6th February 1928

I wait to hear from Dick Bentley all morning and I am climbing the walls of the hotel room. I forgot to ask where he and Dorys are staying. I doubt they're here in the Carlton. If I knew where he was, I'd go to him rather than being stuck here. Cabin fever is setting in and I have broken my habit of never smoking before lunchtime. I'm just extinguishing my second Turkish cigarette when a bellboy knocks on the door to summon me to the lobby for a phone call. I overtake him as we near the desk and lunge for the receiver.

'Bentley?'

'I'm sorry to disappoint, Lady Heath. Mr Cranch here.'

I hesitate. Cranch? Why do I know that name?

'Of the *Rand Daily Mail*.' He huffs. He sounds a little disappointed that his name didn't ring an immediate bell. Of course. Emil's colleague who interviewed me at Baragwanath and wrote a glowing account of me. I must unruffle his feathers.

'Mr Cranch. Apologies. I was catching my breath. I sprinted downstairs when I heard there was a call for me. I'm awaiting some important news.'

'Well, I am calling with some important news. Although why Emil insisted I contact you for your reaction is not clear. It has nothing to do with flying. It concerns the humble motorcar.'

'Do tell.' I smile. Clever Emil. He's gifting me the perfect opportunity to make my own announcement.

'Our mutual friend,' Mr Cranch clears his throat, 'is to embark tomorrow on a tremendous feat at the behest of Sir Abe Bailey. He, a Mr Bouwer and a cinematographer will attempt to drive from Cape Town to London, thus establishing a possible land route running the length of the continent. Do you have a comment?'

There is a long pause as I gather my thoughts.

'Well?' he prompts.

'I think it is very daring and dangerous. They will face all manner of obstacles and threats. But that's what makes it a good adventure. And they will have me to watch over them from the sky above. I'll keep a good eye on them.'

Now it is his turn to pause.

'Are you ready for a world exclusive, Mr Cranch? Do you have a pencil?'

'Always, always.'

There is the rustling of paper and I give him a moment, then I proclaim.

'I, Lady Heath, will accompany the *Rand Daily Mail*, *Sunday Times*, Chrysler Cape to London Motorcar Speed Dash, and simultaneously complete the first solo flight from South Africa to London.'

I hear him breathing heavily and the scratch of pencil on paper.

'Go on.'

'I will depart Johannesburg with the expedition and meet them in Abercorn, then fly to Cairo, directing them all the way.'

'Isn't that a treacherous flight to attempt solo? Across unknown wild lands. What if you crash or you're forced to land?'

'There are risks. Of course there are. But I think I mentioned my marksman skills last time we spoke. I will of course take a gun. And a tube of morphine. That should suffice.'

'That will suffice?'

'We don't need to go into all the details of my wardrobe again, I'm sure.' I hear him laughing softly. 'I will pack a Bible and a few novels to pass the time.'

'You'll depart from here?'

'Yes. I've already completed the Cape Town to Johannesburg flight so I will await their arrival here and, as soon as they are ready to go, I will go with them.'

'One last question, Lady Heath. Why? Why do you want to put yourself at risk and attempt this flight?'

'Why not? I did toy with the idea of accompanying Bert Hinckler on his flight to Australia. But I love Africa. And I recalled Sir Alan Cobham's words about this beautiful continent. He called it "*God's own flying country*". Think of the wonders I will see from the air, Mr Cranch. I can't understand why anyone would not want to do this.'

'That is quite remarkable, Lady Heath.'

'It makes for a good story, I imagine.'

'That it does. I can see the headline. "*An Angel Up Above.*"'

I laugh, giddy with relief and joy that the start of my dream is so close.

'I look forward to seeing it, Mr Cranch. Goodbye.'

I replace the receiver and close my eyes. I need to organise my thoughts. I must check on the adjustments to the plane and pack. I open my eyes and see someone, across the lobby, pointing in my direction. It is Dorys, with Dick, and he is empty-handed.

I cross the lobby and meet Dick halfway.

'Where's your lovely wife going?' I ask. She's sidling away, eyes on the ground.

'She's gone to the Grill Room to see if we can have a table for lunch. Our rooms at the Central are pleasant but the dining there isn't up to much. Let's sit.'

He manoeuvres me to a pair of high-backed chairs surrounded by leafy plants in a quiet corner of the lobby.

'Sophie, I may as well get right to the point. I'm afraid I can't give you my maps.'

I lean forward with my elbows on my knees.

'*Dick*,' I implore, '*I need them.* You have no idea how much. But I can tell you why now. It will be in the papers tomorrow morning. I'm going to fly to London, from here, solo.'

He laughs softly and takes a cigarette box out of his inside jacket pocket. He offers me one and there is a moment of quiet where we light them and draw deeply. I keep my eyes on him but he busies himself replacing the cigarette box and moving a heavy, crystal ashtray to the middle of the small table between us.

'I knew you had something in mind. And it's hard to keep a secret in this town. I heard that Henderson was tinkering with your Avian. You've made some changes?'

'Yes. Taken a seat out to make room and it has a larger tank for petrol. All of that will help but, Dick —'

'I know, Sophie. But, you see, really, my maps aren't all that good. They're just some rough sketches I made along the way.'

'You know the terrain. Those sketches could be the difference between life and death for me.'

'Now, Sophie, isn't that a tad dramatic? It's not like you.'

'Not just me, Dick. I'll be accompanying a motorcar expedition. Three men driving the same route that I'll be flying. That's four lives at stake if you want me to be dramatic.'

'They'll have maps, I'm sure.'

I stub my cigarette into the ashtray. 'A pretty outline of the continent with no detail. Come on, Dick. Why won't you let me have them?'

'You see. Dorys and I thought we'd fly back to London. For a sort of honeymoon. We'll do it leisurely. It won't affect your trip, Sophie. I'm sure you can pull this off without me. A tough girl like you.'

I stand and straighten my skirt. I offer Dick my hand.

'No hard feelings, Dick.'

Then I turn on my heel before he can reply and storm to the lift. The young operator eyes me warily. I'm sure anger is emanating from my pores. Am I to lose my chance at a legacy because Dick's silly wife wants to joyride over Africa?

The lift stops at my floor and I realise I have nothing to give to the operator as a tip. No matter, he looks relieved to be losing his passenger as I step out.

'Is there anything you require, ma'am?' he asks tentatively.

I stop and turn back to face him. 'A map would be lovely. A detailed map of the whole of Africa.'

He pulls across the cage, keen to get away from this madwoman, no doubt, and the lift commences its slow, clanging descent. I storm into our suite, slam the door behind me and let out one long scream.

I'm lying on the bed a while later with a pillow over my face when there is a knock on the door.

'Go away,' I moan into the goose-feather pillow.

'Lady Heath, a message for you.'

I fling the pillow from the bed and leap off. Maybe Dick has had a change of heart. I open the door and a short messenger boy is standing there, dwarfed by a stack of books.

'Where would you like these?'

I am agog. I take two from the top of the pile and back away from the door, permitting him to enter. I read a title as I follow him: *New Pictorial Atlas*.

'Where did you get these?'

He is red-faced and perspiring. 'My manager sent me to the City Library. He said you need some maps. I brought what I could carry.'

I pick up another book, *Citizen's Atlas of Central Africa,* and rifle through the pages. There are some maps showing mountains and rivers. Not a great amount of detail but they might just do.

'Can I get you anything else?'

'Yes, some tracing paper, or greaseproof from the kitchen. And sharpened pencils.'

I clear a side table and spread the books out. The messenger is about to close the door when I remember him.

'Boy, wait!'

I search the pockets of a jacket hanging on the back of my chair and find a silver King George shilling for him. He lights up when I hand it to him.

'Thank you, ma'am.'

I am back at the table focused on my task when Sir James returns. His face is aglow.

'I've been to the Turkish baths,' he announces. 'I feel twenty years younger. You might have to put up with me for longer than you thought. What's all this?'

I look up from the table, one finger on the exact part of Tanganyika that I was tracing. I haven't seen Sir James since last night's dinner.

'Maps,' I say. 'Dick couldn't spare his so I'm making my own.'

I look down at the map in front of me and wonder what hidden dangers lie in the large section marked '*unsurveyed*'. I picture a map of Ireland and wonder how many times my little home country could fit into the expanse of the African continent.

'Dinner?' Sir James throws the question in my direction as he moves towards the dressing-room.

'Can you have them send something up? I need to get these done. The expedition will be on the road the day after tomorrow and I have to be ready.'

He hears me but I am met with silence and a slowly closing door.

I am in a small dark place with a knot of dread in my stomach. There is the most horrendous, banging noise but I cannot raise my head to find its source. I don't want to see. Something stings my nose – is it kerosene?

Now I am flying, laughing and soaring. But the plane pulls away from me and down and I cannot stop it though I am fighting with every ounce of my strength. I am shielding my head with my hands, crying out. I twist my body away from the impact.

And I wake.

There is a pounding, pulsating throb in my left temple. I wonder for a moment if I have banged it on the bedstead. A nightmare. That's all.

But I cannot understand why I have had such a troubled night. Everything is in place for the trip. All day long yesterday I was receiving well wishes and congratulations as word spread and people read the details in the paper. Mr Cranch did a fine job again. I must send him a token from my travels. My plane is in Roberts Heights getting the finishing touches and all I have to do is wait for Emil and the others to get here. They are due to depart Cape Town today, 'launched' by none other than Mrs Lindbergh. I joked with Sir James that if I'm successful soon he will enjoy such honours but it seems his sense of humour has gone astray.

Maybe the strain of waiting is the cause of my fitful night.

I remain still under the covers a while and as my heart slows the pain subsides. The morning chases the dark away as I lie, staring at the ceiling, refusing to draw any premonition or meaning from the terrible night. The only thing I am willing to consider is that maybe I should stick to gin and forgo my beloved wine for now.

As the room brightens I feel the need to do something, so I decide to dress and go downstairs to call Dick. It's worth one final effort to get him to part with his maps. A glass of chilled water with a slice of lemon revives me in the lobby and I smile at the receptionist as she dials Dick's number and passes me the receiver.

I keep smiling so that my voice sounds warm.

'Dick, I hope I haven't woken you up.'

I hear the click of a lighter.

'Not at all. Dorys and I are heading out for a light jaunt before it gets too hot. I saw the papers. Congratulations!'

'Thank you. I guess you know why I'm calling?'

He sighs. 'Sophie. I feel awful, really. I was even reconsidering giving you the maps after I read the news article. I said to Dorys – a woman, flying alone across Africa, she needs them more than we do. I could go from memory or make some copies. We could make out OK, I think.'

I hold my breath. Has he changed his mind?

'But, Sophie, this is terrible. I cannot find the blasted things. I haven't seen them since we got to Johannesburg. Our little chat the other day prompted me to ferret them out and, I swear, they are nowhere to be found.'

My stomach drops. That moment of hope was so delicate. I could almost see the maps, beautifully intricate. I wonder if he is telling the truth. But I can hear the honest frustration in his voice. He wants those maps just as much as I do.

'Oh dear, Dick. I hope they turn up. For your sake.' I force some cheer into my voice. 'Not to worry. I've managed to cobble together a few tracings from atlases and such and there's always local knowledge. That can be a good guide too. This is meant to be an adventure, after all. No point making it too easy.'

'Yes.' He sounds doubtful. 'Have you thought about Sudan?'

I picture the route I have sketched and memorised.

Johannesburg to Bulawayo then Abercorn and on and on all the way to Cairo before crossing the Mediterranean for the final leg home to London.

Yes. I've thought about Sudan but for all I know of its geography from looking at flat pages in an old library book I may as well be thinking about the moon.

'A little,' I respond.

'The authorities there are very slow to let anyone fly over the swamps. Especially solo. And, as for letting a woman fly there, I'd say you'll be very much up against it, Sophie.'

I am starting to dislike Dick. So far he has been responsible for my main disappointments.

'I'll talk them around, Dick. You know how persuasive I can be when I have to.'

I start to tap my foot. I'm anxious to get back to my room and study the swamps of Sudan to find a solution to this newly born problem.

'I could help,' Dick says. 'If I act as escort they might allow you to cross.'

An escort. No. I don't want that. I want to be alone in the air. I want to reject his offer outright but I force myself to hold fire. I might need him after all.

'That's very kind, Dick. Let's see how we go.'

'Alright. We'll catch up with you along the way, Sophie. Good luck.'

Chapter Eleven

Johannesburg, South Africa, 7th February 1928

A small crowd awaits the arrival of the Chrysler outside the Carlton Hotel in Johannesburg. Emil emerges stiff-legged from the Sedan. It is mud-spattered and already wearing the signs of its journey. As are its occupants. I note that they're not speaking to each other as they trail into the lobby in single file. Emil waves to the crowd of onlookers but doesn't stop to talk. I stand back, observing, giving him room to breathe. I know how it feels to step down from my plane, back into the real world, and be immediately swallowed by other people's questions and demands. I wonder who is responsible for the maintenance of the Chrysler. My guess is that it is either Emil or the motor racing driver, Gerry Bouwer. Not the heavy man who is man-handling a camera box with some difficulty.

Emil gets his room key and looks ready to bolt when he sees me. He smiles and beckons me over. He places a hand on the cameraman's arm, stalling his escape to the lift, and talks to the men, nodding in my direction.

'Gentlemen, meet your "eyes in the sky". Lady Heath, this is Mr Bouwer and Mr Noble.'

I laugh. 'Is that my *Rand Daily Mail* codename?' I shake hands with the men.

'It's nice to meet you,' Noble says. 'But you'll have to excuse me. My back is screaming from that ghastly journey.'

He limps away and I raise my eyebrows at Emil, thinking, he's not going to last the course. The Cape Town to Johannesburg leg that they've just completed is probably the best, smoothest run they'll have. Mr Bouwer excuses himself to the bar and Emil and I settle in a small couch hidden from view by an ornamental bush in a pot adorned by native art.

'Was it ghastly?' I ask.

'No. Just long. Made longer by listening to Noble's complaints every time we struck a pebble on the road.'

'Three may become two then if he's already complaining. I couldn't abide a griping passenger. I'd have to fling him out.'

Emil laughs but it turns into an involuntary yawn. 'Don't you mean four?'

'Four? Oh! You're including me. I suppose technically. But I am just shadowing you.'

I consider my flight to be separate, my own individual exploit.

'If you say so. You'll see us off tomorrow?'

'Yes. I'm no Mrs Lindbergh but the crowd will be expecting me. Three intrepid men in their motor car and one crazy lady in her Avro Avian. We have to give them what they want.'

A silence descends. I wonder if the initial spark of our – friendship – was fuelled by our mutual ambitions. And now that the wheels are literally in motion is it fading?

He interrupts my thoughts. 'I'm dull company, I'm afraid. The tiredness has robbed me of my usual wit and charm.'

I stand and he groans out of his chair.

'A nice hot bath and a fresh bed,' I prescribe.

'That sounds like heaven.'

He takes my hand. 'It's good to see you. And it's good to know I'll see even more of you. Goodnight.'

I stay hidden by the ornamental plant and watch him move across the lobby. When I turn away I realise I have not been so well hidden. Behind me is a wall mirror and in its reflection I see a red-faced Sir James.

The door of our suite shuts loudly as I exit the lift. The thought crosses my mind that he can move fast for an old man. I stop outside the door and take a deep breath. I need to have a steady mind to handle this one. What did he see? What is he thinking? I decide to go for the offensive.

I push the door open, allowing it to swing back violently. I slam it behind me and stalk to the bathroom.

'*Can you believe the cheek of that man?*' I shout. '*If I didn't know better I'd swear that Mr Millin was flirting with me just now. Ugh!*'

I am running the tap, washing my hands vigorously, raising my voice to be sure Sir James can hear me over the commotion. He appears in the bathroom mirror and I turn to face him.

His expression is one of confusion. I dry my hands on the towel and lean back on the basin, closing my eyes.

'I think I'll have to call the whole thing off.'

I push past him to the bedroom and fling myself face down on the bed. My voice is muffled by the bedcovers as I say, 'After all my preparations. What a desperate shame!' I sit up. 'What will I tell the press? It's in all of the papers that I am to accompany the expedition. What will they make of it if I cancel?'

Sir James sits in the bedroom armchair and surveys me. He lights a cigarette and offers one to me. I move to sit in the chair opposite and allow him to lean in and light it.

'I'm no fool, Sophie. My last wife thought I was. But I proved her wrong and left her without a penny. Be straight with me.'

I take a breath. 'I am.'

'Sophie!' There is a warning in his voice. 'Stop this diabolical theatrical act. You weren't made for the stage.'

I smile. 'You're far too clever for my silly tricks. Truth be told, I didn't mind him flirting. I'm well used to silly men and fawning men and men who want to make love to the famous aviator. Most of them married, I should add. It used to alarm me but now it bores me. And I'm more than capable of handling them.'

'So why the charade?'

'I saw your face. You looked so angry. So I thought I should act outraged.'

'Don't.'

'Don't?'

'Don't try to pull the wool over my eyes like that. I saw right through it. But the one thing I won't stand for, Sophie, is to have you embarrass me and damage my name. I will not have people sniggering behind their backs about poor Sir James, a fool in love, while his wife flits around the place with other men.'

'I don't. I won't.'

'If you do it will cost you dearly. What matters most to you? I know it is not me so don't patronise me with that answer. What is it?'

'Flying.'

'Yes. You would do well to remember who funds that. You wouldn't want to lose it. Not at this point when you have everything you want within your reach. And, you're right, he is married too. I will drag your names, both of you, through the divorce courts until you wish you'd never laid eyes on each other. Is that straight enough for you?'

'Yes.'

I do feel ashamed. He's right. He's paving the way for me to live my dream. Not to mention all the luxuries along the way. And Emil really doesn't mean anything. I nod and look directly at Sir James. 'I understand what you're saying. You have nothing to fear.'

'Good. Well then, I will go to golf.'

He leaves and I sit a while longer in the chair. The chair he paid for in the hotel room that he paid for. And I start to feel a niggle. An uncomfortable twitch of knowing. This isn't the dream. The flying is, yes. And someone has to pay for it. But the sooner that can be me the better. I don't want to be somebody's possession.

Johannesburg, South Africa, 13th February 1928

Bellin, from the local flying club, waits with me as the crowds cheer for Emil, Bouwer and Noble. They are fêted warmly by the dignitaries of Johannesburg while I stay by the plane. Sir Jeppe, the *Rand Daily Mail* chairman, has instructed that his gifts be added to their cargo: boxes of cigars, a waterless cooler and, for some unknown reason, a portable gramophone.

What is more practical is the roof of the Chrysler which has been painted white with a large black C that will be easily seen by me from the air.

I have kept my distance from Emil, staying busy checking on the DH Moth that I've borrowed from the club for today's occasion. My Avian is still at Roberts Heights for final adjustments.

The men walk down the steps of the town hall and climb into the waiting Chrysler. The crowd swarms and are actually swaying the car. It will be impossible for them to drive off without hitting someone.

'*Come on!*' I call to Bellin. '*Let's draw fire!*'

I climb into the plane, Bellin spins the propeller, the Moth starts and once he is onboard we take off, swooping low over the crowd, diverting their attention from the Chrysler and onto us. I am flying as low as I can, barely within regulations, following the car as it navigates the city streets. It seems that every car in the province of Gauteng has turned out to trail the Chrysler on its historic departure. A slow, snaking column forms a caravan and I delight the motorists by flying barely ten, twelve feet above the ground. The women passengers shriek and wave and the men toot their horns emphatically.

As they reach the outskirts of Johannesburg I dive low again, cruising alongside the Chrysler. Emil and Noble are hanging out of the windows, waving to their followers.

I take my chance and drop a message that I prepared back at the hotel. It is tied to a bottle of beer: '*God speed. Meet you in Abercorn. Don't forget to wear your winter woollies.*'

Emil reaches up and catches the bottle. I see him scanning the message then he waves. I pull back on the stick, pushing the plane upwards then swooping into a broad loop the loop, painting the sky with everything the Moth has to give. I turn back to the city.

It will be many days, if not weeks, before the Chrysler makes it to Abercorn. This fanfare of our departure from Johannesburg is a charade as I have more time to kill before I go. I will return to Sir James for the next while and play the part of a loyal, loving wife. I envy Emil. He has made the break and many weeks of freedom and adventure await him. But I must be patient. My time will come and, for it to be a success, everything must be right with the Avian and my provisions.

I have some public talks to give and there might be another newspaper interview or two. I must keep up public interest in my flight. I'll tell them about the gun Sir Jeppe has gifted me for my protection. I won't tell them how I feel about catching up to Emil in Abercorn. I haven't quite figured that out for myself yet.

I am just leaving the Goodwill Luncheon some days later, having fired up the audience of ladies with a rallying talk on women in sport, when I hear my name.

'*Lady Heath!*'

I turn, expecting it to be one of the attendees and see a well-dressed, fair-haired lady sporting the most obscene bump. She is sweating in the afternoon heat and her bird-like hand strays repeatedly to press on her back. Is this a fan of mine, I wonder? I don't recall seeing her at the luncheon.

She steps closer, offering me an envelope.

'I'm Mrs Emil Millin. I was hoping you could give this to my husband. You will see him sooner than I will.'

I take the envelope then shake her still-extended hand.

'Of course. But it will be a while before I get to them.'

She places her hands on her bump. 'I understand. I'm glad I caught you before you left. I'm going back home today. The heat in the city is ...' She waves a hand through the sticky air. 'I thought this might be a nice surprise for him.' She gestures at the envelope in my hand.

'I'll make sure he gets it.'

'Thank you. Good luck with your flight. Keep an eye on him, won't you? I need him to come back in one piece.' She attempts a smile but her powder-blue eyes dampen.

'I will. All the time,' I answer as she turns and lumbers away.

I mean for that to sound reassuring but as the words leave my mouth they carry a hint of menace. A threat or a promise of ill intentions.

I think about how it would be to swap places with Mrs Millin. Homebound, heavy with child, playing a waiting game while my husband greedily devours all that the world has to offer. Do I envy the small comforts of her life?

No. I want to be in the world, not waiting for it to come home to me.

My encounter with her is a stark reminder though. Regardless of the silly flirtations between myself and Emil, I can have no designs on this woman's husband. I will keep an eye, as promised, but from a distance.

Chapter Twelve

Pretoria, South Africa, 25th February 1928

My departure is more subdued than the Chrysler chaps. But this is just the way I like it. I cannot wait to be in my plane with the beautiful morning sky laid out before me, an infinite carpet. I am so keen to be there that my feet are practically lifting off the ground. The Avian is packed, every corner and cranny that can be found is crammed with my provisions. I will fly away from Roberts Heights with forty-two gallons of spare fuel stowed. That gives me great comfort. There aren't many ways I can protect myself from the risks of this trip but at least I won't run out of fuel soon.

Colonel Sir Pierre van Ryneveld, aviation pioneer of the South African Air Force, has insisted on flying alongside me for the first hour or so. I'd rather be alone but I can't refuse. The aviation folks here have been so helpful and kind to me.

He climbs into his plane, awaiting my take-off. 'I hope you can get off the ground, Sophie. You've got quite the load there.'

I clamber into my Avian and pull on my flying helmet. The sun is already casting its heat across the aerodrome. 'I hope I won't have to resort to fourteen donkeys pulling me.'

He laughs. News reached us yesterday evening that the Chrysler gang had to enlist the help of local donkeys to tow them across the flooded Limpopo River.

'It's a good thing I've been watching my weight!' I add.

He has a point, though, so I make sure to use every bit of runway to my advantage. I taxi to the furthest end and push forward, picking up speed and feeling every judder and shake. The engine is working hard but it sounds strong and hungry for sky. I pass the hangar and estimate that I've gone a hundred or a hundred and ten yards. I concentrate my attention, waiting for the lift, but I'm already doing all I can. It's all down to the plane now and if it fails I'll have to make some tough decisions about what I take out of my cargo. I'm nearing the end of the runway, almost one hundred and fifty yards behind me, when I feel it.

The rise.

My stomach lifts and my soul with it. The ground noise of the wheels disappears in an instant and now there is only the engine. As I level out I raise a hand in the air and whoop. *Finally!* After all the planning and waiting, I am airborne.

Over an hour later I wave goodbye to Pierre who banks left and turns back to Roberts Heights. It is bliss as I glide, solitary, through the air. I tilt my head back, feeling the breeze on my face. I close my eyes for a moment then open them to gaze at the wondrous vista below. Jags of low, green hills and clusters of houses are visible whenever the fleecy clouds part. I think of how life down there must be for those people. Their ordinary days of keeping themselves fed and sheltered. Do they even know that I am up here, surveying it all as though I am its creator? What a shock they would get if I suddenly descended among them from on high. Would they crown me or crucify me?

The elation of this takes me back to my first solo flight in Stag Lane. The sense of power and freedom I had at being able to climb into a machine and compel it to take me where I wanted. By myself and by my own hand. It made me feel as though I was no longer human, as though I had been transformed into something else, something with infinite possibilities. And now I feel it again.

I have the whole of a continent, an undiscovered Africa, at my fingertips. Me, Sophie Peirce-Evans from County Limerick, who was not permitted to leave the house unchaperoned. What would my grandfather, the austere and esteemed George Peirce, say if he saw me now? I throw my head back and roar with delight.

I have been flying for many hours, almost six. I have left South Africa, crossed over into Rhodesia and feel I am nearing Bulawayo. I've just flown over Warm Baths so another hour or so should get me to my destination. I'm looking forward to a swim and a hot bath. My legs are starting to cramp. I shuffle them about in the tight space but get no relief. My neck and shoulders are stiffening too. Being in the open cockpit for hours doesn't usually bother me but maybe all the preparations have made me tense. I roll my head clockwise, then anti-clockwise and feel the muscles crackling but the strain remains. I stretch my arms up over my head, pulling them high, feeling the breeze. It has been relentlessly, stinking hot and I am sitting in a puddle of sweat.

The luscious grasslands below me look like a springy mattress and I imagine lying down there and shutting my eyes for a delicious rest. I do shut my eyes now. A moment's break from the sun's glare. When I open them again black blobs float across my field of vision. I blink and shake my head but they float by again. I look to my left and right but they follow me, trailing into my periphery and now I feel it. A dull pain in my head that is growing to a gnawing throb. I put a hand to the back of my neck to massage it. It feels hot and the skin is tight.

The uneventful flight has lulled me to a trance but now I realise that I am not well. I felt like this once before. The effects of staying too long under a hot sun and I remember now, sickeningly, that last time I passed out. That time I was on the ground and somewhat embarrassed when I came to. If I pass out up here I could die.

I scan the scene below for a suitable place to land but there are none that I can see. It is true wilderness and I don't fancy becoming a leopard's lunch. I recall passing Fort Usher with its lookout tree just visible. I manage to extract my folded, hand-drawn map from my shirt pocket and after a quick glance, with one eye shut for focus, I alter my course north-east to where I might find a place to land.

Curse it! To think I could be in real bother here and in danger of ending my adventure before it's really begun. Why didn't I take more care, wear my rimmed topee helmet to keep the sun off my head and shoulders? All this talking to journalists about how easy and glamorous flying is has distracted me and I have become careless.

Could I get the helmet now? I twist in my seat and try to reach back to the locker where it is stowed but the sudden movement sends a spike of pain out through the top of my head. I have to stop to catch my breath. My heart is skittering like a nervous mare.

I manage to pull out a cotton slip and pull it across my shoulders to protect the back of my neck but it is too late. The damage is done.

I sit as still as a stone so the pain doesn't worsen. I try to breathe softly. I can hear a moaning sound – low and monotonous. My eyelids drag down, beyond my control.

I come to. Stretched on ground under thorn bushes. Something soft cushions me against the hard veldt. There is something wet, like a cold skin, pressed to my head which immediately resumes its throbbing torture as soon as I become aware of it. I smell milk. Strong, warm, bestial, earthy milk and I start to retch. I lean to the side and empty the contents of my stomach onto the grass, narrowly missing the sleeve of my fur coat. How did that get here?

The sound of giggling forces me to look up. The movement and low evening light provoke another bout of purging. I am as sick as a passenger crossing the Channel in rough seas. When I finish I feel a little better or a little less like death and well enough to lean up on one elbow to see my amused audience. Three native girls, mahogany skin gleaming, short brown hair curled tight to their perfect round heads. They are barely clad – only a beaded necklace and a short beaded skirt and their breasts hang free. They fall into each other laughing, covering their mouths with their hands.

There is a large brown gourd on the ground before them. I take the cloth from my head and recognise it as one of my own handkerchiefs. It is stiff with dried milk. I put my hand to my head to check for injuries but find only clots of milk in my hair. I must look a sight. I realise that my fur coat is serving as my mattress. They must have pulled it from the plane. The plane! I quickly sit up straighter to look for it but the world spins and I am forced down again. The girls find this hilarious. They seem to find everything hilarious. I envy them whatever world they live in that they find everything a source of joy. I rise again, slow and gentle this time. The sight of my little plane brings tears to my eyes. Apart from a slight, sad droop in one wing she is intact, nose to the wind, clear of the trees and thorn scrub of the veldt. It was as though I had brought it to land there by choice. But I have no memory of the landing. I was fully unconscious. Some other hand must have guided it there. And, although a fanciful idea like that is unlike me, I am grateful.

I recline again, arm flung across my eyes.

'Am I near ...?'

What was my destination? Where was I going? I close my eyes and concentrate but for the life of me I cannot find the words. Where did I come from? That answer will not volunteer itself either.

I realise they probably have no English. I try Swahili. 'Where am I?'

That will have to do for now. I don't expect an answer from the native girls so I am startled when one says, 'Matabele'.

So this is Matabeleland. That puts me somewhere near Bulawayo. Was that my destination? I don't expect these girls to know if I don't. It is surprising that one of them seems to have some Swahili. It is also surprising that they haven't run away or taken me captive. It must have been a terrifying sight for them. A silver bird descends from the sky with a strange white woman who appears to be dead. I could have ended up in a much worse situation.

My heart warms towards these young girls. I try again with Swahili and they understand my request to see the plane. They help me to stand, patient sentries as I test my legs. When I feel sturdy enough they assist me to the plane. I stagger around it, checking for more damage but there is none. I lean into the cockpit. The watch on the dashboard tells me it is half past five in the evening. How long was I unconscious?

The machine is in good enough nick. I imagine I could fly off in it this very moment. If I could see straight. It, and I, will have to stay the night. A wave of sickness strikes again and I empty-retch onto the ground, my stomach muscles contracting painfully. I fall to my knees, weakened by the effort. The girls help me to a tree where they prop me upright against its trunk. I explain as simply as I can where to find my sandbags then demonstrate how they must fill them with stones and earth to secure the Avian for the night. This seems to be the best joke they have ever heard and as I sit there with every inch of my body aching, the taste of vomit in my throat and the smell of sour milk wafting from my hair, I can't help but smile. Together the four of us weave a slow path back to their kraal, a small cluster of huts. I reckon it to be about a quarter of a mile from where my plane sits. The circular huts with their mud walls and straw roofs are as welcome a sight to me now as any opulent hotel suite. A crowd gathers to observe me but all I want to do is lie down.

We enter one of the larger huts, about thirteen feet across. Two women are inside, one tending to the fire, each nursing a baby at her breast. One of my helpers spreads my fur coat on the floor beside the fire pit. As dusk creeps up slowly outside the hut, the fire is lit and I gladly recline, gazing into the cheerful blaze. The hut is smoke-filled as the only chimney is the door but I feel cocooned. Women and girls come and go, quietly tending to the fire and sneaking glances at me but I am never entirely alone. The smoky gauze over everything I see may be from the fire or my own wooziness but I like how it softens my surroundings into a dream scene. I cannot tell the women apart and they merge into one then separate into three, then two. They leave and return with stealth and purpose and I lose track of who is with me.

I feel a fold of paper in my shirt pocket and, pulling it out, I recognise my map. On it Bulawayo is circled in red ink and now I remember, I was headed for there. I left Pretoria. This morning? Yesterday? I recall seeing the time on the dashboard when I passed Fort Usher. I must have been unconscious for nearly four hours. The knowledge chills me. I lay there, alone, unprotected for all that time. I could have been eaten alive!

One of the women scoots closer to me, the skin of her belly taut as a drum over a large bump.

I point to my chest and say, 'Sophie'. My voice is hoarse from being sick.

She responds with the same gesture. 'Makula.'

I show her the map and point at the circled town.

'Bulawayo. How far?' I ask.

'Ten,' she says, holding up all her fingers.

She speaks English!

'Ten miles?'

'Yes. Ten miles.'

A young girl enters the hut with my small, soft-leather dressing case with silver fittings that was a gift to me from the Johannesburg Light Aeroplane Club and will be my pillow for tonight. She has also brought my mosquito netting. I pull it over me, hoping it will protect me from the thousands of flies that have started to buzz, threatening to land on my eyes, in my ears and even up my nose. No doubt bathing myself in milk like some modern Cleopatra has made me all the more tasty and attractive.

'Your house?' I ask Makula.

'We are wives,' she answers. 'Of the chief.'

Which means that I am in the harem. Now it is my turn to laugh. What would the proper people of Sir James' circle make of this? His new wife, flown away and staying in a harem.

Maybe this is the best way. To be one wife among many, to have female companionship and share the demands of the man between you. And be free to do as you please at other times.

My brain must still be addled.

An older woman enters the hut with a fresh gourd of milk. I take a small sip, unsure whether to trust it, or my stomach. I would hate to defile their home by being sick and my legs are not sturdy enough to take me to the doorway in time if needs be. But it settles well and suddenly I am ravenous. Another brings a whole boiled chicken and offers the plate to me first. I discover that it really is whole as the cavity of the bird is not hollow. It has been cooked with its innards and giblets intact. I try not to think of this, pull off a leg and pass the plate back, nodding my thanks. I pick at the warm, rubbery flesh with my fingers and in no time at all I have devoured it. It is all I can manage but I think it is the most delicious meal I can remember having.

The hut starts to fill with small children. They settle quietly, lying on the hard floor, covered in blankets. And in this warm air, heavy with the scent of bodies and thick with the sound of sleepy breaths I drift off.

Chapter Thirteen

Newcastle West, County Limerick, 1906

They say they can't get the bloodstains out of the wall. She hears them talking. They talk about it all the time and that's what they say. They say the new owners are cleaning the place constantly but every time they return the bloodstains have seeped back out again. They smirk when they talk about the owners, thinking they'd got a fine, big house for themselves. But all they got was a shell. The whole place stripped to barren frames and only one room lived in by the end. And that room had every stick of furniture destroyed. Burnt in the fireplace for warmth. Broken up to beat her with.

And bloodstains on the wall.

They must think the girl is a piece of furniture too. That she sits there, like a side table, with no ears. But she hears even if she doesn't understand.

She hears them saying that he married poorly, the woman was beneath him, a poor Catholic, with a questionable past and a terrible drink problem. Tall, good-looking. They say the child took after her in looks. They say he is a madman. Locked up now for good and glory. That he always had it in him but who could have foreseen it ending like this? They say the child is like him in her ways.

She hears everything they say. How could she not, sitting in this house of silence? The clock on the mantel ticks. Skirts rustle. Outside, on the street, the horse hooves strike against the earth and a child whoops. There is the sound of her own breaths. There is nothing to do, but sit.

She hears what they don't say as well. The concern about money that is there in the stingier fires and the dwindling staff. Her maiden aunts embroider their hours away, stitching themselves in place. They talk in low tones. They furrow their brows as they wonder, what will become of the child? What will become of their father George and their stepmother Henrietta, who are too old to have the burden of rearing another? She hears her grandfather, late into the night, bemoaning the loss of his only son. What more could he have done to get him straight? To keep him out of the drinking dens and away from the gambling and blackguarding. He curses his first wife's father, Old Tom Evans, who took him on hunts and drinking sessions then left him Knockaderry House and free rein to his madness.

George Peirce always kept a tight grip on his family. But now that one child has evaded him and brought them all low, he tightens his grip further until it is a vice. The girl is forbidden to play in the street, or anywhere except for a small patch at the back of the house. It looks onto a vast demesne but she cannot roam there, only stroll, chaperoned, for half an hour daily. She must not run.

She longs to run. But for now, she sits. Sits. Waits. Listens.

She looks out the window. This is one of the things her grandfather does not like her to do. But she is exhausted from all the not doing. She moves the lace curtain to one side so she can see better. The drawing room is on the second floor and below is the Square. Surrounded on all sides by tall, handsome buildings, it is busy today. Some kind of market has brought the country people in. They look different in their dress. And they bring such wonderful things. Her eyes dart about, trying to see everything all at once. Trying to fill up her memories so that she can think about it again later when she is staring at the wallpaper, listening to Grandfather read from the Bible. She drinks in the nervy chickens, the carts of mucky vegetables, the cows, dropping splats under their lifted tails, the men arguing, agreeing, shaking hands. She sees a group of children returning from school and her heart heaves, wishing with every inch that she could dissolve the glass and bricks that separate her from them. She would run alongside them, cast off her leather boots to feel the mud underneath her bare feet. She would climb to the top of the wall with them, with her arms out to keep her balance. She has never done these things but she knows she could. She would seem strange to the other children. Her clothes would mark her out as different. Her aunts dress her in the old fashion preferred by Grandfather. But if she spoke to the children would they not recognise that she is like them? She thinks of what she would say.

'Hello, my name is Sophie Catherine Theresa Mary Peirce-Evans.'

She says this out loud in the empty drawing room. And even though she has never met or spoken to these children, or any children, or anyone outside of these four walls, she knows they would laugh at her.

'Why do you have so many names?' they might ask.

She tries again.

'Hello, my name is Sophie.'

That's better. She smiles, gladdened at the thought of how easy that was, just change a name and change how people see you. They might ask why she is not in their school. What would she tell them? That Grandfather won't allow it. That she is taught by a governess who comes to the house. That she is not permitted to speak with any boy or man, is forbidden to play with other children, even if she sees them in the Demesne. That she can only play in a small part of it, chaperoned. That Grandfather would whip her if he caught her speaking with them. That he is determined to raise the girl as he did her aunts. For here they sit, blameless.

Her heart rate has quickened now, she can hear it beating in her ear and her fingers worry at the edge of the lace curtain. This time she says it louder.

'Hello, my name is Sophie and I am nine years old!'

'Sophie!'

She drops the curtain and jumps back from the window. Will she be punished? Sent to her room without supper? Or worse, sent to Grandfather? There are so many rules and forbidden things in this house.

'Step away from that window this instant.'

Aunt Lou is not happy. She stands with her hands clasped in front of her and frowns at the girl. Her eyes scan her from head to toe and she looks displeased by what she sees. Sophie hides her fingers behind her back, lowers her eyes to the floor. She does not like to displease Aunt Lou. Or Aunt Cis. They are her mothers. In place of her own. And they are only trying to protect her. From her own recklessness, from Grandfather's wrath, and from whatever is in her nature.

'You must not stand by the window gawping out so. It is most unbecoming of a young lady.'

She strides past to fix the curtain back in place then turns to face the girl.

'You know very well that if you are looking out there anyone can see in here. Can see you.'

She is to be hidden, tucked away too. What is wrong with her?

Aunt Lou takes her arm gently. 'Come now. It is time for your lessons.'

She is sitting. Again. Where she has been told to. Where she is expected to. The only sounds are the polite touch of knife and fork on plate. And the ticking of the clock. The house is filled with clocks. All marking time but she doesn't know why. They go nowhere and every day is the same as the one before and the one to follow. She believes that if by some magic or miracle the clocks all ceased, their legs would carry them from bed to table to drawing-room to park to table to bed without the need for any one of them to pause or reflect on where to go or what to do next. The only one who goes anywhere is Grandfather. And Rugs, his dog. Grandfather is the sole resident permitted access to the outside world. And while Sophie hungers for it, he finds it distasteful and brings back only his deep dissatisfaction with it.

She had this conversation yesterday with Aunt Cis.

'Do we not go to church on Sunday?' Aunt Cis posed with that tilt of head that always indicates she finds Sophie comical. 'Do we not visit with our cousins?'

'Yes.'

Aunt Cis smiled, apparently softened by the ease with which the girl agreed. But she should know her better.

'Yes,' Sophie added. 'We go from one cold four walls to another.'

Now Aunt Cis smiles at Sophie from across the polished table, nodding a reminder to finish her vegetables. Sophie sighs loudly and pokes at a stubborn piece of turnip. It flees the dull blade of her knife which clatters onto the plate. This may be the loudest sound heard in this house in the longest time. And she is sorely tempted to repeat it. To fling her fork down, twice as hard, to shatter the plate, to swipe the crystal glasses onto the floor and scream. Henrietta has clutched her hand to her chest. Aunt Lou looks as though she may cry and now all eyes turn to Grandfather for his response.

'Sophie Theresa Catherine,' he addresses her, so formally, his tone low but serious. 'If you cannot conduct yourself decorously at this table I will relegate you to the nursery and you can tend to your food with a wooden spoon.'

At this he lifts his eyes to meet hers. She holds his gaze. What does he see when he looks at her? She displeases him. Although he has been kind enough to take her in. She sees the tremor of his hand, the flicker of an eyelid. He fears her, fears what she will become.

After dinner they sit by the fire. Grandfather reads from his bible and Sophie struggles to keep her head from falling off her neck with boredom. She breathes lightly, pretending to focus on her embroidery. Grandfather closes his bible with a snap and taps his fingers lightly on the cover. 'Sophie, I want you to give this some thought.'

She looks up. Grandfather is staring at her with a grave and furrowed visage.

'Yes, Grandfather.'

'I am concerned at times by your behaviour. You seem to find it difficult to follow direction and I ask myself if we are doing right by you. Maybe there is something in your nature that steers you off course. It would be comforting to think of each of us as a blank slate, on which the best virtues and ideas can be imprinted, thus ensuring a good and proper life. But I fear this is not so. Too often I have seen the son go the way of the father and meet a bad end. Equally, it is possible for the child of a good man to turn bad due to some flaw rooted in another branch of the family. I think it is possible, despite a good environment, for bad traits to surface. Even more reason to never budge from the proper rules and rigidities. These may be the last line of defence against inherited wickedness. Do you understand what I am saying?'

Aunt Cis throws a quick glance in Sophie's direction.

'Yes, Grandfather.'

Sophie doesn't understand. But she thinks Grandfather is saying that she might be bad. That she needs to watch herself lest the badness inside her wins over. Her stomach clenches with shame. Then flushes with anger. She wants to be good. She tries so hard to walk within the rigid boundaries set for her. But if she is naturally bad, then so be it. Maybe that would be better than the rigidity of this life, for it is not a life at all.

Chapter Fourteen

Matabeleland, Southern Rhodesia, 26th February 1928

My rest is broken by constant bites from the winged assailants that get through my net and feast on me. My dreams also disturb me. They are vivid and take me back to days I thought I had forgotten. When I wake at dawn the dream I was in feels so real I almost expect to see Grandfather or Aunt Lou in the hut.

I inspect the bites covering any exposed skin. Why didn't I think of bringing some Keating's Powder to ward off the little buggers? Makula approaches me and lifts the net. She is carrying a dish of water and a piece of soft cloth. She dips it into the water and starts to sponge my face and neck, then my arms and hands. The water is tepid but it is not unpleasant and I am moved by the tenderness of her touch and the pleasant sensation of being clean again. The filth of yesterday: the dust and milk and sick and sweat are washed from my skin. I feel weak but renewed.

I try to sit up but my head is still its own carousel. I quickly lie back down and assess my body. Apart from still having the 'spinnies', my head and neck feel much improved.

I lie in place for the morning, idly aware of the busy comings and goings of the Matabele women as they go about their chores, observed like a zoo animal by murmurations of curious children who scatter when I catch their eye. It is mid-morning when I hear an engine in the kraal. It stops and now I can hear voices. English voices. Help has arrived.

A tall older woman with sun-bleached blonde hair fills the doorway then stoops to enter and stands over me.

'My goodness! I didn't expect to find this on my morning drive. Liza Fletcher.'

She sticks out her hand and I shake it weakly.

'They said you came from the sky. I presume they mean in an airplane.' She looks around the hut as if expecting to find it there.

'Yes,' I croak. 'I managed to land it a little distance away from here.'

'Righto. That was a stroke of luck. I'll send someone for it. But first let's get you out of here before you go fully native.'

'They've been very kind,' I say.

There is a lump in my throat and suddenly, to my shame, I find I am weeping. I should be happy I've been found. Maybe it's the relief. Or the sadness of having to leave this simple world.

Through my tears I try to express my gratitude to the wonderful Matabele women.

I am led to Liza's car where her husband, she introduces him as Pat, sits behind the steering wheel. On the way to her farm she tries to distract from my emotional turmoil by talking as fast as her husband drives. She tells me that they were passing in search of grass for their cattle when she learned of my plight from one of the Matabele men. She promises to send someone by the name of Captain Mail to bring my plane to her farm.

'He's a very good pilot,' she assures me. 'Rhodesian Aviation Syndicate.'

We rattle up the drive of a large farmhouse and I am once again put to bed by strangers. Although it is noon I sleep immediately and deeply until the evening.

I wake to the sound of a plane flying over the house. The light outside the window is almost gone. I lean up on one elbow to check the time on a small clock beside my bed. Five in the evening. Almost twenty-four hours since I came to and I am no nearer to regaining my energy.

There is a knock on the door and Liza peers round.

'Will you take some tea? A bite to eat?'

I am not hungry but I know I need to eat if I am to recover.

'Thank you. That would be lovely.'

'I'll have the maid bring up a convalescent supper. Nothing too heavy.'

'Did I hear a plane just now? Or was I dreaming?'

'That was Captain Mail flying over. He's been to get your plane and he's taking it on to Bulawayo. You can catch up with it there as soon as you feel fit.'

I lean back against the pillows. When the maid brings my bland supper I eat as much as I can. I barely get the covers over me and then I am out like a light again, lulled by the ticking of the bedside clock.

Next morning I'm wakened by a knock on the door and Liza peers round.

'Are you awake?' She comes into the room, speaking in a low voice. 'Captain Mail is here. He just arrived back from Bulawayo. The Lord Mayor sent him to fetch you. Do you feel able?'

I want to say no but I'm anxious to get going again. I've already lost so much time. She leaves me to wash and dress. It takes a lot longer than usual as I have to keep sitting down whenever I feel my legs are about to go from under me.

Liza brings me to a formal sitting-room where a tall, thin man in a brown shirt and pants is standing, looking out the window.

He turns and offers his hand. 'Captain J. Douglas Mail. My friends call me Douggie.'

'Lady Heath.' I shake his hand then lower myself into the nearest chair. The short walk from the bedroom has drained me. 'I believe you've rescued my Avian.'

'Damn fine plane. I fly a Moth myself.'

'You must be quite the pilot to have managed a take-off, Captain Mail. I didn't land on much of a runway out there.'

'I think you are an incredible pilot! You managed to bring that plane down in the only place possible in a fifty-mile radius. And it's a miracle you landed at all. The machine was bone dry of oil. And the port forward flying wire was loose. There's a bend in the undercarriage. That may have been from when you landed. I've tightened the leaking oil connection and topped her up. She'll be good to go as soon as you are. But you'll need to get that undercarriage looked at.'

'I can't thank you enough, Captain Mail. I had no idea how things were going to turn out when I came to on the veldt with the native girls watching over me.'

'You really have been quite lucky. There were crowds waiting in Bulawayo for you to arrive. They expected you after lunch and as the afternoon wore on there was real concern. Once it got dark and there was no word ... well, everyone feared the worst. They'll be happy to see you. And your husband will be happy to get word that you're safe, I'm sure.'

He's right. I need to send Sir James a telegram.

'Can I travel to Bulawayo with you? I want to see the plane for myself.'

'That's why I'm here. Are you up to it?'

Again, the honest answer is no but I must power onwards.

In no time we are in the Fletchers' mealie patch, saying our goodbyes and promising to send Liza and Pat a telegram when I get to London.

Captain Mail is starting to help me into the plane when I have an idea.

'Could I fly it, do you think?'

'Do you think you're able?'

'There's only one way to find out,' I say as I make my way into the cockpit. 'I had a Moth myself before. And if I start to feel woozy you can take over.'

Mr Fletcher starts the propeller. I turn on the ignition switch, open the throttle and taxi down the ploughed field, into the wind. I pull the joystick back and the plane lifts. My hands are shaking. Is it from the illness? Or fear that I would not be able to do this? I bank left and fly over the Fletchers one last time, giving them a wave. Glancing at the instruments I realise that my eyesight is not fully recovered. The numbers are blurred and impossible to read but I can see where the needles sit and all looks to be fine.

We make it to Bulawayo in under twenty minutes and I am bundled quickly into a waiting car with the Mayor. Someone has decided that I'm not well enough to meet any fans. I am relieved.

The car takes me to a quiet part of town where the jacaranda trees shade a squat, nondescript building. I've been lulled by the rumble of the engine on the rough road and the monologue of the Mayor who is insisting on giving me a potted history of the place. My eyes are tired from the flight and I have to battle to stop my eyelids from dragging down. I barely catch the name of the nursing home I am to recuperate in. Sister Rigby's, or Sister Roux' Maternity Home! This tickles me and I want to say something clever to the Mayor but the words refuse to assemble into the correct order to leave my mouth.

Firm hands change me into a light, mauve gown and I climb onto a narrow bed. I am swaddled tightly in starched white sheets and a thermometer is placed under my tongue. A doctor appears by my bedside in a white linen suit. He looks like he should be out hunting game.

'Quite the adventuress, Lady Heath. I'm Dr Wright. I'll be keeping an eye on you here. We need to get your temperature down. Nurse, give the patient something to help her rest.'

I want to tell him that won't be necessary. I need help to stay awake. But my mouth is dried cotton and I am gone again.

I wake in the dead of night. The room is lit by the cold glow of a perfectly bisected half-moon and I can see it contains four beds but only mine is occupied. Whatever they gave me earlier is threatening to pull me under again. I sit up to fix the sheet that is making its way to the floor. I must have been running sprints in my sleep.

There, to my shock and horror, at the foot of my bed, is a tiny white cot. I kneel up and scoot my way along the bed. I peer in, almost petrified at the prospect of finding a baby inside. Have I dreamed my entire life? Was none of it real? Am I not an aviator but, rather, a plain old mother?

The cot is empty. Of course it is. Empty save for a tiny mattress awaiting its next occupant. Fit for a doll. Or a newborn baby.

I settle back onto the pillow and close my eyes. My tears seep onto the white coverlet until I fall asleep.

I wake, confused. The room is dark, the only light a gentle glow from the lamp in the corridor. A nurse passes my door and I call out to her. She enters quietly and presses a finger to my hand, timing my heartbeat with her fob watch.

'What time is it?'

And what day, I wonder.

'Almost breakfast time.' She smiles, not taking her eyes off her watch. 'You slept for almost eighteen hours. Your body needed it.'

'When can I go?' There is a tremor in my voice. Eighteen hours. Another day lost.

'Dr Wright will come by presently. I'll bring you something to eat.'

She leaves and there is nothing for me to do but wait. I can't abide all this waiting. Or being at the mercy of someone else's decisions. I could just discharge myself, I suppose, if it comes to it.

Dr Wright arrives just as I'm finishing my second boiled egg and a glass of cold orange juice. I have wolfed them down with three slices of toast, grateful to be alone in the ward, with no one to witness my appalling manners.

'I hear you are keen to leave?' He places a thermometer under my tongue, making it impossible for me to answer. 'And I presume you plan on resuming your escapade?'

He removes the thermometer and reads it.

'Yes, I do.'

'Your temperature is as it should be. So you are free to go. But I advise you to return to your husband and rest.'

I nod. There is no way that is happening but I don't need to argue the fact with him.

'Could you send for a car? I'd like to go straight to the aerodrome. I haven't seen my plane since the crash.'

'As you wish.'

'Thank you, Doctor. And please forward any bills to my husband. He'll take care of them. I'll be sure to tell him, and everyone, how well you've looked after me here.' I smile brightly at him, knowing he is still assessing me.

He extends a hand. 'I wish you well, Lady Heath. Don't take any more risks.'

As soon as he leaves I get out of bed and start to dress.

Chapter Fifteen

Bulawayo, Southern Rhodesia, 27th February 1928

The red light of morning is starting to bleed into the horizon when the car arrives with Captain Mail at the wheel. He speeds me through a sleeping Bulawayo and we are at the aerodrome in minutes. My Avian is there, waiting for me in the hangar. I take my time checking it over. Everything is exactly as it should be and apart from a tiny scratch on the wing I could have imagined this whole affair. I close my eyes and rest my head on the body of the plane. I am filled with gratitude for the people who got me through this scrape, and for my plane, for being intact.

Captain Mail helps me to wheel her out and we shake hands.

'Oh! Could I ask for one more favour?' I say. 'Do you have some paper and a pen?'

He produces a small notebook and pencil from his jacket pocket and I scribble:

Sorry to have caused worry and trouble. All is well. Lady H.

'Could you send this telegram for me? Sir James must be frantic.'

'Of course.' He slips it into his pocket. 'As soon as the office opens.'

'Thank you.'

I climb into the plane, open the locker and pull out my topee sun helmet. I wave it at him, laughing, and put it on along with my goggles. The morning is still fresh but I have learned my lesson about the African sun.

Mail reaches for the propeller. Just as he does, I remember something I've been meaning to ask.

'*Mail!*' I shout down to him. '*Any word on the expedition?*'

'The expedition?'

'The Chrysler gang. The motorcar expedition.'

'Oh! I haven't heard anything.'

I salute him and he turns the propeller. I taxi, feeling the rush of air hitting me, reviving me. The thrum of the engine kicking into life and the grating of the wheels on the rough runway feel like a part of my own biology. I pull the stick and the plane lifts into the dawn sky and I whoop. I am airborne again!

I wonder if I'll catch up to Emil. I don't really mind whether I do. Once I am progressing onwards, that is all I need.

I glide along, keeping an occasional eye on my instruments and a close one on the country beneath me. I fly between sheets of rain along the broad sweep of the Umgassa River. I look at the thick scrub below with new eyes, seeing how impossible a landing there would be. If I had to come down, I'd have to get as close as possible to the railway and even then ...

I have never been one for faith but I can't help feeling again that something or someone guided me down in Matabeleland.

I come over more open country near Intundhis. I've been flying for an hour and a half, accompanied by an easy wind from the east. The railway peeks out to greet me more regularly here and I am able to follow it almost exactly for thirty miles between N'game and Dett.

My stomach rumbles. It's been a few hours since my hospital breakfast. It seems strange to me that the only other time I was in a hospital was in France. And that couldn't compare, being a field hospital in the midst of a war. I never stayed long there. Just enough time to deliver my dispatch, or on occasion when I was needed to drive the ambulance, a groaning soldier. Or worse, a silent one.

Movement in the scrub below catches my eye. It looks like a small band of eland and I swoop down to investigate. They stop their feeding, breaking off from nosing at the ground to track me. Ears pitched, limbs tensed, they listen to the whine of my engine and they mustn't like what they hear as they canter back under the cover of the trees. The noise of my engine has not only disturbed the eland. From out of the scrub scatters a mother rhino and her baby. She runs off, abandoning it to whatever threat I might pose. How unmotherly! I presumed the maternal instinct was stronger than that. Maybe it is different for rhinos. Lady Bailey pops into my head. She who abandons her five children to take flight. It's different for rhinos and aviators, I decide, chuckling to myself.

A little after eight I spy a train just beyond Dett and guide my nose down to see it. Heads poke out of the windows, followed by arms waving. I wave back then bank left and climb again. Perhaps it's the sense that all of this pleasure was nearly lost to me or perhaps the sheer joy of flying freely over such wondrous country but I'm enjoying myself disgracefully. So much so that when I notice a small white cloud on the ground and know that I am nearing Victoria Falls I am almost disappointed to be so near my destination.

It's nearly nine now and the bright morning rays are trapped in the spray that sits above the gigantic falls, casting rainbow arcs into the blue sky. I fly through this curtain of smoky spray, deafened by the roar of the water as it tumbles over the sudden drop – water that had flown along, knowing only momentum until suddenly the riverbed turned into a gorge. I loop the loop and holler like a madwoman.

When I land in the large aerodrome in Livingstone, my hair is wild with damp and I am fizzing with happiness.

'Sophie! We thought we'd lost you.'

Dick Bentley emerges from behind his Moth and kisses me on the cheek.

'Dick! This is a nice surprise. You don't seem too concerned.'

'Don't be daft. Word came through that you'd turned up. In a hut!'

'A harem,' I tell him, enjoying the look of shock on his face. 'I shared the hut with the chief's wives. Five of them, I believe.'

Dick throws his head back and laughs. 'It could only happen to you. Weren't you tempted to stay? You might have lived happily ever after.'

'I never met the Chief. A lovely chap, I'm sure. But I had more important things to do and a Mrs Fletcher came to my rescue. What's this place like?'

'Well-kept. I'll walk you over.'

'How's Dorys?' I ask. 'Is married life treating you both well?'

'So far so good. We're having a wonderful honeymoon. We plan to make it last as long as we can. I think that's the trick. You look well, Sophie, considering your ordeal.'

I wave my hand. 'I'm sure the tale was embellished far beyond what happened. No doubt I was tied to a spit and about to be roasted by the natives when my rescuer appeared. I was well cared for.'

'And your plane survived the scrape as well? You were damn lucky.'

'I know.'

A stern-looking, tall man with brown hair is in the hangar, busy at work. Dick interrupts him to introduce me. Major Cochrane-Patrick is from Beith in Scotland and seems delighted to see me.

'I've heard all about you, Lady Heath. My wife will be thrilled to hear you've arrived. You had us all on edge, waiting to see if you'd come out of your adventure alright.'

'A minor scrape is all it was.'

'Major here is an expert mechanic. It might be worth letting him give the Avian the once-over,' Dick says.

'Would you? There's a bend in my undercarriage but I'm not sure how serious it is.'

'I'll take a look.'

Together we wheel my plane into the hangar.

Dick slips away to meet Dorys. 'We'll come along with you in the Moth in the morning,' he announces as he goes.

I wave my hand to acknowledge this news. Some company will be nice, I suppose, but I want to make up ground. They'd better not slow me down.

The Major is under my plane. 'There it is,' he calls. He scoots back out from underneath. 'I could fix it,' he says. 'But it would mean taking it back to Bulawayo for a few days.'

I bite my lip, considering. Bulawayo. That's the wrong direction. I want to go forwards, not backwards.

'Could I carry on with it as is?'

He takes his time checking over the rest of the body before answering me, paying close attention to the wheels.

'These look good. You could stick to wheel landings. And there might be a chance to get a new fitting made at the mine workshops in Broken Hill.'

I smile. 'I don't think I've used up all my luck yet so I'll bank on that. Thank you for your help. It's most kind.'

'Well, you can repay me. Have dinner with me and my wife. She's more fanatical about this flying lark than even I am and I know she'd love to hear all your stories.'

I agree and after a pleasant afternoon working on my engine I have a relaxing dinner with them. I do enjoy an encouraging audience.

I arrive back at my room in the Falls Hotel and take a final cigarette on the balcony. I sit, with my feet on the balcony wall, head back to see the glistening stars overhead and make a wish. That my luck will hold. A black cat swishes onto the wall, stares for a moment, surprised to find me there.

I hold out my hand to tempt it over. '*Psp, psp!*'

It looks at my hand with an air of disdain then swishes away again, disappearing into the bushes.

Chapter Sixteen

Newcastle West, County Limerick, October 1906

Sophie is by the window again. The sunlight and the sounds of life draw her to it, no matter the displeasure it causes Aunt Cis or Aunt Lou. She keeps one ear cocked for the slow shuffle of Henrietta's slippers and Grandfather's heavy tread. She is light on her feet, even if Lou calls her a clumsy giant, so they have yet to catch her. She is watching again for the schoolchildren. It has become her habit to track their progress through the Square when she can and join in the lively chatter in her head. Today, she sees a boy walking alone. He crouches by a cart in the street, right down on his hunkers, barefoot! He must have no fear of returning home with dirty clothes or mucky feet. He is trying to coax something out from under the cart but suddenly he takes off, running to catch a friend on the other side of the street. Sophie is curious. She presses in closer to the window wishing she could call out and ask him what he saw there. Now the cart is moving and she can see for herself. A cat. Well, a kitten, sooty grey, a blur of fur almost blending into the stones. She watches the poor thing, slinking along, exposed without the cover of the cart and wonders how it came to be here, with no mother, no father. She longs to go and bundle it up into her arms and bring it home and love it. The kitten disappears behind the church wall.

Aunt Cis agrees to accompany her to the Demesne but first Sophie must take a nap. A nap! She could burst from all the energy inside her. But she has to concede so she lies in her darkened bedroom, willing her fizzing limbs to rest.

She wakes in a strange humour after it. She has had the queerest dream. In it she was a very little girl and she was on a bicycle. Or rather she was on a bicycle that someone else was riding. All she can recall when she wakes is that and the odd sensation of moving at wild speed and the sun and the light and the air rushing by.

'Aunt Cis, was I ever on a bicycle?' she asks, taking her aunt's arm to hurry her along. They are only permitted half an hour by Grandfather before they must return.

'A bicycle? Heavens no, child! Not in all the time I've known you.'

Sophie is about to tell her of her dream when she sees a man approaching. Captain Roger Cunningham, one of the few men Grandfather allows them to converse with, due to his being a neighbour, or his proximity in age to Aunt Cis, or his status as a land agent. Sophie does not share Grandfather's fondness for him and already she feels the outing spoiled by his presence.

'Miss Peirce. Miss Sophie.'

He falls into step beside them, even though he was going in the opposite direction a moment ago.

'Captain Cunningham, what a pleasant surprise.'

He nods in Sophie's direction and she offers him only a sour look but it does nothing to discourage him.

'May I have the pleasure of accompanying you?' he asks.

'Of course. We were just talking about bicycles, Captain. You have been on one, I presume?'

He laughs his thin, reedy laugh. It emits from his small mouth, causing his bristling moustache to twitch but his dark eyes are not altered one bit by it. Sophie switches the focus of her sour look to Cis. Why is she involving him in a private conversation?

'Indeed I have been, Miss Peirce. But I can assure you that was an error I did not repeat. Blasted uncomfortable thing and impossible to control. No, give me a well-bred horse any day. That is the only dignified mount suited to a gentleman, if you ask me.'

He winks in Sophie's direction and her scowl deepens. He turns his attention back to Cis.

'You were not considering getting one for yourself, I hope?' He is feigning concern and Cis laughs politely.

'I was not. I do not fancy it and, besides, I imagine Dr Peirce would be strongly opposed to such an idea.' He nods, a smug expression settling on his yellowy jowls.

Cis continues. 'Miss Sophie was enquiring as to whether she had ever been on one. From what you say it does not sound like the type of encounter one would forget.'

He is silent now, casting glances at Sophie every few steps, until finally he speaks. 'No. One would not forget. Unless one was very young at the time and being transported by another on a bicycle.'

His words hang heavy between them. Aunt Cis throws him a thunderous look. Sophie's stomach turns as she suddenly feels that this repulsive man knows something of her that she does not know herself. The silence has the effect of hunting him away. For that Sophie is glad but now she must know more.

'What did he mean, Aunt Cis? Why would he say that?'

She tuts. 'Who knows, child? I only listen to half of what he says. A lot of empty blather most of the time. Now hurry along or we will have to turn back before we reach the river.'

Sophie knows this about Aunt Cis. Once she has decided not to speak on a subject she is a clam. They reach the bank of the river and Sophie finds a light twig to throw in. She watches as it rushes away from her, tossed and chucked by the fast flow. She loves how the river is changed by the weather. Today there has been some rain and it is freely hectic, in a hurry to be somewhere. She imagines herself shrinking, climbing aboard the twig and letting the river take her. She crouches down beside it so that she can trail her fingers and feel the tug of the current. That is when she sees it: the kitten. He is soaked to the skin, his sooty-grey fur flattened onto his bones. He is gripping the river bank with his front paws while his back legs scramble for purchase. He is in a fight for his life and in an instant she is in the river. The shock of the freezing water stalls her for a moment but she sloshes against the flow until she reaches him. She puts a hand under him, enough to lift him onto the bank, away from the edge. He lies there, spent. She climbs out after him, floods of river water spilling from her boots and skirt. Ruined, no doubt, but she doesn't care. She bundles him into her arms, rubbing at his fur to coax him back to life. She puts her lips to his fur.

'*Sophie! Good Lord above, what are you doing?*'

Aunt Cis is rushing over, dropping whatever leaves she has gathered. She likes to press them in her heavy books.

A sob escapes from Sophie's lips. It stops Aunt Cis in her tracks.

'Let's get you home. You'll catch your death.'

Catch her death? She has never felt more alive. In fact, until this moment, she has never felt alive at all. Now, every cell of her body has ignited. Her heart fills her whole self and her heart is in this tiny, warm creature that stirs now in her arms.

'I'm going to call him Moses.' She laughs. 'Because I found him on the river bank.'

Aunt Cis looks at her with pity and love and hope, afraid to say what she is thinking. That Sophie will not be allowed to keep him.

Sophie tightens her grip and resolves silently that if he does not stay, nor will she.

Back at the house the cook, Mina, coaxes him from Sophie's arms so that she can go and change. 'I'll put out a nice sup of milk for him,' she says.

Sophie thunders upstairs.

She is desperate not to be away from his side for a second longer than she must. On the way back to the kitchen she sees Aunt Cis knocking on Grandfather's study door, straightening her spine and taking a deep breath. She is about to report Sophie's latest escapade, before someone else does.

Sophie hesitates then races down to her newfound love and first friend.

In the following days she spends every spare minute in the kitchen with Moses. Mina grumbles under her breath about cats and children cluttering up her space but that doesn't stop her sneaking scraps to him. Sophie is relieved to see she is not the only one smitten. It may strengthen her case to keep him. Aunt Cis has visited Moses a few times. Each time Sophie hears her footsteps her heart freezes and she fears that Grandfather has made his pronouncement but so far he has not.

The footsteps approach again now. Aunt Cis's face is sorrowful, fixed. Sophie takes her hand from Moses' warm body and stands to straighten her skirts.

'Your grandfather wishes to speak with you in the drawing-room.'

Aunt Cis lifts a hand to tidy Sophie's hair. There are tears in her eyes and Sophie steels herself for what is to come. She will not cry but she will not give Moses up either. Grandfather is at the fireplace, contemplating the flames. Henrietta is seated in an armchair and offers the girl a weak smile. Sophie clears her throat to let him know she has arrived. He regards her for a moment and all she can see in his expression is disappointment. He beckons her to sit. She perches at the edge of the seat, ready to make a run for it and grab Moses if needs be. They can run away together, sleep under the large oak trees in the Demesne and catch fish in the river and —

'Sophie, I despair,' he begins.

He has turned his back to the fire and all she feels now is the cold of the room and of his heart.

'From the day I brought you into this house we have tried our best to raise you well. And clearly we have failed. It was unfair of me perhaps to expect your step-grandmother to carry the burden of a parentless child but I did not anticipate you would be so unruly.'

Henrietta gives him a watery smile and looks at Sophie as though the girl should pity her for what she's had to put up with.

'I truly believed this household would have a civilising effect. I cannot fault the comportment of my own daughters —'

The words 'my son' hang unspoken and heavy in the room but he pushes past them.

'It has taken some time for me to come to terms with your antics and to decide on an appropriate outcome.' He purses his lips as he once again regards her.

Sophie racks her brains to think what else she might have done wrong. Did she not save a defenceless creature from drowning?

'Do you know that you are the talk of the town? That you were seen, sloshing about in the river, fully clothed?' He closes his eyes against the horror of this knowledge.

She swallows down a nervous giggle. She longs to ask him would it have been better for her to remove her clothing?

'No, this cannot go on. I dread to think where it may lead. We have come to a decision.'

He moves to stand beside Henrietta and places his hand on her shoulder. No doubt the decision was his but it seems to please her too.

'You are to be sent away, Sophie. You will attend an appropriate boarding school as soon as one is found and can be persuaded to accept you. I pray the news of your misdeeds will not travel that far. This will be a considerable expense for our family but I can think of no other option.'

He watches her now. She composes her features as her mind scrambles to make meaning of it. Moses is not to be sent away, but she is? This will cost them money. Her aunts will suffer because of this. She will miss them so, especially Cis. But ... she is to be free! She thinks of the kitten. She saved his life and he gave her freedom.

Chapter Seventeen

Livingstone, Northern Rhodesia, March 1st, 1928

We creep out of the hotel in darkness next morning. I am keen to be en route by daylight.

I watch, aghast, as Dick loads his Moth with thirty gallons of petrol, spares, two large suitcases and Dorys. I doubt he will manage to take off so I let him go first. I am impressed when he manages it in two hundred yards and relieved when my Avian, weighed down with fifty gallons and my usual gear, gets off the ground in one hundred and fifty.

I am a little ahead of him all the way in the very good weather, buffeted by a friendly breeze. From the cockpit I see some buck, mostly impala. We cut the railway from time to time and dodge a little rain shortly after half seven in the morning. We climb to seven thousand feet above a layer of cloud to avoid the bumps then drop down as we pass over the abundant plains of Kafue River.

I spot a threatening cloud bank and signal to Dick to drop under it. We get onto the railway line just in time and are forced to fly on top of it for nearly ten miles, getting drenched to the skin in a ferocious downpour. Finally it clears and we are able to climb again.

A thread of smoke from the mines at Broken Hill tells me we are close. I see the aerodrome, laid out in the shape of a cross with a grass fire burning in one corner and at twelve sharp I bring my plane down, landing beautifully on the starboard wheel.

We take our time pegging down the Moth and covering the induction pipe and engines and cockpits of both planes from the constant threat of rain.

'Lady Heath, we are honoured to have you! And you made it before the rain, too. What luck!' A robust, brown-haired woman in a beige skirt and shirt approaches us, talking before she's anywhere near. 'Mrs Moffatt-Thompson. Mr Stevens, the manager, was hoping to meet you but I'm afraid he is unwell today. Is there anything you need?'

I frown. 'Oh, there is! I had hoped to meet with him. I have some damage to my undercarriage and there was some mention of me being able to get a new fitting made.'

'That should be no problem. *Howell! Howell!*'

She summons a nice-looking young man.

'Howell here is the man for the job, ex Air Force mechanic.'

Within minutes we are wheeling the Avian into the yard and Howell is working on getting the root section off. I can see now that my luck really was good. The fitting is bent at a forty-five-degree angle and the bolts are sheared. I must have side-slipped onto the ground in Matabeleland. If I had landed straight on it would have been a different story and my Avian wouldn't have managed another landing. Howell finds a piece of steel and fashions another fitting. He has just finished when the heavens open and a torrent of water is unleashed on us. We push the Avian to shelter and make a run for it ourselves.

I am woken by the pounding of rain on the hotel roof. I know before I put one foot outside my bed that today will not be a day for flying. I am slow to dress and keen to keep my own company so I delay going down for breakfast. It is not to be, however. A fresh-faced Dorys meets me at the entrance to the breakfast room.

'What a pity! We've just finished. But why don't I join you? I can have another cup of tea. It's a day for nothing else. And I have so much to tell you.'

We sit and Dorys calls for tea. I request two soft-boiled eggs with bread and strong coffee.

The food arrives and I begin to eat.

'We've decided to go for it,' Dorys announces.

'Go for what?'

'We're going to fly all the way back to England!' She claps her hands. 'Isn't that something? Dickie and I were talking about it and I said, "Dickie, dear, you know I'd love nothing more but I must have Mother's approval." You know what mothers are like.'

I nod, although really I don't know.

'You haven't met my mother, of course,' Dorys continues. 'But trust me! One does not move without her say-so. *Formidable*, as the French say. I wasn't sure she'd let me, such a treacherous journey, but she's all for it. Thinks it's a novel idea.'

I really am tired and the coffee isn't doing its work yet and my mind is swimming with the meanest things to say. I clamp my lips tight in between mouthfuls of egg to make sure they don't slip out. *Your mother must want rid of you. She seems overly keen for you to embark on this 'treacherous' journey. And it's not such a novel idea. It's my bloody idea. And now you and 'Dickie, dear' are going to steal my thunder.*

I think. I do not say.

She twitters on.

'And there's the passports. We don't have them. Well, not with us. So that will have to be seen to.'

And travel documents, guns, appropriate clothing, maps. All they have is their – my – wonderful idea. I push aside the rest of my breakfast. My taste buds have soured. I light a cigarette and signal to the waiter for more coffee.

'What do you recommend I pack? For wearing?' Dorys asks. She is oblivious to my bad temper.

I take a few more drags then viciously stub my cigarette out in my emptied eggshell.

'Brown coat, brown skirt, brown jumper, fur coat.'

My answer is deadpan. It says 'I do not care'. Already I am seeing the headlines.

Lady Heath, Lieutenant and Mrs Bentley in Joint Venture.

This is not what I want.

It is as though Dorys has read my mind. 'Have you heard about the Chrysler expedition?'

She reminds me about my other joint venture. To my shame I've hardly thought of them since Johannesburg. Between my sunstroke mishap and the worries about my plane, Emil and the others have been so far from my mind it's as though they never existed.

'They've been having a most awful time of it. I was speaking to a man this morning who met them when they passed through. We've only just missed them. They got here a few days ago but only just. They've been plagued by mosquitos and spent most of their time hauling the car out of swamps. Their cinematographer, a man named Noble, was ordered back to Johannesburg by the doctor here. The poor man's back was in ribbons from travelling over the rough terrain and he couldn't go another yard in that car. So it's just Bouwer and Millin now, limping along at snail's pace. I'd rather the skies, wouldn't you?'

'Yes,' I say. 'I don't envy them.'

Dorys starts to wave.

'Dickie, dear' has found us. He plants a kiss on her cheek.

'Passports are on the way. They should get to Abercorn before we do.'

Dorys gives a squeal. She squeezes his hand and smiles at me.

'Sophie has been giving me some wonderful advice on what to pack.'

'I hope the key word was 'less'. I don't think my Moth will make it across the Mediterranean if we keep loading it up like it has been.'

She swats his hand away and I manage a small smile.

'You don't mind us tagging along, Sophie? I doubt we'll be with you all the way but it might come in damned handy for you in parts.'

'I suppose.'

'And you'll still be doing it alone. Solo. In your plane. So the record will still stand.'

My friend understands me, it seems. But that doesn't shift my grumpiness. This is just a jaunt to them, an extended honeymoon. It makes less of my endeavours and threatens to steal my headlines. I will have to make sure I get to London before them, no matter what.

I stand and pat Dick on the shoulder.

'We three will be marvellous company for each other,' I manage to say.

I return to my room and resign myself to watching the rain fall.

Chapter Eighteen

Broken Hill, Northern Rhodesia, 4th March 1928

The rain clears enough for us to depart on the morning of the fourth. The bad weather ahead of us matches my mood and when I look down from my cockpit I see only dense forest and dreary kopjes, the hills stark and rocky. I am unmoved by the occasional rhino and eland but understand the utter disdain with which an eagle treats me as he flies alongside. I allow myself to be distracted by his wingspan and ponder the machinations of his flight compared to mine.

We reach N'dola in two and a half hours. It is a much larger town than Broken Hill and it seems the entire population has turned out to greet us. I do what has to be done then I sleep.

I wake for lunch and do some work on my machine. When darkness falls I refuse all offers of entertainment and claiming fatigue I take to my bed again. But I sleep badly so at first light set out for the aerodrome and begin to ready the Moth and the Avian.

Dick and Dorys arrive just in time to take off, oblivious to the fact that I've been here for hours working. They delay us further, taking too long to say goodbye to the crowds that have turned out to see us off. Really! They're behaving like celebrities and I'm sure it's me the people have come to see. Or it would be if Dick and Dorys hadn't decided to jump on my bandwagon.

I give the briefest goodbye and wait sulkily in my cockpit, ruminating on the impracticality of this aerodrome. Too small and, as it's positioned at four thousand five hundred feet, the air density means it will be hard to get decent lift for take-off.

Finally, Dick assists Dorys into the plane, planting one last big kiss on her lips, drawing roars from the crowd. The people chase after us as we take off, me and the lovebirds. We bump along under low rainclouds for an hour. The bends of Luapula River reveal themselves below us and, shortly after, the raucous drop of the Mambatuta Falls.

We settle between two cloud layers at six thousand feet and my bad humour is starting to lift, washed away by the fresh air and familiarity of flight, when I detect a strong smell of petrol. My stomach twists. Will I have to land? I peer out to see if there is a suitable spot but can see only cloud. I'll have to carry on and hope for the best. The instrument readings are stable, that is a relief. After a while the smell dissipates. It must be the overflow. I'll have to check it when I land.

The space between the layers of cloud narrows with the shifting of the breeze. Now I'm flying blind with only my instruments and the shape of the clouds to guide me. I lose sight of the Moth entirely. The breeze carries the whine of their engine now and again so I can tell they're still there. But otherwise I am alone.

The sight of Dick and Dorys canoodling earlier has made me feel it sharply. The sting of loneliness. I have always striven for independence, been dogged in my pursuit of it and still am. But, it would be nice to have someone. Someone to talk to when I get into bed at night. Someone to hand me my tools and keep me company while I work on my machine. Someone to put their arms around me. Someone to dine with, to dance with. I spend so much time among strangers, new acquaintances, casual friends and it's exhausting keeping my public face on. What I wouldn't give to be with someone who knows me! Just someone and just to be. I had some hope for me and William in the early days but it was lost a long time ago and I wonder if I'll ever have it again. Happiness, love. My arrangement with Sir James contains none of that promise but it never did and I entered into it knowingly. Could I have had it with John? Was that my chance? And have I lost it?

The layer of cloud starts to lift and soon I can see the ground beneath me again. Mostly it is bad forest interspersed with ominous swamps. There's more rain to dodge and more showers visible on the horizon.

The Moth comes into view again and I'm relieved to see it. I'm getting used to having company although it is a headache having another plane to worry about. Our arrival at Abercorn is preceded by drenching rainstorms between the hills. The blue of Lake Tanganyika is visible despite the downpours and the town of Abercorn comes into sight soon after.

We land and tend to the planes then Mrs Jelfe drives us to the magistrate's house where we are to stay. She owns one of the two cars in this small town. But the size of the place has no bearing on the welcome we receive and I am soon ensconced in a charming little bedroom with a free-standing bath that I luxuriate in for most of the afternoon.

I am just dressed and making my way downstairs when I hear the sound of an engine outside and raised voices. Has Mrs Jelfe forgotten something? Or has the other motorcar owner decided to pay us a visit?

I skulk along the dark hallway, trying to see without being seen. I'm not keen for more small talk with well-wishers. From the entrance I see the side of a green car. A man steps out from the driver's side and moves out of my line of view towards the rear. The car is not in good nick. The paintwork is scratched and torn and there is as much caked mud covering it as there is green. The passenger's door opens and a head pops up over the far side of the car.

Emil!

My heart skips a little and I feel my cheeks flushing. I turn to a mirror hanging over a small sideboard. I look decent enough, I suppose. At least I had a chance to bathe and dress. I smile, not at my reflection which isn't that pleasing, but at the prospect of spending time with someone who makes me feel a little giddy. I am about to rush out to the yard to greet him and Gerry when I remember. *The letter*.

Will it dampen his spirits to be reminded of his wife and, maybe by now, his child? If it has arrived. He must miss her. And he has a long way to go yet before he sees her again. Really, it wouldn't be good for his morale or the expedition if he were to be made feel homesick. Or maybe the letter is a tirade, a blast of her resentment towards him for abandoning her in her hour of need. No. That won't do him any good. None at all. I'll give it to him when he's leaving Abercorn. That way at least he'll get to enjoy his time here.

With me.

And the Bentleys.

I fix a bright smile on my face and step out of the dark into the sunlit courtyard. Emil and Gerry are in conversation with Mr Varing, whose house this is, and I wait, not wishing to interrupt. It allows me a moment to observe him. His tan is deeper, his hair has grown longer and his arms ... My stomach tightens. His shirt sleeves are rolled up and I can see how the physical demands of the expedition have defined the muscles there.

I can't wait any longer.

'*Emil!*' I call and he turns, a warm greeting in his brown eyes.

'Sophie.'

He kisses me on the cheek and I shake hands with Gerry.

'Did the other fellow get eaten by lions?' I ask.

'No. Not lions. The roads ate poor Noble up and spat him out. He only made it as far as Broken Hill and had to return to Jo'burg. Doctor's orders. His back couldn't take another hour of driving.'

Dorys was right then.

'So, no more cinematography?'

'He left us his equipment. I've been trying a bit. So has Gerry. But, to be perfectly honest, it's taken all we've got to get as far as here in one piece.'

'I rather abandoned you, didn't I?'

Emil laughs. 'Don't feel bad. You couldn't hang about waiting for us. Some days we barely manage ten miles.'

'That awful?'

'You have no idea! Why don't I freshen up and we can have a good talk over some sundowners?'

'That sounds wonderful. Are you staying here?'

'Yes. Mr Varing has been kind enough to offer. He didn't expect us and you to turn up on the same day. But we'll squash in.'

'The more the merrier.' I smile.

The sundowners on the porch are a raucous affair. I get the sense that Mr Varing doesn't have many visitors. The man is overjoyed at having two feted expeditions arriving to his residence on the same afternoon.

'Cape to Cairo by car!' he exclaims, as though he's just heard. 'And by plane!' He clinks glasses with us all and convulses with delight. His enthusiasm is infectious and it extends to the drinking. His man is run ragged refilling glasses that are drained by us faster than a parched man stumbling across water after a day in the desert.

We are summoned to dine and eat God knows what. I am aware that I am ravenous and that I am having trouble focusing on spearing my vegetables with the fork.

'Bring me an *assegai*!' I demand and everyone finds it hilarious.

We wander out to the porch after dinner and I take to drinking water in between the gins. I like the feeling that my head is floating away from all my concerns but I don't want to lose the run of myself entirely. Dick and Dorys are quieter than the rest of us, sullen even. Has there been a row? A lovers' tiff?

Gerry is nearing the end of a dramatic tale he has been recounting of the expedition's latest escapade. 'And it took thirty of the strongest natives from the nearby *boma* to pull us across the stream. And when we got over to the other side the chief told me we need a new camel because this one is dead. Dead!'

We fall about the place laughing though I'm not even sure that it was very funny. Gerry abruptly staggers to standing and declares, 'I'm going to bed.'

He takes a moment to gain his equilibrium then points his drink-heavy head in the direction of the bedrooms, waving away the offer of assistance from the house servant.

'I want to go too, Dick. My head is ringing.' Dorys is on her feet too. She is looking pasty. She reaches down and removes a whiskey glass from Dick's grasp and helps him up. They slip away.

Mr Varing has fallen into a doze, snoring softly in his chair. It must be a frequent occurrence as the servants don't seem fazed and already they are gathering him up to be carried to bed.

Is the night over? I am in a disappointing midway place between drunk and sober. I feel a gloom settling on me and I know that even if I down three or four more drinks I won't regain the giddy joy of earlier.

The evening has worn away some of my hard shell and exposed a need. A strong need to be with someone.

A servant comes to light the way for me.

'My room is at the top of the stairs,' I say loudly but not for the servant's benefit. 'On the left. Goodnight, Emil.'

I wait inside my closed bedroom door. There are footsteps on the stairs. I tense but they scurry past. A servant? The house is silent and then I hear another, careful tread. It pauses at my door. Then moves away, into the quiet of the night, leaving me more alone than before.

I turn my face to the pillow. What was I thinking, presuming that there would be some illicit *rendezvous* with Emil? I replay every moment of our interactions since we met and see, mortifyingly, that what I had taken for flirtatiousness could just as easily be friendliness and harmful banter. And here I was ready to throw myself at him. Ready to risk my reputation for a meaningless fling. He is a married man after all and I a married woman. Except I do not feel like a married woman and have not felt that way once since I wed Sir James. Being with Dorys and Dick is a constant reminder of that. Tears leak from the corners of my eyes. I am bereft and lonely.

But I must also remember that I have an obligation to Sir James. He has given me the freedom to pursue this dream and it would be foolish to risk losing that. I think of my first taste of freedom and how it can be taken as quickly as it is given.

Chapter Nineteen

Rochelle School
Blackrock, Cork
28th October, 1906

Dear Aunt Cis,

I am sorry for not writing sooner but I have been so busy! My head is simply crammed to bursting with all I am learning: English, French, drawing, history, geography, writing, arithmetic, geometry, needlework. I love it all and each night when I lie down to sleep my mind races through all the new information. I soak it up like a thirsty plant. I think I am doing quite well, except in needlework. That is my Achilles' Heel! My 'point faible', See how my French improves? Miss Marshall, the headmistress, despairs of my sewing skills. She has written me off in that regard due to my 'mannish' hands. Can you believe that is how she described me? But I don't care. What use is needlework at any rate? She manages to be everywhere all at once and we would never even see her coming were it not for the ferocious hats she likes to sport.

We rise early here. Six o'clock! We swallow down a dreadful breakfast then we crowd into our classroom for lessons. We are glad of that for the room warms up nicely and the chill that keeps us awake at night leaves our bones. Miss Marshall lectures us repeatedly on how we are to acquire a ladylike, easy manner and a refined, pleasing accent. Not an easy task, I assure you, when your teeth are chattering from the cold.

I hope you don't think I am complaining, dear Aunt Cis. I am as happy as a clam! At least when the cold keeps me awake I have the other girls to chat with. They were on me for days when I arrived, firing questions. They were intrigued to hear that I have no parents. There is one girl in my form with no mother and a few with no fathers but I am unique in my situation. I told them all about you, my 'mother-auntie', and how well you look after me.

Tell Moses I miss him. There's a big tabby here who likes to sit under the mulberry tree in the garden and chase little birds but he's not friendly at all. Give my love to Lou and Henrietta and Grandfather and Rugs. But most of all I send my love to you.

Your baby,

Sophie

PS We are to start outdoor games as soon as the weather allows and we will share grounds with the boys from the Grammar!

Newcastle West, County Limerick, December 1906

Sophie's heart lifts as she steps down from the coach that met her at the train station. Her grandfather's house stands before her in its haughty grandeur, indifferent to the festive bustle in the town. She is dead on her feet from her travels and longing for her bed. But she knows Aunt Cis and Aunt Lou will want to hear all about Rochelle. She owes them that – they never had this opportunity. But how will she convey to them all that she now knows and how changed she is in these short few months? She has been plunged into the world and it has made her look at this little corner of it with new eyes. She sees herself as others do – little orphan child – no mother or father – blessed by the charity of her family. For this visit she will be on her best behaviour.

Aunt Cis opens the front door and Sophie flings herself into her arms. They hold tight to each other as they make their way to the drawing-room, falling over their words.

'Was the train journey tiring?'

'Your hair looks different, Aunt Cis!'

'Have you learned so much?'

'When can I see Moses?'

The others are waiting for them. Grandfather is in his armchair by the fire. He clears his throat to demand attention and stop the gabbling but there is a hint of a smile on his lips.

'Goodness, child, the peace we have known these past few months is well and truly shattered!'

Sophie drops her gaze and Aunt Cis squeezes her hand.

'But we are glad to welcome you home.' On the last word he convulses into a fit of coughing. Aunt Lou is at his side in a moment and no one speaks while she tends to him. He looks smaller and less fearsome.

'Sophie, I have no idea how,' Henrietta says, 'but you appear to have grown taller again. I do hope you don't intend to keep growing forever!'

Sophie laughs. It is true. Often it feels like she is in someone else's body. But she likes its heft and strength. Except here, with these eyes on her. Now, she feels like she is too big for this room.

'Yes, Henrietta, my uniform will need its hem let down before I return to school. Sophie looks down at her pinafore to illustrate the point. She sees the glance that passes between my aunts. She is reminded how heavily the silence and the unsaid things sit on this house.

Aunt Cis draws her aside and leads her to the door.

'Come, Sophie. You need to wash up before dinner. The Cunninghams are to join us later.' She tuts at Sophie's expression but there is a smile there too.

As they head towards their bedrooms, Cis quietly says, 'I received a letter from your Miss Marshall. She was most displeased with a prank you were involved in. In fact, I fear you were the ringleader.'

Sophie feels her face redden. She thought Miss Marshall had punished her sufficiently already. Writing a letter of complaint home was a bit *de trop*.

'Am I to understand that you and some other girls found a hidden passage?'

'Well, you can hardly blame us for wanting to explore ...'

'And you scattered mutton bones from your dinner about the place?'

'Any fool would have known what those were ...'

'And wrote a message on the wall in red ink? And told some girls it was blood from a prisoner who'd been tortured to death down there?'

There isn't much Sophie can say to that. It's all true. So she says nothing.

'Sophie!' There is a trace of amusement mingled with the disapproval in Cis's tone. 'You frightened one girl, Sarah Gillespie, out of her wits apparently. She had to go home early for Christmas break.'

Now is not a good time to tell Aunt Cis that Sarah is a Nervous Nellie, afraid of her own shadow.

Cis stops walking and places her hand on Sophie's arm. 'I do not want to receive another letter like that, Sophie. Is that clear? The expense of sending you to boarding school is a burden on the family and you need to be respectful of that.'

Sophie is chastened. 'I know, Aunt Cis. I am sorry.' She squeezes her aunt's arm. She'll be good. For Cis. She'll do what she's told.

The table is laden with food and still the servant girl brings more. Sophie's stomach rumbles loudly and she glances at Henrietta, seated on her left, to make sure she hasn't heard it. The room is cosy and twinkles in the candlelight. If she turns her attention to her right her heart lifts, for there is dear Cis and Lou, looking almost youthful in the soft glow. Beside them sit Harriet and Doris Cunningham, two sweet girls, years older than Sophie, at least ten, but as silent as she has always been at this table. When a question is addressed to them they glance at their mother for permission to answer.

Lucia Cunningham, widow of Richard, has aged since Sophie last saw her. She looks unwell – maybe it is a trick of the light, but where her daughters' cheeks are flushed hers are wan and tinged with yellow. She eyes the dishes laid out before her with a look of trepidation, as though they are a mountain she must climb. She, in turn, glances at her adult son, now in his thirties and the head of the household, for permission to speak.

Sophie has managed so far to avert her eyes from him so as to preserve her appetite. Roger Cunningham, more pompous than ever since his father's death, takes over the table with his talk and Sophie has to pinch her fingers under the table to control her rage. There is no real reason for it. It is a thing she feels more than she knows or understands but every time she is forced to be in his company he makes her feel wrong.

He is speaking to her now. 'You must be very grateful to Dr Peirce for this opportunity, Sophie. I hope your schooling is worthy of the expense.'

Her cheeks heat up. He is so brazen and insensitive. She feels Henrietta shifting in her seat. She hates any talk of money, Sophie knows, never mind at the dinner table. He trundles in again, paying no heed to the fact that he is making everyone uncomfortable and is trampling all over her pleasure at being home.

'Well, is it worth it? What have you learned?'

This question is more straightforward but her mind is a blank. What has she learned? She thinks of her friends, those other girls who fill her days with laughter and fun and she wants to say that she has learned how to be alive. But she could never say that to him so instead she is an open-mouthed mute until dear Aunt Cis comes to the rescue.

'Mr Cunningham, in her letters to us Sophie has told us all about the marvellous things she is learning – geography and French and needlework and goodness knows what else!'

'Is that so?' He glances at her but returns the cold stare to Sophie once more. It is as though he is suspicious of her, that she has learned something, gained some knowledge of the world that she is refusing to divulge. 'Well, you seem to have learned to control your tongue, which is a blessing. You used never cease your chattering from what I recall.'

She fights against that tongue now, longs to stick it out at him and shout that he knows nothing about her. She remains silent and still, pinching her fingers harder and harder until they whiten.

After dinner they retire to the drawing-room. Sophie hopes the Cunninghams will leave straight after but they linger. Mrs Cunningham and her daughters sit by the fire with pained expressions. They watch Roger who leans on the mantel, pulling on his pipe and preaching to Grandfather about the slovenly habits of the Irish peasant farmer. Sophie whispers to Aunt Cis that she needs the lavatory. She leaves the room and then races down to the kitchen to bury her face in Moses' fur. His warmth and strength and uncomplicated love fortify her and soon she is ready to return.

She climbs the stairs to the drawing-room and meets Roger on the landing. His face is flushed and when he speaks his words slip, ill-formed, from his lips.

'Sophie,' he steadies himself with a hand on the wall, restricting her path.

She is close enough to smell the brandy and pipe smoke on his breath.

'Mr Cunningham.' She hovers, not knowing how to proceed. She would like to turn and run back downstairs but her feet refuse to move.

'I must say, you are much changed since your departure. I think the schooling suits you.' He steps closer. 'It will be my pleasure to see you blossom into a young woman.' He fixes his dark eyes on hers before sliding them down her body.

Her stomach flips over in disgust. She doesn't understand his words but she knows how they make her feel.

'You are like your mother, you know.'

She has a sensation of the ground slipping from beneath her feet. Nobody has ever spoken of her mother. She knows that she died in childbirth. That her coming was her mother's going. Beyond that she does not think of her, it is too difficult, and she has nothing on which to hang her thoughts – no photograph, no lock of hair. She has never met her family. She knows her name – Kate Theresa Dooling – but that is all. She despises this man even more now for being in possession of something that is hers.

He smirks. 'Let us hope the resemblance is physical only. It is most unlucky to run the risk of inheriting either of those two personalities.' He laughs at his own words.

She does not know what's funny. Her hands are bunched into fists.

'I'll tell you one quick story – you reminded me of it the last time we walked together in the Demesne and you asked if I had ever been on a bicycle.'

Sophie shakes her head. She wants to tell him he is wrong. She did not walk with him in the Demesne. He intruded on her walk with Cis and she has no interest in whether or not he was ever on a bicycle.

He leans closer still and lowers his voice.

'You were on one when you were very small.'

She shakes her head again.

'You were,' he insists. 'Your father, Jackie, put you in a bag, like a kitten. The lunatic! Heading for Queenstown, he told the policeman that stopped him. He was taking you to America!' He spluttered out the last sentence. This was hilarious to him.

She is confused. Cunningham is mistaken. Her father died before she was born. She hears the drawing-room door opening and the light it throws onto the landing pulls her forward, like a moth. She moves to pass Cunningham but as she does he whispers. 'You'll turn out just fine.' She feels his clammy hand brush against hers.

She returns to the drawing-room and quietly takes a seat behind the others.

Her mind races and she barely notices the Cunninghams leaving. She needs to talk to Aunt Cis, to find out what she knows, if he is telling the truth. But before she gets the chance Grandfather addresses her.

'Sophie, I am pleased to see how well you have been doing at Rochelle.'

She glistens in the rare praise, her other concerns fading for a moment.

'However,' he says, 'I'm afraid you won't be returning.'

She stands up, her body reacting to this news before her mind can comprehend it. How can he snatch this away from her now?

He is overcome by a fit of coughing and Lou brings him a glass of water. Henrietta takes up the baton.

'There are other people to think of Sophie, not just you. Your grandfather needs to retire. He hasn't been able to see patients properly in a long time. There will have to be changes.' She looks around the room as if trying to find an example of this change to come.

But it is not necessary. Sophie understands. Her schooling is an expense the family cannot withstand if Grandfather stops seeing patients. She can see that he himself is in need of a doctor and although she is sickened at the thought of being encased again in this living tomb she blinks away the tears. At least now she knows there is a world outside of these walls and she resolves to find her way back to it again.

'Will I continue my lessons at home?' she asks quietly.

Aunt Cis rushes to her side. 'Oh no, dear girl! Father and Henrietta haven't finished. If you will permit me, Father?'

He raises a hand, permission granted.

'You will not return to school in Cork but we have found an alternative. In Belfast. It is more affordable and without the unhealthy preoccupation with vigorous sport. Utterly unbecoming in a school for young ladies!'

Sophie shuts her eyes and takes a deep breath. Her body is collapsing with relief. She is not to be yanked from the world after all.

Chapter Twenty

Abercorn, Northern Rhodesia, 6th March 1928

I wake up late and go downstairs for breakfast, hoping I will be alone. But everyone else is equally as tardy and the full contingent of guests is gathered around the table. Emil sits opposite me and I'm aware that he is trying to catch my eye but I avoid him. My head is starting to throb, a dull ache that threatens to sharpen if I don't appease it with food and sweet tea. Or, if I could manage it, the hair of the dog. I'm fortunate to never suffer with my stomach when I overindulge and am able to manage a decent breakfast.

Mr Varing pushes a full plate of eggs away from him. 'You adventurers know how to enjoy a good time, but maybe a little too much,' he groans.

'You have been most hospitable, Mr Varing,' I say. 'And you will have a peaceful house again once we get on our way. The rains seem to have cleared.'

'Here, yes,' Dick chimes in. 'But north and south of here have taken a beating with thunderstorms. I went down to the postmaster before breakfast to check if our supplies have arrived. Nothing has been able to get through and the telegraph wires are down as well.'

'You went down already?'

'Yes, I was up early.'

'I was so tired this morning. All those flying hours catching up with me.'

'I'm certainly glad of the break from the road,' Emil says. 'Gerry too. He said he's going back to bed and I might just do the same.'

'I think I'll walk over to the aerodrome and check on the planes,' I say. I rise from my place. 'Thank you again, Mr Varing. I'll be sure to tell everyone how kind and generous you've been.'

'Good God, woman! Don't tell everyone. I can only handle so many guests.'

I set out for the aerodrome through quiet streets. The day is muggy. The rain brought some respite from the humidity but the moisture in the air is building already and the sky overhead is full of clouds. I feel like they are closing in, pressing down. I have a sudden longing for fresh sea air stinging my nostrils, an Atlantic breeze whipping at my hair and taking my breath away.

I am almost at the aerodrome when I hear footsteps behind me. I turn and see Emil catching up, the armpits of his shirt stained dark.

'I thought you were going back to bed,' I say when he reaches me.

'I thought I'd come and find you instead. Is that alright?'

'Of course. Why wouldn't it be?'

'I don't know. I got the feeling you weren't at ease this morning. That you didn't want to be around me.'

'It's not personal. I don't want to be around anyone when I'm like this.'

'Like what?'

'Tired, groggy, cranky.'

'Will you tolerate me, do you think?'

'Well, you're here now. You might be of some use.'

We enter the aerodrome and I start my usual checks. I want to make sure we are ready to go as soon as the supplies get here. Emil busies himself, holding tools for me and thankfully not talking.

'Does the Chrysler need some work? I could help,' I offer.

'Gerry is going to give it the once-over. We take care of the routine stuff every evening and I'm not sure there's much else we can do out here with no spare parts.'

I have an idea. 'Could we take it for a spin?'

'Sure.' He brightens.

'I'd like to see some of the country. Up close for a change, instead of from the air.'

'I think that's a splendid idea. Will we go after lunch?'

'Perfect.' I wipe my hands on my oil-stained trousers.

'Are you bothered about the supplies?' he asks.

'I'd rather not have the delay but there's no point sulking about it. It's out of our control.'

'It could take days,' he says. 'Why don't we just allow ourselves to have a little fun?'

I like the sound of that. I pick up my wrench.

'I'll meet you back at the house. And then we can take the Chrysler out after lunch,' I say.

I am dismissing him and he takes it gracefully. He is walking away, an arm raised in concession.

I call after him. '*I'm driving!*'

Emil clings to the inside of the passenger door and I hear him swearing under his breath as I take the Chrysler sweeping around a bend.

'Where did you learn to drive?' he asks, raising his voice to be heard above the engine.

'I did a lot of driving in the war. France and Belgium mostly.'

'Is that where you learned? That explains your technique.'

I laugh. 'I'll take that as a compliment.'

I'm enjoying being behind the wheel again. It's a change from flying which is serene by comparison as we jolt over rough country roads, leaving a column of dust behind us.

'*Slow down, Sophie!*' Emil shouts. '*Gerry will have my guts for garters if I bring this back with damage.*'

He's right. Chastened, I squeeze the brake pedal and bring the Chrysler down to a smoother cruising speed. I wouldn't like if someone went rough-housing in my Avian.

'Actually,' I tell him, 'I learned how to drive on a beach, in County Kerry. And, now that I think of it, that was the day I decided to sign up.'

'Because you loved driving so much and knew you'd be of use in the war?'

'Because I knew I had to get away from my husband.'

'And did you?'

'Eventually. We struggled on for a few more years. But I'd lost my love for him, over time. It was sad.'

'He was a fool.'

'He's a dead fool now.'

'I'm sorry. I shouldn't speak ill of him then.'

We return to Mr Varing's house and I see Dick coming out.

'Good news,' Dick says. 'Supplies have arrived. So we can be on our way. Maybe tonight even.'

'Tonight?' I glance back at the car. Emil has got out and is under the bonnet. I look up at the sky. 'There might be more rain. And not too many hours of daylight left. Let's wait until morning.'

'One more night in Abercorn it is then,' Dick says. 'I'll go and tell Dorys.'

Chapter Twenty-one

Abercorn, Northern Rhodesia, 7th March 1928

I'm packing my bag to leave when I remember the letter from Emil's wife. I will give it to him now, before I go. I sit at the edge of my bed and run my finger across the envelope where she has written, MR. E. MILLIN, in neat, childlike print. I have no strong feelings about her, or him. No jealousy. I'm happy for them and will have to learn to live with my lack of companionship for now. I don't know if it is more or less painful to know that it is a self-inflicted wound. I could be in London right now with John.

But, then, I could not be here.

I take a deep breath and make my way downstairs.

Emil and Gerry have come to see us off.

'Lovely to see you again,' I whisper before handing him the letter. 'Give my best to your family.'

By half past seven we are taxiing along the downhill slope of the aerodrome and lifting into the sky. Abercorn has been an interesting interlude but there is still a lot of sky between me and London. It seems we will never have a day where it is just plain sailing.

The first obstacle is a dirty down-flow as we are passing over a range of hills. My engine protests loudly and I make the decision to reroute around them instead of continuing over. The landscape is endlessly enthralling. I fly over an enormous extinct crater, a maze of swamps and streams flowing into a large lake, the broad sweep of a large, indolent river. I consult my hand-drawn map. Yes, that must be the Ugalla. I swoop low over the villages along its bank but there is no sign of life apart from a herd of fifteen or twenty elephants meandering parallel to the river's path. I fly low to enjoy the sight of these paradoxical creatures. Clumsy and graceful in one. They remind me of myself. My size and stature could suggest inelegance but I hope my style and manner prove that initial impression wrong.

The last one hundred miles are among the easiest I have flown so far as all I have to do is follow the road and the railway line below until the large town of Tabora becomes visible. We circle the town, flying low, drawing out the inhabitants who come running, shouting welcomes in Swahili. I feel a rush of joy and comfort. It is a homecoming of sorts to be back in East Africa. I land on an excellent surface in the large aerodrome.

Pushing through the crowd towards me there are familiar faces. The Wyatts! My oldest friends in Tanganyika, Will and Margaret.

'*Sophie!*' Margaret calls out and envelopes me in a tight embrace. 'What an honour to be here to host you.'

'I had no idea,' I say. 'What are you doing in Tabora?'

'Will is the Provincial Commissioner here now. One of his duties is to welcome visiting VIPs. And here you are! You are to stay with us tonight. I want to hear everything!'

I turn towards the Bentleys' Moth. They have removed themselves a little from the melée.

'And the Bentleys?' I ask.

'We don't have the space, I'm afraid. But they will have very pleasant rooms at the Officers' Quarters of the King's African Rifles.'

I while away the afternoon tinkering with the tappets and filters. The noise of the engine under strain this morning has me double-checking all the routine things. I have to request the use of a car so as to be able to finish my work by the shine of the headlights and before I know it is dark and I am embarrassingly late for a dinner party at the Wyatts'.

'Could you give me a spin to the Provincial Commissioner's?' I beg of the car owner and he graciously does.

I slip into the residence, hoping not to be observed in my oil-stained overalls. I wash as fast as I can and pull on my nicest evening dress. I want to be an entertaining guest for my kind hosts.

The dining-room is full of loud chatter and I can see that they have begun the starter. I'm glad. The only thing worse than making people wait is making them wait hungry.

'There she is!' Will exclaims. 'We started without you. You don't mind?'

'Not at all. I'm very sorry to be so late.'

'Nothing wrong, I hope?'

'Just fine-tuning the plane. It's all ready for an early departure.'

Will stands and raises his glass.

A servant hands me a bubbling flute and I long to pour its contents down my throat. But I must wait for my host.

'All of you here have heard of the daring exploits of our guest this evening, Lady Heath. She stands to make history and forge a new aviation path for Africa with this epic voyage from Cape Town to Cairo. And we are honoured to have her as our guest. To safe travels and history-making!'

He raises his glass, the other guests follow suit and I take a deep sip. He remains standing.

'Not only is Lady Heath a very important visitor, she is also our dear friend. We spent a good time, if not a long time, together when she ran a coffee farm with her husband in East Africa. And I know I speak for both Margaret and myself, Sophie, when I say how wonderful it is to have you here.'

He raises his glass to me and I return the gesture to a chorus of '*Hear hear!*'.

Dinner is served. The Wyatts have an excellent cook and I wolf it down.

'How do you find life in Tabora, Margaret?'

'Very pleasant. It's a privilege for Will to have been made PC.'

She talks at length about their life here and I'm grateful that it allows me time to eat and drink. Finally, as the dinner plates are being cleared, I feel that I've had a chance to catch my breath. I look around the table. The great and good of Tabora have turned out in my honour.

After a dessert of pineapple cake we are served a round of ruby port. The champagne and wine have created a soft fuzz around the evening and I'm filled with a sensation of warmth for these people, strangers apart from the Wyatts and the Bentleys.

An older gentleman downwind from me on the other side of the table calls over, his words slurring a little.

'Why were you so delayed in Abercorn?' He throws his hands up dramatically. 'We thought all was lost. They were nearly on the point of sending a search party.'

I smile. 'It was just a matter of delayed supplies. It pays to err on the side of caution when travelling through Africa. And it would have been foolish to plough on without the essentials.'

'You live for adventure, Lady Heath?' The woman beside the elderly gentleman asks, his wife I presume. 'I much prefer the quiet life, myself, but then I am a little older than you.'

'I believe when we are young we look for adventure and long for it.'

The other guests at the table grow quiet, wanting to hear my words and I feel the weight of responsibility. I must say something interesting and sensible and witty.

'Yes. In our youth we long for it but in reality it is when we are grown up that we are able to have it and often then we do not make the most of our opportunities. I think that is what I crave, the sense that whatever happens I've made the most of it. That I haven't missed my opportunities.'

'But you're not afraid?' she asks.

'Oh, I am. Quite a lot of the time. But I'm not afraid of flying. I know how to keep myself safe there. I'm afraid of the unknown, I suppose. Like everyone.'

I look about the table to see if I'm right. Doesn't everyone fear what they don't yet know?

'But you carry on even so?'

'I do. Fear can be a tonic and danger a stimulant. But like all stimulants it should be taken in moderation.' I raise my glass to emphasise my point. The servant takes it as a sign that I want a refill and I don't stop him.

'There are real dangers of course,' the man says. 'Whole villages near the Ugalla River have been wiped out by this dastardly sleeping sickness. You need to steer clear of that if you can.'

I nod, remembering the silence of the villages we passed over. Emil and Gerry will be headed that direction. I wonder do they know what lies in their path?

'Sophie is well aware of the risks in Africa,' Margaret says.

'Yes.' I smile in agreement.

'And hard times,' she adds. 'Oh! Sophie! You must read us a poem. She published a book of poetry, you know. About her time here. *East African Nights*. I have the copy you sent me in the library. I'll fetch it now.' She stands and leaves the table.

I scan through the contents in my mind, trying to decide what would be most appropriate for this company.

Margaret returns to her seat and hands me the slim, green volume. It is strange to see my old name on the cover, Sophie Eliott-Lynn. Do I remember what it was like to be her? I turn the pages and it falls open on 'Footease'. I recite it, feeling that it captures still the pleasure of rest and the pleasure of hard travel.

The guests applaud and the book is passed around.

A lady to my left holds it aloft on the page with my war photo. 'This is you?'

'Yes, I was a dispatch rider with the WAAC for a while.'

'*Bravo!*'

The book is passed along and makes its way to Will. 'Here is something else you should all know. Sophie donated all proceeds from this book to the Women's Amateur Athletic Association. She was one of the founders.'

There are murmurs of 'Well done'. I am starting to feel the burden of too much praise. If I was here, as one of these guests, would I start to find this over-achieving irritating?

The book has made its way back to Margaret who leans in close and asks me quietly, 'Something I've always wondered, Sophie. Since I got this.'

I know what she is going to ask me.

'Who is this?' She opens the book to the dedication. '*To J. Best friend one ever had*.'

I take a drink and answer. 'A friend.'

'Best friend?'

'Yes. A best friend. An old friend. One you've never met.'

I give her nothing more, no clue as to whether 'J' is male or female. I don't break eye contact and she looks away.

'How curious.'

I don't feel like talking about John tonight. I don't want to have to try to explain him to Margaret or to anyone. I don't have the words or the energy for it. Suddenly I am very tired.

I stand. 'I'm afraid you'll all have to excuse me. My bed is calling. We have an early start. But thank you, Will and Margaret, I'll never forget your kindness.'

I hug them both and bid goodnight to the others. Just as I'm about to leave the table a solitary man to the left of the Bentleys stops me.

'Will you permit me one more question, Lady Heath?'

I nod. It's important to never displease my fans, if at all possible.

'You are most unconventional,' he says and I do not disagree with him. 'What does your family make of it all?'

'My family?'

'Yes, your people, back home.'

They pass through my mind, Cis, Lou, Grandfather, Cunningham. The answer to this question is too complex and too private for this stranger. I reach instead for humour.

'All I can say is I have a cousin in Scotland who was advised to keep her girls away from me, lest I corrupt them with my notions!'

I leave the room to a gale of laughter and take refuge in my bed. I try to put thoughts of my family from my mind, the tangled web of my origins and the lies woven to conceal them. Until it became impossible.

Chapter Twenty-two

Princess Gardens
Belfast
13th January, 1907

Dearest Aunt Cis,

I have so much to tell you I fear my pen will not keep pace with my brain. How are you? And how is dear, darling Moses? I miss him so! I hope Grandfather hasn't kicked him out or Mina hasn't baked him into a pie. Tell her I long for her food. It's only just edible here and they operate a 'clean plate' policy so no matter how revolting it is you have to force it down. It is fortunate they keep us so busy that by dinner-time we are starving. We spend many hours transcribing into our green notebooks. When it is raining we exercise in the indoor gym. I love vaulting over the horse! Once we tire of that we stand on tiptoes to see out over the curtained bit of the window. It thrills us to catch a glimpse of life on the street, even if it is very quiet. It reminds me of Newcastle West and your efforts to keep me from spying on the Square. When it is not raining we troop down to the playing fields in Ormeau Road, two by two like brown ducks in our uniforms.

I am delighted to report that I am as happy in Princess Gardens as I was in Rochelle, if not even more. The girls are nice, apart from a few bossy prefects, and we all get along. Good thing we do – we are packed in here like feathers in a pillow. To think that for years I longed for the company of girls my age and now I would give anything for five minutes alone! We know everything about each other. I repeated my usual tale of woe and they were suitably impressed.

I am starting to tire of that story though. Is that awful? Next time I introduce myself I might add some exciting details. I might say that I am adopted but my real family is royalty. I am laughing as I write because I can just hear you tut and see you shake your head at your silly, fanciful Sophie.

As I think now of my history and stories, I must ask you something. I hate to even write his name but the last time I was home, at Christmas, Roger Cunningham cornered me on the landing. He told me the maddest story of my father taking me to Queenstown. In a bag! On a bicycle! I presume he is mistaken? I always understood that my father died before I was born. Is that not so? Is he confusing me with someone? Or are we to blame the brandy? I hope you can help me understand.

Give my best to Grandfather, Henrietta, Aunt Lou and Moses of course!

Your baby,

Sophie

The Square,
Newcastle West,
Co. Limerick.
18th January 1907

Dear Sophie,

Your letter made me smile but also, I'm afraid, it brought a slight frown. I am not entirely in favour of young girls engaging in vigorous exercise and you know your grandfather is opposed to it. Remember, he sought an alternative school for you once he found out about Rochelle? I will not discuss it with him as his health has not been good this last while. I ask only that you comport yourself with dignity at all times. Ultimately the aim of all this education is to turn you out into the world a cultivated, charming young lady who will make a pleasing companion to an equally charming and cultivated young man.

Regarding your enquiry about Mr Cunningham and the things he said, this is something I would rather discuss in person. We will speak of it when you return for the Easter break.

Moses is well. He is getting fat from too many titbits in the kitchen!

Stay well, and out of mischief!

All my love

Aunt Cis

Ballybunion, County Kerry, April 1907

Sophie puts her hands on her hips, leans her head back and sucks down as much fresh air as she can. Yesterday was spent sitting through an interminable Easter Sunday service at church, a never-ending dinner with Grandfather and Henrietta and an infinite coach ride to Ballybunion. It was all worth it, she thinks now, as she spins around on the sand, taking in the wide open beach, the thrashing waves rolling in from the Atlantic Ocean and the sheer cliffs. She loves it here. The vastness of it. There is so much space. She has gained weight since leaving Rochelle. The food in Princess Gardens is plentiful and there is hardly any sport. But she feels there is actually room for her and she is not too big or too loud for here.

'Sophie, you will make yourself sick if you don't stop that spinning.'

Cis is occupied trying to bring her new pup to heel and keep her hat on in the strong breeze. Sophie took hers off the minute they arrived and the sea air is rifling through her hair, tossing it about. She wonders what the sea would feel like today. She loves flinging herself into the cold shock of it in summer time.

It is as though Cis can read her mind and she steers her up the beach, away from the water's edge.

'Make sure you knock all that sand off your boots and skirts before you go into the house. The D'Arcys have been so kind to host us for the week.'

'But they're family, Aunt Cis!'

'Even so.'

Sophie slows to match her aunt's pace as they walk up the steep cliff path.

'It's so good to be here, Cis. I'm enjoying school, but it's still marvellous to have holidays from it.'

'I hope you're behaving yourself. No more pranks? I wasn't going to tell you but it might have a positive impact on your behaviour. The money for your school fees is coming from my allowance. I am paying for them.'

Sophie sees in a flash how this has come about. Grandfather wanted to keep her home after Rochelle but Aunt Cis knew she'd be miserable and came to her rescue. Again!

Sophie throws her arms around Cis and sobs.

'Come on now! There's no need for that. We all have to learn our lesson at some point.' She dabs at Sophie's tears with her scarf and tucks an arm into hers. 'Your father was a great man for the pranks too, you know.'

She laughs and Sophie stays silent. It is so rare that anyone speaks of her father that she doesn't want to risk losing the moment.

'Your grandfather sent him to Kilrush to work in the bank and he pulled a wicked trick on the policemen there.' Cis shakes her head, remembering.

'What did he do?'

Cis casts a look at her sideways. 'You can't let on I told you.'

Sophie mimes her lips being locked with a key.

'He had a run-in with one of the policemen and decided to get his own back. So he took to going down to the pier, at odd hours, acting strange. The police were sure he was up to no good. Didn't he turn up one evening with a box the shape of a coffin, loaded it into a boat and rowed it out? When he was far enough out he stood up and threw the box into the sea.'

Cis is gasping with laughter and her giddiness infects Sophie too even though she's not entirely sure what the joke is.

'When he came ashore they arrested him. But after they went to huge effort to bring the box up and ashore, they opened it only to find it full of stones! Sure they thought he was after committing a murder ...'

Cis stops. She looks quickly at Sophie, then away. Sophie doesn't get it. It wasn't a bad prank. Hers was better though.

'I suppose the point is, he lost his job in the bank, Sophie. And Grandfather was very angry about it all.'

She's got the message. She's not to get in any more trouble and cause upset to the family. Now that Cis is in a talkative mood and has brought up the subject of her father she decides to ask her about Roger.

'Aunt Cis, what do you make of what Roger said to me? About being on a bicycle? With my father?'

Cis shakes her head and Sophie hears her muttering something about loose lips.

'Your father was alive when you were born, Sophie.'

Sophie stops walking and stares at her aunt. *'What?'*

'I'm afraid he came to an unpleasant end. The family presumed you wouldn't remember, you were so small. So we thought it best to not muddy the waters, just give you a clean slate, so to speak. But the time has come. You are of an age to understand and away at school with people asking questions. It's better that *I* tell you rather than someone else —'

'So, I met him? He met me?' Sophie's mind is swimming in all directions, trying to locate some snippet of memory that will reveal him. 'It was true then, what Cunningham said? About my father putting me on a bicycle, in a bag, to cycle to Queenstown?'

'There is some truth to the story. But Cunningham is fond of drama. And his own voice. And brandy.'

'But, Aunt Cis, he said my father was a lunatic. That's what he called him.'

Cis takes her hand. 'Jackie was an unpredictable man, Sophie. He could be difficult.'

'Am I like him?' She recalls Cunningham's words about her mother.

Cis looks at her for a long moment. 'Maybe, in some small ways you are. But we will steer you right.'

'What happened to him?'

They come to a bench facing the Atlantic Ocean and Cis sits. The conversation seems to have taken the wind from her sails and all the gaiety of remembering Jackie's pranks has disappeared. She looks to Sophie like an old woman, one who could float away on the next strong gust. But Sophie must know. This is her chance to know everything.

She sits, takes Cis's hand.

'Tell me, please.'

'I'll tell you what I can, Sophie. But remember he was my brother and I was fond of him. Even if he was a rogue. I never thought ...' Cis puts the back of her hand to her lips as though keeping down a bout of sickness. 'Your father is in a special hospital, in Dublin.'

'*He's still alive?*' Sophie is on her feet again. She has the urge to run, to get away from whatever Cis is about to tell her. But she must hear it. She has a father? A living one?

'Yes, he is.'

'*In a hospital?* Why didn't you tell me?'

'There are reasons, Sophie.'

'What reasons? How long has he been there? Is he sick? Can we visit him? Do you know—?'

'Let me tell you, please!'

Cis' voice has risen and Sophie hears a tremor in it. She sits back down.

'Tell me.'

'He married your mother, against all of our wishes. She was not suitable. In any way. She was a drinker and a fighter, a complete unknown. Father presumed Jackie would marry well, to someone from a good Church of

Ireland family like our own. Instead he landed back to Knockaderry House with this streel of a woman. She was his housekeeper, he told us. I couldn't tell you where he rose her out of, somewhere near here I think, in North Kerry. No matter. She was a complete unknown and I'm sorry to tell you, my dear Sophie, but they brought out the worst in each other.'

Sophie stands and paces, trying to make all the pieces fit. 'You speak so ill of her. She *died* bringing me into the world.'

'No.' Cis looks up at her with grey-blue eyes brimming with hurt. 'She didn't.'

'What then? What happened to her?'

Tears roll down Cis's face. 'Sophie ... he murdered her. They quarrelled all the time and one night he went too far.'

Sophie sits down hard, heavy with this new knowledge. She has so many questions. 'What did he ...? How did he ...?'

'Oh dear, Sophie,' Cis takes her hand, speaking softly. 'You don't need to know that. You don't need those details in your mind.'

'I do. I need to know everything.'

Cis sighs. 'I suppose you do. He beat her, Sophie. He beat her to death.'

Sophie's mouth swims with spit. Will she throw up?

'He was charged with murder. But the judge decided he was insane and locked him up in the Criminal Asylum for the rest of his days.'

'So I could see him there?'

'*No.*' Cis' voice is harder now, louder. '*No. Never.* I know this is difficult but you must forget he exists. Forget what I told you and carry on as before. Your grandfather was almost destroyed by what happened. He will not have it spoken about. It would kill him. We all struggle with this. You are too young to know this, Sophie, but every family has its secrets. The things that they slide into the shadows and remember to forget forever. This is ours. And I'm sorry but it is yours too. The story we told you, about your father dying before you were born and your mother in childbirth. That's a fine story that will do you no harm in the world. That's the one you need to remember.'

They huddle together on the beach. Hot, salty tears flow down Sophie's face. She hasn't cried like this in front of anyone since she was a very young child. But the tears come now, unbidden and unbowed. When they stop she stands and puts a hand out for Cis and they guide each other back to the house.

Newcastle West, County Limerick, October 1907

Grandfather is dying. He hasn't left his bed in months and is getting weaker by the day. Someone is always at his bedside: Henrietta or Cis or Lou and sometimes Sophie now that she's been brought home from school. That must mean the end is near, she knows. But she finds it hard to sit with him. The room is stuffy, the curtains pulled tight and they sit in silence. Cis sketches Grandfather. She is so good at portraits and Sophie envies her that she can pass the time in this way. She watches as her aunt coaxes to life on the page a friendly soft face, a harmless old man on his deathbed. Sophie looks at the real man before her and does not see him like that. She sees Rugs, Grandfather's dog, exactly as Cis has drawn him, loyal and loving. Cis loves Grandfather in a way that Sophie cannot. He is her father and Sophie never had one to love. She never had the chance. Since Cis told her she feels angry at the Peirces. They are happier to forget Jackie ever existed. And she cannot accept the things Cis told her about her mother. Surely there was some good in her?

But she knows she must be grateful to Grandfather, even if he was always exasperated by her. She hears him now, dictating his dying wishes to Lou and she knows he has her welfare at heart. He tells Lou to take care of poor old Rugs. To consult with Shaughnessy regarding the sale of Knockaderry House. To keep the child straight and care for her.

The child.

Sophie.

She is to be kept straight. She is inclined to crookedness in his mind.

This morning Cis hung black crêpe on the front door. The women all dressed in dark mourning clothes, recently acquired. Sophie would not have believed it possible but the house is even more silent than before. It has seeped now into the fabric on the chairs and the wallpaper on the walls. Even Moses saves his soft *miaows* for outside. Inside, he slinks along, flat to the wall, making himself invisible. The only sound is the gentle weeping of Henrietta or the aunts.

Sophie has not wept. It is sad, she supposes, that the life of George Peirce is ended. But she does not weep.

She overheard Henrietta talking to Cis earlier. Henrietta is worried about the house and money and what is to become of everyone. She is still angry with Jackie. Sophie's ears perked up when she heard his name. Her father! Henrietta said it broke Grandfather's heart when they fell out. And then everything that happened after. And he died of heart failure in the end. So Jackie broke Grandfather's heart and he died from it?

The house is full now of friends and neighbours and cousins and uncles. Some of whom Sophie has met before but many she has never laid eyes on. She was never brought to family events – the garden parties, picnics and pageants were not for her. The way they watch her now, she is like an animal in the zoo to them. Conversations pause when she passes close by then the whispers resume. She hears 'Jackie' and 'housekeeper' and 'tragedy' and 'lunatic'. There it is – that word again!

She is fascinated by these people too. She has heard her aunts mention their names and their glamorous lives and big houses and hunt balls. She would love to be in the thick of it. To sample the excitement. But, based on their reactions to her, she doubts that will ever come to pass.

When the funeral ends and they all retreat to Heathfield House and Castleview or Cahirmoyle, here Sophie will sit. Alone, again, with her step-grandmother and her aunts.

Chapter Twenty-three

Tabora, Tanganyika, 8th March, 1928

I am at the aerodrome early and I watch the morning light creeping across the sky as I wait. And wait. And wait.

By eight o'clock the Bentleys have still not arrived and I am very tempted to just go. I cannot abide being delayed by another person's tardiness.

I make my final checks and am starting to climb into the cockpit when I hear an engine. A car speeds into the aerodrome and a sheepish Dick and Dorys are deposited.

'Sophie, our apologies.' Dick is flustered.

'Well, it wasn't our fault. Not really,' Dorys says. 'The blooming driver overslept. And because the car didn't arrive no one came to wake us. But, anyway, we're here now. No harm done.'

I glance at the time on my watch and take a long, slow breath. How rude of her to dismiss my patience like that!

'I thought you might have gone off without us,' Dick says. 'Good of you not to.'

I smile a tight smile. I will be gracious, even if it kills me.

'Will we make for Nairobi, or Kisumu?' I take the map that I have been studying to pass the time and unfold it onto the wing of my Avian.

Dick leans over me and places a finger on it, nearer to Tabora.

'I think we'll have to make do today with Mwanza. I won't have enough petrol to get any further.'

I nod in silence and refold the map, smoothing it into place with more pressure than is necessary. So, not only have I lost two hours of my day but I am to lose precious miles too because of their fuel situation. I get into the cockpit and signal for Dick to start my propeller. Before it springs to life I hear Dorys complaining.

'You should try sitting in the front cockpit with a stinking petrol container, Dick. It's not a bit pleasant.'

I turn my plane and guide it down the runway. I accelerate and as it lifts into the air I shout, '*No one asked you to come!*', safe in the knowledge that they won't hear me. I feel all the better for it.

I fly along, trying to get over the irritation of the morning. My spirits are lifted by a herd of giraffe, stepping elegantly beneath me. I go down for a closer look but they scatter. As I climb again I realise I no longer have sight of the Bentleys' Moth. Maybe if I can't see them I will be able to feel more kindly towards them by the time we arrive. I am flying now over the dark soil and its green cotton plants that will soon be festooned with nodding white buds. The Mwanza gulf opens up below, flanked regally on either side by towering rock hills.

I circle the large aerodrome. Bentley is on my tail now. Has he been behind me this entire time?

We land and once again we are surrounded by a large crowd of well-wishers. I am heartened to see that they have brought with them glasses of cold beer to refresh us and many tins of petrol. By a quick count there seems to be nearly a hundred tins. That should keep us both going. My machine only uses four gallons an hour.

We are met by Captain Surridge, the Assistant District Officer, his wife and their two small boys. They are to put us up in their residence. Dorys looks utterly exhausted, pale and black under the eyes. Has the initial excitement of the venture worn off? Is she sick? Or expecting? Already? Such things are possible, I suppose. Dick sends her off with the Surridges to rest then he and I do some routine maintenance. Everything is shipshape and very quickly we are freed up with a leisurely afternoon stretching ahead of us.

'Will you rest too?' I ask Dick.

'I could,' he answers. 'Or the Surridges mentioned a game of tennis. I could join you for that?'

'Oh, that would be marvellous – we could play doubles.'

My muscles strain for a good run on hard ground. I feel like a caged tiger, waiting to be set free.

I change into the lightest clothes I have. A game of tennis in this heat will test the stamina of any man or woman. But I am looking forward to it. It feels like an age since I last played.

Captain Surridge and his wife arrive accompanied by a houseboy carrying a cooler. This is shaping up to be a very pleasant afternoon. They come to the net to shake hands.

'This is a real pleasure, Captain Surridge. I'm terribly grateful to you both.'

'It's our pleasure. We love to play so this is a treat for us as much as it is for you. Now please, call me Ernest.'

'And me Roy,' his wife adds.

I'm not sure I heard that right. I've never met a woman called Roy before. It must be a pet name.

'Sophie,' I add.

'And Dick.'

'Right, formalities out of the way. Shall we split up? Roy and I are tired of playing together. If we mix it might make for a more interesting game.'

'Top idea.' Dick vaults the net and takes up serving position.

I do the same on our side not offering Ernest the choice of serving first. I am itching to start.

We play a tentative first set, getting used to our partners' pace and movements. Ernest and I take it by a small margin and we break for a drink.

The ice in my gin and tonic is melting fast and the cooling fizz slakes my throat. I know my face is flushed and bathed in sweat but I'm happy and couldn't care less how I look. I can make myself presentable later.

We are about to begin our second set when we're interrupted by a man in military uniform. Ernest introduces him as the Officer Commanding of the local King's African Rifles.

'I wonder would you folks like to partake in a hunt? We could try to fix a buffalo shoot for tomorrow? Unless you are to depart, that is.'

I look at Dick. It's tempting. I haven't enjoyed a good hunt in years but we should also try to make up some lost time.

'What do you think, Sophie? Dorys isn't feeling so good. A day in bed might be just the tonic.'

I consider this a moment. I might have to leave the Bentleys behind if these delays continue. But, then again, if there is a hunt on the cards it won't be such an inconvenience.

'Why not? When in Africa!'

'Splendid,' Ernest says. 'Do you know? There's a chap in the town, he's staying on his yacht, an Italian trader by the name of Bonini. He might be happy to take us by boat. We'll get there and back much faster.'

'Not as fast as by plane,' I say.

'That is true. But the plane would scare the buffalo.'

We finish out our second set and call it a day. Ernest and I trash poor Dick and Roy off the court so they're happy to concede and retire.

'You've played a lot of tennis?' Roy enquires. She's younger than me, by at least five years is my guess, but she is breathless and wan after the game. I feel like I'm brimming with more energy than when we started.

'I played everything. Hockey, tennis, athletics. Everything I could do, I did in boarding school.'

She laughs. 'I did everything I could to avoid it. We had a horrid teacher and I never liked getting into such disarray. Let's meet at six on the porch and we can make a visit to this Bonini chap and see if he will help us out.'

We part and I return to my room to wash and dress.

Funny, I think, how some people try to avoid physical exercise while for others, like me, it's as necessary as breathing. I think I would go utterly mad if I couldn't use my body in this way. For so long I wasn't allowed. Nothing more strenuous than a gentle stroll in Newcastle West. Grandfather abhorred the thought of women in sport. But once he made the mistake of sending me off to school there was nothing he could do about it.

The sun is low in the sky as we arrive at the port. It is crammed with boats of all sizes but one in particular stands out. *The Otter*. It's a powerful beauty with gleaming wood that catches the glow of the setting sun and towering masts, proudly erect, waiting to bear her bulk across Lake Victoria.

Ernest boards and has a few words with a crewman. He turns and waves to us all waiting by the car.

'Come up!'

I lead us aboard with Dick following behind me and Roy at the rear. Dorys really is missing all the fun, taking to her sickbed like this.

Inside, beside a scattering of cushioned chairs, Ernest is speaking in fluent Italian to a small, balding man with round glasses in a navy blazer, white shirt and trousers.

'Signor Bonini, may I introduce my guests? Lady Heath, Lieutenant Bentley – and this is my wife, Mrs Roy Surridge.'

The small man takes my hand and bows low over it. I am comically taller than him and feel as though I am in the company of a courteous child.

'*Piacere*. Captain Surridge tells me you are an aviator.'

'Yes, Dick — Lieutenant Bentley and I both.'

'And you are flying to London! *Brava!*'

Signor Bonini chuckles delightfully and my spirits lift. What an effervescent little man he is. He settles now and turns to Ernest.

'You want to hunt?'

'Well, we don't want to impose but if you're going anyway we would love to join you. Might we?'

'*Sì, sì*. Tomorrow at eight. We will have our own *avventura*.'

We are clad in the shirts and shorts of safari and settled comfortably into our guest cabins next morning by nine o'clock. We gather on deck as the steamer glides out of port and begins its crossing. I am trying to focus on a conversation Bonini and Dick are having about the funeral of Marshal Diaz, Mussolini's former Minister of War. But the roiling and rolling of the boat has turned my stomach askew and all I can think about is the gelatinous slime of the egg that I had for breakfast a few short hours ago. It's rebelling against me and all of a sudden I realise I'm going to be sick. I stand and grip the railing.

'Are you OK, Sophie?' Dick asks.

I wave him away with one hand. 'I'm going to go below for a rest.'

I've broken into a sweat and my mouth fills with rancid spit. I really do not want to void my stomach onto this polished deck. As I stagger below I hear Bonini comment.

'*Mal di mare*.'

I want to correct him, this is not the sea, it's a lake. But I have to concede that while his description is not accurate his diagnosis is. I lie on my bed, one arm stretched over my eyes and try to focus on my breathing. If I lie very, very still and keep my breaths shallow I might be OK.

The Otter continues its onward journey. The rocking has taken on a side-to-side momentum and I feel as though my brain has come loose in my head and three times already I've had to dash to the toilet. The third time produced nothing but bile and I hope that means I am done with it. My stomach muscles ache from the strain and my throat is raw.

Finally, I doze off in my cabin. The boat has steadied or maybe I have found my sea legs. Lake legs. I'm exhausted from the exertions of my sickness and when I wake again I am parched.

Someone has left a jug of water on my bedside table. I never heard them coming in. What must they have made of me? Asleep in my clothes and the entire room in disarray. I go to the bathroom and brush my teeth. My breath is rancid. I wash up as best I can with the facecloth and scrub at a vomit stain on my shirt. I look at the woman reflected back at me from the mirror above the basin. A madwoman. There can be no doubt. Her hair standing up from her head, a snail's trail of drool unfolding from one corner of her lips, her eyes bloodshot, her clothes untucked and stained. It can all be put to rights, of course. The external appearances. Amazing what a vigorous hair-brushing, a wash and a change of clothes can achieve. But what about what's on the inside? What kind of state is that in? And can that be put to rights? And what if someday none of this can be fixed? What if I end up at the point where things have gone too far and I'm not able to present an acceptable face to the world anymore? Will I even know? Did my father know he was mad?

A knock on the door jolts me from my maudlin musing.

'Lady Heath.'

'Yes?'

'Signor Bonini requested that I check on you.'

I pat my hair once more and wipe my mouth. I open the door to a young crewman and give him what I hope is a warm smile but may be the grin of a lunatic.

'I'm feeling much better, thank you.'

He takes a step back. 'We are nearing Kimi Island. The Signor thought you might like to see it if you were able.'

'I'll be right up.'

I shut the door, change my shirt and ascend to the world again. This time, again, I can do it.

For now.

Chapter Twenty-four

Kimi Island, Uganda, 9th March, 1928

'Feeling better?' Dick asks as I join him, Bonini and the Surridges on deck.

'Yes, thank you. I don't know what came over me.'

'Do you suffer from seasickness usually?' Roy asks.

'I rarely am on the sea, to tell the truth. In it, when I can. I enjoy that. But hardly ever by boat. So it seems maybe I do suffer. Hopefully I'm over it now.'

I take a seat on a deckchair, my legs still weakened, and Roy joins me. She pours me a glass of white wine from a bottle cooling in a silver bucket and I accept it gladly.

'I try to avoid flying over water when I can,' I tell her. 'I had a fright early on in my flying days and nearly lost my way in heavy fog over the Irish Sea.'

'Oh, how terrifying! I do admire you. Your courage and your strength. How do you keep yourself in such good shape?'

'I really don't give it much thought. I live very simply. I never diet. I eat what I want and plenty of it. I have a cigarette whenever I want one and I believe in the advice given by St Paul – to take a little wine for thy stomach's sake.'

Roy laughs and clinks her glass to mine.

'Ernest!' she calls her husband over to join us. 'Did you know that Lady Heath has a fear of flying over open water? Ernest here proclaimed that you didn't seem to be afraid of anything.'

'Well, now you know the truth,' I say.

'How will you manage crossing the Mediterranean?' he asks.

'I haven't given it much thought. I've been thinking only day to day but I suppose I'll just have to do it when the time comes. There's no other way.'

'Alone?'

'If needs be.'

'Maybe Signor Bonini can help.'

Our rotund Italian host has joined us on deck and takes a seat.

'Lady Heath might need some help to cross the Mediterranean.'

I bristle. I never said I needed help. And what can anyone possibly do for me when I am alone in the sky?

'You must contact my friend. He will help,' Bonini says.

'Your friend?'

'Benito.'

'Mussolini,' Roy supplies.

'Mussolini? *Il Duce?*' I ask.

'*Sì*. I will send a telegraph and let him know to expect you.'

'Thank you.' But still I wonder what anyone, even *Il Duce*, can do. I must be gracious. 'One can never have enough friends,' I say.

'She's afraid of the open water,' Roy tells him. She seems thrilled to have identified my weakness.

'I don't blame you,' Bonini replies. 'You cannot tell what is in there. Come. I will show you.'

He stands and we follow him to the railing.

'Watch,' he says.

We follow his gaze to the shoreline. Along the edge of the water and in the shallows lie indolent crocodiles. The only movement an occasional indifferent swish of a tail. But their indifference is a ruse. They like to give the impression that we are of no interest to them. I know if any one of us was foolish enough to enter the water they would spring into action and take us down to the bone in minutes.

'Frightful,' I say. 'Pangani River, near where my first husband and I farmed, was full of them.'

'At least there aren't any in the Med,' Dick remarks. 'One less thing to be frightened of.'

I nod but my jaw tightens. Why is everyone so obsessed with this topic? I'm sorry I said anything.

We sail past Kimi Island, its shoreline dotted with small fishing boats and thatched mud huts, and into a shaded bay. It's evening and after almost ten hours of sailing we have traversed Lake Victoria. We stroll on the shore to stretch our legs and I am relieved to be on *terra firma* again. We return to *The Otter* for dinner and I am suddenly starving. This must mean I am on the mend. I enjoy every mouthful, plenty of good Italian wine and fall happily into my bed, eager to rest ahead of tomorrow's hunting.

Lake Victoria, 10th March 1928

I am on deck before any of the others and it is a flurry of activity. The porters are getting all of our supplies ready. I long to dive in and help them. Anything to speed things up.

Finally we are rowed in to shore just as the sun is rising. I shut my eyes and listen to the birdsong. I feel myself enveloped by the natural world.

As soon as everything is ashore we strike off into the bush. We are a large party, two agile trackers out front of us and nearly fifty boys behind. All eyes are on the ground as we hike in near silence, looking for a trail.

Suddenly the tracker to the fore stops, squats and word is whispered along the line. They have a fresh trail. This bodes very well. We have only been walking for two hours and already there are footprints – recent ones too. My blood quickens. I take a sip of water and check my rifle. We move off again, leaving most of the boys behind us to allow for pace and stealth. We must not make too much of a disturbance. In total silence we creep after the trackers for ten minutes, fifteen minutes. They freeze. A hand is raised. We cock our rifles, barely daring to breathe. Then all around us a sound, like waves breaking on the beach, as the tall grass stirs and shudders with the stampede of a big herd.

So close, I can almost smell the beasts. My heart is thundering. This is the most thrilling moment of my life. The most thrilling moment on the ground.

We drop to our knees and, hidden by flora, we crawl nearer. I can see at least sixty buffalo chomping at the grass. They seem oblivious of our presence but then the wind shifts and they catch our scent and scatter.

The chase is on again.

We follow their trail for half an hour more and again as soon as we come upon them they startle and take off. Fat drops of rain fall from the sky and this is a gift as it deafens the herd to our creeping footsteps. This time we get closer, a hundred yards. We fire off a couple of shots and they bolt.

A tracker waves me forward and I fall into position behind him as we track again. We spot a single footprint and pick up the trail. He stops. Beckons me to the front. There, not seventy yards from me, is a fine bull. He looks young but the spread of his horns is already impressive and intimidating. He stills, sensing us, and as he tosses his head I take my chance and fire two shots.

The first gets him in the back, turning him to face me. The second goes right through his head and he thuds to the ground, instantly dead. A clean kill.

I stalk across the glade to his fallen bulk and crouch, placing my hand on his still-warm hide. The boy joins me and mimes wiping his fingers on his face. He dips into the dark blood pooling at the bullet wound. I follow suit and dash a stripe of red across my cheeks and forehead.

'*Asante!* Thank you!' I join my hands together then stand, wiping my blood-stained fingers on my shorts.

We set off again, leaving some boys behind to cut up my prey. It is a longer hike this time and we can see and hear nothing in the densely vegetated gully we are forced to follow. I hear Ernest grumbling behind me but I have every confidence in these trackers.

And rightly so. As we emerge from the donga the herd is before us again, grazing. I crawl to the top of the ridge and take aim. My shot hits a young bull, breaking his leg. He swings towards us and someone else gets off a shot, getting him right through the head.

We go again. I love the feeling of the ground beneath my feet. It is welcoming, hard enough to support me but with some give, an almost encouraging bounce that propels me onward.

I am sweating heavily but not one muscle in my body is tired. We clamber up ridges and down through narrow ravines, hemmed in by trees and plants. The rain is heavier now and I taste salty metal as buffalo blood washes onto my lips. We reach the top of a steep, thick gully. The party stops, deliberating. I push my way to the front to where the first tracker is surveying the path ahead. I point to the gully and raise my hands to my head in imitation of the buffalo horns.

'They're down there,' I say. 'I can feel it. I've been watching the hills and there's been no sign of them. That's where they are.'

He doesn't understand a word I've said but my gestures are clear. He freezes now and sniffs the air. I can smell it too. The damp undergrowth and rain bring a heavy, beefy smell. We advance down into the donga. As we emerge from the overgrown thicket the path in front of us darkens. I think for a moment that it is a trick of the light, a cloud crossing out the sun but then I hear a snort. A great, black-horned head rushes at us. He is no more than ten yards away and about to trample us into the ground. I lift my gun and shoot. My bullet hits the base of his horns, nearly lifting him off his feet. He stops and we wait. I hold my breath. If he charges again we are done for. Before anyone can get another shot off he turns and the bushes quake with the herd stampeding either side.

The trackers start to shout and I turn to see them clambering up trees. I spin around as two more black shadows thunder out from the bush, headed straight for me. A shot rings out. I pull my trigger and both buffalo drop before us. I'm panting and my rifle shakes in my hands.

Bonini pushes past me to claim his kill.

'Mine went through the head,' he says, pointing at his own forehead.

Ernest whoops. '*A stellar shot, signor! Bravo!*'

I drop down beside the other animal. It is slightly smaller, a cow. My shot got her in the shoulder.

'Did I get that first bull?' I ask.

We search for any trace of the blood in the undergrowth but there's none. Maybe I just scared him off when the bullet hit his horns. We wander through the flattened bush, following his path and there, most curiously, is a dead calf with its head thrown back, spindly legs splayed out. Dick lifts the head.

'See here, a bullet hole.'

It's on the throat. Dick looks around then points to a nearby rock.

'Must have ricocheted from here. Another one for you, Sophie.'

'No,' I shake my head. 'It doesn't count. I never meant to kill this one.'

It's a shame. I had such a clear shot and ended up with this accidental victim. I'm tired now and sit on the dented rock. I watch as the hunting men unsheathe their knives and open up the calf like a package. They shout out their excitement when they find my bullet, lodged just under the spine. The man hands it to me. I wipe the blood off and slip it into my shirt pocket.

The other man has got a small fire going and in minutes the calf's liver is spitting on a pan. We wolf it down with fried fat as the rain soaks us through the canopy overhead.

We retrace our steps until we make it back to our camp. The houseboys we left behind have been busy in our absence. The tents are up, the fire is lit and the cook has prepared some dishes to which he now adds buffalo steak.

I change quickly and wash my face and hands. I plan to eat then fall into my makeshift bed. I am delightfully weary, my body happy with the feeling that it has worked hard today and earned its rest.

I have just finished devouring everything on my plate when Roy Surridge says, 'I thought you were a lady, Sophie, but today I have seen another side of you entirely.'

I sit back and look at her. Her petite frame is backlit by the glow from the campfire. Her hair is perfect and, I only notice this now, she is wearing a pristine white shirt and trousers. Maybe I should have made more of an effort. I am still a guest.

'What do you mean?' I ask, keeping my tone level.

'Oh, I don't mean any offence. It's just seeing you out there today, in the jungle, you fit right in!' She laughs, her voice like cut glass.

'With the buffalo?'

'No, no. With the natives. You were up the front, telling them where to go, tracking with them. I think you could have led the whole thing without them.'

'I really don't think so. We'd have been like headless chickens in the jungle without them.'

'You're an excellent shot,' Ernest interjects.

I get the sense he's trying to head his wife off at the pass. I also get the sense that this is a private conversation they had that he expected to stay private.

'I was just saying to Ernest earlier,' she continues.

I was right.

'I was just saying, when I saw you crouched by the fire, with blood streaked across your cheeks, chomping down on that calf's liver, its body still warm. Why – you brought to mind those cannibals one hears of.'

Dick bursts out laughing. 'It was rather savage, Sophie.'

I glower at him. Can I not enjoy a day's hunting without being held to some invisible standard?

'When in Rome,' I say, fixing Roy with a hostile stare.

She lowers her eyes. 'I just ... I don't mean any offence. It was quite impressive actually.'

I stand. 'Thank you. I must take to my bed now. All this playing savage has me bone-tired.'

I signal to the cook.

'That steak was cooked excellently. Could you prepare the rest for breakfast? Some soup with the tongue and the brains?'

He backs away, nodding and beaming.

'*Brains for breakfast!*' I call as I stride away to my tent. Let them chew on that one for a while.

But I'm mad as hell. Who does she think she is? No matter how much I achieve or how much money I have I will always find myself being measured by women like Roy. Well, I'll be damned if I let her spoil today. Or tomorrow. I resolved long ago to carve my own path and worry less about whether or not it would be acceptable.

Chapter Twenty-five

Ballybunion, County Kerry, August 1914

Sophie reclines as the sun's rays wash over her. It has rained steadily since they arrived in Doon Bay four days ago. But this morning it was as though they woke up on a different planet, or at least in a different country. She gobbled down breakfast, grabbed a book, a sunhat and a picnic rug and escaped to the beach before her aunts got up and started devising visits to this, that, or the other cousin. Sophie has no intention of letting the glorious day slip by with her gazing at it out of a drawing-room window.

The light breeze shifts the seagrass in the dunes, creating a pleasant shushing noise and she feels that her holidays have truly begun. Before they left Newcastle West, she got word that she was successful in her entrance exam and will start at the Royal College of Science in a few weeks. All that hard work and study has been worth it. So now she will relax and enjoy a summer in Ballybunion.

A cloud obscures the sunlight. At least she thinks it is a cloud until she hears the voice.

'*Ah! There she is now. The scientist.*'

Cunningham! Why must he also holiday here? She sits up and is about to stand but he drops down on the other side of the rug. He nibbles at a piece of seagrass between his lips and looks at her until she feels compelled to converse.

'The weather is much more pleasant today,' she says.

'Yes.' He stares at the water. He shrugs his arms out of his jacket. Seeing him sitting there, in just his shirt, is disconcerting and utterly ruinous of the beautiful setting.

'Will you swim?' she asks.

He turns to look at her then drops to one elbow. 'Perhaps. And perhaps I'll have company.'

Sophie's mouth fills with spit. Is he suggesting she might swim with him? The very thought repulses her. She doesn't trust herself to speak so wrinkles her nose and shakes her head.

He smiles. 'Well, Miss Sophie. I must hear it all. You are to be a university student? Of science, no less. Why have you chosen this area of study?'

She begins to tell him, more comfortable with this topic. If she must speak to him then this isn't so bad. The only way to avoid speaking to him is to invent an excuse to leave the beach. She is loath to allow him to steal this lovely day away from her.

'Well, you may be aware, or maybe not, that initially I had thought to follow in my grandfather's footsteps.'

'Your father's footsteps?' His voice is loud and he regards her with alarm.

Sophie feels he is mocking her.

'*My grandfather!*' she almost shouts.

'Oh!'

She continues. 'I had thought to study medicine and qualify as a doctor.'

He snorts, then gestures for her to continue.

'But after my time in St Margaret's Hall, working in the laboratory there, I became fascinated with all that science has to offer. It's so exciting. When you think of all the modern developments, even just in the last few years – photography and motorised vehicles! It's such a fascinating sphere to delve into. Don't you think?'

In her enthusiasm she finds she has been carried away with the topic and forgotten who her audience is. He looks at her now, bemusement tempting the corners of his lips into a smirk.

'Sophie Peirce is to be the next Madame Curie? Well, I will say I'm honoured to have known her.'

She reddens and curses herself for engaging with this man. No good ever comes from a conversation with him.

'And, Sophie, pray tell, have you given any proper thought to the most important ambition of a young woman?'

She stares at him now, lost.

'Marriage!' he pronounces. 'Motherhood!'

Now it is her turn to snort. 'Certainly not. I have only just left school.'

'You are eighteen. Am I correct?'

She nods.

'Well, that is just the right age. You are like a fruit in the orchard. Ripe for the picking. Be careful you don't stay on that tree too long or you may end up rotting on the ground.'

She is speechless. There is so much wrong with what he is saying. His impropriety, his audacity, his tortuous metaphor. She looks out to sea, wishing she was on a boat, floating away from Roger Cunningham.

'Your sisters are not married,' she counters.

'My sisters,' his lips twist in disgust, 'are too choosy. They seem to believe they are a rare prize. It would be an honour for any gentleman to marry into the Cunningham family, of course, but my sisters must accept that they are no oil paintings. They waste their time on foolish romance stories and sit, waiting for a young dashing suitor to sweep them off their feet. Youth is not the most desirable trait in a suitor, I tell them often. A good wine is of a good vintage.'

Another metaphor. Sophie looks around the beach, hopeful for some distraction to remove her from this nightmare.

'You lack parental guidance, Sophie. So I will import to you some advice I have given to my sisters.'

She is not looking in his direction but feels him shift closer on the rug. Her muscles stiffen.

'Do not overlook the benefits of age. An older gentleman can be of much assistance in educating a young lady in the ways of romance.'

She can smell something sullying the sea breeze. His soap, a stale tarry smell. Is he propositioning her? She turns to face him and, yes, his eyes have taken on a hungry gaze and his lips are pursed. She is tempted to laugh into his face but opts instead for outrage.

'*Mr Cunningham!*' She jumps to her feet, swiping the sand from her skirt. 'I am shocked! This really is very inappropriate.'

There is silence in the aftermath of her outburst and she watches as he changes. The soft gaze hardens, he straightens up and stands, not too close thankfully. He must know she his equal in height. He throws the stalk of seagrass to the ground.

'*Miss Sophie!*' he shouts. '*How dare you accuse me?*'

She is stunned. She thought he would be contrite, embarrassed even. He takes a step closer.

'Do you presume that I have some romantic intentions towards you? You stupid child! I am more than twice your age! I was giving advice. As I said, you lack parental guidance. You lack parents. God knows what will become of you. I do not admire you. I pity you. You're not much better than the orphans abandoned at the workhouse door. I am a Cunningham. I would not dream of associating with the likes of you.' His eyes are pure hatred now as he spits his words at me. 'Your father was a madman. He beat your mother to death right in front of you.'

Sophie covers her mouth with her hand and steps back. She is going to be sick.

'And your mother.' He laughs. 'She was no better.'

No. She cannot hear this. It is too much. She grabs her things, turns and runs, scrabbling to gain purchase in the sand. She hears him calling out and the words follow her across the beach.

'*Your mother was little more than a whore!*'

Chapter Twenty-six

Lake Victoria, 11th March 1928

We break camp in the morning to hunt closer to the shoreline. I keep my distance from the trackers and from Roy. I am happy enough to work alone today picking off guinea fowl with the gun gifted to me by Sir Jeppe. I make sure to mention this to Roy when she falls into step beside me.

'Do you know him? He owns the *Rand Daily Mail* and goodness knows what else besides.'

'No.'

'Lovely man. Very generous but then again he is very, very wealthy.'

I know I'm being a bore but I hate that her silly words last night wounded me sufficiently that I'm not myself today. Instead I am watching myself, making sure I am not being too outlandish, too unpredictable.

There it is again. That concern. Does everyone have to consider it? That someday their natural way of being will tip from being a little eccentric into full-blown madness? My own family worried about it. About me.

I stomp along the track lost in my thoughts. I cannot let people like Roy have such an effect on me. Where is my thick skin gone?

I hand the cook a full bag of guinea fowl when we return to camp. We sit for a while under the setting sun but the talk is subdued. Bonini holds court at length about the ambitions of the Italian Republic and this serves as an excellent sedative.

We set sail early next morning. Bonini has had his men adorn *The Otter* with dark, bloodied buffalo heads. They festoon the prow and the masthead, macabre evidence of our hunting skills.

We glide into Mwanza under a tangerine sun bobbing low in the sky. I change into a beaded dress, get my hair under control and add some rouge to my cheeks and colour to my lips.

When I join the others on deck they are in high spirits. Roy hands me a glass of Frascati. It teases my tongue with its fizz and tastes of more.

'Sophie, I want to apologise,' she begins.

'There's no need,' I say. 'I was in a huff. Tiredness, nothing more.'

'No, what I said came out all wrong. I meant to say how much I admire you. You swoop in on your plane, interrupt your cross-continent epic to thrash us at tennis then pick off a couple of buffalo like you're swatting at flies. Really, you're remarkable. And you seem so comfortable with yourself. I wish I could be more like you. Just getting on with things and not caring what people think. It must be so freeing. Are the Irish all like you?'

I drain my glass of Frascati and signal for another. I think about her words before I answer. 'That's kind of you, Roy. And really there's no need to explain. You and Ernest have been wonderful hosts. Sometimes I forget there even are other people and I lose the run of myself. I don't even think of myself as a man or a woman at times. Or even an Irishwoman. I'm just me.'

My glass is refilled and Roy raises hers.

'Well, here's to you! I'm delighted to have met you and I will boast to anyone who'll listen how I watched Lady Heath fell a herd of buffalo.'

'Oh, please do embellish,' I say, laughing.

We enjoy the party far too much and have much difficulty staggering up the hill to the Surridges in the early hours. A sour-faced Dorys greets us and complains of how ill she's been.

'I'm not fit for flying yet, that's for sure.'

I sigh. More delays. Dick reads my mind.

'More hunting, Sophie? Bonini is going down the Gulf tomorrow to try for some leopard. We might as well join him.'

I spend the next morning traipsing after roan, koodoo and speckled leopard. Miles before breakfast and nothing much to show for it. I never thought I would say it but I've had my fill of hunting. My thoughts have turned again to the sky and I'm anxious to be up there.

'Don't forget,' Bonini says as we return again to Mwanza. 'You must go and see Mussolini when you get to Italy.'

I smile. He is insistent. I just hope I will get there. At this point I had hoped to be much further along.

I go to the aerodrome to check on the Avian. I hate being away from my baby for so long and I spend hours checking over every inch of her. I have some concerns. There's a slow, steady petrol leak that needs to be seen to. And my undercarriage is bent again thanks to the waterlogged grounds here. I hope I can take off tomorrow. I'm annoyed with myself for the hours spent carousing and taking my leisure instead of tending to these tasks. I will have to trust that it will be OK until our next stop.

We leave after breakfast. I barely dare to breathe until I'm safely in the air. We follow the curve of the lake, its placid blue shimmer giving no hint of the ravenous creatures that lurk within it, or the relentless churning that sickened me. I feel like I've come home to myself as I go through the usual motions of checking my instruments and feeling the air beneath the wings. I missed it so.

After an hour or so the ground begins to slope upwards and so must we, climbing higher and higher until we are at ten thousand feet. The plateau of the Serengeti Plain sweeps below me and I duck under the cloud ridge for a clearer view. Here the villages are in enclosures surrounded by wooden fences for protection.

Ten miles further north I see what they seek protection from. A pride of lions bounds alongside a panicked herd of antelope. The topi is swifter but light and easier to take down. The eland stand taller but seem ungainly, their dewlaps flapping clumsily. The lions are unhurried, taking their time to run their prey to exhaustion before they strike. I should feel pity for the antelope but my heart races alongside the lions, urging them on. I am past them before this game reaches its inevitable conclusion but there can be only one.

I bump along for the next while, buffeted by a down draught and am glad to see the large Nairobi aerodrome to the south of the town. I have crossed into Kenya.

My contentment is abruptly shattered by a sight no pilot ever wishes to see. Beneath me as I descend is the crushed body of a crashed airplane. I cannot help but think of the lions, feasting on the carcass of the felled antelope.

I land and climb down from the cockpit, unable to keep my eyes off the crash site. It looks to me like the plane hit the ground nose first and I would be surprised if anyone survived it.

Dick lands immediately after me and a young man comes out of the clubhouse to meet us.

'Henry Bevan.' He extends his hand to us each in turn. His clothes look unkempt, like he might have slept in them and there are bags under his eyes.

'You've had a mishap here,' Dick says.

Bevan puts his hands on his hips and releases a long, slow sigh. When he speaks again his voice is shaky.

'No mishap. A tragedy. Terribly, terribly sad. A young lady, only twenty-two, I believe. And a mother too, to a little girl. Terrible!'

'Who was it?' I scan the crash site again. Do I recognise the plane? It's a Moth but its registration, G-EBSQ, isn't familiar to me.

'Lady Evans-Freke. Or Mrs Carberry since her husband dropped the title. He saw the whole thing —'

'Not Maia? Maia Carberry?' I take a step back and Dorys puts her hand to my elbow.

'You knew her?' she asks.

I spin about, shaking off her elbow. 'Of course I knew her. She got her licence last year in Stag Lane. A damn good pilot. Her husband is an Irishman, from Castle Freke in County Cork.' I turn to Bevan. 'What happened?'

'It seems that —' Bevan starts.

'Wait! I need a drink.' I stalk into the clubhouse and accost a servant. 'Brandy.'

I throw it back, feeling the burn of it down my throat, the heat spreading to my face, flushing my cheeks. My legs are numb as I lower myself into a chair.

'Go on,' I motion to Bevan who leans on the table beside me.

'Not much to tell, really. Mrs Carberry was here all day yesterday, taking people up for rides. Then, a young chap by the name of Dudley Cowie went up with her. She'd been teaching him to fly. She took him up and all looked fine. But then the noise of the engine stopped. We all heard that. They lost speed and got into a spin and couldn't get out of it. All we could do was watch and it can't have been more than a minute later they ploughed straight into the ground. Her husband saw the whole thing. He was first to the plane, but ...' He shakes his head. 'It was no good. They were both killed instantly.'

I nod. It's hard to understand. Maia was well able to fly and even if they were using dual control she should have had time to get them back level or even manage a better landing. To be killed outright on impact. It's horrific.

'Awfully sorry, Sophie,' Dick says.

I manage a small smile. 'Poor Maia.'

'And her poor husband,' Dorys mutters. 'Imagine seeing that happen to your own wife. Were they long wed?'

'A few years,' Bevan answers.

An unkind thought enters my head. I had heard people talking about John Evans-Freke, or Carberry, or whatever he was calling himself these days, in London and took an immediate dislike to him. His reputation was one of cruelty to animals and children and wives. Maia was his second. She wouldn't have had an easy time with him, money aside. I couldn't summon sympathy for him. But her poor little girl – motherless. It didn't bear thinking of.

A silence has descended and suddenly I want only to be alone. I feel dreadfully worn out from everything. It's as though Bevan reads my mind.

'Sir Grigg is sending a car, it should be here any moment. You are to stay with him at the Governor's House.'

Chapter Twenty-seven

Nairobi, Kenya, 14th March 1928

Next morning I lie on the large bed in my flying clothes, not caring if I stain the pristine white cover. I am overcome by despair and inertia. The news of Maia's death has drained me of the desire to do anything, even wash. I didn't know her all that well. She was quite a bit younger than me and moved in different circles. But our paths crossed more than once in Stag Lane and I recognised her love of flying and her passion for charting new paths. She spoke to me once of turning Kenya into a centre of aviation where people could fly to Nairobi from their remote farms to shop and dine before returning home in the same way the English pop in and out of London in their motor cars. And last November, when I was back home, still planning my Africa trip, she flew from Mombasa to Nairobi. The first person to do it and now ... Dead. All that ambition and desire and hunger for life, gone in an instant.

I need to know more. What happened? Had she become careless? Was it a technical problem? Sir Grigg will surely have answers. He is the Governor of Kenya, after all. I move fast now, suddenly filled with an urgency to be where I can get more information.

Once I am presentable I make my way downstairs. In the hallway I encounter a servant who tells me in hushed tones, 'You can wait in the drawing-room, Lady Heath. I will let Sir Grigg know you are there.'

I pace the room, idly picking up ornaments and staring, non-seeing, at the portraits on the wall.

'Lady Heath.'

I turn at the sound of a crisp English voice. Sir Grigg is tall, late forties or early fifties, with greying hair and a neatly trimmed moustache.

I shake his outstretched hand. 'Thank you for your hospitality.'

He waves my thanks away and motions for me to sit. A china tea set is awaiting us on the small table and the servant girl brings the teapot now. He signals to her to pour. I wish he was offering something stronger but then I realise it's not yet lunch.

'I'm afraid I must apologise for the circumstances of your arrival.' Sir Grigg sits back in his chair, the delicate teacup looking ridiculously dainty in his large hand.

'It really is awful,' I say.

He stares blankly. 'Oh! The crash! Of course. I was referring to my wife's absence. Lady Grigg is up-country and will be so upset to have missed you. We had no word of your arrival.'

'You didn't get my telegram?'

'Not a word.'

This confuses me. I've been spending quite a bit of money, nearly ten pounds already, sending telegrams ahead when possible. Where can they have gone to?

'But not to worry,' he continues. 'Yes. Dreadful business at the aerodrome yesterday. It's so sad to lose young lives. That can't have been a pleasant sight for you today when you landed. And of course such dangers must be always on your mind.'

I nod. I don't dwell on the risks of flying. They are fewer than the dangers of driving. But it is true I suppose that a plane crash is more likely to be fatal, if it occurs.

'What was the cause of the accident?'

Sir Grigg puts down his teacup and goes to his desk.

'There is talk, of course. There's a bit in the newspaper today, mere speculation if you ask me.'

He hands me a copy of the *East African Standard*. They must have worked late to get the story into today's copy. There it is on the front page. A large headline, '**Woman Flyer Dies**'.

Woman flyer.

Is that how I would be known if anything happened to me?

Underneath: '**Mrs Carberry and Passenger Killed Instantly**'. So brutal and abrupt. And of course the main paragraph begins with '**Wife of** ...' There is a line or two on the accident itself, followed by a lengthy description of her husband, John Carberry, his lineage, connections to the Barony of Carbery in West Cork and the controversy surrounding his giving up the title and becoming a citizen of America. The event itself lost in the tittle-tattle. How enraging!

'It says nothing here about the cause,' I say.

'Yes. Not much. Apparently she took this chap, Cowie, up for a lesson. They were to fly dual control. It can only be that he panicked and she hadn't time to get the plane back under control before it crashed.'

I stay silent, thinking. Yes, I suppose that could happen. It's not a scenario I will find myself in, crossing Africa. But someday, maybe. I resolve to remind myself of poor Maia if ever again I am in the position of giving tuition.

'Sir Grigg, a pleasure to meet you.' Dick comes in, spruced up and looking refreshed. 'My wife is resting. She'll join us for lunch.'

'Wonderful, would you like a cup of tea?'

The servant girl is dispatched for a fresh pot and I pass the newspaper to Dick. He examines the article.

'A nice tribute.'

I bristle. 'It says more about her husband than it does about her. You'd be forgiven for thinking it was he who died.'

Dick turns the pages and reads silently for another moment. He passes the paper back to me. 'You won't like this much either.'

I scan through the paragraphs. The editor of the paper is pontificating on the needless danger of flying. There is a roll-call of recent losses. Lieutenant Kinkead off the coast of Southampton, trying for a new air speed record. Captain Hinchliffe, presumed missing attempting to cross the Atlantic with Elsie McKay. And poor Maia.

I hate that she's being made an example of in this way. The blood rises to my face as I read on. The editor speaks of pioneering aviation as 'a form of suicide' and accuses women pilots of doing it 'purely for the thrill or the notoriety'.

I toss the paper onto the table, knocking over the sugar bowl.

'Who is this arrogant fool?' I demand.

Sir Grigg laughs. 'He is quite insufferable. One of those types who likes to sit in his office and cast judgement on the world without ever really doing anything. Pay him no heed.'

'I would like to pay him a visit.' I stand as though I'm about to go there this moment and haul him over his desk to answer to these scurrilous lies. 'I should tell him what I had to go through to become a pilot. How I had to harangue official after official until finally they gave in and let me take the test for my licence. How they refused to let me fly commercially which meant I couldn't earn a penny from it. I think they only gave in finally in the hope that I would kill myself flying and then I wouldn't be a nuisance to them anymore. But you can take my word for it, there are easier ways to do away with oneself.'

'Sophie.'

Dick's voice is soft. He wants me to calm down, no doubt, to not disgrace myself or him in front of our host. But my blood is up. How dare this newspaper man!

Sir Grigg decides to ignore me. He turns instead to Dick. 'Do you know we received no word you were coming? Lady Heath says you telegrammed.'

'That's another thing!' I interrupt. 'Maybe that's what this editor should fill his columns with. We are flying the length of Africa, for the good of the Empire, and we can't even get a simple telegram through! The one thing that could safeguard us. At least if we are expected then someone will know we have gone astray. But, no! The great Empire can take over almost an entire continent but can't guarantee a working telegraph line.'

Sir Grigg laughs, although I am certain I said nothing amusing. 'You are correct on that front, Lady Heath. Please do sit, won't you? You're making me nervous with this pacing. How about an aperitif? Lunch will be served shortly.'

The servant girl clears away the tea tray and soon small glasses of Dubonnet appear.

I raise my glass. '*To Maia!*'

They respond and drink.

'What exactly is the issue with the telegrams?' I ask, after I drink. 'I have spent a small fortune on them and you tell me they aren't getting through. My husband will be frantic not having word of my safety.'

'You're not alone. We often get telegraphs that are completely unintelligible. The line is down between N'Dola and Abercorn. In fact that line is down more often than it's up. They suffer damage from storms, the giraffes wander into them and of course the natives are a huge problem. Do you know, they steal the wire from the lines to make copper bracelets? They see more value in using the wire for adornments. There is no line at all between Abercorn and Tabora.'

'That is simply depressing,' I say. 'One thinks this continent is under British control when really we control nothing. We have barely scratched the surface. And it is a shameful disservice to the pioneers. Us and the Cape to Cairo motor-car expeditions and anyone else trying to open up this territory.'

'I have to agree with you, Lady Heath. But unfortunately the powers that be prefer to lay the blame elsewhere. I must show you something.'

Sir Grigg leaves the room. Dick leans towards me.

'Sophie, keep your head. We can't burn any bridges with the authorities. Not yet. You can give your opinion free rein once we finish our journey.'

I don't respond but I slit my eyes at him. People like him are part of the problem if you ask me. Keeping quiet when they should shout from the rooftops.

Sir Grigg comes back in, holding a file marked '**Expeditions**'.

'I sent a telegram myself to Amery's office to enquire if they knew when to expect you.'

He hands me the file. Inside on a single page '**Owing to her slackness in letting us know her movements we are unable to keep pace with the vagaries of Lady Heath**.'

My slackness.

Vagaries.

My hands shake as I scan the page for the name of the official who put this offensive statement to paper. But of course there is none. Cowards all!

I hand the file to Dick and don't react when I hear a snigger.

'Sir Grigg,' I say. 'Is the line working adequately in Nairobi?'

'Yes.' He takes the file from Dick, resumes position in his armchair and places it on his lap.

'Then I would like to send a telegram to London. And a letter to the *East African Standard*. And I would like to lay a wreath for Maia.'

He opens the file again and hands me another page.

'Some more news, I almost forgot.'

I scan the page. Another official missive dated March 8th, it states simply: **Lady Bailey commences London Cape Town flight.** I read and reread the words, trying to make sense of it. When did she decide to do this? Why didn't she let me know? Why is she trying to steal my glory?

I suddenly feel like crying. All of my efforts have been for nothing. My closest friend is undermining my biggest achievement to date. I could be dead and rotting in some undiscovered wilderness and London would neither know nor care. *Well, damn them all to hell! I won't stand for it.*

I excuse myself from lunch. I'm being a poor guest, I know. But I am tired of being the perfect, gracious aviator and getting nothing for it in return. If I want to stay in my room and sulk then that is what I will do.

My thoughts snag again on Maia, the tragedy of her young death, only twenty-two. When she married John Evans-Freke, as he was then, at only eighteen, did she have any sense of what was before her? Or was she full of naive optimism, as I was?

Chapter Twenty-eight

Rathfarnham, Dublin, November 1916

The wind whips her veil around her legs as the wedding party steps out of the Holy Trinity Church. Violet, my friend from college, rushes forward to fix it. William and his best man Roddie are trying to light cigarettes but the November gale is determined to prevent them. They huddle together, a merry band of four, and hurry down the street for the wedding breakfast. Sophie feels glad that it is done and she is a married woman.

'Good job,' Violet raises a glass of champagne. 'You know, this war is stealing so many of our men, you've done well to snag a lovely husband for yourself.'

It's true. There is a dearth of young men but regardless none ever caught Sophie's eye before as William did at the Officers' dance. He looked handsome in his Royal Engineer's uniform. So did all the other men but what drew her to him was his calmness of presence. He wasn't peacocking or gadding about trying to be noticed. He sat, quietly, sipping his drink, not talking too much, nodding to his companions who were much more raucous. When he led her to the dance floor for a waltz she discovered some more about him and it made sense why he stood out. He was much older for a start, twice her age, over forty, and he had lived and travelled the world.

'From Liverpool, originally,' he told her.

Sophie saw a chance to boast. 'My uncle, my grandfather's brother, was a doctor in the hospital there. He left a bequest that if anyone from Newcastle West ever needed a bed there would be one there for them.'

She blushed when she finished telling him. Her words sounded so childish and he didn't seem impressed. But she felt safe in the quiet of his firm grasp. All the boys who'd flirted with her before bored her, and they were like children compared to him. And she had a sense that she terrified them. They fled at the sight and sound of her once she got going. William was a strong, steady man.

And now he is my man, she thinks. And Violet is very correct. She doesn't have to worry about losing him in the war. He has already served and even lost part of his finger in a motorcycling accident. So hopefully he will stay put here, safe and sound in Ireland. Well safe enough, as long as the Irish revolutionaries can be kept at bay.

Sophie catches his eye and raises her glass to salute him. He leans across the table and strokes his thumb over the plain, gold band on her ring finger.

'Are you well, Mrs Eliott-Lynn?'

'Quite well, Mr Eliott-Lynn.' She blushes a deep red. She hasn't allowed her mind to stray to tonight. As a married woman some intimacy will be expected. It has been the subject of many hysterical conversations with her friends ever since boarding school. But until she experiences it for herself she dreads it a little. William takes her hand in his warm grasp and her jitters subside. I am safe, she thinks.

Later that night he asks again, 'Are you still well, Mrs Eliott-Lynn?'

She sighs and brings the bedcovers over their bare bodies. She is well. And, if she is being honest, she is relieved. What a lot of fuss about something so straightforward! Now that the reality of what goes on between a husband and wife, in the privacy of their own bedroom, is known to her, she feels she might rather enjoy it.

'I am very well, William.' She lifts his arm so that she can tuck up tight underneath it. Her hand ruffles the hairs on his chest. 'What do we do now?'

'We could talk about the future? Make some plans? I'll start. How many children should we have?'

Her hand stops moving. She knows children are the expected outcome of a marriage, happily anticipated no doubt. But she is only twenty. Why did we not discuss this already? she thinks. Our courtship was brief. Best we do it now, so. She plays it safe and tosses the question back to him.

'How many children would you like to have?'

'I quite like the idea of two. A boy and a girl. Tall and strong and joyous like their mother.'

She smiles. 'And clever like their father.'

She thinks he is clever. From what he has told her of his engineering work in Africa he must be. She knows she is clever too, top of her class at the Royal College of Science, but she doesn't say it.

'Well?' he asks, running his fingers through her hair. 'How does that sound? A nice house in the country where they can run and be free, away from the noise and squalor of the town.'

'That sounds very nice indeed. I think it is impossible for someone to be unhappy living among nature.'

'You admire its beauty?'

'I do.'

'I admire its power. I like to do battle with it, take from it what I desire. Civilise it.'

'Oh!' She sits up. That isn't her understanding of nature. He pulls her back down.

'Of course, I'm speaking of Africa. That is a place that needs to be tamed. For its own good. You should see the changes, the prosperity a bit of civilising can bring to the savages there.'

'I must take your word for it, I suppose. I am in favour of working with nature but then I can only refer to Ireland.'

'We don't need to quibble. So that's all agreed? A boy and a girl in a nice house in the country?'

'It is. But first — there is something niggling at me. It's not that I dislike the vision of our future or that I don't want it, it's just — not yet.'

'My dear, you married an old man! A delay could be costly.' He tickles her ribs to show that he is joking.

But she is serious. 'There are things I want to do first.'

'Such as?'

She comes up on to her elbow so she can look him in the eye, so he can see that she is in earnest. And to see if he is on her side.

'My studies, for one. I want to finish them. I want to graduate. And then, who knows? The world is dizzy with change, William. I want to be in the thick of it.'

Is there a hint of disappointment in his smile? He tucks some hair behind her ear.

'In the thick of it? I wish I were ten years younger with half your energy. But I know what you are saying. There are things I want to do too. That's why I never married before. All the marriages I saw scared me off the idea. The way two people could flatten each other, drain all the fizz out of their lives. But I feel that you and I, we can do it our own way. You can have all the time and freedom you need to follow your dreams and I'll follow mine. And, do you know?'

'What?'

'I think we can do it. We can be really happy and have everything we want. What do you think?'

'I think I love you.'

She means it. From the top of her toes to the tip of each hair on her head. She swings one leg across so that she is astride him then leans down and kisses him hard on the lips.

'Shall we do it again, Mr Eliott-Lynn?'

Ballybunion, County Kerry, April 1917

'*Are you trying to kill us?*' William shouts, taking the wheel, steering away from the rocks and pulling the brake.

Sophie is in fits of laughter and there is no way for her to stop.

'How about I drive us back?'

He climbs out of the car and comes around to the driver's side.

'William. Don't be such a bore. I've barely started.'

'Yes. I know. And you've nearly finished us off too. Twice.'

She gets out and bangs the door shut. 'I didn't have you down as a coward, Captain Eliott-Lynn.'

She stalks off across the beach, trying to move fast in spite of the sand. Ballybunion beach was the perfect place to learn how to drive. The D'Arcys were kind enough to lend their motor. William was kind enough to offer instruction, or so she thought. But his patience and courage were in shorter supply than she imagined. He overtakes her before she makes it back to Doon Cottage and calls from the window as he passes by, 'We can try again tomorrow!'

Sophie flings herself into a chair in the kitchen. Cis shuffles in with her dog at her heels. 'Someone's in a sulk, Mop.'

She hates when Cis talks about her to the dog. Or talks to her like she's still a child. Or when William treats her like a child.

'I'm not a ruddy child,' she mutters.

'Stop sulking then,' Cis retorts. 'What's the matter? Lesson didn't go well?'

'You could say that. I make one small mistake and he carries on like I tried to murder him. Confiscates the motor car.'

'Did you listen to him? Follow his instructions?'

Sophie shoots her a dark look. 'Of course I did. Maybe that's where I went wrong.'

William is out in the porch banging the sand off his boots. He smiles at her when he comes in.

'We'll try again tomorrow. Don't be cross.'

'Did you take the car back?' She refuses to look at him.

'No. They said to keep it until we're done. They don't need it today.'

Now she doesn't dare meet his eyes in case he reads the idea that's brewing in her mind.

'Good,' she says. 'I do want to try again.'

'Of course.' There is relief in his voice. He hates it when she's cross with him. 'Tomorrow. Now, I'd best wash up for dinner. What time are the D'Arcys expecting us?'

'Anytime after seven, they said. Captain Cunningham is expected around then too.'

Sophie groans and bangs her head on the table. 'I'm not going!'

William puts his hand on her back, rubbing up and down. 'Poor you. Having a rough time of it. Tell you what. How about we take a walk up to the hotel afterwards and have a drink, just the two of us?'

'That sounds nice.'

'Wonderful.' He consults the kitchen clock. 'In that case I might chance a short siesta before dinner. Wake me in an hour?'

She nods then waits until she hears the bedroom door shutting.

'I'm too keyed up after all that,' she tells Cis. 'I'm going to walk the beach.'

'Don't be late back.'

'I won't.'

She slips out the back door to seize her chance.

She completes one lap of the car to assess the situation. Yes, she thinks, I can do this. She leans in and moves the lever to 'spark'. What did William do next? She thinks for a moment. The crank! She rotates it, gingerly at first. Then when nothing is happening she goes at it vigorously. The engine jumps to life. It is so loud. Surely this will bring William and Cis and everyone out of their houses. She gets in behind the wheel, her heart thumping. There's no sign of anyone. She takes a deep breath and talks herself through the next steps. Then she does them. Hands on the wheel, feet on the pedals, ease it forward. It shudders and jumps a little. She responds, easing off one pedal and down on another and now she is moving. Driving! And it is filling every vein in her body with exhilarating joy. She feels as though she is flying. In reality she is moving quite slowly. But that's fine, she'll get faster. For now she is thrilled to have got this slab of metal to move, at her command. And, my goodness, how much easier it is to do this without William fretting and barking at her every two seconds. I'm a natural at this, she thinks. He just didn't recognise it. She applies the brake as she reaches the end of the road. It's a junction where she must commit to a left or right turn and her nerve fails. If she goes left or right she might not figure out her way back to the house. The engine senses her indecision, sputters and fails. She makes an attempt to start it again but she cannot.

She gets out, leaving it where it is, and walks back to the house.

William is in the kitchen, yawning and stretching.

'Where have you been?' he asks. 'You're as red as a tomato.'

She puts her hands to her cheeks. It's true, they are hot to the touch. The rush of blood has inflamed them.

'Driving,' she answers in as casual a tone as she can muster.

'With whom?'

'With myself, dear man. And, I think it is fair to say, I made good progress. Although ...'

He is looking at her in horror, his braces at half-mast where he has paused in pulling them to his shoulders. He is probably waiting for her confession that she has buried the D'Arcys' precious vehicle in a wall or squished a small child into the road.

'I got to the end of the road but I couldn't figure out which way to go and then the ruddy thing cut out and refused to start again. Would you be a darling and bring it back up? Oh, look at the time! I'd better change for dinner.'

She scampers up the stairs, wincing at the slam of the back door. He is annoyed. For a moment she is sorry. Then she is not. He cut short her lesson and all she did was finish it off herself. And a damn fine job she did too.

Chapter Twenty-nine

Nairobi, Kenya, 15th March 1928

I rise next morning and after a quick breakfast I return to my room with writing paper, and pen an impassioned letter to the editor of the *East African Standard*. My words are measured but I hope my true feeling pushes through them to be heard.

Maia was not just 'a woman flyer' or somebody's wife. She was a deeply loved and admired human being. And she was not flitting about the sky for novelty. She was engaged in serious pioneering. I remind the editor of the courage of her flight from Mombasa to Nairobi. I press upon him the suitability of naming a new aerodrome for Mombassa in her honour. I sign my name *Lady Heath, Aviator*, puncturing the page with the force of my concluding punctuation mark.

I then turn my fiery attention to the Secretary of State for the Colonies. A curt, tongue-in-cheek riposte.

Pleased to report — alive and well.

Unlike postal system. Telegraph lines slack.

Vagaries will continue as will updates.

An expensive message to send but a necessary one. Let them know I'm aware of their insulting communication and that I don't like it one bit. I dash off a quick one-liner to let Sir James know I haven't been eaten by wild animals.

The next day I take a wreath to Maia's freshly dug grave. I shed a few tears there for the waste of her youth and the loss of what she could have accomplished.

'I'll keep my stick forward,' I whisper.

I think that my journey could be a homage to her in some way. All us women aviators are links in the same chain toward progress.

Dick has got word that his maps have turned up in Johannesburg. I feel bad for doubting him when he told me they were lost. We have agreed they are worth waiting for and so we sit here day after day waiting for the damnable postal system to deliver them to us. I hope it will be worth it.

My mind cannot adjust to this slow pace. I cannot bear to stand still. At least when we lingered in Mwanza we were occupied with hunting. Here we sit and read. Nairobi is having an unusually hot spell and nobody even wants to play tennis.

Dick and Dorys seem happy with the arrangement, dashing off to their bedroom after dinner as soon as it is polite. Sir Grigg is busy with his work and Lady Grigg still has not turned up.

This leaves me idle and an idle Sophie is not a good thing. I cannot stop thinking about Maia. Her death is forcing me to confront the actual risk of flying and I don't want to. Maybe I am being superstitious but I'm afraid that if I think about what could go wrong, it will.

I fall into a routine of sundowners, drinks with dinner, drinks after dinner and when I feel I am sufficiently sedated I take myself to bed. I think if I were to live here permanently I would be a dipsomaniac within the year out of sheer boredom.

I am in a plane but it is not my plane. This one has a fat body and there is a man behind me in the back seat. I cannot turn my head to see who it is. I am flying at a low altitude, about a hundred feet, and I want to please the people below me on the ground. They expect something spectacular from me and I won't disappoint them.

I'll give them a dead-stick landing – with my propeller dead. I drop the nose a little and switch the engine off. Now it is just me, the air and a metal tube silently gliding through the air. I feel like a bird, testing out my wings. I keep my landing point in sight and start to bank left, flying over a large building. There are large smokestacks to navigate but I am fully in control.

My nose dips forward, just a little, then more and now I am pulling hard on the joystick to bring it back level but it fights against me. Now the plane is diving, diving. My arms shake, muscles screaming at the effort of pulling it back. The wing glances off something, a wire maybe? And we are spinning, diving, hurtling towards a roof. I try to move but I am strapped into the cockpit. I raise my arms to my head as the world turns to splinters, wood, shards, glass and screams.

I open my eyes. My legs are shaking and the sheet beneath me is stiff with sweat. I put my hand to my heart. It is thumping like a runaway stallion.

Dick's maps have arrived and I am more than ready to leave. I trundle down the runway feeling the weight from my extra supply of petrol. Every time our journey is interrupted or delayed I feel sluggish getting going again and my Avian seems to be suffering the same. It takes almost two hundred and fifty yards before I can rise up. The furthest yet. I need to lighten my load at the next stop.

Soon after leaving Nairobi a steep escarpment looms in the distance ahead of me. I need to get over it and I do my best to get to a sufficient altitude but it proves impossible. I would need to reach ten thousand feet by my reckoning and the Avian is just not up to it today. I retrace my flight path over and back for nearly half an hour taking numerous runs at it. Eventually I have to admit defeat and carry on following the railway below, looking for an easier spot to get across.

I detour for about fifty miles to where the escarpment looks lower and take another go at it. But, no, I'm still carrying too much weight. Something has to give. I twist in my seat and pull items out of the locker. There's no time for deliberating and, anyway, everything here is replaceable. My plane less so and I am definitely not.

My stomach twists as I remember my dream. Was it a premonition? Is this the moment of my death? Smashed into an escarpment, miles off route, alone, where I won't be found for days, if ever? I shake my head to clear the thought. The dream was of a crash into a building and that's the one thing that won't be found here. I start to throw things out of the plane with abandon: a pair of shoes, a tennis racket, my books. I point my nose up and the altimeter starts to climb. Slowly, slowly, pulling up. It might just be enough. I scrape over the top of the escarpment, leaning forward as if that might help. There can't be more than twenty feet between it and my undercarriage. I clear it, only just.

Dick is nowhere to be seen. I lost him when I detoured and I hope he made it across too. I land at Kisumu to fill up but there is no sign of him there. I fly onwards to Jinja and after another two hundred miles I am very glad to see the little aerodrome, the only one in all of Uganda.

Jinja, 22nd March 1928

After I land I start my routine checks and repairs. The brief stop at Kisumu has revived me so I don't need a rest yet. It may be also that the adrenaline from my near-miss over the plateau is still fuelling me.

I hear the low hum of an engine and see Dick coming in to land.

'Now, how did you beat us to here?' he asks, laughing as he climbs out of the cockpit.

Dorys disappears into the basic clubhouse. It amuses me that she shows no interest in our mechanic errands. Her interest in flying seems to extend only to the moments of elevation.

'I don't know. I thought you'd be here well before me. I had to detour to get over that escarpment. I calculated that I added about fifty miles onto the trip. How did you fare?'

'I managed to get across early on. The Moth must be flying lighter. I'm going to stay around for a while,' he says. 'I need to get this engine out and give it a good going over. I wasn't happy with the sound of it today.'

'I'll stay too. I want to check my gaskets. I think one of the cylinders might be blown.'

We pass a few pleasant, companionable hours with no need for talk. I replace a few gaskets. That should have everything shored up for another few hundred miles at least. I clean my hands on a rag and pack away my tools. It will be nice to fly out of here tomorrow knowing I am in good nick.

'Dick, I'm going to see if I can borrow a motorcar and drive down to visit with Sir William Gowers. Grigg suggested it. He's a friend and according to Grigg very knowledgeable about aviation in these parts. It might be good to talk with him.'

'Splendid. I'll stay on here with Dorys if you don't mind. She mentioned a visit to the market. I'd better go with her or we won't have any weight advantage tomorrow.'

A young man at the aerodrome sources a motor car for me and I zoom to Entebbe. The native women catch my eye as they wander along the road. So graceful and regal, their glistening, mahogany shoulders left bare to the sun by the long, flowing draperies they wear. Those not burdened with pots on their heads hold a sunshade, matching the colour of their robes.

Government House at Entebbe takes me completely by surprise. Positioned on a hill overlooking the town it would not be out of place in an affluent, modern English suburb. Not at all what one expects to find in remote Uganda. It's a vast redbrick, trimmed with white timber with gabled roofs and verandahs. A pleasant manservant takes the motorcar away to be parked and I'm escorted into a large drawing room crammed with hunting trophies. My breath is taken away when I turn and see that the door I have just entered by is framed by magnificent elephant tusks, towering above the doorframe.

A tall man with neatly groomed grey hair and a weather-hardened face walks through it now.

'Lady Heath, an honour to welcome you.'

'Sir William, thank you for having me.'

'I cannot tell you how delighted I am to have such an accomplished aviator as my guest. The first woman to fly across the equator, yesterday no less!'

'Oh!' I am taken aback. 'I hadn't taken note of that but I guess I am. I have been so busy with the difficulties of the trip it's hard sometimes to keep track of the successes.'

'Then I'm delighted to have been the one to remind you. Would you like some refreshments or shall I give you a tour?'

'A tour would be lovely. I may only stay the one night and I would love to see the place.'

'Yes, I am fortunate. It's very comfortable.'

I smile at his understatement. This place is a mansion. I wonder if he lives here alone, without family.

A timid knock interrupts us.

'Come in. Lady Heath, may I introduce my private secretary, Winifred Paul.'

I shake hands with the neat lady. She is slim with brown curls and lively eyes. I turn away and walk to the large window as she hands Sir Gowers papers to sign. They talk quietly while I admire the view of rolling lawns outside. I sense an intimacy between them and feel that my presence is an intrusion even though she interrupted us.

'You'll join us for dinner?' Sir William asks her.

'Yes, if you think ...' Winifred says.

'I insist.'

She leaves and there is another moment of silence. I can see in the reflection of the window that he is watching her go. My intuition is accurate, I think.

'Now, that tour.'

He whisks me around tennis courts and a golf course outside and a multitude of rooms inside. Finally he suggests I might like to rest.

'Yes, I think that is in order. I want to be well-rested before I carry on tomorrow. Although I feel the worst of the journey is behind me.'

I am brought to an opulent guest room and gratefully nestle onto the large, white bed.

I am asleep in minutes.

I wake, famished, and dress quickly for dinner. Sir William is seated at the head of a large dining table beside Winifred and there is another place set opposite them. I take my seat, feeling again as though it is an intrusion. Even the soft glow of the candlelight envelops him and her while I am cast in shadow. Sir William and Winifred enquire about my travels so far. When I mention the villages ravaged by sleeping sickness that we flew over, unknowing, Sir William becomes animated.

'My predecessor, Bell, practically eradicated that scourge here. Do you know all the rooms here are mosquito-proof? It was part of his design.'

He places his glass of wine down heavily on the table and sighs.

'I have found, Lady Heath, and maybe this is something you have also noticed, but there is a burden placed on us here in the colonies to carry on life as though we were in dear old England. That all the same rules and norms should apply. As though we should forget that we are in a wild place, with death at every turn. That is why I have decorated the dining-room with my trophies.'

He gestures at the walls from which loom the mounted heads of Africa's finest predators.

'They are a reminder of where we are. The powers that be forget that at times.'

I take my time before I answer. I'm surprised that Sir William feels comfortable enough to speak so openly to me. Most governors are obedient creatures, keen to toe the line and work their way up the ladder to more and more attractive appointments.

'But is that not the purpose of colonisation, Sir William? To imprint our civilised ways onto a wild place, to bring it into harmony with how a good society runs?'

'That is certainly what they say.' He smiles ruefully. 'I don't mean to be belligerent, Lady Heath. I'm a cranky old man. But I've had some difficulty this past while, been the target of some vicious rumour-mongering. It seems I have survived this bout, so we should celebrate.'

He raises his glass to me.

Winifred raises hers too. 'To Naughty Willie!'

I almost choke on the sip of wine I have just taken. Did I hear her correctly?

Sir William roars with laughter, then places his hand on hers on top of the linen tablecloth. 'You'd best explain, my dear.'

'I'd rather not,' she says, blushing now.

'Then I shall.' He props his elbows on the table and leans towards me. 'I hope you will excuse my frankness, Lady Heath. My first wife and I are estranged. Winifred and I are together and as soon as it is possible and proper we will be married.' He sits back, gauging my reaction.

I see her hand creep across the cloth again to hold his.

I raise my glass. 'I wish you every happiness!'

And I do. I know how it is to be trapped in an unhappy marriage. The way out is not always clear or possible.

Sir William nods. 'See?' he says to Winifred. 'I knew an adventuress like Lady Heath would be open-minded enough to accept our situation. Unfortunately not everyone feels the same, hence the moniker, Naughty Willie, and the accusations of debauchery. Debauchery! I only wish I had the energy.'

He laughs again and Winifred and I join him.

'Now that is out of the way, let us discuss your trip. Where to next?'

'Well, I hope to get to Cairo.'

'Crossing the Sudd?'

I nod.

'Have you secured permission?'

'Do I need it? I rather thought I might just keep going until someone stopped me.'

I expect him to laugh but he is quite serious.

'Let me send some telegrams in the morning. I'll see what I can find out.'

I go to my bed, sobered. Is there to be more difficulty? At least I have an ally in Sir William.

Chapter Thirty

Entebbe, Uganda, 23rd March 1928

I am fully refreshed and eager to get back to Jinja, rally the Bentleys to get themselves organised and be in the sky at dawn tomorrow morning. I regret losing these two days unnecessarily even if Sir William and Winifred have been good company.

I enjoy my breakfast, having a pleasant conversation with Sir William about the future prospects of aviation in Africa. I'm suffused with energy and excitement for what lies ahead and proud of my contribution to it. And who knows? The next time I visit, Africa may be abuzz with commercial routes crisscrossing the wildernesses.

A manservant deposits a silver letter tray by Sir William's elbow. He reads it, his glance flitting over it then returning to me, still giving me his full attention as I ramble on. But I can see in his eyes that his thoughts have been pulled elsewhere by the post.

'Would you like to come onto the verandah?' he asks as I finish my meal.

It's a beautiful morning outside. The heat is not too intense yet, more a bathing than a baking warmth. Sir William leans forward to light my cigarette and I recline on my chair.

'What do you know about the Sudd?' he asks.

I blow out some smoke. 'I know it's a vast swamp in Southern Sudan. If a plane goes down it's likely to sink, or be stuck fast. And given the size of the place, never again found. But I don't intend to go down.'

'There are other dangers.' He is watching me closely. 'Have you heard what happened to District Commissioner Ferguson?'

'I'm afraid I've never heard of the man.'

'He was massacred. Stabbed to death by Nuer tribesmen in the Sudd just last month.'

'That's awful,' I say. 'I'll make sure to avoid that tribe.'

I don't mean to dismiss the poor man's death but Sir William seems to be lining up an argument against me crossing over this area. I am surprised. He seemed very enthusiastic about my journey.

'That would certainly be my advice. But even in the air you may not be safe. Ferguson had gone to negotiate with the tribe when things turned nasty. The tribesmen retreated into the swamp and it was too dangerous for anyone to go in there after the attack. So planes were sent to fire on the tribesmen and bomb their sacred monument.'

'This is all very interesting, Sir William. But might I ask what this is leading up to?'

He sighs and stubs out his cigarette in a heavy crystal ashtray with more force than necessary.

'The authorities have refused you permission to cross the Sudd. Apparently they sent a telegram to that effect to Jinja yesterday but of course you'd already left for here.'

'They have no right!'

'I'm afraid they do.'

He passes me a telegram. I scan the words, my eyes burning holes in the paper. So official and curt:

No woman permitted to fly solo between Juba and Wadi Halfa. Permission denied to Lady Heath.

No woman permitted! Damn them all to hell! This rules out all of Sudan given that Juba is in the south and Wadi Halfa is in the north. I scrunch up the paper and toss it into the ashtray where it starts to smoulder.

I stand, offer my hand for him to shake. 'Thank you for your hospitality. But I must be off.'

'You can't fly without permission.' He ignores my outstretched hand.

'You of all people should appreciate why sometimes rules must be broken.'

'Not if they're likely to get you killed. You'll be shot down.'

'Won't they want to check first that I'm a woman? How will they be able to tell if I'm in the air?'

'That's the whole point. Of course they won't know. Any airplane will be seen as a threat. And they won't spare anyone.'

'Yet it says there,' I jab my finger in the direction of the half-cremated message, 'that no *woman* can fly solo. Are you telling me a man would fare better? If Dick Bentley goes down on his way across what will happen? Is it presumed that he will fight off a whole tribe of Nuer warriors? Single-handed? It's beyond ridiculous. What difference does it make if it's a man or woman in the cockpit? Either it's safe for everybody or it's safe for nobody. *And I can assure you, I've been hunting with Bentley and my shot is a damn sight more accurate. And my flying is a damn sight better too!*'

I am shouting and beads of sweat have formed on my upper lip.

'Let me make some more enquiries. I might be able to figure out a way for you to carry on,' Sir William says in a calm voice.

'Thank you,' I say stiffly. 'But if you could have my car brought around, I really must be off.'

The dust swirls around my car, making it hard to see clearly as I race along the road. I have an urgent need to get back to Jinja, to sort all this out, although how I don't know. Will I just get into my plane and fly away before anyone notices?

No, I must calm my mind and think my way through this. I strike the steering wheel with my hand. It's beyond infuriating. I want to meet the man who signed off on this edict.

I would let him know exactly who he is dealing with. He would be made to understand that he has picked an argument with the wrong woman. I have fought for my right to be here and no one is going to take that from me now.

Dick is at the aerodrome when I swerve in. I stop and am already talking before I am out of the motorcar.

'Have you heard? I can't go on!'

'Yes. I got the telegram yesterday after you left.' He wipes his oily hands on a rag. 'What do you think happened?'

'The same thing that happens every time a woman tries to get ahead in this world. A man stops her.'

I kick an oil can and it rolls across the grass. I shut my eyes and try to calm my breathing. I am angry. No. I'm mad as hell. But I know I won't come up with a good plan when I'm like this.

'I can't cross the Suud solo. Too dangerous apparently. For a woman at least. Men, it seems, are immortal.'

Dick smiles then quickly erases it from his lips. 'Let's head back to Dorys and the three of us will figure this out. There has to be a way. You can send a telegram. Or a letter. Write to them and put forward your argument.'

We meet Dorys on the verandah.

'*Dick!*' she calls. 'Another telegram for you!'

I immediately fear bad news. It's been a non-stop spate of delays and mechanical problems and bureaucracy getting between me and my destination. What now?

He takes it and reads it silently.

'News about Lady Bailey.'

I plop down into a chair. I am sweaty and oil-stained and not ready to hear something terrible about my friend. I survey his face. He looks the same as ever so it can't be too awful.

'What is it?'

'It's from the *Johannesburg Star*, on Lady Bailey's behalf. She's made it from London to Cairo but she's been stopped too. The authorities are refusing to let her fly on solo and they've impounded her plane in Heliopolis aerodrome. This might put a finish to her reaching Cape Town.'

'That's outrageous.'

My blood rises at the thought. I don't know what I'd do if someone kept my plane locked up and away from me. It would be like confiscating my legs.

He continues. 'They want to know if I will agree to escort Lady Bailey southward from Wadi Halfa.'

'Over the Sudd?'

'Yes. If I agree they will release her plane and allow her to fly south to Khartoum where we would meet her.'

'Well, yes, of course you should agree. She will need a lot more help, you know. Mary's plane has always been maintained by De Havilland so she's never had to do much at all herself. Which is all well and good when you're flitting about England but out here it's a disadvantage.'

'I'm going to agree. Once we get to Khartoum, Dorys can stay and wait for me to do the run south with Lady Bailey. I'll go with her as far as Juba on the Ugandan border. Dorys feels ready for a break anyway. I'll telegram and tell Lady Bailey to wait for us if she gets to Khartoum first.'

'I imagine we'll be there before her.'

Dick bursts out laughing.

'What?' I ask.

'You can't help it, can you? Everything is a competition.'

I redden. I hadn't meant for it to come out like that. I'm looking forward to seeing Mary. But I will get to Khartoum before her, and I intend to be in London long before she reaches Cape Town.

The telegram from the *Johannesburg Star* has given me an idea. If an escort is deemed acceptable in Lady Bailey's case then surely it will be in mine too.

I sit down to write a convincing letter. Should I try to emphasise my flying abilities? Tell them of my athletic prowess to prove that I am no wilting daisy? Talk of my courage in France riding my motorcycle close to the front lines? I write and cross out and toss the pages into the bin and after an hour I still haven't managed anything satisfactory.

What if I appeal to their logic and science to point out that nowhere is it proved that a man would fare better were he to be shot down or have to crash-land in this dangerous territory? See poor DC Ferguson for a case in point.

No. That page goes in the bin too.

These are all men I'm appealing to after all so that argument is the least likely to get me a good result. I must comply, submit, play by their rules, give them what they want.

I sit again and write. I tell them it is a wonderful regulation. I am grateful that they want to safeguard my safety and the safety of all women. I wish all governments took the same paternalistic — no, I can't say that. I wish all governments took the same care with travellers passing through or over their territory. They are models of protection and responsibility and should be emulated all over Africa.

Bastards!

I light a cigarette and smoke it down to the butt in a succession of deep drags.

I tell them that in light of recent events it would of course be foolhardy, stupid even, to allow me, a woman, to fly solo across the Sudd. What might happen should I be forced to land, as happened early in my journey when I had sunstroke?

I propose instead that I will have an escort. I will hire Lieutenant Bentley to accompany me over this dangerous stretch. I will remind them of his expertise, having already flown the route southwards from London. He will be my knight in shining armour should anything go wrong. I hope this will be to their satisfaction.

I fold the letter and seal it in the envelope before I change my mind.

I stomp downstairs.

'Could you send this immediately?'

The houseboy gratefully accepts the coin I give him and darts out the door.

I find Dick on the verandah.

'Is it too early for a sundowner?' I say.

He glances up from his book and surveys the sun, still blazing but inching closer to the horizon.

'I won't judge,' he says. 'In fact, I'll join you. Any word?'

'I've just sent a letter, with a proposal that you escort me across.'

Once Dick stops laughing, agrees to my plan and we have been served drinks I feel I can relax a little.

Dick clinks his glass against mine. 'To my boss!'

'To my escort!' I reply.

'Do you think they'll go for it?'

'They'd better. Otherwise I shall have to go and see them in person.'

'I wouldn't fancy being in their shoes,' Dorys says.

I look at her for a moment, wondering how many hard times she's had to go through. Or has life just provided for her, without hardship?

'Quite right,' I tell her. 'I've fought tougher battles than this.'

'And you've always won, Sophie.' Dick raises his glass again.

Chapter Thirty-one

Leinster Road, Rathmines, Dublin, 1917

William has let himself into her digs by the time Sophie arrives back from her last lecture. It has been a trying day and she would rather be alone. She only sees her husband at the weekends, as he is stationed in the Curragh during the week, and feels a twinge of guilt that she is not more pleased to see him. He is sitting in her favourite armchair with his shoes off, feet resting on the coffee table, her library books moved to one side to make room.

She pauses at the door – his breathing is heavy. If she moves about quietly he might stay sleeping and she can have the best of both worlds. He will be here and not here at the same time. But as soon as she closes the door he stirs.

'My darling wife ... I have returned.'

His tone is aiming for humour but she can only manage a small smile as she watches him groan to standing, bearing all the signs of his further years. Sophie is surrounded daily by fit, young, lively, quick-witted men in the Royal College of Science and finds she is less tolerant of the old man she married. She should have waited. She shouldn't have allowed herself to get so carried away with the first man to show her affection. Looking back now, she can see she was in a panic. Henrietta was dying, the house in The Square was to be sold and so William was her safe haven. But now, barely six months after their winter wedding, she wishes she could travel back to the moment he proposed and say no or, at least, not yet. She hardly knew herself then. She has learned so much since. The little living-room feels too small for them both.

'Shall we go out for supper?' Sophie suggests. Somewhere noisy, she thinks. We might even get in with a fun crowd.

William threads her arm through his and she feels a little silly strolling into the city like this. She shouldn't feel silly. They pass lots of couples out similarly enjoying the early summer evening. But her pace won't match William's and they keep bumping hips. She is relieved when they reach a hotel with a suitable evening menu. William's wage as army officer is modest but it allows for outings such as this. She should be grateful, she thinks.

'Shall we have wine?' she asks, before they decide on their main dish.

'Why not?' William beckons the waitress and orders a bottle for them.

When it arrives Sophie takes a generous swallow from her glass and William raises an eyebrow. The alcohol stirs her bloodstream and the more she sips, the more she talks. She's not even sure that he is listening – he is more attentive to his lamb chop dinner.

He scrapes his plate clean, the shriek of the fork on the ceramic highlights the silence that falls between them. Sophie looks around, trying to think what else she can talk about to fill the space. Then she remembers the hilarious prank she pulled in college during the week. She wasn't going to tell him, but what's the harm?

'William, I did the daftest thing this week.' Her words are a little slurred and she takes a sip of water. 'I was dared by Tim and Abbie – you've heard me mention them? Anyway, we were talking about heights and I said I have no fear of them. They didn't believe me so to prove them wrong I said I would climb out the first-floor window. They dared me to do it. So I did!

And not only did I climb out but I hopped from windowsill to windowsill, going nearly around the whole building, then popped into a laboratory through an open window and nearly frightened the students there half to death!' She is laughing now, uncontrollably, her cheeks are flushed and she has an urge to throw her head back and cackle.

William is not laughing. His cheeks are red but not from amusement. He reaches across the table and removes her wine glass, placing it beside his own. He calls for the bill and they leave in silence.

All the way home she has to endure this silence until she can take it no longer.

'It was just a silly prank, William, don't be such a bore.'

'I don't think I am behaving like a bore, Sophie. Rather, I am being an adult. Imagine if you'd fallen. You could have killed yourself or ended up a cripple that I would have to care for, for the rest of my days. Do you ever stop to think of how your actions might affect someone else?'

He is marching her along now, her arm trapped in his.

They are at her door again when he says, 'It's time you settled down, Sophie. You are a married woman, not a silly schoolgirl! Maybe it's time to reconsider if college is the appropriate place for you.'

She reaches the bedroom before him and shuts the door firmly. He is not welcome. Let him go back to his barracks if she is too silly for him. She cannot sleep and is still staring at the ceiling a while later when William comes in, stepping over the pillow that she flung to the floor. The bed dips as he sits down. He puts his hand on her leg, outside the covers and she jerks it away.

'Let's not be cross, Sophie. We only have two nights together, it's a shame to waste them arguing.'

'I'm not arguing. I'm insulted. How dare you call me those names? And threaten my studies.' She sits upright. 'Do you really think I should give it up? To do what? Play house?'

'I suppose we should consider what college is all for. It's not cheap and once we have children you will have to stay home anyway.'

She pushes back the cover and stands. 'That is a long way away. I intend to finish my studies and there are lots of other things I want to do first. You said as much yourself. That we could allow each other to follow our passions.'

'But not forever, Sophie! You have to accept your place – as a married woman, certain things are expected.' He offers her a thin smile, as if to say, that's how it is. You have to accept it.

But she won't.

'I'm going to sign up.'

William laughs. She picks the pillow off the floor and throws it at him.

'*Stop laughing at me!*

'I will laugh. You're being impulsive again. And silly!'

She paces the length of the room, talking as much to herself as to him. 'No, it's been on my mind. For a while now.'

'What on Earth would possess you to do that?'

'I know I can be as much use out there as any man.'

'So that's it? You're going to war to prove a point. That you're equal? You're wrong, Sophie. You can't be as much use as any man. You'll only be in the way. You are ignorant of the reality. Because you haven't been there but I have.'

'Edward Pullin.' She stops pacing as she says the name. It drops reverently into the fraught room.

'Who?'

'A student. I knew him, William. He has a wife and a daughter. Had. He died out there.'

'And now you must die too? Do you hear how stupid all of this sounds?'

'I won't be near the frontline.'

'You know nothing.'

'There was an ad, in the paper, recruiting young women like me to sign up for a special auxiliary corps. Cookery, administration, transport. And I can already drive. I'll be freeing up a fit man to fight.'

'To die, you mean. Or be disfigured.'

He stands up and holds his hand close to her face so that she can see his missing finger.

'I've been fighting to stay here,' he says. 'And you are racing to the front?'

'What do you mean? Fighting to stay here?'

William goes to his case and tosses a file of letters onto the bed. She scans them. He has been deemed fit to return to active duty. France. She reads on. He has argued his case, made the argument to be sent to Africa, to use his skills in road and railway construction instead.

'Oh, William!'

'I didn't want to worry you. Until I knew for sure. If they grant me permission you'll come too.'

She wavers. Africa. That would be an adventure. But she realises now that her words were not just in anger. She wants to go where she can be useful. She shakes her head.

'I will. But not yet.'

Chapter Thirty-two

Jinja, Uganda, 28th March 1928

I sit and wait. There is no other choice. I have spent hours at the hangar and if I do any more work to my airplane I will be doing more harm than good. There is no more tinkering I can do.

So I sit and wait. It brings back an uncomfortable feeling of that time when this was how I spent my days. Every day the post arrives but there is no letter. I have visited the post office and spent more silly money on telegrams to London, Cairo, Sir James, Sir Abe Bailey, anyone I can think of who might be able to get me out of this quagmire.

The authorities are worried about me sinking into the swamps of the Sudd. I feel like I am sinking into this swamp of wasted time.

Did I take the wrong approach in my letter? Was I too obvious?

I can't help but think of all the times in my life I had to tell a man what he wanted to hear in order to get what I wanted. And the times when I failed to do that. And the consequences.

Those are the two common threads running through my life, I realise. The need to placate and appease to just be allowed to live my own life. The flight away from who I am, where I really come from.

I am storming back towards the house when I capsize the houseboy. He hits the ground with a thud. I offer him my hand but he waves it away. He gets up with ease, unfolding his long brown limbs. In his left hand is a stack of letters.

'Anything for me?'

He hands me the bundle to check for myself and yes! *There it is*. A letter from the office of the Governor-General of Sudan. I tear it open and scan the contents.

'*Yes!*' I punch the air, startling the poor boy again. '*Permission granted!*'

I take the steps up to the verandah two at a time.

'*Dick! Dick!*'

Dick and Dorys come out of their room onto the upstairs landing.

'What is it? We were resting.'

I take them in – their dishevelled hair and flushed faces – and laugh.

'No more time for that, I'm afraid. We've been granted permission. Come on, my protector! Time to go!'

I am back on the verandah when Dick catches up to me.

'Sophie, stop!'

I turn to face him.

'That's wonderful news. What did they say?'

'Just that they are happy for me to cross the Sudd with you as escort. So, come on!'

'You can't just expect a person to jump at your command like that. We're not ready.'

I sigh. But I can't risk upsetting Dick, or Dorys.

'Let's go in the morning,' he says, 'bright and early, when we're all ready.'

'OK,' I say. 'I'm sorry, Dick. I'm starting to lose my patience, all this waiting around. And I want to get going before they change their mind.'

He takes his cigarettes from his shirt pocket and offers me one.

'I know. It's been frustrating. But we can stay tonight and head out in the morning.'

I take a cigarette and lean in for him to light it. 'And I'll be a happy woman if I never see Jinja again.'

Next morning I am pleased to see Dorys up and ready for departure when I arrive downstairs. 'Good morning, Sophie.'

'Good morning, Dorys. Is Dick ready?'

'He's gone ahead to make sure everything is organised. I think he's taking his new role quite seriously.'

'It's daft really, isn't it? We've flown all this way as companions and now, just by mere fact of me having to pay him, he's an official escort and the powers that be pave the way for me to fly.'

'Yes, but it's probably for the best, isn't it, should anything happen?'

'*Hmmm.*' There's no point debating the idiocy of her statement, the notion that Dick can do anything for me that I can't do myself!

We catch up with him at the aerodrome. The planes are still in the hangar.

'There's a problem.' Dick's face is stony. 'The runway isn't long enough.'

'*What?* We landed fine.'

'You know we needed plenty of yardage to take off last time. I've had a look and we are at least a hundred and twenty yards short to be safe.'

I put my hands on my hips and look at the sky. The sky I long to be in. A little light is starting to bleed up from the horizon. I cannot take another delay. But he's right, I know. We are both carrying extra fuel and the weight that comes with it. There's no point trundling about wasting petrol and failing to get airborne.

I throw my flying helmet on the ground. '*Damn it!* OK, get the blasted thing cut then!'

'There are men on the way, Sophie. Be reasonable.'

'It needs to be done today, Dick. We need to get going. *Today*. I'll cut the damn thing myself if I have to.'

I allow Dorys to lead me inside to the clubhouse where she finds us both a cup of tea. I hold the handle tightly, watching as the men arrive then take an age to measure. They take turns walking up and down and across and disputing, arms waving about.

Eventually Dick stands in the centre of them and I can see from his gestures that he is giving instructions. Now the men are dispersing and starting to dig. As the morning creeps in and the sun climbs higher I feel a little guilty that these men are sweating hard, breaking ground to allow our planes their required distance. A hundred and twenty yards of digging the hard ground in this heat is no easy task. I request that some cool drinks be sent out to the men. They pause to drink then resume the work with vigour.

After what feels like an eternity Dick beckons to us. He is paying the men.

I thank them profusely in Swahili and they seem to understand.

'Did you give them enough, Dick?'

'More than. Good job you're paying me generously.'

We wheel out the planes, unfold the wings, swing the propeller blades and finally, finally, we are taxiing down our newly crafted runway and lifting into the blue sky. We climb through a delicate mist that swirls about, cooling and ethereal.

After about forty miles I can see, through gaps in the laced haze, that we are over the Nile. It unfurls like a blue ribbon weaving through the land.

I whoop and shout. '*You lovely river! I'm going to follow you all the way to Cairo!*'

I look around for the Bentleys. I want to wave to them and make sure they've seen the majestic river below. I see the Moth but it's turning. Where are they going? It's turning back, back towards Jinja.

'*No!*' I thump the dash. I can't believe this is happening. Jinja is cursed. A wicked spell has been cast on us, trapping us there.

I turn my plane around and drop down to a lower altitude alongside Dick.

He waves and gestures. 'Oil.'

He waves again and circles with his hand, indicating for me to turn around and carry on.

But can I? Won't the authorities see that as a breach of our agreement? If they see only one plane they'll think I'm intending to continue on alone and fly over the Sudd unescorted. I'll have to go back with him. I'll have to hold my tongue when I get there and not ask why in blazes he didn't spend all that precious time in Jinja making sure his plane was ready instead of 'resting' with Dorys.

I offer to help Dick with his repairs and manage to pass away a few hours without mentioning my frustration. Then I sit and walk and wait for night to come and return Dorys' guilty smiles with my own tight grimaces.

Finally it is time for bed.

Morning comes and I am at the aerodrome before everyone else. Will we ever get out of Uganda?

'How wonderful that we get to enjoy our bespoke runway for a second take-off!' I snipe at Dick when he arrives.

'Safety first, Sophie. You know how it is,' he retorts.

We leave Jinja. Again. And this time I vow never to return. My poor humour starts to lift as I fly along, following the blue Nile below. All of life is drawn to her banks. There are great herds of elephants meandering alongside her. I fly low to see what I think is a white rhino. It is! Very rare but also disappointingly grey, despite its name. I suppose titles can be deceiving in all species.

A little after nine o'clock the Nile turns lazily. The bend here is occupied by Nimule, the first sign of my crossing into the Anglo-Egyptian territory of Sudan. I turn and twist in my seat, trying to see where the Bentleys' Moth is now. I am above them, that I can tell from the sound of his engine. I throttle down and drop my speed to under fifty miles per hour but still he lags behind. I must have a much more favourable air current up where I am. Why doesn't he climb too?

All this slow-running is terrible for my engine and there is a real risk that I will over-heat it and have to land to allow it to cool. I'll have to push on without him. After all, I tell myself, I've kept my promise. I am flying escorted. It's not my fault my escort can't keep up with me.

I pick up the pace and follow the twists and turns of the Nile as far as Mongalla.

My plane is barely on the ground when I'm swarmed by an officer from the Sudan Defence Force and natives carrying water to cool my engine.

'No, thank you! Not hot. Cool!' I try to communicate by miming shivering. 'Could I get some sandbags instead? To weigh down the plane?'

Finally I am understood and the Avian is secured for the night. These native men are tall and seem thrilled by my stature. They take turns standing beside me for comparison, laughing delightedly. I long to trace a finger over the parallel lines that have been etched on either side of their foreheads. Signs of manhood or strength. I like how they can communicate their status so simply to anyone who sees these markings.

Whatever about my engine, it is boiling hot here, in the mid-forties. I retreat to Government House where I am to be put up but even here every surface is burning to the touch. I drag a chair into what little shade I can find. It feels as though the air I breathe is itself scalding hot. It fills my lungs like hot steam.

I have a light lunch with the governor, Arthur Skrine, all I can manage in this heat and start to wonder where Dick and Dorys have got to. Should I have waited for them? Have I abandoned them? Did they get into difficulty and have to land? It would be a tragic irony if my escort came out the wrong side of the journey. Now that I've had the thought that something awful has befallen them I cannot shake it. The worry or the guilt. I didn't wait for them. My annoyance at the delays they've cost me has caused me to behave carelessly.

I trudge to the post office and send numerous cables, to Jinja and Entebbe and Nimbule. At least if they don't turn up by nightfall everyone will have been alerted to the fact of their disappearance. We left Jinja, cursed Jinja, together, and I doubt they travelled backwards so they must be somewhere between here and there.

I return to the house and doze on the verandah, unable to do another thing in the dead heat, until I am woken by the sound of a car engine.

'*Dick! Dorys!*'

They seem intact, refreshed even.

'I was worried!'

'We stopped at Nimbule. Dorys needed a break.'

'Thank goodness. I thought I'd lost you.'

'And be honest, Sophie. Would you be more sad that you couldn't fly on without me or that I was missing?'

I swat his arm. 'Don't be daft. You're only my escort since today. And not a very good one at that. I flew most of the way alone.'

He laughs. 'That's true. Have you had lunch? We're starving.'

'Yes. Now that you've turned up in one piece I'm going to attend to my routine work on my engine. I'll see you later for dinner.'

I am relieved they're safe. I must try to be more tolerant.

The officer in charge insists on accompanying me on my errands, handing me the spanners and tools that I require. The biggest risk with undertaking this work here is that the tools will grow red-hot under the sun and blister the hands.

Chapter Thirty-three

Mongalla, 30th March 1928

I sleep well and am happy to be at the aerodrome early, ready to go. I'm even happier to see that Dorys and Dick are on time and appear to be ready as well.

I climb into the cockpit and start to taxi. There is a beautiful amber glow in the sky. A good omen for the day's travel. I turn my eyes back to the runway and see, too late, that there is a deep channel running across it, completely unmarked. I switch the engine off, hoping to stop before I reach it but instead I drift clumsily into it. The plane lists to one side then settles. I place my head on the dash.

Is anything going to go right for me? Will any day just be a good, eventful day where I get from A to B unmolested and unbothered by mishaps?

My cheeks burn with embarrassment as I am forced to sit in the cockpit while Dick, the helpful Commanding Officer and ten of his troops labour to pull me out. I shout a quick 'Thank you!' then taxi again. I cannot get into the sky fast enough.

The Bentleys' Moth rises behind me and I make sure to keep it in my sights. Today is the day we fly over the Sudd. I can't afford for anything to go wrong, not over this stretch of country. The government's hesitance about letting me fly and all the bad luck we've had have made me extra cautious. Landing here would mean having to contend with a voracious swamp, hostile natives, hornets' nests and honey badgers whose cute name belies the fact that they could savagely dismember me in minutes.

Finally, after about four hours of flying, out of the wilderness I spy the aerodrome at Malakal. A large, scorched spot. I bring my plane down, guiding it onto the cracked runway. I am almost home and dry when I hear a loud bang. I bring the plane to a complete stop and look around.

Gunshots?

No, there was only one.

Dick has landed and jogs up to the side of my plane.

'*You hit a crack. Your tyre's burst.*'

I pull off my helmet. This is irritating but a problem I can easily fix. I take my spare tyre out from under the cockpit floor and get on with the job of changing it.

'Shall we stop here?' Dick asks.

Dorys is sheltering from the midday sun under the wing of the Moth. I consider his question. We have lost so many flying days by now. If we stop here we will have a whole day and evening in Malakal. I'm not sure I can manage another civil meal with a District Commissioner who I'm unlikely to ever meet again. I have that feeling again that I need to keep moving, stay ahead of the bad luck that's been trying to catch me.

'There's a good wind behind us,' I say. 'Let's get some petrol and oil on board and keep going.'

The midday sun is an angry globe at the highest point of the sky when we take off again. But the Nile shimmers beneath me, a friendly guide. I take out my novel and enjoy a few pages of it, glancing out now and again to make sure the loyal river is still there.

I'm sweating hard. Flying in midday sun is hard on the engine, and the pilot. I am starting to regret my decision to continue on but I had hoped I could reach Khartoum today. I've started to think of it as the end of my troubles. And if I can get there before Mary Bailey does I will feel much better about my prospects of reaching Croydon before she arrives in Cape Town. She is on her way south and I am headed north.

I drop down, trying to put some distance between me and the blaring sun. Dick follows suit and we continue on at three thousand feet. My head is pounding and my stomach churns, reminding me of my sickness on Lake Victoria. The thermometer reads forty-five degrees. It's madness to be out in this heat. I listen for my engine and detect a struggle in it. I'm asking too much of it to stagger on. I have the sudden idea that my plane could drop from the sky at any moment like an exhausted bird. A sudden wave of nausea hits me and I lean out of the cockpit to be sick. I can't go on. It will be an absolute embarrassment if I crash-land with sunstroke again.

I wipe my mouth on my sleeve and shut my eyes for a moment. I must land. I open my eyes again and peer over the side. There, beneath me, traversing the majestic White Nile, is a beautiful truss bridge with an even more beautiful aerodrome beside it. I consult my map. *Kosti.* The end of my journey for today.

I climb down from the cockpit, lean against the side of my plane and close my eyes. Then I hear hooves.

Hooves?

I open my eyes to see some stray camels stepping indifferently across the runway and in the distance a man on horseback, leading a second by the rein.

I shield my eyes from the sun and wait for him to reach me.

'District Commissioner Arkell, at your service.'

The slight, bespectacled man jumps down from his horse to shake my hand.

'I wasn't expecting you but I'm very glad to see you. Lady Heath, I presume?'

'Thank you. Yes. How do you do?'

'I heard you passing over and then coming in to land and I asked myself which of the intrepid ladies might that be. I've been following the news closely and I figured you'd be closer to me than Lady Bailey.'

I nod. I'm not sure I can feign interest in this exuberant chatter but I don't mean to be rude.

'Are you ready to come up to the house? You must need a rest after flying in this heat.'

'Yes,' I say. 'I certainly do. Just give me a moment to secure my plane.'

I fold back the wings and push the Avian into a sheltered spot. I secure it for the night although the air is as still as treacle so I doubt there will be any breeze to trouble it. Then I mount the pony and canter after Mr Arkell.

I'm afraid I make for a disappointing, if unexpected, guest as I'm still feeling wretched. I manage some small talk over dinner which is not attended by the Bentleys. They arrived after me and are being put up in another officer's house.

I rouse Mr Arkell's household early next morning and make use again of his pony to make a speedy return to the aerodrome.

There is no sign of the Bentleys and I take to the skies without them. I cannot tolerate waiting around for them another minute. All that is on my mind now is Khartoum. Will I get there before Mary?

I leave Kosti just before sunrise. I figure there is about two hours of flying time between me and Khartoum. I keep an eye on the Nile meandering along beneath me. The brightening sky becomes foggy and bit by bit my visibility shrinks. I'm in the middle of a dense sandstorm, alone. I check my instruments and veer westerly. I am flying blind, barely able to see the tip of the wings. The sandstorm looms ahead, like a vertical cliff face. I keep my course and my nerve and gradually get myself out of it. I check and yes, my good friend the Nile is there again. A second sandstorm means a second diversion but this one is easier to navigate away from and I spot the aerodrome at Khartoum just before nine o'clock.

I bring the plane in to land smoothly. I have the same feeling I get at the end of a tight race. It's as though I have reached some sort of finish line. Silly, I know, I still have some of Africa and all of Europe between me and the actual finish. But I am through the Sudd, intact, and the next steps shouldn't pose as much difficulty.

I am cheerful and exhausted as the welcoming committee of Air Force troops take me to the Sudan Club. An imposing and fanciful structure of white arches, it welcomes me into its open arms and I alternate between the bar and the cool swimming baths.

I can feel every knot and muscle in my body start to unwind. I must be careful not to relax too much. There is still a way to go. But for now I'm happy to be here. And I'm delighted that I am the first to arrive. When Mary gets here I will be the definition of warmth and generosity.

Khartoum, Anglo-Egyptian Sudan, 1st April 1928

I am reclining by the pool when I hear her unmistakable voice. I sit up to see Mary striding into the Club followed by an RAF officer.

I've had my morning swim and was enjoying the heat of the sunshine melting my bones but am propelled now out of my chair and towards the changing rooms. I must pull myself together.

I find her in the dining-room having a late breakfast.

'Mary, how wonderful! You made it!'

She stands and gathers me into a tight embrace.

'Sophie! Please, join me for a coffee.'

She signals for another pot and I settle in opposite her. I watch as she drains her cup and refills it. She looks weary. The lines around her eyes are deeper and there are dark circles beneath them.

'You are a dark horse, Mary! You kept your plans close to your chest. Not a word to me in London before I left about your plan to fly to Cape Town.'

'Last-minute decision. And, believe me, there have been moments when I've regretted it.'

'Has it been very tough?'

'Tougher than I imagined, to be honest. I really thought this would be a nice holiday. A little jaunt, to get me away from the family. A change of scenery, that kind of thing. I didn't expect there to be so many problems.'

The waiter arrives with the coffee and I gratefully accept a cup.

I feel awful that this is good news to my ears. I shouldn't be so ghastly to my friend but I resent how she minimises what she is doing, and by association what I am doing. Carrying on as if she's popping to the next airfield for an afternoon picnic. I'm glad it's been hard. Maybe it will teach her to respect the endeavour this is.

'It's been one thing after another,' she sighs. 'You name it, I've had it. Horrendous weather on my way to France, gale-force winds that I thought were going to blow me back to London. Fog so thick I couldn't even find Paris. Snowstorms all the way to Lyon. None of that was helped by the fact that my compass was malfunctioning but I managed to get it fixed.'

'Oh dear,' I mutter. I could have fixed it myself, I imagine.

'It wasn't too bad from there on. I got across the Med OK and on to Cairo and then those beastly men shackled my plane.'

'That was outrageous, Mary. They tried to stop me too. I had no intention of allowing them.'

'Nor I. Abe was straight on the phone, of course, calling all and sundry. He even got Lord Lloyd to have a word but the wise souls of the Anglo-Egyptian Sudan administration wouldn't hear of it. Then Abe had the bright idea of enlisting the help of Dick and here we are!'

She brushes her hands together to show me how easily the solution was found. I bite my lip. How breezy life is for Mary!

'You're lucky to have Abe to fight those battles for you,' I say. 'I wrote to the authorities myself and convinced them to allow Dick to escort me across.'

'You could have asked James to help,' she says.

For a moment I am lost. James?

'Sir James. Your husband.' She regards me slyly. 'You know, the one I found and convinced to marry you.'

I place my cup down on the saucer, louder than I intended to.

'I believe I had no small part in that arrangement myself.'

'Have you heard from him?'

'No.' I feel a twinge of guilt. I have been utterly remiss at staying in contact. 'I was just heading out to the post office to send him a telegram, in fact.'

'And John? Anything from him?'

I shake my head. I had almost convinced myself I could forget him. But now, at the first mention of his name in months, I can conjure the smell of his skin and the touch of his fingertips.

I don't like it. I change the subject.

'But you got my telegram. Congratulating you?'

'Oh yes, Sophie. How kind of you. I was relieved when I got it. I had been worried.'

'Why?'

'That you might be cross. After all, you are probably more deserving of that title. You taught me to fly, for heaven's sake! But it's just a silly thing for the papers and probably came down to someone hoping to get on the right side of Abe.'

She waves her hand to dismiss it. This honour of being named Champion Lady Aviator of the World. It's nothing to her.

'I think it's wonderful,' I say quietly.

'You'll have plenty of accolades no doubt once this trip is over. The press will be falling over themselves to speak to you.'

I sit up straighter. 'Has there been a lot about my flight in the papers?'

'Not a word. Isn't that ridiculous?'

'Not one?' I push my chair back. 'The communications on this continent are dire. At times one would forget we are in British lands. This won't do. Thank you for the coffee. I'll see you later.'

'Did you hear they're giving a dinner in our honour? Tonight at the Club.'

'I heard. I'll see you there then?'

'Yes. I need to go down to the aerodrome now. The mechanics there are doing some maintenance on my plane.'

We walk out together into the glaring sunlight.

'You must miss the De Havilland mechanics,' I say. 'You've never had to get your hands dirty with your machine thanks to them.'

'Yes. That's true. But then we can't all be mechanical experts as well as pioneering aviators like you, darling. See you tonight.'

She leans in for a kiss on the cheek and I feel the crackle of tension between us. I march down the street, saddened by it, towards the post office. I am to blame as much as she is. I never wanted her as a competitor. Not in this.

At the post office I spend far too much money demanding attention by way of telegrams. I send a short one to Sir James, letting him know of my whereabouts and welfare. Then, to the London papers and the Secretary of State for the Colonies, Lord Lloyd and Sir Brancker, I send effusive, celebratory news of my incredible progress in the face of unending difficulties. I make myself a heroine and a pioneer and a success story that they should embrace and celebrate.

May God help them if they don't. When I get back to London they will hear of it.

I return to my room and try to rest. But it is useless so I take a long bath and choose my most elegant evening gown, a sea-green satin affair. I style my hair carefully and apply some powder, rouge and lipstick. By the time I complete the ensemble with my one pair of high heels I feel like a real lady, happy to be feted at this dinner in my honour.

Our honour.

It is a good thing that we are to be acknowledged in this way. I push aside the feeling that I would rather it just be me and the knowledge that, if it wasn't for Mary and her connections, it probably wouldn't be happening. Or it wouldn't be such a grand affair.

She had to mention John too. For the first time in weeks he is back on my mind.

Chapter Thirty-four

Boscombe, England, 1917

Sophie wheels her motorcycle into the yard at base. It's late, after ten. She's covered in mud and furious at the flat tyre that has forced her to walk the last few miles back. She brings the motorcycle under the one dim light outside the cycle shed and pushes the stand down with her foot. Crouching down, she can see something protruding from the rubber. A flinty fragment of stone. It must have caught the tyre with the pointiest end to puncture it so quickly.

'Rotten luck!'

She stands. Through the shadows she can make out a figure walking towards her.

'Did you have to walk it back far?'

The voice is quiet but casts out strongly in the chill, night air. The only other sound is a distant strain of music and voices. There's a party on somewhere and the sound of people having fun makes her feel even more miserable. The man steps into the tiny pool of light. He is the same height as her with brown eyes and a neat moustache. From the insignia on his shoulder she can see that he is a lieutenant.

'Too bloody far. I don't suppose there's any grub to be had?'

'I'm afraid not. The officer's mess has been turned into a dance hall for the evening.' He pauses. 'Would you like to go?'

She looks down at her filthy trousers and boots, indistinguishable from the mud all around. No doubt it is splattered all up my back too, she thinks. The rain has stopped now but since she left base just after lunch she has travelled miles through an incessant downpour. Her arms are tired from wrestling with the bike, stopping it from skidding all over the awful clayey roads.

'I don't feel much like dancing,' she tells him.

'That's the best time to dance.'

He steps out of the light and she hears his footsteps heading in the direction of the mess.

She retreats to her room in the 'Married Quarters'. There is no one else there. She stands, paralysed by indecision. She's too cold and too hungry to get into bed. She thinks of what the lieutenant said about dancing.

There is a basin of cold water in the communal washroom. She gives herself the roughest of cat licks, just her face and hands to deal with the worst of the mud.

Dancing will warm me up, she thinks, and she might get a gin for a nightcap. She pulls off her boots, trousers and shirt, kicking them under her cot until the morning. She dresses in a clean skirt and shirt, avoiding her reflection in the window and the disaster that undoubtedly is her rain-frizzed hair. It'll be dark in the mess, she hopes.

Body heat and a not unpleasant odour hit her when she opens the door. The mess hall is packed. She hears her name and someone puts a gin into her hand. She closes her eyes and takes a deep drink, savouring the liquor heat travelling down her throat and into her empty stomach. It scratches an itch she didn't know she had. She opens her eyes and sees that she's drained half the glass. One more of these and I'll sleep like the dead, she thinks.

The gramophone is playing a lively number and her feet start to shuffle and step in time to it. The record stops and the makeshift dance floor empties. A slow waltz starts to scratch out.

She looks around trying to see where a second gin might come from and sees him. The man who spoke to her outside. He walks over.

'May I?'

He takes her right hand in his and places the flat palm of his left hand firmly against her back. She rests her hand on his shoulder and they start to sway, barely moving their feet.

'What's your name?' he asks.

'Sophie.'

'I'm John.'

Then they move, in harmony and silence, until the record ends. She's moved closer to him. Close enough to feel his heart beating through his shirt. Like a cat that has found a warm, safe spot she is loath to leave him. But the room brightens as the C.O. declares the evening to be over. They stand apart to sing 'God Save the King' and when they finish he is gone.

She returns to her dorm and climbs into bed. Before sleep captures her, she tries to conjure again the warmth between them and she drifts off wondering why she felt so at home in the arms of that quiet man.

Abbeville, France, June 1917

A vigorous game of hockey is coming to a conclusion. The commanding officer encourages this kind of thing, says it's good for the morale. He might be right. It feels wonderful for the body after days of riding around the French countryside, hunched over the handles of a Harley Davidson. All good fun but fiercely competitive too. Sophie's team, all from the Married Quarters, defends its status as reigning base champions. The other women on the team all played hockey at boarding school, like her, and it is a joy to be transported back to those relatively uncomplicated days. Far away from the muffled sound of distant bombs, the threat of air strikes and crouching for hours in trenches, covered in loose soil, waiting for the all clear.

It's true, she thinks, I'm covered in mud now but it is in pursuit of fun. The puck comes to her stick and she strikes it, hard and accurate. It flies to Elinor's stick and she taps it neatly into the goal, securing their victory.

They commiserate with the losers and stroll off the field, arm in arm. The few spectators have drifted away. All except one, a lone man whose eyes follow Sophie. It takes a moment for her to recall his face. She swears under her breath. This will be my second time meeting this man, she thinks, and both times I've resembled a street urchin or cave-dweller or pig farmer, top to toe in filth and sweat.

'I thought that was you. Sophie, isn't it?'

He smiles. Is he enjoying her discomfiture?

'Hello, John.'

'When did you get here?' he asks.

'A few weeks ago. We left Folkestone in mid-May. Spent a miserable day in the harbour stuffed into stinking life-jackets waiting until it was safe enough to cross the Channel.'

'How are you finding it?'

'Not so bad. I'm kept busy and when I'm not I play ...' She gestures to the field behind. 'And I help with the gardening. It's good to take the air.'

'Shall we walk? '

They move off towards the living quarters.

After a few moments of silence, he speaks again.

'I got here a few weeks before that. The town is nice. I've done some touring around when I can. Have you tried the baths?'

She glances down at her shins, more mud than flesh and throws him a questioning look.

'Do you think I should? I do wash, you know. Daily.'

He roars with laughter. 'I wasn't implying that. Only I've heard they're worth a visit. I'm trying to get around to asking if you'd like to come with me, on an outing.'

'To the baths? I don't think that would be approved of, Lieutenant.'

'Something else then.'

They have reached the section of Nissen huts grandly referred to as Married Quarters. She sees him looking at the sign, frowning, realisation dawning. She doesn't wear her ring anymore. Tells herself she'll only lose it in the chaos if she does.

'Unless you don't think we should,' he says.

She looks for a moment at this quiet, assured man, remembering how it felt at their last, brief encounter, thinking it would be nice to feel that again.

'I think we should,' she says. 'Most definitely. I have leave this weekend. There might be a dance, or something ...'

His features relax into a soft smile. 'I'll come find you on Friday evening.'

She saunters into the hut, humming a popular tune.

'Someone's happy with herself!' Maggie calls from her bunk. 'Another victory?'

Sophie grins. Yes, that's what it feels like. A small victory.

Abbeville, June 1917

Since he found her again on the hockey field, John and Sophie are inseparable. They have to be careful, of course. Fraternising between members of WAAC and officers is discouraged. Her waking hours are consumed with plans for them to find ways to spend time together. There are friends who are happy to act as cover. After all, a group of young men and women gardening or caring for the fresh graves in the cemetery or carrying out routine mechanical work looks innocent enough.

They find stolen moments but every kiss and touch is becoming torture. They want more. He is a gentleman, always, and steps delicately around her complicated situation. She never mentions William. To him or anyone. Apart from the occasional letter she could forget entirely that he exists. Wartime France is another planet and every ambulance load of shattered soldiers that she sees reminds her that her own husband is actively fighting against his return to war and using a pathetic injury as his excuse. She feels shame. For him. For herself as his wife. But never for her deepening feelings for John. They are beyond shame.

They fit together so naturally. She has never before known the delicious comfort of spending time with someone who understands her. And she is crazy for him. That is a first too. When she chose William as a suitor it was on the basis of a conscious appraisal of his character and inoffensive appearance. It wasn't so much that she was attracted to him as that she couldn't identify anything about him that repelled her. Not then, anyway.

With John, there is no need for conscious thought. It is all feeling and she is compelled to follow it to whatever end.

Yesterday he got word that he will be on the move soon, so today they are going on an outing. 'A day of normal life,' he called it and so she has borrowed a cream blouse to wear with her khaki skirt and is wearing a straw hat she found in the local marché. She doesn't quite pass for a civilian but is less like a military woman. John has the same idea. He has borrowed a motorcar and looks handsome behind the wheel, his white shirt contrasting with his tanned skin.

They drive out of town until he stops by a little stream and takes a picnic from the back seat. He leads her to a shaded spot, overhung on three sides by sycamore trees and invisible from the road.

'How have you managed all this?' She gasps as he produces a small carafe of wine, some bread and cheese and vivid, ruby strawberries.

'I have my ways.' He keeps his eyes on the tin mugs as he pours the precious wine but she can tell that is very pleased with himself.

They feast on the picnic, then on each other's mouths. Behind, the stream tinkles gently and the peace is disturbed only by the insistent quacking of a duck. It makes Sophie laugh.

'I don't think the duck approves,' she says. 'That quack sounds like a reprimand.'

'He's just jealous,' John replies.

She stretches her legs out on the rug and props herself up on her elbows to watch the trickling water. She is suffused with joy.

'Sophie.' John takes her hand and presses something into her palm, bending her fingers down to cover whatever it is. 'Please don't think me foolish. I know things aren't straightforward. But I saw this at the *marché*. The woman told me the stone came from an Egyptian temple dedicated to Hathor.'

'The Egyptian goddess of love, among other things.'

She sits up and opens her fingers. On her palm is a silver ring with a single turquoise stone. She thinks of chastising him. Of saying he's been had. The woman in the *marché* probably has a box full of these 'ancient' stones ready to fob off on the next love-struck soldier trying to impress his girl. But that voice, the cynical one, is silenced by other feelings and questions. *What does it mean? And how can it be? And does he know I love him? Because I have just admitted it to myself in this moment.*

She goes to speak but he shushes her.

'I want us to spend the evening together. I know a little auberge. Very private and discreet.'

Her cheeks flush. She understands what he's asking. She slips the ring onto the fourth finger of her left hand and offers it to him. He gazes at it, then looks up. She meets his eyes.

'Yes,' she says. There is no other answer possible.

The auberge is on the edge of Abbeville, surrounded by farmland. John parks the car some distance away and they walk up to the front door, wanting to give the impression of having arrived by train, to cover their tracks. A small, elderly lady, composed of more wrinkles than skin and with no discernible teeth, greets them. She summons a younger woman — her daughter? She is flushed, pulling off an apron and shooing a child as she approaches.

'*Une chambre?*' Sophie asks. '*Pour la nuit.*'

One night is really more than they could have hoped for. The French classes in St Margaret's stand her in good stead but her accent is unmistakably not French.

'*Anglais?*' The woman asks. 'Army?' She looks at John.

'Yes,' Sophie says. It is easier than trying to explain that, in fact, she is Irish. And the less known the better. The woman's eyes narrow and Sophie can see that she is unsure of the situation and whether it is proper to rent them a room for the night.

'From Paris,' Sophie says, pointing in what she thinks is the correct direction. 'Our ...' she scours her brain for the phrase and miraculously it comes to her. '*Lune de miel.*'

If John's gesture at the stream was a betrothal of sorts then this is the honeymoon.

The lady smiles, her eyes softening. She beckons them to follow her upstairs to a sunlit bedroom with a large white bed. I hope she doesn't expect us to display the blood-stained sheet from the window in the morning, evidence of our consummation and my virginity, Sophie thinks.

John palms some francs into her hand. From her expression it is more than the cost of the room. Discretion acquired.

She leaves and suddenly Sophie becomes aware of the sounds. Outside, a farmyard bird clucks and somewhere in the house a baby is crying. Inside this room her heart thumps and she can hear John's quickened breathing. They are both unsure, having come this far, of how to make the next step.

Sophie unbuttons her blouse and skirt, letting them fall to the floor and that is enough to stir him to action. He guides her to the bed.

Their movements are frantic. She feels as though she is trying to absorb him so that even if they are parted, they will always contain a piece of each other. She responds to his every touch, as he does, noisily. They finish in moments, sweating and breathless. Sophie laughs out loud suddenly and falls into such hysterics that it takes many minutes before she can try to explain.

'I had a silly thought that the woman of the house would want confirmation of our consummation in the morning, but I am sure now no one within earshot of the house will be in any doubt that it has been achieved.'

John smothers her with kisses and she settles on his shoulder. It seems there is a spot right there that was carved out for just her. She could not wish to be anywhere else in this world.

In the morning, John presses more money on the old woman. She smirks at Sophie as they leave.

The mood in the car becomes sombre as they near the base. Sophie lets go of his hand, hating having to relinquish his touch, feeling the loss of the body she has claimed as her own in the last few hours.

He brings the car to a stop and turns to face her.

'It might be better for us to return separately. Do you want to go on ahead?'

He is right, of course, but it is hard to remove herself from his company. He leans in to kiss her, quickly.

'I will try to see you later,' he says.

Sophie returns to her hut and pulls on her uniform. The day is filled with routine duties. As soon as she is free to do so she takes her Harley onto the open road on the pretext of it needing a test drive. She tears along furiously, trying to find a release for the energy flooding her, feeling that her heart has been made whole and is about to break all at once.

Next morning a message arrives. John has received orders and is already gone.

Sophie twists the ring on her left hand and tries to calm her breathing. She will try to keep busy. She will try to stay where he can find her. She will pray every night that he will come back. And she will find a way out of her situation with William.

Chapter Thirty-five

Khartoum, 1st April 1928

The Sudan Club is illuminated by soft candlelight and low lamps that reflect the white sweeping arches in the still pool water. It looks like liquid velvet. How lovely it would be to submerge myself in its coolness, gown and all!

I meet and greet and accept congratulations and receive glasses of champagne and finally I am led to the top table where the guests of honour are to be seated.

'Mary! You look ...'

I burst out laughing. Mary, in typical fashion, has not changed or made any effort to tidy herself up. She is wearing the same dusty, tweed flying suit she had on today. And probably every day since she sat into her plane.

She laughs along with me as I take my seat beside her.

'Well, you look exquisite. I feel like a right frump next to you. I didn't think to pack any evening gowns! Silly me.'

'One must always be ready for an occasion,' I say.

The clash of our fashion sensibilities breaks the ice between us and once the formal speeches are over we spend a most enjoyable evening, oblivious to our hosts, exchanging news from London and stories of our flights.

The evening ends and we sit together on the verandah for a nightcap. Our hosts have got the message that we would rather converse together and they leave us alone.

'I want to toast you, Sophie,' Mary says. Her hair is askew and I wonder if she wears a toupée now to cover the mark made by the propeller that nearly scalped her.

'We can toast each other.' I raise my glass unsteadily.

'*No!*' Her voice is louder than it should be in the dead of night with only the waiting staff pottering quietly about. 'I want to toast *you*. You have been so courageous. You have fought every battle. You've never given up. Did you ever want to?'

I sit back and consider the carpet of stars overhead. I feel like life has been a succession of battles. Or rather hurdles. And what choice did I have? Overcome them or stay stuck.

'No,' I say. 'I never wanted to give up. Because what then? What would I do? Play house?'

'What will you do next?'

I sigh. This is something that I've thought of on occasion but each time I push it away. First, I must finish this.

'I don't know,' I tell her. 'But definitely something.'

She leans her elbows on the table and looks closely at me. 'Are you happy?'

I look again to the stars. Am I happy? What is happiness? A sense that something has been won? Or peace? Am I at peace?

'No,' I tell her. 'But I am not unhappy.'

'I wish you happiness, Sophie.' She raises her glass and downs its contents.

Next morning, we say goodbye at the aerodrome with tender heads.

'Godspeed, Mary. Don't let them stop you.'

'I won't. You neither.'

She turns away to climb into the cockpit but turns back, laughing.

'I forgot to tell you. I am to be a convicted criminal.'

'*What?*' I shout.

'I'm to be fined in court tomorrow in Brentford for driving on the Great West Road without a licence.' She can barely speak for laughing. 'And for speeding.'

I screech in hilarity as she climbs in. I'm still laughing and waving as she taxis down the runway and lifts into the air, followed closely by Dick, now her escort.

I miss my friend. Hopefully it won't be long before we're reunited in London.

I won't miss the Bentleys, truth be told. Dick has been most useful to me but I am keen to paddle my own canoe, so to speak.

I am still hobbled by the nonsensical authorities. It is not enough that I made it all the way to Khartoum in one piece. They prefer me to not fly alone until I reach Wadi Halfa south of the Egyptian border, little woman that I am, and my escort has absconded with my best friend. Word reaches me that a Fairey service airplane is leaving, headed north. I seize the chance and take off with them.

Within a matter of minutes I have left the slower machine behind, its service rendered.

I'm glad to be alone, without having to keep tabs on the Bentleys. But I can't help but think about Mary's question. What next? And am I happy? What would make me happy?

I find it easier to consider the first question. There is so much that could be next. A whole world out there for me and my plane to conquer. America calls to me. I like the vastness of that continent and their thirst for adventure. My chances of making a living as a commercial pilot are slim. It's a sad reality that, while I have earned my licence, the public appetite does not yet exist for a female pilot of commercial flights. And they are too few anyway for now. I don't think that Sir James would like his wife to be thus employed at any rate. It wouldn't do his reputation good for me to be out earning a crust. So I will stick at what he does like – my daredevil flying. For as long as I can.

What about Sir James? Can I face back into domestic life in London with him? No. My stomach turns at the thought of having responsibility for the mundane daily demands of his household. There has to be more to life.

If I am honest, I care little for him. Less and less the more time I spend away from him.

And John? Is there a chance of reconciliation there? My heart feels heavy when I think of how I've treated him. Discarded him. For this opportunity. But, no. It had to be done. And I must put him out of my head. He can't have any part in my future. My world is different now. We are no longer out of the same drawer, if we ever were.

Will I love again? Will I ever be happy?

I think of what I told Mary. That I'm not unhappy. And this is true. For as long as I can keep moving, keep flying, I can stay that way. Not happy but not unhappy. That's more than most people have.

I land in Atbara, in the north-east of Sudan, after two and a half hours of deep contemplation. Utterly sick of the thoughts in my own head and still feeling the effects of my reunion with Mary I jump at the offer of a game of tennis. I sweat my thoughts and feelings and gins out in the act of walloping the ball and racing around the court.

The vigorous tennis game does the trick and I sleep like the dead. I rise early the next day, still delighting in the fact that I can leave when I'm ready and set my own pace.

I follow the Nile and keep an eye out for Station 10. But I can't locate it or the aerodrome nearby so I bring the Avian down onto the banks of the river.

It's peaceful here, only the song of the birds and the rustle of the papyrus on the banks to break the silence. The midday heat is relentless so I dangle my feet in the cool water while I relieve my thirst with my canister.

Refreshed, I take off again and follow the railway line happily for more than five hours. I'm ready again for company when I bring my plane down in the aerodrome at Wadi Halfa where I am met by Henry Cecil Jackson, the Governor.

'Two gallant women aviators in the space of a week. What are the odds?' he exclaims as he shakes my hand.

'You mean Lady Bailey? We just parted company in Khartoum.'

'On good terms, I hope.'

'Of course.'

'That's good. A bit of healthy competition never hurt anyone.'

'I don't regard it as a competition. We are each of us engaged in our own flight. In opposite directions and I think for different reasons.'

'Is that so? I would have thought that both of you flying the length of Africa at the same time would have given rise to a contest. Who will reach their destination first?'

'Well, I will. There is no question of that.'

'Really?'

'Yes, I am much further along. I have completed the most challenging section and will most definitely conclude before Lady Bailey.'

My voice has risen in pitch.

He laughs. 'I detect a hint of urgency.'

'You do not. And besides, Lady Bailey is simply on a holiday. She said as much herself. I am striving to change the nature of aviation on the African continent and for women in general.'

'So you feel she is quite relaxed about it all?'

'I do.'

'That's not the impression I got. She was quite exercised when she got here. All in a fizz about her plans being held up and the authorities refusing to allow her to cross the Sudd without an escort.'

'Well, I was happy to let her have mine. I had no more use for him.'

'I heard. Lieutenant Bentley has given great service to you ladies. I must say I admire Lady Bailey. She could sit at home in the lap of luxury but she forges on in the great British spirit of discovery. Remarkable.'

I remain silent, waiting for him to add my name to his praise but he says no more.

I seethe in silence as Mr Jackson delivers me to his impressive home. I am cross with myself for allowing these comparisons to spoil my enjoyment. I decline his offer of a tour of the town and return to the aerodrome after lunch.

Hours of sorting out my tappets and fillers, topping up the oil and grease puts a stop to any more rumination. I take off the propeller boss and discover a looseness. I'm able to turn the bolts two full turns each. I am lucky it didn't cause me trouble, I should have checked sooner.

I take off before sunrise the next morning, happy that if nothing else my plane is in good order.

As the sky brightens around me I feel full of life. I have the sense that today will be easy flying and I imagine the continent that I have traversed laid out behind me. I may even push on to Cairo, even if it means more hours of flying. Close to nine probably. But I will do it.

I position myself over the Nile and with my friendly river as guide I'm able to open my novel and enjoy some chocolates, keeping an eye on the page before me and an occasional glance out of the cockpit. I'm maintaining a good height, my engine sounds perfect and nothing more is required of me.

The sights below me soon pull me away from my novel. There's no way it can compete with the vast grandeur of the palaces of Luxor. I drop down, coming in low for a better view. I pass over the Winter Palace on the banks of the Nile. Traditional felucca wooden boats with a single sail skim across the serene surface of the river. What a beautiful way to travel! So graceful. The fertile green of the Nile valley stretches below me, tapering into endless golden desert.

I consult my map, a page torn from an atlas, and decide, yes, I will push on to Cairo. I have enough petrol on board, maybe just enough. I will take the chance.

The air starts to cool as I near the city. Can I detect a hint of sea freshness? I realise that my legs are bare. I couldn't bear the thought of wearing stockings in the heat but now I want to be presentable. I am at the end point of my journey across this dangerous continent.

I intend to make a good impression and get noticed.

I poke my silk stockings and suspender belt out of the locker and using the tow straps to keep the rudder bar steady I manage to pull them on.

I get my feet back on the rudder bar and swoop down to get closer to the step pyramid below. It is an impressive structure but I am no sooner awed by it than the Pyramids of Giza come into view.

My breath is stolen from me by the sheer size. How did they come to be? Did their builders know they would last so long and be known around the world? Was there a desire for the next one to be bigger and better? That is the problem always. And it is what drives us all, I suppose. But look, Sophie, I tell myself, they remain and they are known. All great achievements are. Take solace.

The air is bumpy. I'm at six thousand feet and torn between keeping my plane steady and getting a good look at the sprawling vista of houses and minarets unfolding below me.

I reach the aerodrome and despite the fatigue of having completed nine hours in the air I can't resist a little showing off. I swoop and turn into a loop the loop, then another and another. If I could hug and kiss this plane I would. It has been my constant, unfailing companion through all the mountains and deserts and swamp and jungle. It has been more faithful and reliable to me than any living person I have known.

I land smoothly and climb out of the cockpit, ready to be welcomed with open arms.

'*No, no, no!*'

A uniformed man is jogging towards me, waving his hands.

'What are you shouting at me for, man? I'm Lady Heath, arriving on my solo flight from Cape Town!'

'You can't stay here.'

He stands, hands on hips, shaking his head. Is he mad?

'This is Heliopolis, is it not? The aerodrome? That generally is where I land my plane.'

'This is the wrong one. This aerodrome is for multi-engine planes. You need to be at the other aerodrome, for single-engine planes. Do you not have a map?' he demands in his cut-glass, English accent.

I think of the torn atlas page in my shirt pocket and decide not to produce it.

'Well, this is a bother. Do I really have to move it? I've been flying for nine hours.'

'Wait here.'

He turns on his heel and leaves me on the boiling hot runway. When he returns another man has joined him.

'Mr Emerson.' He shakes my hand. 'Lady Heath, we are most honoured to welcome you to Heliopolis. It's quite a feat you've pulled off. We had Lady Bailey here not so long ago.'

'I heard.' My tone is cutting. But I can see why Mary was so irritated by what transpired here, with her plane being impounded in a hangar. The officials seem to be very pernickety. 'Must I move my plane? Really?'

'No, no. I wouldn't dream of it. You must be exhausted. Leave it to us. We'll take care of everything.'

'Oh, that is a relief! You know, I'm not so much tired as famished.'

'Then please allow me to take you to dinner.'

'That would be wonderful.'

I follow Mr Emerson, throwing a snide smile at the uniformed official who's tutting and muttering under his breath about regulations.

The restaurant tinkles with chandeliers stirred by a gentle breeze from large open windows sheathed in flowing white drapes. The wine glasses and silverware on the table sparkle and I am loath to touch the stark white linen for fear I will sully it. I feel dusty and grubby after my journey but my appetite takes over and soon I forget everything except my need to fill my stomach.

Sated, I ask Mr Emerson to accompany me to the post office. I transcribe celebratory telegrams to Messrs A.V. Roe and Company to congratulate them on the excellence of their machine that has transported me. Next to the Aircraft Disposal Company to thank them for the efficiency of their Cirrus engine that has not let me down once. To Sir James to announce my successful and safe arrival in Cairo and to let him know I will see him soon in London. And, finally, to the Stag Lane and the Associated Press I send an announcement.

'Lady Heath has arrived in Cairo. Her successful solo flight from Cape Town means she has set three records. First solo flight from Cape Town to Cairo. First light plane flight from Cape Town to Cairo. First flight by a woman alone the full length of the African continent.'

If the newspapers have forgotten about me and my flight, as Mary suggested, then I will damn well remind them.

Errands complete, I settle into my room at Heliopolis House and sleep for fifteen hours.

Chapter Thirty-six

Cairo, 4th April 1928

I am enjoying a leisurely breakfast when a tall, sallow man with a thick moustache approaches.

'Lady Heath? Group Captain MacLean. At your service.'

He executes a stiff bow and I sit back to take in the full, handsome length of him.

'And what service might that be?' I ask, a cheeky smirk skirting around my lips.

'Whatever is required.' He holds my gaze. Brazen. 'May I?'

I nod and he pulls out a chair. He extends his hand so I shake it.

'Mind if I smoke?'

'Not at all.'

He offers me a cigarette from a silver case so I take one.

'The authorities thought it might be useful for you to have a guide of sorts, here in Cairo.'

'A guide? And of the charming New Zealand variety too. How chivalrous of them! But, Captain MacLean, be honest. Are you here to guide me or keep an eye on me? I have rather the reputation, I'm afraid.'

'Reputation?' He leans across with a flaming lighter.

I light my cigarette on it, suck in.

'I seem a little inclined to get in trouble. Though I try very hard not to.'

'That's unfortunate.'

'Yes, but it is quite fun too. I think therein lies the problem.'

'*Hmmm.*' He leans back and expels smoke towards the ceiling. 'Then how about I help you have lots of fun but keep you out of trouble at the same time?'

'That sounds like a wonderful plan. What do you have in mind?'

'That depends. Would you rather rest or see the city?'

'I can rest when I get back to London. I don't mind a jot if I don't sleep for a week. I want to see everything.'

'Marvellous. I have a few ideas. Meet me in the lobby in an hour.'

'Should I bring anything?'

'What have you got with you?'

'Some books. An evening gown. My bathing suit. A Bible.'

'Just the bathing suit.'

I scurry back to my room, fizzing with excitement at the thought of having the company of this dashing man for my time here in Cairo. I've had no thoughts of any romantic entanglements. But, who knows? Maybe this could be a fun encounter.

Captain MacLean is waiting for me in the lobby and leads me outside to his motorcar.

'Where are we off to, Captain MacLean?'

'I was thinking a spot of tennis at the club in Gezireh before lunch. Would that be satisfactory, Lady Heath? Word has it you are a fan of sport.'

'I am. Please, call me Sophie.'

He drives on in silence and I steal glances at his side profile, the strong jaw, slight dimples in his cheeks. He points out local sites of interest. I'm waiting for him to tell me his first name but I grow impatient.

'What should I call you?'

'You don't like Captain MacLean?'

He's toying with me.

'It seems a bit formal. It makes me feel like I should sit in the back and treat you like my driver.'

'Cuthbert.'

'Oh! I see now why you didn't want to say.'

He guffaws. 'My friends call me Cuppy.'

'OK, Cuppy. Are you any good at tennis?'

It turns out he is. Very good. And he doesn't mind showing me. He comes at me with everything he has in his arsenal, holds nothing back. And I like him all the more for it. I detest anyone who softens their game for me. I make them pay for it every time. But Cuppy and I are evenly matched and we exhaust ourselves in the morning sun before we decide it's best to call it a draw before one of us dies.

We have a quick cooling dip in the pool and a delightful lunch on the verandah. My mind turns to my plane and I ask him to drive me out to the aerodrome. The Avian is being seen after by a Flight Lieutenant Lord and while I prefer to do all the maintenance myself I decide to allow myself a little holiday. After all, I have worked very hard to get to Cairo. I deserve a rest. And some fun.

Cuppy has me out dancing late that night. And the next. The following evening he instructs me to wrap up warm and meet him out front of my hotel at seven. I follow his instructions to the letter.

I've taken to calling him 'my little Kiwi' even though there is nothing little about him. But he hails from New Zealand and I love to hear him talk in his slant accent of his boyhood days there. That is another country I will visit. The world is at my feet.

He stops for me and I get in before he can come around to open my door. He speeds away from the hotel.

'Where are we off to?' I ask.

'It's a surprise. Enjoy the ride.'

I close my eyes for a moment, luxuriating in the breeze created by the acceleration. It is a welcome relief after days of hot, blistering heat. The evening is cooler and our surroundings grow quieter as we leave the city behind. The houses get smaller and further apart and soon it feels as though there is just the two of us in the world. Will I reach across and put my hand on his? I am weighing up how he would react when I see it. It rises before the windscreen. First a shadow, a silhouette. And if I hadn't seen it from the air I would have doubted it was real. It takes shape and form and becomes solid. The Great Pyramid.

Cuppy stops the car a distance away and I sit, speechless. When I find my voice I ask, 'Are we not going closer?'

'Wait.'

I sit and keep my gaze turned in the same direction as him. Behind the pyramid it comes creeping. A full circle of glowing light, so bright it seems to pulsate. It makes its way stealthily up, stalking the pyramid until it crowns the apex.

'*Oh!*'

I can think of nothing to say. And this is good. Any words now would be a disappointment. I wish I had brought my camera but, no, it would never have been able to capture the beauty of this illumination. My heart is beating fast and all I can think is: this world! This world is beyond our comprehension. It is so wondrous.

Minutes pass in silence as we drink it in. Cuppy breaks the awed stillness and hands me a hip flask. I take a sip. Strong whiskey stings the back of my throat and I hand it back. I don't want any of my other senses to distract me from the sight before me. I blink quickly and reluctantly, not wanting to lose a moment of this. I will always remember it.

'Do you want to go for a closer look?' he asks.

'No. Let's just stay here.'

I need nothing else.

Later, Cuppy drops me back to the hotel and I lie awake, my eyes full of the moon.

Next day he takes me to the bazaar and I laugh at the crazy chaos of the place. I buy bracelets and a silk tie in teal for Sir James. I suppose it would be wrong of me to return empty-handed. Cuppy and I dine together that night, laughing over our adventures, and finish the evening with a cocktail on the verandah. The moon is lower in the sky tonight and he is cast in shadow.

I take my chance.

'Would you care to walk me to my room?'

His non-answer drops achingly into the silence.

Eventually, he says, 'I don't think that is a good idea . Though it might be great fun. It could also spell trouble.'

I am grateful for the shadow hiding the burning blush of my cheeks. I swallow and aim for a light tone.

'How true! Your loss, Cuppy. See you in the morning.'

I stand and pass by his chair. His hand reaches for mine but I ignore it.

'Sophie.'

'Goodnight.'

I walk briskly to my room, hoping I don't meet anyone. The corridors are empty and once inside I put my back to the door. I tap my head against it.

'Silly girl.'

I tap again.

'Silly girl, talking to herself now.'

I prepare for bed, mulling over the possible reasons for his refusal. He is married. Although there is no ring. Maybe he doesn't like women in general. *Or*. I have to face it, I suppose. It might just be that he doesn't like me. I flop into bed annoyed at my foolishness. I have been swayed into romantic notions by Cairo and her full-moon glory. Enough! I will return to my plane tomorrow and get back on track.

I'm pretending to read the newspaper in the lobby next morning when he arrives. I wasn't even sure he would come. There was a strong chance he would leave me high and dry today. Or send someone else to escort the madwoman. I have already run through all these possibilities and all the things I might say if he does show up.

The words of the news articles swim before my eyes and I find that now he is here I don't want to say anything. Will he be gentlemanly enough to pretend it never happened?

He sits. 'How are you this morning?'

'Very well.' My voice is too loud, too bright. I signal to a waiter for more coffee just for something to do with my hands. Eventually I have no choice but to look at him. 'And you?'

He is sheepish, refusing to catch my eye. Have I mortally embarrassed him? Or offended him? I thought he was made of tougher stuff.

The coffee arrives and I request an extra cup for him without checking if he wants some. I pour for us both and pass him the cup.

'So, what's on our schedule today, Captain MacLean?'

'That is going to depend,' he says.

'On?'

'How you react.'

I put my cup down on the coffee table at my knees. He leans across and moves the cup to the side, out of my reach. He glances around, hitches his trousers up his thighs so he can sit forward, closing the gap between us.

'I'm afraid I have some difficult news.'

'Mary?' My stomach turns. Has my friend met with an accident?

'No. Your plane.'

'My plane?'

'Your plane. It's been impounded.'

'By whom? What do you mean? Why would my plane be impounded?'

I stand, knees jostling the table and he rises to meet my full height.

'The authorities. They won't allow you to fly solo across the Med.'

I look down at the table. The coffee has slopped out of my cup onto the linen napkin and is seeping across its fibres. I see now why he moved it because I am itching to throw something. Or break something.

'*Ugh!*' I stamp my feet. 'This is gone beyond ridiculous!'

I storm out of the lobby and onto the street.

'*Bastards!*' I say loudly.

An older couple, dressed for touring, startle and move away from me.

Cuppy takes my elbow and leads me to his car.

'Get in,' he says. 'I'll take you wherever you want. You might need to give this a few days to blow over.'

I get in and slam the door hard behind me.

'I want to see for myself. Take me to the aerodrome.'

He drives in silence until we reach the hangar. I can see from the car that it is closed. I get out and run to the door. Threaded through the handles is a large chain, padlocked. A hard lump sits at the back of my throat and my head starts to spin. I feel so trapped. Amputated. My vessel, my baby, taken from me, imprisoned on the other side. If I could break down this door I would. Start her up and take to the skies. Let them shoot me down! I am pulling at the chain, metal screeching on metal, but nothing gives.

Cuppy is beside me now.

'It's no use, Sophie. Let's go.'

'Take me to the High Commissioner.'

'He's not expecting you. I can go ahead and request –'

'You said you'd take me wherever I wanted. Take me to the High Commissioner.'

I fume in silence as he navigates back to the city and through the erratic streets. What was I thinking, hanging around, playing tourist, flirting, dancing, staring at moonlit pyramids? *Damn it all.* I've given them time and opportunity to stop me in my tracks. Again! And it doesn't matter if the 'them' this time is different from last time or if their illogical reasons are new or the same old rubbish. This is my fault. I shouldn't have taken my eye off the prize. I should have fixed up my plane, stayed the night, then left on the dawn next day before they even knew I was here.

I slap my hand against the dashboard.

Cuppy glances at me.

'*Drive faster!*'

We turn in the gate of the opulent residence and I am out of the car before it even comes to a complete stop in front of the pillared portico. I pound up the steps, leaving Cuppy behind, passing startled staff.

I come to a secretary tapping furiously on a typewriter.

'I am here to speak with Lord Lloyd.' I tap my finger on the polished mahogany desk.

'Is he expecting you ...?'

'Lady Heath. And whether he is or not is not relevant. I am here to speak with him, and speak with him I will.'

I stare her down, dare her to challenge me. She quails and scurries away into the shaded bowels of the vast building.

After a few moments she returns and beckons me to follow her, still scurrying, presumably to maintain a safe distance from my stomping feet.

A small man, with a tidy moustache on a pleasantly round face, is seated behind a large desk. He stands as I enter and the secretary vanishes, easing the door shut as she goes.

'Lady Heath! How wonderful to meet you in person! I have been following your exploits. My goodness, what an adventure! Please, sit.'

I perch at the edge of a dark-green leather chair.

'Lord Lloyd.' I take a breath to calm myself. Turn on the charm, Sophie. You'll catch more flies with honey. 'Thank you for those kind words. And thank you for seeing me. I appreciate my arrival wasn't expected. But I am confused.'

'About what?'

'My plane has been impounded.'

'Apparently so.'

'There is no apparently. I saw it with my own eyes.'

I swallow to clear the lump again. Would he soften if I break down in tears? No. I cannot be weak. I must get him to see the ludicrousness of this situation.

'I just have no idea, Lord Lloyd, why this has happened. Obviously there has been an error. A grave error. My husband, Sir James, will not be pleased. He is waiting for me, you know, in London.'

He eyes me over the desk. 'You've been enjoying yourself in Cairo, Lady Heath. From what I've heard. Why not relax, enjoy yourself a bit more and when a suitable escort is available you can cross?'

I scoff, my tone all vinegar now. 'This escort nonsense again? Really, Lord Lloyd, I humoured the authorities regarding the Sudd crossing. I can understand their nervousness, given recent tragic events. But are you now telling me I must have an escort to cross the Mediterranean?'

'Yes. That is exactly it.'

'By whose orders?'

'By the orders of His Majesty's Royal Air Force.'

'My escort is gone. You know that, surely. He was required to accompany Lady Bailey in her crossing of the Sudd.'

'Yes.'

'So I have none.'

'For now.'

'I'm not prepared to wait.'

'You have no choice.'

'Lady Bailey was permitted to cross.'

'And in hindsight that was foolish. There is too much at risk. If you were to get into difficulty ... No, it can't be encouraged.'

'What, may I ask, is my escort to do for me if I come down in the Mediterranean? Will his plane be able to float? Or transform into a sailboat, perhaps?'

Lord Lloyd laughs. 'I understand your frustration. Really, I do. But you must see it from our side. It's too great a risk. And we can't spare the resources to go searching for any aviator that decides to chance crossing solo and goes down somewhere in the sea.'

He rises so I must too. He leads me to the door.

'You can be angry and write letters complaining of this awful treatment, Lady Heath. Or you can relax and enjoy one of the best cities in the world until an escort becomes available. And you must come along to a dance here at the Residency, on the eleventh. It will be a splendid evening. Keep your mind off these matters and I'm sure all will be resolved.'

He smiles at me as though I'm a child looking to stay up late who he has convinced to go to bed.

'How kind,' I mutter through gritted teeth and follow the skittish secretary out.

Cuppy is leaning against the car, smoking. I get in, slamming the door behind me.

'Went well?' he asks as he gets in.

I put my head in my hands. I need to think. There must be someone who can escort me. I hate that I have to even consider it. What an utter waste of my time! And meanwhile Mary is speeding towards Cape Town. She's not my rival, or hasn't been, but if she gets there before I make London then all of this will have been in vain. I will be second fiddle in the papers again.

'**Wife of Abe Bailey in Daring Flight**.' That's all anyone will want to talk about. I might appear somewhere in the second, or third paragraph. If I'm lucky.

'Take me back,' I say to Cuppy, quietly. 'Please.'

Yet another unnecessary obstacle for me to overcome. I'm growing very tired of them.

Chapter Thirty-seven

London, 20th November 1925

'Congratulations, Sophie. Getting your 'A' licence is quite an achievement.'

Sophie pours tea from the pot into both of their cups. She's been so looking forward to this interview with Stella Wolfe Murray. Now the slight journalist, ten years her senior, regards her with earnest brown eyes. It is her first time meeting Stella but Sophie has a feeling that she is a woman after her own heart, striking a path in a man's world. And with such kind eyes, Sophie can't help her emotions from pouring out of her.

'I suppose it is, Stella. But I have to tell you, I'm rather deflated.'

'Oh? May I?' Stella gestures with her pencil and notebook.

'Yes, of course. I thought we would be having a lovely chat about the prospects for women pilots but I'm afraid the wind was taken out of my sails yesterday, in no uncertain terms. I'm not sure how to even proceed from here.'

Stella nods at her, maintaining an encouraging silence.

Sophie straightens her spine. 'Did you know that there is a ban on women pilots flying commercially?'

'No, I can't say I did. Why on earth would that be?'

'Why indeed! Apparently, the Commission for Air Navigation made the decision last year but it's only now come to light. Poor Madame Bolland in France is fighting to retain her licence. And here I was presuming it would be the next obvious step for me. Otherwise, how can I ever earn a living from flying?'

Sophie slumps back into her chair.

Stella regards her, chewing the inside of her cheek. 'I only have one weapon in my arsenal, Sophie. But I'm happy to lend it to your cause if it's any good.'

'Thank you, Stella. Will it do any good, do you think?'

Stella nods slowly. 'It's worth trying. And you don't strike me as a girl who goes down without a fight.'

Sophie gives her a small smile. A fight. *Another one*. Yes, OK, if she must.

'Tell me what you know,' Stella says, 'and I'll put together a good strong piece about the unfairness of this situation.'

Two days later Sophie is striding across the aerodrome at Stag Lane, the *Leeds Mercury* with Stella's article pinned under her arm. Harold Perrin, the club secretary, is walking towards her. Just the man she was hoping to see.

'Harold!'

'Hello, Sophie. Heading up?'

She thrusts the newspaper towards him. 'Read this.'

He removes his pipe from between his lips and glances briefly at the article headed '**Enthusiastic Airwoman**'.

'Oh yes. A damn shame.'

'It is!' She's waiting for him to say more but he looks as though he is going to just continue on his way.

'Harold! We can't allow this.'

He scoffs. 'I'm afraid it's not up to us.'

'So you are OK with all your woman pilots being made obsolete?'

'That's rather harsh, Sophie. You still have options.'

'Very few, Harold. What would you suggest? Since my first flight I've been dedicated to working towards my commercial 'B' licence and now you're telling me it's not going to happen?'

'It's not my decision, Sophie. I have no say in the matter. But, yes, I suppose there's little point in continuing with that for now.' He sighs. 'Follow me.'

He turns away from her and she chases after him into the little hut that serves as his office. He rummages in a drawer, produces a page and hands it to her.

'Take a look at Resolution 146. I think that puts an end to any argument.'

He sits down behind the desk and she reads, the paper shaking in her hands.

'Candidates must be of the male sex, must have complete use of his four limbs, must not be completely deprived of the use of either eye, must be free from any active, or latent, acute or chronic, medical or surgical disability or infection.'

She places the paper on the table and smooths it out. Then runs her finger along the words again.

'This rules out every woman. So that is a disability? Her sex?'

'I believe that is what they are implying.'

'On what grounds?'

'Read the next one.'

She scans the paper again. Resolution 147. She reads it twice, trying to make sense of its references to the concerns of a medical subcommittee.

'What does it mean?'

'There are concerns that women may not be suitable to flying at certain times, that their, *uh*, nervous reactions may be affected, that at certain times …'

She stares at this man spluttering and stammering in front of her. Then the penny drops. *Menstruation*. That is the problem. They don't trust women to fly at that time of the month. She chews on her bottom lip.

'Did they conduct a study? Do they have proof of this?' she asks.

Harold raises his hands. 'I don't know. You'll have to ask them that yourself. Sophie, I know this is a shock. But you still have options.'

'Do I? I suppose I can do some more stunt-flying, wing-walking, keep taking people up for joy-rides, for pennies! This is meant to be my career, Harold. That daredevil carry-on does nothing for aviation and you know it. Far better to show people that flying is a sensible activity, not some circus act.'

She scrunches up the paper and flings it across the table then strides out. She will do as he suggested. She will ask them herself.

Leighton Close,
Edgeware,
London
21st November 1925

Dear Sir,

During the summer of this year I became much interested in the advance of Civil Aviation, and decided to devote myself to it. I decided to learn flying, and discovered in doing so that I possessed a natural ability for aviation.

I have found that the majority of women pilots have won their way to recognition by daring feats, and 'stunts' which, although very indicative of the ability of the ladies in question, are not of real practical value. I therefore decided that the best procedure would be to fit myself for a 'B' licence, and, if possible, show that a woman could do a commercial pilot's work.

My first difficulty presented itself in the resolutions No's 146 and 147 of the 6th sitting of the Commission in which women are debarred from this profession. I see, however, in No. 147 that the Medical Sub-Commission was directed to continue its study of the matter, and it is on this account that I write to you.

I realise that the decisions of the Commission were made with most laudable intentions, but the very lack of suitable material in the shape of women pilots to examine and test means that the Medical Sub-Commission did not have before them all the data.

I would be intensely grateful if you would put me in touch with the President of the Medical Sub-Commission personally, or lay my views before him. I hold the Government degree in physiology, have worked for years among women and girls, as I started the Woman's Amateur Athletic Association of Great Britain and have been myself a member of every International Women's team since then.

In addition I am a member of the Medical Sub-Commission of the last Olympic Congress, being the only woman to attend and give evidence at Prague, in June 1925, on the question of the advisability of women's entry into the world of athletics which I am delighted to say has progressed favourably.

I appreciate that the decisions arrived at by your Sub-Commission were due to the very great differences that occur in the nervous and mental systems of some women at certain periods.

Having dealt for some years with hundreds of girls and women of all ages and nationalities, I have seen that when a woman is sufficiently fine and healthy to enter the first class of athletes her periods of nervous difference are imperceptible, even to the acute measurements of such an instrument as the Reid indicator, which is accepted by our Air Ministry for measurements of the nervous reactions of intending pilots.

I would like to offer myself as material for any set of experiments that the Medical Commission would care for me to undergo.

I will be very grateful if you will let me know as soon as possible your own views on this subject and any other move I might make to forward the matter before it again comes up under the deliberations of the Medical Sub-Commission.

Yours truly,
Sophie Eliott-Lynn
Associate of the Royal College of Science

Chapter Thirty-eight

Cairo, 8th April, 1928

To his credit, Cuppy gives me a wide berth for the rest of the day and the evening. I stay in my room, smoking, pacing. By nightfall I am no nearer a solution and have returned to my earlier fantasy of breaking the lock on the hangar and absconding.

I change into my nightclothes and lie in bed, not sleeping. I mull over Lord Lloyd's comment about writing letters. Something in his tone tells me my appeals this time will fall on deaf ears. But I will try anyway.

I rise early the next morning and fortify myself with a decent breakfast. Cuppy joins me. He bears the same sheepish look as yesterday so I put my fork and knife down and light a cigarette.

'More news?'

He nods and slides a bundle of newspapers over to me.

The headline, although small, above a single paragraph, jumps off the page at me. '**Women Fliers Lose.**' My blood rises to my face as I scan the article.

'Oh no!'

Mary has crashed. Outside of Tabora. Her plane is wrecked but she is uninjured. Thank God! I forget for a moment my jealous thoughts of her beating me to the finish. Will she be able to go on? Or is that the end of her adventure?

I put the paper aside and pick up another.

'Rival Women Fliers Fail.'

It's an assault, half fact, half opinion. It says I've been halted by authorities and rightly so. Mary is lucky to have escaped unhurt. The phrases leap at me. '**Doomed to failure**.' The words are gleeful. These journalists, these men, are delighting in our mishaps. Women must be prevented from doing solo flights over dangerous territories, according to another article. I read it, fling it down, pick up another. It tells me I might have the skills, I just might, but I lack the experience required to cross a body of water. I have only crossed a vast, dark continent, but that counts for little or nothing. Furthermore my stunts offer nothing useful and make people nervous of flying.

The decision is now with the Air Ministry.

'Right,' I say, standing. 'Thank you for that. Now, if you'll excuse me, I must make contact with the Air Ministry.'

I march to the post office and compose a volley of telegrams. I dispatch them to everyone I can think of with any influence, including Sir James. Surely someone will intervene on my behalf? Surely someone can see the value of what I am doing?

I return to my room and wait for news. Tennis and swims and even food are not enough to tempt me out of my funk. The only thing that can do that is permission to fly. My mood is further soured by the hot cramp arrival of my menses. The thing that is supposed to affect my ability to perform as a pilot. I lie in bed, holding my stomach, wishing hot piercing cramps on everyone who stands in my way.

I approach breakfast with trepidation. This one meal seems to be the locus of bad news. I have almost completed it safely when a telegram arrives on a silver tray. It is from the Air Ministry.

Permission has been denied. A dangerous precedent would be set. Cannot be allowed.

I must find an escort. That is the only solution left to me. The dance at the Residency. That might be a good place to start.

The large ballroom heaves with the great and the good of Cairo. They are framed artistically by roof-high arches enveloping the dance floor and bathed in the shimmer of glittering chandeliers. I strain my neck to see over the bodies. Where is Lord Lloyd? I have no intention of letting him off the hook so easily regarding my predicament. Surely the High Commissioner has some clout, some ability to influence the RAF?

I spy him, leading his wife through the throng. I elbow and squeeze until I reach him.

'Lord Lloyd.'

'Ah, Lady Heath.' His tone is warm but there is no denying the glimmer of disappointment that crosses his face. He doesn't want to get into an argument with me, I presume. Not here, not now. I realise there's nothing to be gained from that.

'I just wanted to thank you again for inviting me. What an incredible evening!'

His features relax. 'I hope you will enjoy it. Have you seen the programme? There's to be twenty-five dances. No doubt you'll be on the floor for them all.'

'I've reserved the first for Captain MacLean. He was good enough to escort me this evening and he has been so kind since I arrived in Cairo. And haven't been able to leave.'

He raises his eyebrows so I backtrack.

'I couldn't help myself, Lord Lloyd!' I laugh gaily and pluck a glass of champagne from a passing tray. I raise it in salute and turn back into the crowd.

Time to find Cuppy and ferret out some potential escorts.

By dance number sixteen I am bereft. Not one dance partner has offered any hope of being able to chaperone me across the Mediterranean. I hate having to even ask. It is humiliating.

My dance partner, an RAF officer whose name evades me, is guiding me through a frustratingly slow waltz.

'Tell me again what you need.'

For the sixteenth time that evening I repeat my story.

'And one of their stupid reasons is that Malta is apparently difficult to find from the air. Who said I have to go to Malta? And am I to get no credit at all for having flown the length of a continent, picking out aerodromes from the sky that are no more than a pinprick in a vast wilderness?'

'Lady Heath ... *Lady Heath!*'

I haven't answered him. He must think me rude, or deaf.

'Yes?'

'Would you mind loosening your grip?'

I redden and release him from my clutch. He rubs at his left hand then takes me again to circle pointlessly around the floor. I sigh.

'Where are you heading for when you get across?'

'Sicily.'

'Then why don't you ask the French or the Italians for an escort?'

I stop. Oblivious to the sea of dancers meandering around me.

'Do you think I could?'

'They could only say no. It's worth a try.'

'Yes. It is. Could you take me now?'

'To where?'

'To send a telegram.'

He consults with his watch. 'It's very late. I doubt you'll find anyone there to send it.'

I pull at his arm. 'It's worth a try.'

He's a good sport. Abandoning his wife without even a word, he loads me into his car and drives me to the post office.

'I met a man in Mwanza.'

'That's how all the best stories start,' he says.

I shriek, giddy now. 'He was an Italian merchant. A good friend of Mussolini's. He told me to make contact with Mussolini, if I needed.'

'He must have had a premonition.'

At the telegraph office we find two clerks, ready to be of assistance. They help me to convey my message in Italian. I address it simply to **'Mussolini, Italy'**. That should reach him.

'We had Lady Bailey here too, sending many, many messages,' one clerk says. He seems to enjoy the drama of our situation. 'If there is an answer we will bring it to your hotel, post haste.'

I tip them generously. The RAF and Air Ministry should congratulate themselves on creating much business for the Telegraph Office, I think.

My new friend and I race back to the Residency. It's in complete darkness, the ball concluded, and two very angry attendees are standing on the path outside, wondering where we are. I apologise profusely to my friend's wife. How unnerving for her husband to disappear from a formal dance with another woman and leave her high and dry!

Cuppy is angry because he is responsible for keeping me out of trouble.

I coax them all back to my hotel and they are won over by my tale of international nocturnal cabling. We part with kisses and promises to let them know if I have any success.

I rise late, exhausted by the high drama. At the end of my second coffee a tray appears.

Bearing a telegram.

It says simply: '**Have put a seaplane at your disposal. Mussolini**.'

What a marvellous gentleman!

I request a car to take me to the aerodrome. It's time to get everything in order and get out of here. I have enjoyed myself despite the circumstances but I can never swallow being kept in one place against my wishes. I am a bird and I must be allowed to fly.

'Sophie,' Cuppy comes across to meet me as I exit the motorcar, 'I was about to come over to your hotel. I have some news.'

'So do I.'

'The ministry is granting permission.'

'I don't need it anymore.'

'But you're free to go, at your own risk.'

'They're willing to let me kill myself, you mean? That's good of them. But, Cuppy. I don't need it. I've arranged my own escort.'

'Anyone I know?'

'Mussolini.'

'Pardon?'

'Mussolini.'

'The Prime Minister of Italy is going to escort you?'

'Don't be silly. Not him personally. Of course not. But he is arranging for me to have an escort. He's putting a seaplane at my disposal.'

'How did this come about?'

'I sent him a telegram. We have a mutual friend so he was happy to oblige. Now would you be so kind as to tell the Air Ministry that I have no further need of their help. I've made my own arrangements. Thank you.'

I find a man to unlock the hangar. Cuppy has to work hard to convince him that I have been granted permission and he insists on making a phone call to confirm it. Finally, I am inside. I arrange all of my tools for the usual routine check and turn my back to Cuppy now as I begin to tighten the nuts and bolts. I can sense him still there. I ignore him for as long as I can tolerate it. He has been a good friend to me but does he not understand that now I need to focus on leaving? And quickly, before something else prevents me from doing so. Eventually I turn to face him.

'What is it?'

'I'm surprised, that's all. I thought you had some principles.'

It shakes me. The use of the past tense. As though I am without principles now in his mind.

'Has that changed?'

'Do you know the kind of man Mussolini is?'

'Yes. From what I've heard he is a good leader and from what I know of him now, an obliging man.'

'From what I've heard he doesn't tolerate the rights of workers or women.'

I sigh. 'It's just a seaplane, Cuppy. Not a seat in his government.'

'Once you've got what you wanted then. That's fine.'

He turns and leaves the hangar, leaving me with the empty space where his accusation lingers. Is he right to point the finger? Should I be more choosy who I take help from? No! Maybe if the authorities here hadn't made all of this so damn difficult I wouldn't have to. I seethe. Who does he think he is, standing in judgement over me? He barely knows me. He doesn't know that I flew newspapers all over England during the General Strike of '26. With a broken arm! Or that I did a flyover for the women's march in London that July. How could he know? But I'm disappointed that he doesn't have a sense of me. Of who I am. I bang my wrench on the work table. Is this what it means to be alone? To never have anyone to truly understand me.

I think of Mary. My friend. Does she know me?

An officer is passing through the hangar and I call to him.

'Any news of Lady Bailey?'

'She's due to set off again. Sir Bailey is arranging a new plane for her.'

How nice, I think, for Mary to have someone like that in her corner. Someone who understands, who doesn't tell her to come home now, it's over. No. He is making sure she has a plane, a brand new plane, to replace the one she wrecked so that she can continue.

I have only myself.

The day passes with maintenance. The plane needed more than I realised. And I am being extra-cautious, conscious of the sea crossing that lies ahead. I return to my hotel smeared with engine oil and caked with sweat. It's a pleasant, work-induced tiredness that pleases me much more than late nights at silly dances.

A telegram has been slipped under my door.

I never again want to see another telegram. I read it, afraid of the news it might bring.

Mussolini has changed his mind?

My licence has been revoked?

But, no. It tells me the Bentleys are due to return to Cairo and want to cross over to Europe with me. I am loath to have them delay me again. It means I can't leave tomorrow if I am to wait for their arrival. But maybe a Plan B is a good idea. The way my luck has been lately it might be for the best.

I get between the pristine white sheets without cleaning off the grease and grime of my day's efforts. I will decide in the morning.

I am suspended in a state of readiness and caution. I'm keen to go but sense tells me to wait for the Bentleys. I settle it by giving them two days to get here.

'**I will leave Cairo April 15th. Happy to travel together if you are ready then. Otherwise will proceed alone**.'

That puts it to rest for now. I make another trip to the bazaar, this time alone, and gather a few trinkets. In a short while I will be gone from Africa, back in Europe. It will be nice to have some mementoes.

Cuppy seems to have abandoned me. That's fine, I don't need him. Now that I think of my time here I am irritated that I was so easily distracted by his entertainment. I feel that I have been manipulated by him, that he was sent to keep me busy and not kick up a fuss about my impounded plane.

Chapter Thirty-nine

Cairo, 15th April, 1928

I am at the aerodrome early. The Bentleys have failed to appear so true to my word I push on. I wheel my baby out of the hangar.

'I'm sorry,' I soothe it. 'You've been kept locked up in that stuffy shed. Time to set you free.'

It's daft I know to be speaking to my airplane. But my muscles relax and my jaw loosens. I am speaking to myself too.

'There,' I say as I unfold the wings.

A few final checks before I spin the propeller and climb into the cockpit.

'Ready?' I press the ignition button and listen. Yes. My baby is ready and so am I.

Without a backward glance at my Egyptian prison I accelerate down the runway. I pull back and start to lift, laughing and whooping.

Never again. Never again. Never again will I be stopped.

Sunlight opens up the sky ahead of me as I turn my nose to head for the north-west coast of Egypt. I am attentive to my plane, listening for sounds, feeling the smoothness of the engine under my hands. All is well and I feel I could fly for months without stopping. It's a shame that I ever have to go to ground.

Beneath me I see black dots. I drop down to look closer. Bedouin tents. Soon after, I fly over Mersa Matruh, where Cleopatra had her country villa. Palaces or the encampment? Which would I choose? Right now, the freedom of the nomads calls to me more than any gilded mansion.

Thick white clouds hide the coast as I approach, tantalising me with seductive glimpses of the blue Mediterranean.

Despite flying for six and a half hours non-stop, I am sad to see Sollum on the border between Egypt and Italian Libya as it means it is time for me to land. I circle the cliff behind the town where the aerodrome is, waiting for someone to notice me and light the fire so that I can see the direction of the wind.

Eventually they do and I guide my baby down. We are tossed about by the worst surface I have yet encountered. I clamber out, sure that my plane has been damaged. How could it not be? The runway is comprised of boulders set in loose sand.

I am lying on the ground, checking the undercarriage when a small group of army officers arrives.

This rocky runway and this tragic band is all Sollum has to offer. That's good. I won't be tempted to delay.

'Welcome to Sollum!'

I clamber out from under the plane, wiping the dust from my overalls.

'Thank you. I had rather hoped to find a runway.'

The English officer who greeted me looks confused.

'This is ...'

I laugh. 'My attempt at humour. But I'm rather shocked at the state of the surface. Have many planes made it in and out in one piece?'

He contemplates his boots for a moment then looks me in the eye. 'Colonel Green is in charge here but I'm afraid he is away at present. You're welcome to stay in the Rest House and if you have complaints you may address them to him when he returns.'

The officer turns on his heel and marches off. I roll my eyes. So tetchy! He could hardly disagree with my assessment of the place. Basic doesn't begin to describe it.

A car arrives from the Rest House to take me to lunch. I am famished and devour an Egyptian dish, a vegetable resembling a cucumber stuffed with all sorts of delicious food. It improves my humour and I'm happier again when I ride back to the aerodrome on an army horse to finish my routine maintenance.

Tired in the best way from good hard work, I return at nightfall.

'Lady Heath. I believe you have a matter to raise with me.'

A neat man in uniform is leaning against the doorframe of the Mess where I had my lunch.

'You must be Colonel Green. Yes, I do actually.'

I offer him my hand. It is caked with dust and grease.

'Would you like to wash up and we can discuss it over dinner?'

I blush, feeling like a grubby child who's been tumbling about in the mud. My hackles are up and I'm wondering if Colonel Green is going to be unpleasant company for the evening. Combative, defensive.

A table has been set for two and he pulls out my chair for me and pours a glass of wine.

'Now,' he says, 'your complaint.'

I take a sip and fold my hands in front of me on the table. 'I'll state it simply, Colonel Green, as I like to. The surface of the runway is appalling. It's only a matter of time before a machine is badly damaged. And really the Air Force has no business recommending it to pilots if they're not going to prepare a suitable landing place. I would have been better off continuing on to my next stop.'

He looks down and traces the path of a tiny dark bug that is making its way across the tablecloth.

'Yes. And where is your next stop?'

'Most likely Benghazi. Conditions permitting.'

'The aerodrome there is very well maintained by the Italians, I believe. But then, we are just a frontier post. Our attentions have been focused more on troubles on the border here. But I will pass your message on to my superiors.'

Dishes start to arrive and I feel like an ungrateful guest. Here I am, being fed and watered and housed for the night and all I can do is gripe. I fear my difficulties in Cairo have made me cranky. I don't want to be remembered as a sullen whiner.

I take another sip of my wine and coax a smile onto my face.

'Tell me, Colonel Green, what is life like here at the frontier? Is it very difficult?'

He launches into a long description of the warfare happening across the border between the Italians and the Senussi Arabs they are trying to put down in their efforts to gain control of Libya.

'They're bloodthirsty,' he pronounces.

The wine is making me sleepy and I have been so enthralled by his stories that I have almost forgotten where I am.

'The Italians?'

'Well, yes,' he guffaws. 'But the Arabs more so. They will fight to the end, the bitter end. Maybe it's for the best if they all end up all dead. That will be the end of the matter.'

There is a silence and into it creeps a terrible thought. Is this what the officials back in Cairo are saying about me right now? Are they sitting around a dinner table, guffawing and telling stories about how persistent I am? How in the end they had to let me have my way? And if I end up dead, at the bottom of the Mediterranean Sea, then so be it? Good riddance.

A shudder runs through me. I stand.

'Thank you, Colonel Green. You've been most entertaining company. But I'm afraid exhaustion has won out.'

He stands, looking a little taken aback by my sudden change of tone.

'Of course. I hope you rest well. And don't worry. We'll have you on your way tomorrow without difficulty.'

I don't bother with lights when I get to my room, undressing in the dark and sliding between the cool sheets. I feel a sense of urgency. I need to sleep and get up early and get going and put this damn sea behind me as soon as possible.

Of course, I dream of it. How could I not? I am in the sky and in the water, all at the same time. I toss and turn in my bed and among the clouds and through the waves. The blue of the sky outside my cockpit becomes the blue water of the sea. The tufts of air knocking me about and making me drop down to a calmer altitude are the push and pull of the current making me dive under. Deeper to where the water is still. And now I am under it turning and twisting, trying to find my way out. There is a light in the distance but no matter how I move my arms and kick my legs I can get no closer. I kick out furiously, feeling rock wall all around me and I understand that this is the Virgin Rock in Ballybunion. I kick hard once and now I am falling through, crashing down and bringing a roof in with me. I land and the thump wakes me.

I am in Sollum. I have been kicking the footboard and my heels are sore. The sheets are twisted and halfway to the floor. I am covered in sweat.

I rise and turn on a light, pick up the sheets. What a terrible image! I cannot tell if the dream was a memory of my near drowning or a premonition. I check the time. It's only three o'clock. I straighten out the bed. I need to get more sleep. But I see now a line of little ants, like our friend from dinnertime, tracing a route across the bedsheets. I brush at them but there are more and more and eventually I concede.

'Have the bed,' I tell them.

I take up position in an armchair by the window and watch the sky until there is a little brightening. At half past five I let myself out of the Rest House and make my way to the aerodrome, happy to leave Sollum behind me.

I taxi the Avian slowly, cursing at the bumps and knocks it is receiving from this horrendous surface. My kind feelings towards my hosts have vanished and I am composing an angry letter to the Air Force as I go. My wheels stick, something is blocking them, more rocks. I push forward, more power to get the wheels over them. They do, with a loud bump, but as I pick up speed the bumping follows me.

Something is wrong.

I twist in my seat to see what the problem is and my heart sinks. There, trailing behind me like a broken limb are the remains of my mangled tail skid. I halt the machine and climb down.

Damn! The whole rear quarter is damaged. Just from taxiing. I had less damage from my unconscious landing in Matabeleland. I pull off my helmet and fling it to the ground. At first examination I can see that four longerons are completely ruined. The whole back of the plane will need to be rebuilt.

The sound of a motorcar makes me turn. Colonel Green is arriving, to see me off no doubt but he will get more than he bargained for.

'*Colonel!*' I shout, marching towards his car. '*Your runway has destroyed my plane! This is unacceptable!*'

He stands up in the battered screen-less Ford. It's not only planes that fare badly here.

'Is there a lot of damage?'

'Enough that I will have to rebuild a whole section. And where in this godforsaken backwater am I to get materials?'

'Get in.'

I am torn between my wounded machine and his order.

'Get in,' he says again. 'I'll take you to the Italians.'

I perch my hands on my hips. 'What will they do for me?'

'They'll be able to help. They fly planes all over this area.'

I climb in and maintain a sulky silence all the way. It is the only option anyway as Colonel Green rattles the Ford across the desert at an insane speed, hurtling over rocks and ridges and bushes and potholes as though it was a tank. The man has no respect for vehicles. No wonder his aerodrome is in such bad condition.

We pull into a small whitewashed fortress, passing a sign that reads Amsiate. There is no sign of life.

Colonel Green beeps. 'This will get them up. They're on Italian time here so they're an hour behind.'

I am mortified at our rudeness. Turning up unannounced and getting them all out of bed by hooting the horn. So vulgar.

An officer leads us into the mess and presents us with liqueurs while we wait for his commanding officer.

I have never drunk alcohol before my breakfast. But with the way my luck is going I decide it might perk me up so I throw it back. The glasses are quickly refilled and my humour is much improved by the time the C.O. appears.

'Matoni,' he introduces himself, kissing the back of my hand.

Yes, I think I like these Italians.

Colonel Green brings him up to speed, leaving out the detail that my plane was perfectly intact arriving to Sollum and would still be if it weren't for the rock-strewn runway.

Matoni gestures for more drinks to be brought and disappears for an hour. When he returns my limbs have softened to butter. I like Italians, I am sure of it now, and I like their morning liqueurs.

A dark-eyed man has returned with him.

'Edouard D'Alia,' Matoni announces. 'The best air mechanic in Italy.'

I am so confused. How did he get to Italy and back so quickly?

'Where was he?' I manage to slide off a thick tongue.

'Another base, forty-five miles from here.'

I giggle, amused at my own silliness. But I must pull myself together.

We return to Sollum but this time I travel with the Italians in a hostile-looking car with mounted machine guns. I close my eyes and try to figure out if I am still in my dream.

But no, there is my poor plane.

D'Alia requests a trestle so that he can get at the underside of the Avian. The Italians are still my favourites but it must be said that Colonel Green rallies his men. The trestle is erected, a carpenter is loaned to D'Alia and materials are sourced. Mostly soap boxes, scraps and empty tins but this little dark-eyed man fashions what he needs from them.

I hover about, being as helpful as I can. I avoid despair by raging. I hold nothing back on my opinion of the authorities that allowed this aerodrome to descend to this condition or the authorities that recommend this as a stop. And when I think of the fact that these are the same authorities that tried to prevent my progress for fear of my safety my blood boils.

I may have overdone my criticism, as on the second day stuck in Sollum a shamefaced Colonel Green approaches me.

'I've wired headquarters in Cairo,' he tells me. 'I've told them about your plane and attributed fault to this.' He gestures at the runway.

I don't know what to say. I manage a curt 'Thank you' but all I can imagine is the men in Cairo, howling with laughter at the fact that I only made it this far before coming a cropper again.

Chapter Forty

London, 18th March 1926

The room is large and very cold. Bright lights glare and she feels goosebumps breaking out on her skin. She is down to her slip and underwear. She breathes deeply to stop herself from shivering. She would hate for them to think she was afraid. She places her hands on the metal rim of her chair and squeezes. She must present as strong and unwavering. Indestructible. But feminine and inoffensive. It is a fine line but she has walked it before.

They confer in lowered voices then the Chief Examiner clears his throat and peers at her over the rim of his glasses.

'Mrs Eliott-Lynn, we are conscious of the cold this morning so we will conduct the physical examination first then allow you a chance to dress before with the interview.'

He smiles as though he is her benefactor and she returns it with as much warmth as she can muster.

She is led to a corner of the room with a blue examination couch and other medical equipment. She is weighed and her height is measured.

'Please bend over and touch your toes, Mrs Eliott-Lynn.'

She could do a hundred of these if they needed her to.

'Raise your arms above your head.'

Another man in a white coat circles, making marks on his paper.

'Thank you. Any wounds? Surgeries?'

'No.'

'You served with the WAAC?'

'Yes, France and Belgium, nineteen seventeen to nineteen.'

'You must have had a quiet war.'

She bites her lip. She wants to say that she was lucky enough and skilful enough to avoid injury. A bright light is shone into each of her eyes. She is instructed to read a letter chart and she makes it almost to the end. She knows her eyesight is good, perfect in fact, but she's starting to worry now. What if she fails over something as simple as that? She starts to shake again and squeezes her knees together to stop it.

The chief examiner bangs a tuning fork on his elbow and places it in the centre of her forehead.

'Where do you hear the tone?' he asks.

'Both ears.'

He retreats from her, six feet. 'In a moment I will say a number. Please cover your left ear and repeat the number when you hear it.'

She puts her hand over her ear and waits.

'Forty-seven.'

She repeats it back to him.

'Now the right ear.'

She hears him say, thirty-nine. Or was it thirty-five. She's not so sure. Can she ask him to repeat it? No, that might call her hearing into question. She thinks it was thirty-nine. She's almost certain.

'Thirty-nine?'

He doesn't respond.

She hopes all those years of silence and listening intently to hear what was being whispered behind closed doors in Newcastle West have stood to her, sharpened her hearing.

'Open your mouth wide, please.'

Her tongue is flattened by a depressor then a light is shone down her throat then up her nose. Another examiner approaches with a stethoscope.

Its cold metal disk pressed against her skin is oddly reassuring. She focuses her attention on the sensation.

'Breathe in. And out.'

More writing on paper.

'Please stand on your left leg. Arms out. Eyes closed.'

She is trying not to giggle but she wonders how this looks. A barely clad women imitating a flamingo surrounded by earnest men in white coats taking notes. She must look like an asylum inmate. An acid taste comes up her throat.

'Now the right leg.'

She performs the action. Are they making fun of her? Is it all a charade to give the impression of a serious test? Do they intend to deny her the licence even after she's jumped through their hoops?

'Mrs Eliott-Lynn!'

She jumps and opens her eyes. She didn't hear what was just said. She has to be careful not to let her thoughts run away with her.

'Please take a seat.'

An examiner taps her knee with his little hammer. Her leg shoots out obediently. A cuff is slipped up her arm and inflated. She breathes deeply, hoping she hasn't driven her blood pressure up with her silly mental rambling. She focuses on this sensation now, the pressure building until it feels like her arm could burst then the sudden, welcome release. She wishes her whole body could be squeezed in a cuff like that then let go. A finger is on her pulse now, silent enumeration of her heartbeat.

'Could you stand?'

She stands.

'Please run on the spot for one minute.'

She starts to jog, feeling foolish again, going nowhere despite being the only moving part of this weird tableau. She focuses on a water stain where the ceiling meets the wall.

'Please sit.'

Her heart rate is measured again. She is confident it barely stirred. She could run for hours like that without feeling winded.

'On the table before you, Mrs Eliott-Lynn, is a board on which is a rod. Will you please stand now, lift the board to shoulder height and replace it on the table without disturbing the rod.'

She stands and takes a long slow breath. She looks at her hands. There is no sign of a tremor. Why should there be? There never is. But now that she knows they are about to test it, she fears she can see a slight movement. She lifts the board, the rod moves. She freezes and it stills. Fluidly but not rapidly, she lifts it then lowers it, holding her breath until it is safely returned to the table. She rolls her shoulders and twists her neck left and right.

'In a moment we will begin the Reid reaction test. Before that, may I ask if the dates you supplied previously are accurate still?'

The dates? She is confused. Why did she provide dates?

Her silence runs on.

'Your monthly cycle, Mrs Eliott-Lynn. It is of great import for today's investigation.'

'Oh. Yes. Still accurate.' Her cheeks burn.

'Then according to those dates your menstruation has begun?'

No, she suddenly realises, it hasn't. She doesn't track these things as closely as these men apparently do. But what should she tell him? A lie? She'd better not.

'It has not.' She does her best to answer in a clear voice, chin up.

'Oh!'

The examiner glances at the others and there is some quick conferring. Has all of this been a waste of time?

'But,' she interrupts, 'the information I have provided is accurate to the day, not the hour or the minute. That is not possible.'

The chief examiner frowns.

'I expect it to begin today, as predicted. It just hasn't, as yet.'

This is by far the longest conversation she has ever had on this subject and she is keen for it to end. There is a hot, dull ache in her womb – proof is on the way should they demand it.

Again, they confer.

'Very well. There is some evidence that the three days before and after menstruation are of equal import in these matters so we will proceed.'

She is led to the other side of the room where she recognises the Reid Reaction Apparatus. She suppresses a smile. She knows this is the part of the test where they will test her flying reactions and she will pass with flying colours.

The apparatus is a strange-looking device, almost like a tall coffin. The end of it is taken up with a recording device: a roll of paper and a stylographic pen. The top end is a replica cockpit. She takes her seat inside. There are sets of vertical lights embedded to the left and right and in front of a vertical set and a horizontal set.

She places her feet on the rudder bar, her hand on the joystick and prepares for her imaginary flight.

'Move the joystick to the extreme right.'

She complies, waits for the lights and as soon as they illuminate, even before the order is given, she moves the joystick back to neutral. It is like a game. The lights, when operated by the instructor turn red and it is her job to extinguish them by getting the aircraft back into a neutral flying position. She repeats this exercise with the joystick ten times on each side. Then it is the same for the rudder bar. And finally the vertical lights in front are illuminated and extinguished by moving the joystick forwards and back. In all it takes no more than ten minutes and she enjoys it so much she almost forgets where she is.

She is helped out of the cockpit and has to stop herself from glancing at the report, confident it will achieve the A grade.

'The final part of the physical exam now, Mrs Eliott-Lynn. If you would please remove your undergarments and lie on the examination couch.'

The hairs on her arms stand up.

'Excuse me?'

'This is the final hurdle, so to speak, for the physical exam anyway. And I must say you have impressed us.'

There is a hum of consensus. Are they all going to attend this element of the test?

She walks as though in a dream to the couch. One of the examiners pulls across a light curtain. She stoops, pulls her knickers down, steps out of them, folds them neatly and looks around. There is nowhere to put them. She holds them in her fist and lies on the couch. It is cold beneath the light material of her slip and she starts to shiver again.

Two men appear around the curtain. The chief examiner and another who has donned a pair of surgical gloves. He moves up along the side of the bed until he is parallel with her outstretched left arm.

'My colleague will perform a brief examination of the abdomen and internal organs.'

The doctor starts to press hard on her stomach. She holds her breath.

'Please breathe normally, Mrs Eliott-Lynn.'

She release the breath in one long controlled exhalation, annoyed that he noticed.

'Any noted abnormalities in the breasts?'

Is he asking me? There is silence so she answers.

'No.'

She gasps as the doctor presses on her breasts and nipples, prodding with his fingers as though kneading dough. She squeezes her knickers tightly in her fist.

'Is there any chance of pregnancy?'

She is confused. Is he asking is she pregnant now? Or if there is a chance in the future?

'I'm not pregnant and I don't expect to be.'

There is another silence. She seems to have surprised them.

'You don't want children? Is your husband of the same mind?'

Her husband. She hasn't thought of him in a long while.

'We are estranged.'

'*Ah.*'

She thinks of John, waiting in their warm bed. He might want children. It's not something they've discussed. Neither of them have done anything to prevent it. But it hasn't come about.

The doctor with the prodding fingers speaks now. 'I will perform a brief, standard pelvic examination now, Mrs Eliott-Lynn.'

He moves to the end of the couch and puts his hands on her knees.

No!

She clamps them shut.

'Just relax.'

No!

Her knees remain tightly shut.

The chief examiner sighs loudly. He moves along the side of the couch until he is at her shoulder.

'Mrs Eliott-Lynn. You presented yourself voluntarily, did you not, in order to be tested for the benefit of yourself and other women pilots?'

She nods, squeezes her eyes shut. He is right. She must be brave.

'And you understand, do you not, that in order for us to be reassured we must ascertain that you are not pregnant.'

'I'm not. I already told you.'

'You wouldn't be the first woman to be mistaken. It would mean immediate disqualification, of course. And we must ensure that the pelvis and organs within contain no deformities that may limit the range of motion.'

She nods. The doctor presses with his hands and she wills her knees to open. There is a cold sensation of something metal. A sound of something metal being turned. She opens her eyes a slit and wishes she hadn't as the doctor is no longer visible between her legs and that must mean he is at eye level with her most private parts. He puts a gloved finger, then two inside her and presses with his other hand on her abdomen. Presses down until she feels that he may push her through the couch. The sensation is overwhelming, painful. She feels invaded and wriggles her hips. The hand on her abdomen clamps down.

'*Don't move!*' he barks.

She freezes. There is some more rummaging then he is out. She hears the snap of the gloves and the metal implement is removed.

The chief examiner speaks. 'Very good! Please take some time to dress and use the facilities, Mrs Eliott-Lynn, and we will reconvene in fifteen minutes for the interview.'

They leave and she turns her face to the couch, letting the coolness of it calm her burning cheeks.

Thankfully the room is empty when she draws the curtain back. Internal exam followed by a tea-break, she presumes. She wanders down the hall and finds a bathroom.

Nearly there, Sophie, she tells herself. *The worst of it is behind you.*

She shuts her eyes and imagine herself in the cockpit of a full passenger plane. She is a professional pilot earning her living and this will all have been worth it.

She sits before the men, fully dressed, with a cup of sweetened tea going cold before her. She will not show need. She sits rod-straight and meets their eyes. She presumes the one who cannot meet her gaze is the one who performed the internal exam. She hope he feels shame. Her shame has turned to anger. How dare these men reduce her professional abilities to the mere functioning of her body! When has a uterus ever affected the flying of a plane? She is ready to demonstrate her extensive knowledge on how to fly, land and maintain her plane. She knows there is no question they can ask me that she will not be able to answer.

'Is there any history of madness or mental infirmity in your family, Mrs Eliott-Lynn?'

'I beg your pardon?'

Her tongue feels too big in her mouth and she is finding it difficult to swallow.

'Is there a difficulty, Mrs Eliott-Lynn?'

'I understood that this would be a test of my aviation knowledge.'

The examiner sits back in his chair and folds his hands across his stomach.

'I think you have proven yourself in that regard.' He leans forward, elbows on the table, his fingers templed at his lips. 'And family history is very relevant. We must be thorough.'

She can't allow him to think that he's hit a nerve.

She laughs. 'I just didn't expect it. To answer your first question. No. Absolutely not, no history of madness.' She laughs again. It sounds too loud. And her answer was too emphatic. *Breathe, Sophie.*

There is silence.

'What did your father do?'

Do they know? If they know then she is a liar in their eyes. Untrustworthy.

'What line of work was he in?'

She laughs again and now they look at her, confused. Of course they are. She's acting deranged.

'He was a farmer.'

She sees one of the men smirking. She can imagine what he's thinking. An Irish farmer. Peasant stock.

She clarifies her vowels. 'He was a gentleman farmer, with a very large country estate in the west of County Limerick.'

'I've never heard of the place,' the examiner remarks.

Good, she thinks. That's good.

'Is he living?' he asks.

'I'm afraid not.' She bows her head in an attitude of bereavement. They might take pity on her and move on from this line of questioning.

'How did he die?'

'Old age. Comfortable, at home, thank goodness.'

She says a silent prayer that he is as ignorant of the existence of the Central Criminal Lunatic Asylum in Dundrum as he is of County Limerick.

'And your mother?'

'Oh ...' She breathes out. 'That is a tragic tale. I'm afraid she passed in childbirth. I am an only child.'

They put the pieces together and now, good, she sees a hint of sympathy in the chief examiner's features.

'Do you suffer from nerves in any way? Bouts of depression? Anxious thoughts?'

Only now. She is quite anxious now.

'No, never. I have a very upbeat temperament.'

'Always? Is it never disrupted? By, say, the time of the month?'

What is their obsession with this? She is angry again now. They want to examine her mental state, not because they need to have knowledge of her family background but because she is a woman.

'Always. Except when I lose a few pounds on a horse.'

She aims for laughter but it falls flat.

'You gamble?'

'Rarely. Only when I have the chance to attend a meeting which is, at best, once or twice a year.'

'You consume alcohol?'

'Only occasionally. I like to follow the advice given by St Paul – to take a little wine for thy stomach's sake.'

She thinks of the glasses of gin she was downing until three in the morning. She's sure it's oozing from her pores as she speaks.

'Do you smoke?'

'Again, on occasion. Not regularly.'

She would give her left arm for a cigarette right now.

'You would say you are in good shape overall?'

'I'm sure my test results will prove that. I've been very active for many years in women's athletics. I believe very strongly in the importance of remaining fit. It benefits the body and the mind.'

There is more writing on paper then the men exchange glances. The chief examiner nods.

'Thank you, Mrs Eliott-Lynn. We are satisfied that is all we require from you for now. Thank you for your attendance today.'

She stands and discreetly wipes her hand on her skirt. She doesn't want them to notice the sweat. She shakes each of their hands in turn, thanking them profusely, even her invader.

'When will I hear?' She is giddy with relief that it is over and keen to know.

'We will be in touch.'

She turns to leave but just as she reaches the door the chief examiner calls out.

'I forgot to ask. What were your parents' names?'

She freezes and turns.

'John and Catherine.'

There is a lump in her throat. Will they check what she told them?

'Full names?'

She lifts her head.

'John Peirce-Evans and Catherine Theresa Peirce-Evans of Knockaderry House.'

She hopes her voice conveys pride in her wealthy, respectable, sadly deceased parents.

'May they rest in peace,' she adds. 'Thank you, gentlemen.'

She is praying again as she leaves the building. *May they rest in peace, unbothered by the curiosity of these men. May they lie forgotten in their graves and their deeds with them.*

John is sleeping when she opens the bedroom door. She tries to go in quietly, slipping off her shoes and coat.

He stirs and sits up. 'I tried to stay awake, to wait for you. How was it?'

She crawls into his outstretched arms and lays her face on his warm chest and sobs. He runs his fingers through her hair.

'The beasts. You didn't have to go.'

'I did. I had to. It's done now.'

Chapter Forty-one

Sollum, 18th April 1928

On the third day of constant repair and rebuilding, the blue sky over our work area darkens and fills with a Vickers Victoria. It lands without incident and disgorges a Squadron Leader, a Flight-Lieutenant, a Flight-Sergeant, a Corporal and a couple of mechanics.

Colonel Green consults with them then comes to tell me, 'They're here to inspect the aerodrome.'

'Good. I like to think something will come of my trouble here.'

I watch as they erect a couple of tents on sandy scrub beside the aerodrome. I am on the sidelines, looking for an opportunity to help, to be part of the effort. But there isn't a tool left idle and I become more awkward at my uselessness. I could do plenty but there are more men than tasks at present.

Colonel Green arrives in his Ford.

'I'll run you up to the house,' he says. 'You have a bathing suit?'

'Yes.'

'Get that. I want to show you that we have more to offer than rocks and sand.'

He takes me to more sand. But it is finer and whiter than the coarse desert. And it is lapped by water the same turquoise as the ring John gave me. I slip into its cool folds, submerging myself and feeling the grit and sweat of my troubles washing away.

When we return to the aerodrome more Italians have arrived from Amsiate. Their uniforms are impeccable and they drive their armoured cars with pristine white gloves. How do they manage it? My hair is matted with saltwater, standing in peaks on top of my head and I can feel the tightness of too much sun on my cheeks that are no doubt blazing red.

This won't do.

I wash up in the Rest House, change into my black silk dress and heels and request a car to take me back to the aerodrome. I totter about for the rest of the evening, conversing with the charming Italians and overseeing the work like the lady that I am.

By the 20th the work is almost complete and I am very pleased with it. This could have spelled the end of my flying. *Again*. Who would have thought such a talented crew could be rustled up out of the desert?

Colonel Green seems happy too. It may be that his pride has been restored and the embarrassment of his aerodrome causing the problem turned to pride in the efforts made on the repairs. Or he may be happy that the madwoman in the black-silk dress will soon be out of his hair.

'We must have a dinner party before you go,' he announces at breakfast. 'To thank the Italians for their assistance and to wish you well.'

'That sounds marvellous,' I reply.

I rinse my dress and leave it to air-dry which it does in minutes. That evening, with everything packed into my plane in preparation for an early departure, I put it on, slip my feet into the heels that were never destined for the desert. I adorn myself with lipstick and kohl on my eyes and hope the Mess will be lit by candlelight to soften my features. I have no interest in romancing Colonel Green or the Italians. But I want to leave them with a memorable and appealing image of me. Not the grumpy woman in overalls complaining about rocks or the sand-matted, sunburned woman tramping about the aerodrome in an evening dress. Tonight I will be wit and charm and maybe beauty and in years to come they will remember me fondly as that wonderful, daring aviator lady.

The floor of the Mess is sand but it is a large airy room and yes, thankfully, lit by soft candles. As I arrive some soldiers are filling the empty space with the swelling sound of bagpipes. The music triggers some national pride or homesickness for Ireland in me and my eyes fill with tears. I am so grateful for these Italian men who have got me back in the sky again when they could just as easily have shrugged their shoulders and told me it was hopeless.

Dish after dish of delicious local food is passed along the table and my wine glass never empties. To my left is Colonel Green and to my right Matoni. I am happy to just listen as they recount the adventures they have had here, at the lip of the Mediterranean.

The room, despite its airiness and open doors and windows, is sweltering. The heat sits heavily on us all, my silk dress sticks to my skin and once the meal is over we slip into a lull. It has been a busy few days and we are all exhausted, the deadness of the air sapping what is left of our energy.

I am about to excuse myself when I hear a low thundering sound outside. I look at Colonel Green and am about to ask him if it is a thunderstorm when all the men get to their feet. Chairs clatter to the ground and they are wrapping scarves about their faces then running.

'Stay here,' Colonel Green shouts back.

I am left alone, apart from a server. I grab his arm as he reaches for a plate.

'What is it?'

'*Ghibli*. Wind.'

He mimics the sound I can hear outside, making it louder and more fearsome.

A devastating wind. *The plane.*

I kick off my shoes and run from the room. A white scarf lies on the ground, dropped by one of the Italians, and I wind it about my mouth and nose. I squeeze myself into the last space in the final car to leave, ignoring the protests. I don't speak Italian but I can guess that they are telling me to stay.

No. It is my plane at risk. *Again!* And after everything that has been done to get it right I won't sit idly by hoping it will come through the storm intact.

At the aerodrome the wind is stronger. The hot air blasts and I feel I am at the centre of a powerful oven. A group has formed around my Avian and the Victoria Vickers, laying all their strength on the ropes and sandbags holding them down. Someone is digging holes under the wheels. I run across to my plane, the sand whipping against my bare legs, stinging me. I take up position on a rope, putting my full force on it. The plane shifts restlessly, like a racehorse at the starting gate.

No, I tell her silently, *not yet.*

As the wind washes over us it becomes impossible to see. I close my eyes for minutes at a time, wishing I could reach for my goggles. I hardly ever wear them but I know they are there, at arm's length practically but useless to me now. Every time I open my eyes again, scratched by the sand, the visibility is less until finally it seems I am alone.

Alone and at the centre of a universe made of deafening sound and blinding haze.

My hands are sweating and the rope bites into them.

Blink.

I can barely see my own feet.

Blink.

A figure ducks under the plane.

Blink.

It is gone again.

Blink.

Someone is walking towards the plane. But not from the direction of the Mess. Coming from the desert.

Blink.

There is no one there.

Blink.

The figure appears again, closer now. Is it a man or a woman? It is shrouded in layers of cloth so it is impossible to tell. It is not an English or Italian officer – no uniform. It must be a native.

Blink.

It is a woman. But her clothes are not that of a native.

Blink.

She looks to be wearing a woollen shawl. In this climate?

Blink.

She passes by me, no more than three or four feet away then vanishes into the haze.

The sound stops, the world stops in the silence. It is as though the storm has taken a breath and then it unleashes again. I tighten my grip on the rope, shut my eyes and keep them shut.

Morning breaks and the wind dies down. It's coming in gusts now but the planes are secure and we can leave them. We pile into the cars to return to the Rest House, mute in exhaustion.

I want to ask if anyone else saw the woman. The woman in the shawl. But I know that she was only there for me to see. And I don't want them to think me crazy.

I pad barefoot into the house and to my room. The mirror over the bathroom sink shows a terrifying sight. My eyes are red and swollen, sand crusted at the corners, bleeding into the kohl that meanders down to my cheekbones. My dress is ripped and my legs are spotted with pinpricks of blood. I should wash but I lie on the bed and disappear into dreamless sleep.

The storm has passed but the wind is still too high for me to leave.

Colonel Green is terse when I enquire.

'The *Ghibli* usually lasts for three days. You'll just have to sit tight.'

It feels as though everyone here is avoiding each other, the relentless assault of hot wind and sand making us all too tense to behave civilly.

Finally, a week after my arrival, the wind stops. It disappears as abruptly as it came, making me wonder who controls it. Who operates the switch?

I have to wait for a heavy mist to clear from the aerodrome and the pilot of the Vickers Victoria insists on making a brief flight to test the air. But then I am free to go.

I take off carefully, conscious that our repairs were a lot of guesswork and making do and we haven't had a chance to try them out. But the Avian flies well and I relax.

I stay low until I reach Amsiate where I drop a bag containing a note of thanks for all their help and a request that they alert their stations along the north coast of my approach. I fervently hope this is the last time I need such help, but this journey has taught me that anything is likely.

I have a good wind behind me and fly over Derna in north-eastern Italian Libya after only two hours. The message I dropped in Amsiate has clearly been acted upon as there is a fire lit for me at the aerodrome but I dip my wings in greeting and fly on.

The wind changes direction and comes against me, making progress slower. But despite this I am happy here. This is the environment I can control. I have no power, I have learned, over men and their decisions, or the weather but I have the power here to fly on or stop at my own discretion.

Evidence of time passing unfolds beneath me. There is Cyrene, nestled into the hollows of the hills among lush green vegetation since the time of the Greeks and Romans.

A light rain falls and I am glad and turn my face to it. I never thought I would miss the grey damp of London but I have had my fill of searing temperatures and howling hot, blasting winds. The raindrops are gentle and familiar and fall lightly so I can still see Benghazi as it reveals itself below, a large, well-organised town. I head south-west to the aerodrome, dropping down to prepare for landing.

My plane is caught by gusts that I was oblivious to higher up. My friend, the *Ghibli.* I am tossed about like a leaf. Will I be able to steady myself enough to land? The plane drops suddenly, about twenty-five feet by my reckoning and I have to power up quickly to avoid bumping to the ground.

Finally I glide in, tipping onto one wing, then the other, then coming back to centre, grounded and steady. Another near miss!

Chapter Forty-two

Benghazi, April 23rd 1928

A car awaits me at the aerodrome and a well-dressed officer strides towards me.

'Comandante Morabito.'

He extends his hand.

'Lady Heath.'

'We have been expecting you. The winds were not a problem?'

'Not today.'

'Yes, we are at the mercy of the *Ghibli* this time of year. May I request your camera?'

'Of course.'

I root about in the locker behind my seat and take it out. He hands it to another officer.

'It will be sealed and returned to you on your departure. For security.'

I am taken aback but he disarms me with a broad smile, teeth glistening white in his tanned face.

'Procedures. Tiresome but necessary. Now let me take you to the Mess for lunch.'

I walk in with him and have to shake hands with every man there. I am seated and handed a stiff vermouth. It is delicious and fortifying. We all laugh as my hosts try to teach me to twirl the pasta with my fork and wind the long strands up to get it into my mouth. Mostly it slips off and when no one is looking I cut it into shorter lengths with my knife. My hunger trumps etiquette but no one seems to mind.

I finish every bit of food that is put before me but then immediately start to feel unwell. Have I stuffed myself like a pig? Is that the problem? I put a hand on my forehead. It is burning hot.

'Lady Heath? You are unwell?'

Comandante Morabito is peering at me from across the table. I nod, weakly. I am afraid if I open my mouth to answer the lovely Italian food will re-emerge.

The Comandante, who is only slightly taller than me, stands and with the assistance of another officer, manages to carry me to a bedroom. The shutters are closed and a gentle breeze flows through the darkened room. I am laid on the bed and, not caring whose it is, I immediately slip into a deep slumber.

At tea-time I wake and splash some water from a basin on a side table onto my face. My fever seems to have eased. I am embarrassed to have been such a burden to my hosts. I glance around the room, peek into the narrow wardrobe. This is the Comandante's bedroom. I blush. Will people talk if they see me leaving it? He is a gentleman, as all the Italians I met have been. It is such a kindness of him to let me rest here.

Feeling a little restored, I take a car to the aerodrome and manage to do my daily maintenance on the Avian.

Morabito comes and the car takes us to the palatial home of Governor Teruzzi, who has asked to meet me.

I am led into an ostentatious drawing room. The gilt and shine of the place hurts my eyes and I perch at the edge of a plush chair, feeling every nerve in my body prickling.

Governor Teruzzi is a stout man with an alarmingly extravagant moustache. It is all I can focus on while he talks. Thankfully he likes to talk so little is required of me beyond nodding and smiling.

'Please,' he is scribbling an address on a piece of paper, 'go see my wife in Rome. She will be happy to meet you.'

Back in the car with Comandante Morabito I remember to ask.

'Who is the Governor's wife?'

He glances at me. I have missed some information, it seems.

'A famous opera singer. American actually and very rich.'

'Oh.'

I still don't understand why I am holding her address. Every sight and sound is murky to me, as though I am under water. Morabito directs his driver around Benghazi, trying to show me the sights. It is a lovely town, with stunning architecture that would not be out of place in Rome. But my teeth are chattering and I cannot keep up with the conversation.

I am taken back to bed.

I wake to a doctor checking my temperature. Nearly forty degrees. I am burning up. I sleep again. My last thought, where will the Comandante sleep?

I wake feeling cooler but hollowed out in stiff sheets, as though something essential of me sweated out during the night. I pull myself slowly from the bed. It is past seven.

I make it to the aerodrome and do the usual routine. I cannot get my engine above sixteen hundred revolutions. It is as weakened as I feel. I tinker with the petrol mixture until I get the desired result then take off at nine o'clock, wishing I could fix my own body as quickly and efficiently.

I fly along the coast, spotting aerodromes every fifty miles or so. The Italians have organised this colony beautifully. Around midday I see El Agheila below and decide to land. My head is still fuzzy from the high fever and I am finding it hard to stay focused.

I am greeted by Colonel Garelli, an immaculate gentleman with a sparkling monocle. He leads me to the mess and within minutes I am presented with poached eggs and asparagus and a large bottle of champagne is opened to celebrate my arrival. This confirms that I was right to stop here. I am utterly restored by the time I head back to the aerodrome to take off again.

Every man here turns out to see me off, many of them signing their names and messages in the dust on my wings. I scan them, taking note of the kind words when I see a phrase that strikes my heart.

'*It is better to travel alone than badly accompanied.*'

I am contemplating that when Colonel Garelli appears by my side. I gesture.

'Wise words.'

'An Italian proverb,' he says. 'But I don't think you travel alone, Lady Heath. We are all with you.'

He takes his green scarf from around his neck and presents it to me. I wind it about mine and climb into the cockpit. I take off with scores of men waving and whooping.

The words travel with me. Is it true? Am I happier alone than with someone who is bad company? I was happy with William, at the start, but the fact that towards the end I preferred to be in Aberdeen while he was in Kenya says it all. Sir James. I've barely had a chance to test the theory. Apart from the sailing to Cape Town, we haven't had to spend much time together. John. Whenever I was with him I didn't have to think about whether or not I was happy. I just was. And now, now that I've shrugged him off, I think I would rather be alone. It's easier. No one to worry about and no one to blame for my own feelings. It is lonely. But it is familiar.

I take out a copy of last month's *Pearson's Magazine* to get my mind off the subject. Trust an Italian to stir up a philosophical dilemma!

I arrive to Sirte just after four o'clock. I almost expect problems now and am somewhat bored when things just go to plan. I've grown tired of repeating the same stories to different men in similar places. I perform my usual tasks and go to bed early.

But I lie there, completely awake. Nothing will entice my mind to quieten. It tosses about that riddle. Is it better for me to be alone? Should I seek a divorce from Sir James? Would I have to accuse him of adultery? I giggle in the darkness of my room. Imagine Sir James engaging in a sordid affair while I fly across Africa. At his age!

I'm starting to worry about flying tomorrow, with a dead brain after a sleepless night. No. I have to remedy it.

I tiptoe downstairs and search the mess for the pleasant wine that was served at dinner. There, the bottle marked Scala. I fill up a glass and gulp it down. It is delicious. Another glass should do the trick. I fill it right to the brim and take long sips, finishing it in four mouthfuls. A warmth spreads through me and I hurry back to bed before it wears off. The last thing I notice as I sit on the bed is the moon. It is dancing around the window. Strange. Usually it is quite still.

The morning sun reaches in cruelly through the same window where I saw the dancing moon. It pries my eyelids open and my head is immediately pierced with stabbing pain. I sit, feeling the contents of my skull slide about.

That was no wine. I have never known a wine strong enough to take me down in two glasses and I have never known a headache like this. It must have been brandy.

I struggle to the aerodrome, squinting, holding my head tightly on both sides.

Tenente Bondolfi, my host here, holds court as I stand by my plane, dying to leave.

'We wish you a safe and prosperous journey, Lady Heath!'

He pauses for breath and I grab my chance. 'Thank you,' I say. 'Goodbye!'

I hop up into the cockpit and motion for the man to spin my propeller. I taxi, sure that Bondolfi is still there, open-mouthed.

This is one place I won't have made a good impression with my conviviality. But I need the open sky.

It works a charm. The fresh air takes away my headache and I can open my eyes fully again. I vow to stay away from strong liquor for the next few days.

My speed is good and consistent and I reach Tripoli without incident. This is to be my last stop in Africa, all going well. My next step will be to cross to Europe with the help of Mussolini's escort.

I land comfortably and climb down from the cockpit.

Another Italian in yet another impeccable uniform awaits me. He bows. 'Comandante Matzini.'

'Lady Heath.'

'We are pleased to welcome you, Lady Heath. Please.' He gestures to a waiting car. 'I 've been instructed to take good care of you. There is a room reserved for you in the Grand Hotel, the best here in Tripoli.'

I sit in beside him. That sounds nice. But now that I am here I want to know when I will leave. I seem to be cursed in getting stuck for longer than I intend.

'Have you heard news of my escort?'

'Yes. All is ready. The seaplane will meet you here tomorrow. You have one day to enjoy our beautiful city. We always said Tripoli will be Italian. And now, look!'

I stare out the window. It's true. I could be in Rome. The streets are immaculate and the architecture is unmistakably Italian. But it saddens me to think that this city is so European in its look. Where are the Arabs? The Bedouins? I want to feel that I am still in Africa. For one more night at least.

'It's beautiful,' I mutter.

My room is opulent and spacious. I forgot to ask Matzini who instructed him to take care of me. Mussolini? I look forward to meeting this man. What will he be like? Will he be the same as the other polite and charming Italians I have met? Or does a leader such as him have something additional? It will be very interesting and I intend to ask him many questions.

I am enjoying a delicious breakfast of fresh fruit and eggs and good Italian coffee when a young officer approaches.

'Lady Heath, a message for you.'

It's from Matzini. Good news. Tenente Cola and two mechanics have left Syracuse in the seaplane and should arrive later today. We should be ready to depart tomorrow then at the very latest. I relax my shoulders and signal for more coffee.

Today can be a day of rest. I will take a stroll about the broad streets of Tripoli, enjoy the food and maybe some wine. That's not strong liquor. I will not think about the sea. I will not think about what I will do when I get back to London.

I'm at the aerodrome early, ready to meet my escorts. Comandante Matzini walks out to meet me and I flinch at his expression. I've seen it before, too many times. It is the expression that tells me I cannot fly, my plane has been impounded, I need another escort. What will it be now? I feel anger rising, ready to attack and fight yet another battle.

I stand, hands on my hips. 'What is it?'

'There is a problem.' He spreads his hands out, as if to say it is not his fault.

'I guessed as much. What is it?' I demand again.

'The seaplane. It has not arrived.'

Oh. This is different.

'Tenente Cola and the others left yesterday, they should have been here by evening. But so far there is no sign. And,' he looks at me, 'no communication.'

This is my worst fear realised. Flying over an open body of water. Running into difficulty. Being lost and knowing that no one has any idea where you are.

At least when I crash-landed in Matabeleland I could be confident of a person appearing at some point. I stare at the ground but it starts to quiver. I blink hard, blocking the tears, then face him.

'Is someone looking for them?'

He runs a hand across his chin, which I see now is unshaven. The first time I've seen one of the Italians less than perfectly turned out.

'It's too soon. If they haven't turned up by tomorrow they will ...'

It hangs in the air. This uncertainty. If they haven't turned up by then a search will be sent out. If they haven't turned up by then we'll know it's really serious. If they haven't turned up by then they might be lost forever.

And it's all my fault.

Chapter Forty-three

Tripoli, 27th April 1928

I spend a night staring at the ceiling, not one minute of sleep. My maps are spread out on the table in my bedroom and I pore over the blue expanse of the Mediterranean as if this piece of paper holds the key to where the seaplane is.

It could be at the bottom of the sea.

I send for a glass of brandy and gulp it down, hoping to silence my thoughts.

All I can think is: *I am Death*.

I must have been tainted, marked by the murder of my mother. And I have carried it all through my life. Now, these men are lost, because of me and my vanity. Does this trip warrant the lives of three young men?

I haunt the aerodrome, standing to attention every time someone new walks in. Is there news?

'Seaplanes and destroyers are out looking. If they're to be found they will find them.'

If I hadn't been ill in Benghazi ...

And if I hadn't damaged the plane in Sollum ...

And if I hadn't been held up in Cairo.

They might not be lost.

Or it might have been me who disappeared.

'Is there news?'

'No. The British have sent a plane from Malta to search.'

If I hadn't telegraphed Mussolini ...

If I had waited for the Bentleys ...

'Anything?'

'Nothing.'

'Some news. Lady Bailey has arrived in Cape Town.'

That doesn't matter.

My room fills with flowers and platters of fruit. The distress I am feeling must be showing on my face because everyone is being so kind. But I deserve none of it. I keep a solitary vigil in my room now. There is nothing to do except wait.

A knock at the door. More flowers?

A young man hands me a folded card.

From Matzini.

They have been found. Forty miles off the coast. Engine trouble. Crew is alive.

I shut the door and sink to the ground, pressing the card to my forehead.

I make contact with Dick and confirm that he will be in Tunis on the 5th of May and plans to cross the shortest way to Sicily. I will pay him the usual fee, five pounds an hour, to allow me to cross with him. I feel so foolish.

I could have just stuck to this plan all along. I need never have contacted Mussolini nor set those men off on a journey that nearly killed them.

Mary has made it to the end of her flight before me. It will be weeks still before I make it back to London. And so what?

My ego and my arrogance in Cairo have been for nothing and I am crossing the Med with Dick anyway. Which is exactly what the authorities advised in Cairo. But I couldn't be told. *Sophie! You have to face it. You're not always right.*

Comandante Matzini isn't happy. He wants me to wait for the Italians to go back with me. But I can't wait any longer.

I wake at five. There is no one about the hotel. Last night I tried to arrange an early breakfast but they wouldn't hear of it. Poor form for such a renowned place.

The night porter appears to be sleeping with his eyes open but jumps to attention when I appear at his post.

'Could you find me a taxi? Good man.'

I wait until he is out of sight then dash into the restaurant and backstage, as it were, to the pantry. I watched last night when I was having dinner to confirm the location of the food stores.

I fill my pockets with fruit and breadsticks and am innocently in the lobby when the porter returns, taxi secured. I tip him well.

As I'm taking off my port wheel hits against a pile of stones. What are they doing on the runway? I fly on, listening for any knock-on effects but my Avian sounds fine. I head west, the wind behind me.

Everything feels good again now that I am airborne. No authorities. No accidents. No illness. No interference.

Just me, my engine, my wings and the sky.

I relax into it, enjoying the beauty of the vista. The green shoreline, turning to white where small waves reach it and beyond the deepening blue of the Mediterranean, my final hurdle.

After an hour I see below me a destroyer, towing a seaplane. Those must be my Italian escorts. They are still a distance from the shore but I dip my wings in salute. I hope they see it.

I make a stop in Sfax, having to land on the racecourse because I can't find the aerodrome. I am immediately swamped by the town's inhabitants. I have a quick look at the damage from my take-off. The spar is strained but holding. I will fly on.

I follow the coast then climb to three thousand feet to get over the hills. I cannot land without first having an aerial tour of the ruins of old Carthage. And when I do land it is the wrong place. The aerodrome has been relocated to the north of the town.

As I bring my plane in to land on the starboard wheel after six hours of flying my heart lifts.

There, waiting for me, is the Bentleys' Moth. My companion, who I had been so keen to shake off only a few weeks ago.

How fickle I am!

I come out of my plane to find the place all locked up and there seems to be no one about.

A lone man eventually makes himself known.

Am I in the wrong place again?

'*Le Commandant*?' I ask.

This is French territory and I silently thank Miss Badham for her instruction in Margaret's Hall on the Mespil Road all those years ago, because this gentleman will not speak English.

I am made to understand that the Commandant is not at the aerodrome. Although I had already worked that out.

'*Un mécanicien?*' I enquire. The damage to my spar needs to be addressed. I am not willing to risk another landing with it.

Apparently I need the Commandant's permission to have the assistance of some mechanics. I send the man off with that request and the offer of payment. One hundred francs here and there should motivate a few men to lend me a hand.

They struggle in, their day of freedom disrupted, and sullenly assist me. The work is not to my standard and I am about to let them know when a shout goes up.

'*Régardez!*'

I push my way through the small group that has gathered around my wing.

There, a small round hole, bullet-shaped.

I smile but my hands shake. I was shot at. Unknowingly. It must have been as I came along the north coast of Africa. I try to recall if I heard or saw anything that would solve the mystery of who was shooting at me. Of course, they didn't know it was me. Or care. They were shooting at my plane.

I return to my work and encourage the men to do the same. But the thought whirs about my head. Another few feet, a different target and they would have hit my petrol tank and blown me out of the sky.

I catch up with the Bentleys at dinner. Dick stands and performs a deep bow.

'At your service again, Lady Heath.'

'And you have no idea how glad I am of it,' I reply. 'It's been a bit of a nightmare.'

Dorys places her hand on Dick's arm as he sits back down. 'Really? We've been having the best time. Haven't we, Dick?'

'You have,' he says. 'Relaxing in luxury hotels while I ricochet around Africa escorting crazy women pilots.'

I shoot him a look. What does he mean by that remark?

'Can we get going early tomorrow?' I say.

Already I am fretting about them holding me back. Dorys is yawning. Good, that means she will have an early night.

'Are you ready to cross the Med?' Dick asks.

I smile at him. 'With you, Dick? Of course. You're a pro at this stage. I know I'm in good hands.'

And it's true. I know I can trust him. But what good will he be if I go down in the middle of the sea? I decide to take some extra measures for my safety. Flotation. That's what I'll need. To be able to stay afloat for as long as necessary until I am found.

I locate some motorcycle tyres and fully inflate them.

I'm already in my cockpit the next morning when the Bentleys arrive. Not just out of impatience but a sense of embarrassment. This fear I have is mortifying to me. I know it's not entirely rational. And if they see that I have wrapped these tyres around my waist then they would definitely mark me down as a madwoman. We take off and I climb as high as possible, almost seven thousand feet. This is another part of my strategy. If I run into trouble being at this height gives me more time to find land on the descent. At least, I hope so. The air is cool and I am starting to relax. After all, it is only a short hop across to Sicily.

A loud pop nearly lifts me out of my seat. My heart races as I check the instruments. Nothing looks amiss. Another pop. I glance out of the cockpit but from what I can see of the wings and general body of the plane all is fine. Another pop. There is only one explanation.

I am being shot at. *Again.* Except this time it is close enough for me to hear. It must be another plane. I twist about in my seat to see who is shooting at me. Are they above or below on port or starboard?

Another pop and something hits my neck.

My hand goes up to feel. I am expecting hot, liquid, blood.

But, it touches rubber. Shredded rubber.

I start to shriek, tears trickling from my eyes. The tyres that were to be my lifeline have popped under the pressure of the high altitude. I fly on, with shredded rubber decorating me and a strong feeling that I'm going to make it.

I twist around once more to see where Dick is. I can hear his engine but he must be flying lower. My high altitude allows me a rare glimpse of Africa behind me just as Sicily comes into view.

Africa behind and Europe ahead. My epic quest behind, the end of the journey ahead. I want to go back and start it all again because once my plane comes down in London, it's over. Everything I've planned for and worked for finishes. And I have to return to that question again, then what? A trip like this is only good while it is underway. Soon, like everything, it becomes old news and the feeling of questing after something fades. The only way to recapture it is to go again. Is this my fate? To have to chase after new adventures year after year until I am too old for it all.

'*Farewell, Africa!*' I call. '*I will return!*'

Maybe there is more for me to do in this continent. Or maybe, as I thought before, I should turn my attention to America.

It's easier to say what I don't want. I don't want to stay still. Not for any length of time.

Soon the verdant green of Sicily is beneath me and I'm relieved. The watery depths of the Mediterranean are behind me. I have to climb higher to get to the aerodrome in Catania, soaring over the beautiful pockmark of Mount Etna gaping up at me.

I land and am having a quick lunch in the officers' mess when the Bentleys arrive. They need lunch too but I won't wait for them. I refuel and take off again, alone.

My plane bumps about as I cross the Straits of Messina but I don't worry. There are emergency landing spots every twenty miles or so, each marked with their name in white chalk. Such brilliant and reassuring organisation.

The sky starts to darken as I approach Naples. I check my instruments. Is a storm imminent? It's hard to imagine that as I have been flying through mostly blue skies. It is not cloud, but smoke, billowing up from Mount Vesuvius, coming to me on the wind. It thickens and I have to drop down. I end up almost on the ground, following the roads for guidance. Suddenly I am through and out of the smoke and the little aerodrome of Naples is before me.

My hosts, Comandante Cancianotti and his wife, welcome me into their home and don't protest when I excuse myself straight after supper. I get into bed on European soil for the first time since November and sleep dreamlessly.

Chapter Forty-four

Naples, 7th May 1928

I take off at eight in the morning, barely making it over the trees surrounding the aerodrome. I've been spoiled by the vast openness of Africa and must readjust now to the smallness and crowded spaces of Europe.

The wind is with me and my flight follows the ancient road, the Via Appia. I must remember to mention this when I speak to the press. What I have been doing, flying across Africa, trying to prove the potential and need for a route there, echoes these strategic roads of the ancient Roman republic. Yes, that's good. I will make a note when I land so that I don't forget it.

I glide into a beautiful, new civil aerodrome, so huge that it takes me ten minutes to taxi to the right hangar. I am endlessly impressed by Italian organisation and construction.

I'm escorted to the office of Generale Balbo, Secretary of State for Air.

A round-faced man with a tidy beard, wearing the smart blue uniform of the Regia Aeronautica.

'Lady Heath, welcome.'

I extend my hand but he raises his arm, stiff, palm down, then drops it to his side and takes a seat behind his desk.

I sit in a green leather armchair opposite, feeling awkward.

He leans back and smiles. 'You have been a long time in Africa, Lady Heath. You will have missed the news that handshakes are no longer acceptable. Il Duce has declared, and he is correct, that it is not hygienic. The Saluto Romano is preferred.'

'I'm sorry, General. I didn't mean to cause offence.'

'No need for apologies. I am just educating you. In case you are in the presence of more esteemed men than I. Maybe even Il Duce himself.'

'Do you think it would be possible? I am very keen to meet with Il Duce.' I bow my head as I say it. The term inspires reverence. 'I am anxious to tell him how impressed I have been by Italian organisation and hospitality in Africa. Far superior than our own, and don't mention the French!'

Balbo laughs heartily. 'It might be possible.'

'Is he interested in aviation? He was most helpful in arranging my seaplane escort. I would like to thank him.'

Balbo sits to his full height. 'At present we are more interested in military aviation than civil. But Il Duce is always happy to hear of courage and adventures. You have had some?'

'A few.' I drop my gaze, not wanting to appear arrogant.

'I will have a car to take you to your hotel, Lady Heath. If there is news of a meeting I will send for you there.'

'Thank you.' I stand and am about to offer my hand again when I remember. I raise my arm, instead, self-consciously. I will need to practise.

I barely have time to unpack my bag before I am bombarded with messages.

Lilliana Weinman Teruzzi wants to dine with me tomorrow night. I strain to remember who she is. Oh yes. Governor Teruzzi, in Benghazi. I didn't think I made much of an impression, ill as I was, but I recall his enthusiasm for me to meet his wife.

The Marquis de Pinedo wants to host a dinner in my honour before I leave Rome.

And, a cream card, raised blue lettering announcing '*Il Duce*'.

My presence is requested. Tenth of May. Villa Torlonia.

I am greeted by the now familiar salute and return it with confidence. I have been practising in front of the mirror in my hotel room.

My hair is neatly curled. My blue silk dress is free of creases. My black satin shoes click cleanly on the marble floor as I am led through rooms of beautiful stained glass, splendid chandeliers, gilded mirrors. Everything is pristine and gleaming.

But my palms are sweaty. I need to wipe them on something before I shake his hand. I remember again that I don't need to and a snort of nervous laughter escapes me.

Il Duce is seated behind a huge desk that dwarfs him somewhat. I dined with Lillianna Teruzzi last night after enduring *La fata delle bambole* at the Teatro Reale dell'Opera. I stifled yawns throughout the performance while Lillianna blinked away tears. She told me she hasn't sung since her marriage and my heart broke a little for the robust, blue-eyed beauty. She has given up the love of her life for a 'good' marriage. She grew more effervescent over dinner but dropped her voice to a whisper to tell me that Mussolini is quite short. I feared I would be towering over him so I am relieved now when he doesn't stand. I have found that men do not like to be towered over by me. Especially men with power.

He and I and the secretary who led me here perform the salute and I take a seat.

I wait while he moves some papers around, looking very serious. I have to lean slightly left to see him behind an enormous tasselled lamp. I shift, discreetly. He is balding, his forehead encroaching like the desert sands. His little wet lips pout as he signs some papers with a flourish then puts his pen down.

'Lady Heath. My apologies. I have some important work.'

I bow my head. 'Thank you for taking the time to see me. And thank you, sincerely, for providing me with the seaplane.'

He leans back in his chair. 'I am happy to help. I do not like when *burocrazia* stops adventure. And Signor Bonini liked you.'

I beam. Signor Bonini, who saw me at the height of my seasickness. Governor Teruzzi who saw me knocked low by fever. How did any of these men speak well of me?

'He says you like to hunt.'

'I was lucky.' I shrug.

'And a good pilot also.'

'It is not so difficult. Your men made it much easier, with their exquisite organisation and hospitality. It has a wonderful civilising effect on the colonies.'

'I'm glad. What is next for you?

Oh! That question.

I smile coyly. 'First, I must return to my husband.'

'You have children?' He frowns.

'No. I do not.'

His features relax. 'Then you are free to have adventures in the air. I think if you had children you would remain at home. No?'

No.

But I don't need to tell him.

'A woman's primary role is that of mother. Unfortunately, I was not blessed. So, as you say, I am free to have my adventures.'

'I wish you luck.'

He nods firmly at me, picks up his pen and starts to shuffle more papers. After a moment I stand. He raises his arm. I raise mine and I walk out, trying to quieten the clip of my heels now. Il Duce is working.

My car returns me to my hotel. I take a seat in the garden room and request a vermouth. I shut my eyes and feel the warm sunlight on my face. When I open them a tidy, wiry man with a notebook in his hand stands before me. A waiter?

'Lady Heath. Some questions?'

An American. A newspaper man. Really! I just want to have my drink. But I nod and gesture for him to sit.

'You met with Il Duce? How did it go?'

I wonder how he knows. 'He is a most impressive man. More of a national monument than an individual. I really wanted to thank him for all his assistance.'

'He was impressed with you?'

'Perhaps.' I look away.

'What did you talk about?'

'Mostly my adventures.'

The newsman writes 'Adventures' and underlines it. He looks up, waiting for me to continue. My drink arrives and I take a generous sip. I sit up and lean my elbows on the table. I want to give him the impression that we are speaking confidentially, conspiratorially even.

'Shall I tell you what I told him?'

'Yes.' The pencil is poised.

'I told him how I was almost gored to death by buffaloes. And spent five nights in a harem with native women tending to me when I crashed, unconscious in the wilderness. Then I discovered a bullet hole in my wing. Another inch or two and poof!' I wave my arms. 'I would have been blown sky high.'

He scribbles furiously and I sip my drink.

'Where was the harem?'

'In the veldt.'

'And someone had been shooting at you?'

'Evidently. Angry natives.'

'Who discovered it?'

'I did. I found the bullet hole. Right beside the petrol pipe.'

'I thought you said the wing?'

'Oh no. Right next to the pipe. A near miss.'

'And this was when you crash-landed.'

'That happened more than once.'

I finish my drink and gesture for another.

He stops writing and scans his notes.

'I'm not sure I have everything here. Can you clarify? I want to get the story right.'

I reach across and put my hand on his arm.

'My dear man,' I say. 'I have just flown thousands of miles across darkest Africa. Evaded wild jungles and savage beasts and hostile natives. I'm tired. Just write the most exciting story.'

He shakes my hand. He must not know the new rule.

'One more question,' he says. 'A little morbid, if you'll excuse me.'

I nod.

'Did you ever think of death? What would you want your legacy to be, if the worst happened?'

I take a moment to consider this. I watch a bead of condensation trickling down the outside of my glass. I trap it with my finger.

'I thought of death every day,' I tell him. 'But I am more afraid of not living than I am of dying. A living death. That is much worse.'

'And if you did die?'

'Then I would want my ashes to be scattered over a little quiet town in County Limerick where I grew up.'

He writes this down. I have a thought.

'At midday. When a man I used to know likes to take his daily walk.'

He takes note. I take a sip. What in the world put that idea in my head? And why is Roger Cunningham still lurking in the back of my mind?

The night before I leave Rome I attend a formal dinner in my honour. It is a late night so I am not ready to leave next morning until well after eight o'clock. The flight to Marseilles is easy, a pleasant wander along the Riviera coast. I arrive in the afternoon, dying for my bed.

I am tinkering with my engine when I hear a familiar voice.

'Sophie.'

I turn and cannot believe my eyes. My good friend from London, Stella Wolfe Murray, is walking towards me.

'Stella! What are you doing here?'

'I've been lying in wait. For three weeks! Waiting to meet the heroine. I can't believe you made it.'

She holds up a newspaper.

'**Lady Heath: Narrow Escape From Death**.'

I scan the article. It tells how I was shot down by hostile natives, a shot that almost blew me up, then taken captive until freed by passing motorists. I laugh. Close enough and it won't hurt my image.

I wrap my arms around her. It is so nice to see a familiar face after months and months of meeting strangers.

'Are you staying nearby?'

'I took rooms in a nearby village. There's one for you too.'

'That sounds perfect. Would you mind if I had an early night. Rome was a little too much fun.'

I can't even manage a decent conversation with Stella before sleep takes me. Next morning she waves me off, a pinched look of concern on her face. The weather report gave cloudy conditions and rain and she would prefer that I wait until it clears. But I am in no mood for waiting and I'm not worried about getting a little wet. I wave one last time as I take off in the direction of Lyons.

I curse my impatience as I pick my way through dense clouds. How quickly I have forgotten what it is like to fly with no visibility! Now I am lost in fog, barely able to see the nose of the plane. I drop down, only five hundred feet above the Rhone Valley, winding through hills and keeping the water below me. Any higher and I won't know where I'm going, or which way is up or down. I can fly blind, with only my instruments to guide me but months of clear blue African skies has spoiled me.

I decide to keep going and aim for Dijon. If I stop at Lyons the weather tomorrow might be even worse. I pick up the railway line and hover over it for four hours.

When I finally land every muscle in my body is stretched tight and I have a pounding headache right behind my eyes. The concentration that flight took has exhausted me more than my longest journey in Africa.

I take care of my engine then retreat once more to my bed over a little *estaminet* nearby. If the officers here were hoping to be entertained by me I'm afraid they're out of luck as its lights out by six o'clock.

I wake to clearer skies. The fog and cloud have lifted and while there might be a chance of showers it looks to be a better day for flying.

I make my way from Dijon to Paris, climbing to a comfortable height to cross the hills. I am almost there when the sky darkens and I am assailed by thunder, lightning and hail so fierce is cuts my face. I drop down, closer to the ground, as my wings are battered by the hailstones. If one of them were to break, could I land?

The flight comes to and end and as I arrive to Le Bourget aerodrome outside Paris I wonder if I can adapt to flying in European weather again. I am frozen to the bone when I climb out of the cockpit.

'*Hello!*'

A strong American voice calls out and I turn to see an older man running towards me with a coat over his head.

'You made it! Clifford Harmon, President of the International League of Aviators.'

'Delighted.' I shake his hand.

'Would you do us the honour of attending a luncheon? We have made arrangements at the clubhouse in the Bois de Boulogne.'

I smile. They expect me to say yes if the arrangements are already made.

'It is the second anniversary of our League. We were hoping you could join us for the celebrations.'

I am beyond exhausted but I agree. This is the man who crowned Mary Lady Champion Aviator of the World. I will put on my dress and my heels again and my best smile and maybe next year the trophy will be mine.

Chapter Forty-five

Paris, 17th May, 1928

Next morning Mr Harmon calls for me at Claridge's and drives me to Le Bourget. I perform my usual routine work and take off on my last lap.

I cross the Channel, battling an irritating little storm. I yearn for dust and searing sun and even, maybe, my foe the *Ghibli*. I thought this would be the most exciting part of my flight. The last lap. But the closer I get to England the less I want to reach it.

I am cold, I tell myself. I must have tea. I don't want to arrive in London looking like an icicle. I will warm myself and tidy myself up.

I land at Lympne, much to the surprise of the small few going about their business at the aerodrome. I am expected in Croydon, not here. But they make me tea and I sit with it, looking out at my Avian.

It has been such a constant for me. And I know I took good care but has anything in my life been so loyal? Cis, maybe. I need to telegram her first thing, to let her know I'm alive. I will hop over to see her, to spend a few quiet days in Ballybunion. To remember who I am and where I come from. Before I leave and forget it all again.

I finish my tea and retrieve my leather duffel bag. It has been through the wars with me and shows the signs. I will need a new one. Maybe a London shopping trip is called for. Myself and Stella, we can traipse around Harrods and replace my silk dresses and satin shoes.

In the chilly ladies room I change. I fold my cretonne overalls, stiff with grease, into my bag and pack away Sophie the aeroplane mechanic.

I slip on my silk stockings, making sure the seam marches a straight line up my calf.

Something glints at me from a forgotten corner of the bag. A bead from the headdress given to me by the Tsolo witch doctor. I roll it between my fingers then tuck it into an inner pocket of the bag. It's time to pack away Wild Sophie.

I slip my feet into my shoes and shimmy into my brown tweed suit. Sensible Sophie.

I pull my brown cloche hat on and pull my expensive fur around my shoulders.

Lady Heath's furs.

I slide my hands into my beige kid gloves. The right-hand glove catches, refuses to budge. I take it off. The turquoise stone of my flea market ring sits obstinate. I pull. It is tight, unrelenting. I slide a bar of soap across my finger and try again. I grunt as it scrapes across my knuckle. Without it my finger looks naked, forsaken.

I tuck the ring into the pocket with the bead without looking at it.

It is time to pack that away too. There can be no more past, only the future.

A swipe of lipstick and I am ready now. I stride to my plane and take up position. I spend more time than I need checking my instruments, running my finger across each dial, stroking the smooth wood panelling.

I bring her to life and taxi. I open the throttle, pull back the joystick and lift. My stomach rises and I wonder how I will survive not flying every day. Will Sir James try to ground me? Will I have to ground myself for a while? Talk to the press, give lectures, make my name?

Maybe no one cares. That is possible. I think of all the money I spent sending telegrams from Africa only to be ignored. Until it seemed I would fail. Then the papers were full of my efforts.

I will have to make them see me. Sit up and take notice.

I am nearing Croydon. Two dots in the distance become two airplanes. They are circling. Waiting for me. They come to meet me and fly alongside. I climb, I can't help it, and sketch a wide loop in the sky. My tail skid might fall off, but I don't care. This is my moment and look! A crowd of people below. A huge crowd. I can't disappoint them.

I loop again then follow with a banking manoeuvre to the left before I steady the plane. I bring her in smooth. A perfect landing. I fix my hat and rise up from the cockpit to wave.

The cheers of the crowd rise up too, floating up into the clouds above.

I am helped down. Cameras flash. A bouquet of flowers is thrust into my hands. Sir James is by my side. He presses his lips to mine. I allow it for a moment then pull back, gesturing that we must pose for the cameras.

The newsmen fire questions at me.

'What was your scariest moment?'

'Is it true you were shot at?'

I can't answer them all.

'Now that you're home, are you finished with flying? You've flown ten thousand miles. Have you had enough?'

'*No!*' I shout an answer at this one. '*I'll never have enough!*'

To the Editor of the *Times*

10th April, 1928

Sir, I read in the Press a three-line paragraph to the effect that 'Lady Heath has completed her lone flight from the Cape to Cairo on a 30 horse-power Avro-Avian light aeroplane'.

I wonder if the average reader has the slightest idea what a tremendous individual feat has been accomplished in the above

notice – and by a woman. I am aware that Lady Heath was escorted over the central portion of the journey, namely, from Northern Nyasaland to Khartoum, by Lieutenant Bentley, but that fact should not minimise the brilliance of the performance.

Those of us who have walked hundreds, almost thousands of miles through the bush country of Tanganyika and East Africa know that that bush country is an endless area of scrubby desolation, divided only by oceans of grass well over a man's head. The chances of rescue if a forced landing occurred are little less hopeless than if it took place in the Atlantic. This lady has shown an intrepidity of spirit comparable in every way with either Sir Alan Cobham or Mr Hinkler and without all their well-prepared ground organisation.

I submit that public notice should be taken and recognition given to Lady Heath's performance, and that aviation is richer for the demonstration of what courage and a well-piloted light aeroplane can do. I understand that the engine employed was a Cirrus Mark II. At any rate I should like to be among the first to take my hat off to this gallant lady on her return from a most hazardous, transcontinental flight.

Yours faithfully,

Frederick Guest

Knockaderry House, County Limerick, 6th December 1897

The policeman pushes open the heavy kitchen door. It swings back, knocking against the wall. The sound echoes in the silent room.

He hopes the room is empty. The man, Jackie Peirce, came to him, wild, manic. Ranting that he's done it. He said he'd do it and he's done it. Now he'll swing for it and it's all their fault. He told them he'd do it and nobody stopped him.

Sergeant Mongey eventually understood. The dogs in the street knew that Jackie was violent and cruel to his wife, former housekeeper Kate. It seemed he only married her so he'd have something to beat whenever the mood came on him. And now he's saying he's killed her.

The second policeman creaks into the room behind him. There was no way he was facing this alone.

'Anything?'

Mongey doesn't answer. His practised eyes rove around the room. There are signs of a struggle. Broken glass. A chair in smithereens. A stick. A bloodied stick. On the floor a bundle of rags. It moves.

'Jesus, Mary and Joseph!' His comrade is blessing himself, backing for the door.

'*Stand!*' Mongey shouts. '*If it's moving it's alive.*'

'*What is it?*' the man pleads, terror in every syllable.

Mongey doesn't know. But it's his job to find out. He puts one foot in front of the other until it is beside the bundle. He gently moves a piece of clothing. A woman. Dead. Kate. How does it move then? He pulls her shawl away, still gentle.

The child is curled like a bean. Knees tucked up to her chest, nestled against her dead mother. She is in a nightdress, wet, cold.

He lifts her into his arms. Her legs won't unfurl, they stay tucked, so he holds her like that. His hand around her ankles, her face burrows into his neck.

He turns to his comrade.

'Who is it?' he asks, his face bloodless.

'The daughter. Sophie, I think her name is.'

'Poor cratur! What will become of her?'

Fairy Grass

Wherever a stream has flowed,
Or a winding road may lead,
That's in the blood of my breed.
The lust of the open road.

From *East African Nights* (1925), by Sophie Eliott-Lynn

Author's Note

I grew up very close to Knockaderry House, where Sophie Peirce-Evans came into the world, but remained oblivious to her story until I was in my twenties. Then, I couldn't understand why her story was not known to everyone in County Limerick and across the world. She was a rule-breaker, a record-breaker, a pioneer every bit as significant as the names that still trip off our tongues, such as Charles Lindbergh and Amelia Earhart. In fact, she sold her plane to Amelia Earhart in 1928 with an exhortation painted on the side: '*Always think with your stick forward*.' But her star faded too soon and my motivation in telling her story was to remind everyone of what an incredible woman she was, one who we should proudly claim and proclaim as a real Irish heroine.

This novel charts her most epic achievement: a solo flight over an uncharted, wild, treacherous continent in an open-cockpit biplane. It tracks this flight along with her memories of her childhood in County Limerick, studying in Dublin, driving a motorcycle in World War One and battling for equality and fair treatment for women athletes and aviators.

It was difficult to find a manageable structure for her story. If I attempted to tell a 'cradle to the grave' version of her life this book would have become several tomes. There is no easy way to encapsulate Sophie's incredible life and, considering that it was a relatively short one, this says a lot about her achievements.

Most of the story presented here is factual. I relied heavily on newspaper accounts of the time, and passages about Sophie in biographies of athletes, aviators and pioneering Irishwomen. What was most invaluable to me in discovering her story and more so her personality, was an archive of material entrusted by Sophie's descendants to Limerick solicitor and amateur historian, John Cussen, into which he kindly allowed me to dive. This was enhanced further by family memorabilia which a distant relative, Richard Langford, generously permitted me to access. Reading Sophie's own words in personal letters to her family and in her own writings – her poetry collection, her extensive guide for female athletes and her account of the Cape Town to Croydon flight in *Woman and Flying* – was very special. Add to this her many newspaper articles, her frank interviews, and letters between family members discussing her, and I had a wealth of material which all helped to form a more complete picture of the person rather than the persona.

She was a complexity. The daughter of a landed gentleman farmer from a respectable Church of Ireland family who caused scandal through his drinking, gambling and frequent clashes with the law – and then the ultimate shame: marriage to his poor, Catholic housekeeper Kate Dooling, Sophie's mother.

After her father murdered her mother and was himself committed to an asylum, Sophie was raised in the strictly Victorian household of her grandfather, the local GP, who was heartbroken by his only son's downfall. Sophie encountered much love and kindness from her aunts but her childhood was severely restricted. She did not attend local school, was only allowed out of the house chaperoned and exercise was limited to sedate walking. No doubt this was in an effort to protect Sophie from gossip and shame, but it may also have been an attempt to protect her from her own suspected innate wildness. If this was the aim then it backfired spectacularly. As soon as Sophie escaped to boarding school, she spread her wings and flung herself wholeheartedly into everything life had to offer. But the shame was still there and she frequently lied about her origins, telling people that she was an orphan whose mother died in childbirth.

She excelled in athletics and academics, married Major William Eliott-Lynn who was twenty years her senior, ran away to war, was estranged from William after a stint farming together in East Africa, then widowed, excelled in aviation, married for money, completed her epic flight and was celebrated across the world as the brave pioneer she was. This is where this book ends because I wanted her incredible success to be the focus of this story.

However, it is not the whole story and I know people will be curious to know what happened next. Lindie Naughton's *Lady Icarus* is an excellent factual account of Sophie's life, from the cradle to the grave. I highly recommend that those interested in reading more about Sophie should seek it out, but I will summarise here.

In the aftermath of her great success, Sophie tried to gain employment with KLM as a commercial pilot but public opinion was still too negative regarding women in this role. She left for America in November 1928, without her then husband Sir James Heath, who a few weeks later denounced her publicly, sending letters to a number of newspapers saying he would no longer be responsible for any debts incurred by her. Unsurprisingly, the marriage failed and Sophie was granted a divorce in 1930, citing cruelty in financial matters as grounds. She stayed in America, living the high life and being celebrated.

Then in August 1929 disaster struck. This meticulous pilot crashed during an exhibition flight in Cleveland National Air Races in Ohio. With a fractured skull, broken nose, fractured jawbone and traumatic brain injury, it was feared she would not survive but after brain surgery and a long recovery she returned to England. She had to reapply for her pilot's licence and prove her abilities once again. The recovery was incomplete and she blamed the brain damage for a slide into alcoholism. She married again – another scandal as her third husband was G.A.R. Williams, a coloured man from the West Indies. The marriage was registered in a civil office in Tralee, County Kerry. This union, I believe, was for love but it didn't survive her drinking and the failed business attempt of establishing a flying school and airline in Dublin.

Eventually, in 1939, Sophie was living in London and, where before the newspapers were full of her successes, now her name appeared in short paragraphs detailing her encounters with police, arrested for drunk and disorderly behaviour, being brought before the courts and incarcerated. Few remembered who this woman had been.

In May 1939 Sophie, aged only 42, fell down the stairs of a London double-decker tram and died. The newspapers spoke again of her achievements but it was a sad and ignominious end for a woman who changed the world.

This novel is a work of fiction and, to this end, details have been altered. For example, the Lady Champion Aviator of the World award was granted a week earlier than in my account here. One significant element is my own creation. This is the romance between Sophie and John. There are two references to somebody in her life by this name. In the dedication for her collection of poetry published in 1925, *East African Nights*, it says '*To J. Best friend one ever had.*' And in a letter to her aunt Cis, dated July 29th 1923, she says, '*John, the one good man in my life, is passing through London on Wednesday – tomorrow – and going to stay the night. It will be very sad and poignant seeing him again but God is very good to have let me have such a pure and beautiful thing in my life as my love for him.*' All other details of their romance are invented but it made sense to me that she must have fallen truly in love at least once and made a choice between love and ambition in order to achieve her dreams.

The character of Roger Cunningham and his behaviour towards Sophie are completely fictional. For this story he serves the function of being the mechanism by which she discovered the truth about her parents although it is unknown when, where and how she learned this.

I have used the names of the countries in Africa as they were known in 1928 but, of course, most of these countries have been renamed since gaining independence. Sophie's views on imperialism and colonisation were very much of her time, unacceptable in today's world.

As a work of fiction, I hope this novel has breathed new life into the character of Sophie Peirce-Evans aka Lady Heath. I hope it brings her story to new audiences and that in future tallies of amazing, inspirational Irishwomen, her name ranks high.

Acknowledgements

I want to first thank the readers of my debut novel, *The Lighthouse Keeper's Wife*. It is scary bringing your work into the world where people can read and critique it. Writing a book is only one side of the communication. Without readers, the job would be only halfway there. So I am very grateful to everyone who read the book and contacted me with their comments.

Again my sincerest thanks to all those, family and friends, who continue to encourage me in my writing. Thanks to Vickie, Joe, Avril for your support. To my husband Declan and children Layla, Dylan and Joni – thank you again for your belief in me and for your patience when I lose a weekend to editing.

Thanks to the writing community across all of Ireland and especially the Plague Writers Group who've listened to me rhapsodising about the "flying woman" for a few years now. Thanks to the UL Creative Writing faculty who gave wise guidance on an early excerpt from this novel, in particular Sarah Moore Fitzgerald, Donal Ryan, Fíona Scarlett, Joseph O'Connor, Emily Cullen and Eoin Devereux.

Thanks to my fantastic agent, Francesca Riccardi, of the Kate Nash Literary Agency. To my editor, Gaye Shortland, who once again worked hard to keep me on track and to Paula Campbell and all the team at Poolbeg Press who really understood my vision for this story.

I am deeply grateful to those with personal knowledge of Sophie Peirce and her story who were so generous in sharing information with me, especially John Cussen and Richard Langford.

And finally, thanks to Sophie Peirce herself, who left a trove of letters, articles, photographs and publications in her wake, which made this task fascinating and enthralling.

Printed in Dunstable, United Kingdom